Enid Blyton

THE FAMOUS FIVE

COLLECTION 3

Have you read all
THE FAMOUS FIVE books?

Enid Blyton

THE FAMOUS FIVE

COLLECTION 3

FIVE GO OFF TO CAMP

FIVE GET INTO TROUBLE

FIVE FALL INTO ADVENTURE

Illustrated by Eileen A. Soper

Hodder
Children's
Books

HODDER CHILDREN'S BOOKS

Five Go Off to Camp first published in Great Britain in 1948 by Hodder & Stoughton
Five Get Into Trouble first published in Great Britain in 1949 by Hodder & Stoughton
Five Fall Into Adventure first published in Great Britain in 1950 by Hodder & Stoughton
This collection first published in Great Britain in 2016 by Hodder & Stoughton

9

A CIP catalogue record for this book is available from the British Library.

ISBN 978 1 444 92970 6

Typeset in Times by Avon DataSet Ltd, Bidford-on-Avon, Warwickshire

Printed and bound in Great Britain by Clays Ltd, Elcograf S.p.A.

The paper and board used in this book are made from wood from responsible sources.

Hodder Children's Books
An imprint of Hachette Children's Group
Part of Hodder & Stoughton
Carmelite House
50 Victoria Embankment
London EC4Y 0DZ

An Hachette UK Company
www.hachette.co.uk
www.hachettechildrens.co.uk

Five Go Off to Camp

CONTENTS

CHAPTER ONE

Holiday time

'TWO JOLLY fine tents, four groundsheets, four sleeping-bags – I say, what about Timmy? Isn't he going to have a sleeping-bag too?' said Dick, with a grin.

The other three children laughed, and Timmy, the dog, thumped his tail hard on the ground.

'Look at him,' said George. 'He's laughing, too! He's got his mouth stretched wide open.'

They all looked at Timmy. He really did look as if a wide grin stretched his hairy mouth from side to side.

'He's a darling,' said Anne, hugging him. 'Best dog in the world, aren't you, Timmy?'

'Woof!' said Timmy, agreeing. He gave Anne a wet lick on her nose.

The four children, Julian, tall and strong for his age, Dick, George and Anne were busy planning a camping holiday. George was a girl, not a boy, but she would never answer to her real name, Georgina. With her freckled face and short, curly hair she really did look more like a boy than a girl.

'It's absolutely wizard, being allowed to go on a camping holiday all by ourselves,' said Dick. 'I never thought our parents would allow it, after the terrific adventure we had last summer, when we went off in caravans.'

1

'Well – we shan't be *quite* all by ourselves,' said Anne. 'Don't forget we've got Mr Luffy to keep an eye on us. He'll be camping quite near.'

'Pooh! Old Luffy!' said Dick, with a laugh. 'He won't know if we're there or not. So long as he can study his precious moorland insects, he won't bother about us.'

'Well, if it hadn't been that he was going to camp, too, we wouldn't have been allowed to go,' said Anne. 'I heard Daddy say so.'

Mr Luffy was a master at the boys' school, an elderly, dreamy fellow with a passion for studying all kinds of insect-life. Anne avoided him when he carried about boxes of insect specimens, because sometimes they escaped and came crawling out. The boys liked him and thought him fun, but the idea of Mr Luffy keeping an eye on them struck them as very comical.

'It's more likely we'll have to keep an eye on *him*,' said Julian. 'He's the sort of chap whose tent will always be falling down on top of him, or he'll run out of water, or sit down on his bag of eggs. Old Luffy seems to live in the world of insects, not in our world!'

'Well, he can go and live in the world of insects if he likes, so long as he doesn't interfere with *us*,' said George, who hated interfering people. 'This sounds as if it will be a super holiday – living in tents on the high moors, away from everybody, doing exactly what we like, when we like and how we like.'

'Woof!' said Timmy, thumping his tail again.

'That means he's going to do as *he* likes, too,' said Anne. 'You're going to chase hundreds of rabbits, aren't you, Timmy, and bark madly at anyone who dares to come within two miles of us!'

'Now, be quiet a minute, Anne!' said Dick, picking up his list again. 'We really must check down our list and find out if we've got every single thing we want. Where did I get to – oh, four sleeping-bags.'

'Yes, and you wanted to know if Timmy was to have one,' said Anne, with a giggle.

'Of course he won't,' said George. 'He'll sleep where he always does – won't you, Timmy? On my feet.'

'Couldn't we get him just a *small* sleeping-bag?' asked Anne. 'He'd look sweet with his head poking out of the top.'

'Timmy hates looking sweet,' said George. 'Go on, Dick. I'll tie my hanky round Anne's mouth if she interrupts again.'

Dick went on down his list. It was a very interesting one. Things like cooking-stoves, canvas buckets, enamel plates and drinking-cups were on it and each item seemed to need a lot of discussion. The four children enjoyed themselves very much.

'You know, it's almost as much fun planning a holiday like this as having it,' said Dick. 'Well – I shouldn't think we've forgotten a thing, have we?'

'No. We've probably thought of too much!' said Julian. 'Well, old Luffy says he'll take all our things on the trailer behind his car, so we'll be all right. I shouldn't like to carry them ourselves!'

'Oh, I wish next week would come!' said Anne. 'Why is it that the time seems so long when you're waiting for something nice to happen, and so short when something nice *is* happening?'

'Yes, it seems the wrong way round, doesn't it?' said Dick, with a grin. 'Anyone got the map? I'd like to take another squint at the spot where we're going.'

Julian produced a map from his pocket. He opened it and the four children sprawled round it. The map showed a vast and lonely stretch of moorland, with very few houses indeed.

'Just a few small farms, that's all,' said Julian pointing to one or two. 'They can't get much of a living out of such poor land, though. See, that's about the place where we're going – just there – and on the opposite slope is a small farm where we shall get milk, eggs and butter when we need them. Luffy's been there before. He says it's a rather small farm, but jolly useful to campers.'

'These moors are awfully high, aren't they?' said George. 'I guess they'll be freezing cold in the winter.'

'They are,' said Julian. 'And they may be jolly windy and cold in the summer, too, so Luffy says we'd better take sweaters and things. He says in the winter they are covered with snow for months. The sheep have to be dug out when they get lost.'

Dick's finger followed a small winding road that

made its way over the wild stretch of moorland. 'That's the road we go,' he said. 'And I suppose we strike off here, look, where a cart-track is shown. That would go to the farm. We shall have to carry our stuff from wherever Luffy parks his car, and take it to our camping place.'

'Not too near Luffy, I hope,' said George.

'Oh, no. He's agreed to keep an eye on us, but he'll forget all about us once he's settled down in his own tent,' said Julian. 'He will, really. Two chaps I know once went out in his car with him for a day's run, and he came back without them in the evening. He'd forgotten he had them with him, and had left them wandering somewhere miles and miles away.'

'Good old Luffy,' said Dick. 'That's the sort of fellow we want! He won't come springing up to ask if we've cleaned our teeth or if we've got our warm jerseys on!'

The others laughed, and Timmy stretched his doggy mouth into a grin again. His tongue hung out happily. It was good to have all four of his friends with him again, and to hear them planning a holiday. Timmy went to school with George and Anne in term time, and he missed the two boys very much. But he belonged to George, and would not dream of leaving her. It was a good thing that George's school allowed pets, or George would certainly not have gone!

Julian folded up the map again. 'I hope all the things we've ordered will come in good time,' he said. 'We've got about six days to wait. I'd better keep on reminding Luffy that we're going with him, or he's quite likely to start without us!'

It was difficult to have to wait so long now that everything was planned. Parcels came from various stores and were eagerly opened. The sleeping-bags were fine.

'Super!' said Anne.

'Smashing!' said George, crawling into hers. 'Look! I can lace it up at the neck – and it's got a hood thing to come right over my head. Golly, it's warm! I shan't mind the coldest night if I'm sleeping in this. I vote we sleep in them tonight.'

6

'What? In our bedrooms?' said Anne.

'Yes. Why not? Just to get used to them,' said George, who felt that a sleeping-bag was a hundred times better than an ordinary bed.

So that night all four slept on the floor of their bedrooms in their sleeping-bags, and voted them very comfortable and as warm as toast.

'The only thing is, Timmy kept wanting to come right inside mine,' said George, 'and honestly there isn't enough room. Besides, he'd be cooked.'

'Well, he seemed to spend half the night on my tummy,' grumbled Julian. 'I shall jolly well keep the bedroom door shut if Timmy's going to spend the night flopping on everyone's bag in turn.'

'I don't mind the flopping, so much as the frightful habit he's got of turning himself round and round and round before he flops down,' complained Dick. 'He did that on me last night. Silly habit of his.'

'He can't help it,' said George at once. 'It's a habit that wild dogs had centuries and centuries ago – they slept in reeds and rushes, and they got into the way of turning themselves round and round in them, to trample them down and make themselves a good sleeping-place. And our dogs go on turning themselves round now, before they go to sleep, even though there aren't any rushes to trample down.'

'Well! I wish Timmy would forget his doggy ancestors were wild dogs with rushy beds, and just remember he's a nice tame dog with a basket of his own,' said Dick. 'You should see my tummy today! It's all printed over with his foot-marks.'

'Fibber!' said Anne. 'You do exaggerate, Dick. Oh, I do wish Tuesday would come. I'm tired of waiting.'

'It'll come all right,' said Julian. And so it did, of course. It dawned bright and sunny, with a sky that was a deep blue, flecked with tiny white clouds.

'Good-weather clouds,' said Julian, pleased. 'Now, let's hope old Luffy has remembered it's today we're starting off. He's due here at ten o'clock. We're taking sandwiches for the whole party. Mother thought we'd better, in case Luffy forgot his. If he's remembered them it won't matter, because we're sure to be able to eat them ourselves. And there's always Timmy to finish things up!'

Timmy was as excited as the four children. He always knew when something nice was going to happen. His tail was on the wag the whole time, his tongue hung out, and he panted as if he had been running a race. He kept getting under everyone's feet, but nobody minded.

Mr Luffy arrived half an hour late, just when everyone was beginning to feel he had forgotten to come. He was at the wheel of his big old car, beaming. All the children knew him quite well, because he lived not far away and often came to play bridge with their father and mother.

'Hallo, hallo!' he cried. 'All ready, I see! Good for you! Pile the things on the trailer, will you? Mine are there too but there's plenty of room. I've got sandwiches for everyone, by the way. My wife said I'd better bring plenty.'

'We'll have a fine feast today then,' said Dick, helping Julian to carry out the folded-up tents and sleeping-bags, while the girls followed with the smaller things. Soon everything was on the trailer and Julian made them safe with ropes.

They said goodbye to the watching grown-ups and climbed excitedly into the car. Mr Luffy started up his engine and put the lever into first gear with a frightful noise.

'Goodbye!' called all the grown-ups, and Julian's mother added a last word. 'DON'T get into any awful adventure this time!'

'Of course they won't!' called back Mr Luffy cheerfully. 'I'll see to that. There are no adventures to be found on a wild and deserted moor. Goodbye!'

Off they went, waving madly, and shouting goodbye all the way down the road. 'Goodbye! Goodbyeeeeee! Hurrah, we're off at last!'

The car raced down the road, the trailer bumping madly after it. The holiday had begun!

CHAPTER TWO

Up on the moors

MR LUFFY was not a good driver. He went too fast, especially round the corners, and many times Julian looked behind at the trailer in alarm, afraid that everything would suddenly leap off it at some sharp bend.

He saw the bundle of sleeping-bags jump high into the air, but fortunately they remained on the trailer. He touched Mr Luffy on the shoulder.

'Sir! Could you go a bit slower, please! The trailer will be empty by the time we arrive, if the luggage leaps about on it much more.'

'My word! I forgot we had a trailer,' said Mr Luffy, slowing down at once. 'Remind me if I go over thirty-five miles an hour, will you? Last time I took the trailer with me, I arrived with only half the goods on it. I don't want that to happen again.'

Julian certainly hoped it wouldn't. He kept a sharp eye on the speedometer, and when it veered towards forty he tapped Mr Luffy on the arm.

Mr Luffy looked supremely happy. He didn't like term time, but he loved holidays. Term time interfered with the study of his beloved insect-world. Now he was off with four nice children he liked, for a holiday on a moorland he

knew was alive with bees, beetles, butterflies and every other kind of insect he wanted. He looked forward to teaching the four children quite a lot. They would have been horrified if they guessed this, but they didn't.

He was an odd-looking fellow. He had very untidy, shaggy eyebrows over kind and gentle brown eyes that always reminded Dick of a monkey's. He had a rather large nose, which looked fiercer than it was because, unexpectedly, it had quite a forest of hairs growing out of the nostrils. He had an untidy moustache, and a round chin with a surprising dimple in the middle of it.

His ears always fascinated Anne. They were large and turned rather forward, and Mr Luffy could waggle the right one if he wanted to. To his great sorrow he had never been able to waggle the left one. His hair was thick and untidy, and his clothes always looked loose, comfortable and rather too big for him.

The children liked him. They couldn't help it. He was so odd and gentle and untidy and forgetful – and yet sometimes unexpectedly fierce. Julian had often told them the story of Tom Killin the bully.

Mr Luffy had once found Tom bullying a small new boy in the cloakroom, dragging him round and round it by his belt. With a roar like an angry bull, Mr Luffy had pounced on the big bully, got him by the belt, lifted him up and stuck him firmly on a peg in the cloakroom.

'There you stay till you get someone to lift you down!'

Mr Luffy had thundered. '*I* can get hold of a belt too, as you can see!'

And then he had stalked out of the cloakroom with the small, terrified boy beside him, leaving the bully hung up high on the peg, quite unable to free himself. And there he had to stay, because not one of the boys who came pouring in from a game of football would lift him down.

'And, if the peg hadn't given way under his weight, he'd be stuck up there still,' Julian had said with a grin. 'Good old Luffy! You'd never think he could be fierce like that, would you?'

Anne loved that story. Mr Luffy became quite a hero to her after that. She was pleased to sit next to him in the car, and chatter about all kinds of things. The other three were squashed at the back with Timmy on their feet. George firmly prevented him from climbing up on her knee because it was so hot. So he contented himself with trying to stand up with his paws on the window-ledge and his nose over the side.

They stopped about half past twelve for lunch. Mr Luffy had indeed provided sandwiches for everyone. And remarkably fine ones they were too, made the evening before by Mrs Luffy.

'Cucumber, dipped in vinegar! Ham and lettuce! Egg! Sardine! Oooh, Mr Luffy, your sandwiches are much nicer than ours,' said Anne, beginning on two together, one cucumber and the other ham and lettuce.

They were all very hungry. Timmy had a bit from

everyone, usually the last bite, and watched each sandwich
eagerly till his turn came. Mr Luffy didn't seem to
understand that Timmy had to have the last bite of any
sandwich, so Timmy simply took it out of his hand, much
to his surprise.

'A clever dog,' he said, and patted him. 'Knows what
he wants and takes it. Very clever.'

That pleased George, of course. She thought that
Timmy was the cleverest dog in the world, and indeed
it did seem like it at times. He understood every word
she said to him, every pat, every stroke, every gesture.
He would be much, much better at keeping an eye on

the four children and guarding them than forgetful Mr Luffy.

They drank ginger-beer and then ate some ripe plums. Timmy wouldn't have any plums, but he licked up some spilt ginger-beer. Then he snuffed up a few odd crumbs and went to drink at a little stream nearby.

The party set off again in the car. Anne fell asleep. Dick gave an enormous yawn and fell asleep too. George wasn't sleepy, nor was Timmy, but Julian was. He didn't dare to take his eye off the speedometer, though, because Mr Luffy seemed to be very much inclined to speed along too fast again, after his good lunch.

'We won't stop for tea till we get there,' said Mr Luffy suddenly, and Dick woke up with a jump at the sound of his booming voice. 'We should be there about half past five. Look, you can see the moorland in the distance now – all ablaze with heather!'

Everybody looked ahead, except Anne, who was still fast asleep. Rising up to the left for miles upon miles was the heather-covered moorland, a lovely sight to see. It looked wild and lonely and beautiful, blazing with heather, and shading off into a purple-blue in the distance.

'We take this road to the left, and then we're on the moors,' said Mr Luffy, swinging violently to the left, and making the luggage in the trailer jump high again. 'Here we go.'

The car climbed the high moorland road steadily. It passed one or two small houses, and in the distance the children could see little farms in clearings. Sheep dotted the moorland, and some of them stood staring at the car as it drove by.

'We've got about twenty miles to go, I should think,' said Mr Luffy, jamming on his brakes suddenly to avoid two large sheep in the middle of the road. 'I wish these creatures wouldn't choose the centre of the road to gossip in. Hi, get on there! Let me pass!'

Timmy yelped and tried to get out of the car. The sheep hurriedly decided to move, and the car went on. Anne was thoroughly awake by now, having been almost jerked out of her seat by the sudden stop.

'What a shame to wake you!' said Mr Luffy, gazing down at her kindly, and almost running into a ditch by the side of the road. 'We're nearly there, Anne.'

They climbed steadily, and the wind grew a little cold. All around the children the moors stretched for mile upon mile, never-ending. Little streams sometimes splashed right down to the roadway, and ran beside it.

'We can drink the water in these streams,' said Mr Luffy. 'Crystal clear, and cold as ice! There's one quite near where we're going to camp.'

That was good news. Julian thought of the big canvas buckets they had brought. He didn't particularly want to carry those for miles. If there was a stream near their camping place it would be easy to get the buckets filled with washing-water.

The road forked into two. To the right was a good road,

leading on and on. To the left it became not much more than a cart-track. 'That's the one we take,' said Mr Luffy, and the car jerked and jolted over it. He was forced to go slowly, and the children had time to see every little thing they passed.

'I shall leave the car here,' said Mr Luffy, bringing it to a standstill beside a great rock that stood up bare and grey out of the moor. 'It will be sheltered from the worst winds and rain. I thought we'd camp over yonder.'

There was a little slope just there, backed by some enormous gorse bushes. Thick heather grew everywhere. Julian nodded. It was a good place for camping. Those thick gorse bushes would provide fine shelter from the winds.

'Right, sir,' he said. 'Shall we have tea first, or unpack now?'

'Tea first,' said Mr Luffy. 'I've brought a very good little stove for boiling and cooking things. Better than a wood fire. That makes kettles and saucepans so black.'

'We've got a stove, too,' said Anne. She scrambled out of the car and looked all round. 'It's lovely here – all heather and wind and sun! Is that the farm over there – the one we shall go to for eggs and things?'

She pointed to a tiny farmhouse on the hill opposite. It stood in a small clearing. In a field behind it were three or four cows and a horse. A small orchard stood at the side, and a vegetable garden lay in front. It seemed odd to see such a trim little place in the midst of the moorland.

'That's Olly's Farm,' said Mr Luffy. 'It's changed hands, I believe, since I was here three years ago. I hope the new people are nice. Now – did we leave something to eat for our tea?'

They had, because Anne had wisely put away a good many sandwiches and bits of cake for tea-time. They sat in the heather, with bees humming all round them, and munched solidly for fifteen minutes. Timmy waited patiently for his bits, watching the bees that hummed round him. There were thousands of them.

'And now I suppose we'd better put up our tents,' said Julian. 'Come on, Dick – let's unpack the trailer. Mr Luffy, we don't intend to camp on top of you, sir, because you won't want four noisy children too near. Where would you like your tent put?'

Mr Luffy was about to say that he would like to have the four children and Timmy quite close, when it suddenly occurred to him that perhaps they might not want him too near. They might want to make a noise, or play silly games, and if he were near it would stop them enjoying themselves in their own way.

So he made up his mind not to be too close. 'I'll pitch my tent down there, where that old gorse bush is,' he said. 'And if you'd like to put yours up here, where there's a half-circle of gorse bushes keeping off the wind, you'd be well sheltered. And we shan't interfere with one another at all.'

'Right, sir,' said Julian, and he and Dick began to tackle

the tents. It was fun. Timmy got under everyone's feet as usual, and ran off with an important rope, but nobody minded.

By the time that dusk came creeping up the heather-covered moorland, all three tents were up, the ground-sheets were put down, and the sleeping-bags unrolled on them, two in each of the children's tents, and one in Mr Luffy's.

'I'm going to turn in,' said Mr Luffy. 'My eyes are almost shut. Good night, all of you. Sleep well!'

He disappeared into the dusk. Anne yawned widely, and that set the others off too. 'Come on – let's turn in, too,' said Julian. 'We'll have a bar of chocolate each, and a few biscuits. We can eat those in our sleeping-bags. Good night, girls. Won't it be grand to wake up tomorrow morning?'

He and Dick disappeared into their tent. The girls crawled into theirs with Timmy. They undressed, and got into their warm, soft sleeping-bags.

'This is super!' said George, pushing Timmy to one side. 'I never felt so cosy in my life. *Don't* do that, Timmy. Don't you know the difference between my feet and my middle? That's better.'

'Good night,' said Anne, sleepily. 'Look, George, you can see the stars shining through the opening of the tent. Don't they look enormous?'

But George didn't care whether they were enormous or not. She was fast asleep, tired out with the day's run.

Timmy cocked one ear when he heard Anne's voice, and gave a little grunt. That was his way of saying good night. Then he put his head down and slept.

'Our first night of camping,' thought Anne, happily. 'I shan't go to sleep. I shall lie awake and look at the stars and smell that heathery smell.'

But she didn't. In half a second she was sound asleep, too!

CHAPTER THREE

Anne's volcano

JULIAN AWOKE first in the morning. He heard a strange and lonely sound floating overhead. 'Coor-lie! Coor-lie!'

He sat up and wondered where he was and who was calling. Of course! He was in his tent with Dick – they were camping on the moors. And that wild cry overhead came from a curlew, the bird of the moorlands.

He yawned and lay down again. It was early in the morning. The sun put its warm fingers in at his tent opening, and he felt the warmth on his sleeping-bag. He felt lazy and snug and contented. He also felt hungry, which was a nuisance. He glanced at his watch.

Half past six. He really was too warm and comfortable to get up yet. He put out his hand to see if there was any chocolate left from the night before, and found a little piece. He put it into his mouth and lay there contentedly, listening to more curlews, and watching the sun climb a little higher.

He fell asleep again, and was awakened by Timmy busily licking his face. He sat up with a start. The girls were peering in at his tent, grinning. They were fully dressed already.

'Wake up, lazy!' said Anne. 'We sent Timmy in to get you up. It's half past seven. We've been up for ages.'

21

'It's a simply heavenly morning,' said George. 'Going to be a frightfully hot day. Do get up. We're going to find the stream and wash in it. It seems silly to lug heavy buckets of water to and fro for washing, if the stream's nearby.'

Dick awoke too. He and Julian decided to go and take a bathe in the stream. They wandered out into the sunny morning, feeling very happy and very hungry. The girls were just coming back from the stream.

'It's over there,' said Anne, pointing. 'Timmy, go with them and show them. It's a lovely little brown stream, awfully cold, and it's got ferns along its banks. We've left the bucket there. Bring it back full, will you?'

'What do you want us to do that for, if you've already washed?' asked Dick.

'We want water for washing-up the dishes,' said Anne. 'I suddenly remembered we'd need water for that. I say, do you think we ought to wake up Mr Luffy? There's no sign of him yet.'

'No, let him sleep,' said Julian. 'He's probably tired out with driving the car so slowly! We can easily save him some breakfast. What are we going to have?'

'We've unpacked some bacon rashers and tomatoes,' said Anne, who loved cooking. 'How do you light the stove, Julian?'

'George knows,' said Julian. 'I say, did we pack a frying-pan?'

'Yes. I packed it myself,' said Anne. 'Do go and bathe if you're going to. Breakfast will be ready before you are!'

Timmy gravely trotted off with the boys and showed them the stream. Julian and Dick at once lay down in the clear brown bed, and kicked wildly. Timmy leapt in too, and there were yells and shrieks.

'Well – I should think we've woken up old Luffy now!' said Dick, rubbing himself down with a rough towel. 'How lovely and cold that was. The trouble is it's made me feel twice as hungry!'

'Doesn't that frying bacon smell good?' said Julian,

23

sniffing the air. They walked back to the girls. There was still no sign of Mr Luffy. He must indeed sleep very soundly!

They sat down in the heather and began their breakfast. Anne had fried big rounds of bread in the fat, and the boys told her she was the best cook in the world. She was very pleased.

'I shall look after the food side for you,' she said. 'But George must help with the preparing of the meals and washing-up. See, George?'

George didn't see. She hated doing all the things that Anne loved to do, such as making beds and washing-up. She looked sulky.

'Look at old George! Why bother about the washing-up when there's Timmy only too pleased to use his tongue to wash every plate?' said Dick.

Everyone laughed, even George. 'All right,' she said, 'I'll help of course. Only let's use as few plates as possible, then there won't be much washing-up. Is there any more fried bread, Anne?'

'No. But there are some biscuits in that tin,' said Anne. 'I say, boys, who's going to go to the farm each day for milk and things? I expect they can let us have bread, too, and fruit.'

'Oh, one or other of us will go,' said Dick. 'Anne, hadn't you better fry something for old Luffy now? I'll go and wake him. Half the day will be gone if he doesn't get up now.'

'I'll go and make a noise like an earwig outside his

tent,' said Julian, getting up. 'He might not wake with all our yells and shouts, but he'd certainly wake at the call of a friendly earwig!'

He went down to the tent. He cleared his throat and called politely: 'Are you awake yet, sir?'

There was no answer. Julian called again. Then, puzzled, he went to the tent opening. The flap was closed. He pulled it aside and looked in.

The tent was empty! There was nobody there at all.

'What's up, Ju?' called Dick.

'He's not here,' said Julian. 'Where can he be?'

There was silence. For a panic-stricken moment Anne thought one of their strange adventures was beginning. Then Dick called out again. 'Is his bug-tin gone? You know, the tin box with straps that he takes with him when he goes insect-hunting? And what about his clothes?'

Julian inspected the inside of the tent again. 'OK!' he called, much to everyone's relief. 'His clothes are gone, and so has his bug-tin. He must have slipped out early before we were awake. I bet he's forgotten all about us and breakfast and everything!'

'That would be just like him,' said Dick. 'Well, we're not his keepers. He can do as he likes! If he doesn't want breakfast, he needn't have any. He'll come back when he's finished his hunting, I suppose.'

'Anne! Can you get on with the doings if Dick and I go to the farmhouse and see what food they've got?' asked

25

Julian. 'The time's getting on, and if we're going for a walk or anything today, we don't want to start too late.'

'Right,' said Anne. 'You go too, George. I can manage everything nicely, now that the boys have brought me a bucketful of water. Take Timmy. He wants a walk.'

George was only too pleased to get out of the washing-up. She and the boys, with Timmy trotting in front, set off to the farmhouse. Anne got on with her jobs, humming softly to herself in the sunshine. She soon finished them, and then looked to see if the others were coming back. There was no sign of them, or of Mr Luffy either.

'I'll go for a walk on my own,' thought Anne. 'I'll follow that little stream uphill and see where it begins. That would be fun. I can't possibly lose my way if I keep by the water.'

She set off in the sunshine and came to the little brown stream that gurgled down the hill. She scrambled through the heather beside it, following its course uphill. She liked all the little green ferns and the cushions of velvety moss that edged it. She tasted the water – it was cold and sweet and clean.

Feeling very happy all by herself, Anne walked on and on. She came at last to a big mound of a hill-top. The little stream began there, half-way up the mound. It came gurgling out of the heathery hillside, edged with moss, and made its chattering way far down the hill.

'So that's where you begin, is it?' said Anne. She flung herself down on the heather, hot with her climb. It was nice there, with the sun on her face, and the sound of the trickling water nearby.

She lay listening to the humming bees and the water. And then she heard another sound. She took no notice of it at all at first.

Then she sat up, frightened. 'The noise is underground! Deep, deep underground! It rumbles and roars. Oh, what is going to happen? Is there going to be an earthquake?'

The rumbling seemed to come nearer and nearer. Anne didn't even dare to get up and run. She sat there and trembled.

Then there came an unearthly shriek, and not far off a most astonishing thing happened. A great cloud of white smoke came right out of the ground and hung in the air before the wind blew it away. Anne was simply horrified. It was so sudden, so very unexpected on this quiet hillside. The rumbling noise went on for a while and then gradually faded away.

Anne leapt to her feet in a panic. She fled down the hill, screaming loudly: 'It's a volcano! Help! Help! I've been sitting on a volcano. It's going to burst, it's sending out smoke. Help, help, it's a VOLCANO!'

She tore down the hillside, caught her foot on a tuft of heather and went rolling over and over, sobbing. She came to rest at last, and then heard an anxious voice calling:

'Who's that? What's the matter?'

It was Mr Luffy's voice. Anne screamed to him in relief. 'Mr Luffy! Come and save me! There's a volcano here!'

There was such terror in her voice that Mr Luffy came

racing to her at once. He sat down beside the trembling girl and put his arm round her. 'Whatever's the matter?' he said. 'What's frightened you?'

Anne told him again. 'Up there – do you see? That's a volcano, Mr Luffy. It trembled and rumbled and then it shot up clouds of smoke. Oh quick, before it sends out red hot cinders!'

'Now, now!' said Mr Luffy, and to Anne's surprise and relief he actually laughed. 'Do you mean to tell me you don't know what that was?'

'No, I don't,' said Anne.

'Well,' said Mr Luffy, 'under this big moor run two or three long tunnels to take trains from one valley to another. Didn't you know? They make the rumbling noise you heard, and the sudden smoke you saw was the smoke sent up by a train below. There are big vent-holes here and there in the moor for the smoke to escape from.'

'Oh, good gracious me!' said Anne, going rather red. 'I didn't even *know* there were trains under here. What an extraordinary thing! I really did think I was sitting on a volcano, Mr Luffy. You won't tell the others will you? They would laugh at me dreadfully.'

'I won't say a word,' said Mr Luffy. 'And now I think we'll go back. Have you had breakfast? I'm terribly hungry. I went out early after a rather rare butterfly I saw flying by my tent.'

'We've had breakfast *ages* ago,' said Anne. 'But if

29

you'd like to come back with me now I'll cook you some bacon, Mr Luffy. And some tomatoes and fried bread.'

'Aha! It sounds good,' said Mr Luffy. 'Now – not a word about volcanoes. That's our secret.'

And off they went to the tents, where the others were wondering what in the world had become of Anne. Little did they know she had been 'sitting on a volcano'!

CHAPTER FOUR

Spook-trains

THE BOYS and George were full of talk about the farm. 'It's a nice little place,' said Julian, sitting down while Anne began to cook breakfast for Mr Luffy. 'Pretty farmhouse, nice little dairy, well-kept sheds. And even a grand piano in the drawing-room.'

'Gracious! You wouldn't think they'd make enough money to buy a thing like that, would you?' said Anne, turning over the bacon in the pan.

'The farmer's got a fine car,' went on Julian. 'Brand new. Must have cost him a pretty penny. His boy showed it to us. And he showed us some jolly good new farm machinery too.'

'Very interesting,' said Mr Luffy. 'I wonder how they make their money, farming that bit of land? The last people were hard-working folk, but they certainly couldn't have afforded a new car or a grand piano.'

'And you should have seen the lorries they've got!' said Dick. 'Beauties! Old army ones, I should think. The boy said his father's going to use them for carting things from the farm to the market.'

'What things?' said Mr Luffy, looking across at the little farmhouse. 'I shouldn't have thought they needed an army of lorries for that! An old farm wagon would carry all *their* produce.'

'Well, that's what he told us,' said Dick. 'Everything certainly looked very prosperous, I must say. He must be a jolly good farmer.'

'We got eggs and butter and fruit, and even some bacon,' said George. 'The boy's mother didn't seem worried about how much we had, and she hardly charged us anything. We didn't see the farmer.'

Mr Luffy was now eating his breakfast. He was certainly very hungry. He brushed away the flies that hung round his head, and when one settled on his right ear he waggled it violently. The fly flew off in surprise.

'Oh, do that again!' begged Anne. 'How do you do it? Do you think if I practised hard for weeks I could make my ear move?'

'No, I don't think so,' said Mr Luffy, finishing his breakfast. 'Well, I've got some writing to do now. What are you going to do? Go for a walk?'

'We might as well take a picnic lunch and go off somewhere,' said Julian. 'How about it?'

'Yes,' said Dick. 'Can you pack us dinner and tea, Anne? We'll help. What about hard-boiled eggs?'

It wasn't long before they had a picnic meal packed in greaseproof paper.

'You won't get lost, will you?' said Mr Luffy.

'Oh no, sir,' said Julian, with a laugh. 'I've got a compass, anyway, and a jolly good bump of locality, too. I usually know the way to go. We'll see you this evening, when we get back.'

'*You* won't get lost, Mr Luffy, will you?' asked Anne, looking worried.

'Don't be cheeky, Anne,' said Dick, rather horrified at Anne's question. But she really meant it. Mr Luffy was so absent-minded that she could quite well picture him wandering off and not being able to find his way back.

He smiled at her. 'No,' he said. 'I know my way about here all right – I know every stream and path and er – volcano!'

Anne giggled. The others stared at Mr Luffy, wondering what in the world he meant, but neither he nor Anne told them. They said goodbye and set off.

'It's heavenly walking today,' said Anne. 'Shall we follow a path if we find one or not?'

'Might as well,' said Julian. 'It'll be a bit tiring scrambling through heather all the day.'

So when they did unexpectedly come across a path they followed it. 'It's just a shepherd's path, I expect,' said Dick. 'I bet it's a lonely job, looking after sheep up on these desolate heathery hills.'

They went on for some way, enjoying the stretches of bright heather, the lizards that darted quickly away from their feet and the hosts of butterflies of all kinds that hovered and fluttered. Anne loved the little blue ones best and made up her mind to ask Mr Luffy what all their names were.

They had their lunch on a hill-top overlooking a vast stretch of heather, with grey-white blobs in it here and there – the sheep that wandered everywhere.

And, in the very middle of the meal, Anne heard the same rumbling she had heard before, and then, not far off, out spouted some white smoke from the ground. George went quite pale. Timmy leapt to his feet, growling and barking, his tail down. The boys roared with laughter.

'It's all right, Anne and George. It's only the trains underground here. We knew they ran under the moors and we thought we'd see what you did when you first heard them rumbling, and saw the smoke.'

'I'm not a bit frightened,' said Anne, and the boys looked at her, astonished. It was George who was the scared one! Usually it was quite the other way round.

George got back her colour and laughed. She called Timmy. 'It's all right, Tim. Come here. You know what trains are, don't you?'

The children discussed the trains. It really did seem strange to think of trains in those hollowed-out tunnels down below the moors – the people in them, reading their newspapers and talking – down in tunnels where the sun never shone at all.

'Come on,' said Julian, at last. 'Let's go on. We'll walk to the top of the next slope, and then I think we ought to turn back.'

They found a little path that Julian said must be a

rabbit-path, because it was so narrow, and set off, chattering and laughing. They climbed through the heather to the top of the next slope. And at the top they got quite a surprise.

Down in the valley below was a silent and deserted stretch of railway lines! They appeared out of the black hole of a tunnel-mouth, ran for about half a mile, and then ended in what seemed to be a kind of railway yard.

'Look at that,' said Julian. 'Old derelict lines – not used any more, I should think. I suppose that tunnel's out of date, too.'

'Let's go down and have a squint,' said Dick. 'Come on! We've got plenty of time, and we can easily go back a shorter way.'

They set off down the hill to the lines. They arrived some way from the tunnel-mouth, and followed the lines to the deserted railway yard. There seemed to be nobody about at all.

'Look,' said Dick, 'there are some old wagons on that set of lines over there. They look as if they haven't been used for a hundred years. Let's give them a shove and set them going!'

'Oh, no!' said Anne, afraid. But the two boys and George, who had always longed to play about with real railway trucks, ran over to where three or four stood on the lines. Dick and Julian shoved hard at one. It moved. It ran a little way and crashed into the buffers of another. It made a terrific noise in the silent yard.

A door flew open in a tiny hut at the side of the yard, and a terrifying figure came out. It was a one-legged man, with a wooden peg for his other leg, two great arms that might quite well belong to a gorilla, and a face as red as a tomato, except where grey whiskers grew.

He opened his mouth and the children expected a loud and angry yell. Instead out came a husky, hoarse whisper:

'What you doing? Ain't it bad enough to hear spook-trains a-running at night, without hearing them in the daytime, too?'

The four children stared at him. They thought he must

be quite mad. He came nearer to them, and his wooden leg tip-tapped oddly. He swung his great arms loosely. He peered at the children as if he could hardly see them.

'I've broken me glasses,' he said, and to their astonishment and dismay two tears ran down his cheeks. 'Poor old Wooden-Leg Sam, he's broken his glasses. Nobody cares about Wooden-Leg Sam now, nobody at all.'

There didn't seem anything to say to all this. Anne felt sorry for the funny old man, but she kept well behind Julian.

Sam peered at them again. 'Haven't you got tongues in your heads? Am I seeing things again, or are you there?'

'We're here and we're real,' said Julian. 'We happened to see this old railway yard and we came down to have a look at it. Who are you?'

'I told you – I'm Wooden-Leg Sam,' said the old man impatiently. 'The watchman, see? Though what there is to watch here, beats me. Do they think I'm going to watch for these spook-trains? Well, I'm not. Not me, Sam Wooden-Leg. I've seen many strange things in my life, yes, and been scared by them too, and I'm not watching for any more spook-trains.'

The children listened curiously. 'What spook-trains?' asked Julian.

Wooden-Leg Sam came closer. He looked all round as if he thought there might be someone listening, and then spoke in a hoarser whisper than usual.

'Spook-trains, I tell you. Trains that come out of that

tunnel at night all by themselves, and go back all by themselves. Nobody in them. One night they'll come for old Sam Wooden-Leg – but, see, I'm smart, I am. I lock myself into my hut and get under the bed. And I blow my candle out so those spook-trains don't know I'm there.'

Anne shivered. She pulled at Julian's hand. 'Julian! Let's go. I don't like it. It sounds all peculiar and horrid. What does he mean?'

The old man seemed suddenly to change his mood. He picked up a large cinder and threw it at Dick, hitting him on the head. 'You clear out! I'm watchman here. And what did they tell me? They told me to chase away anyone that came. Clear out, I tell you!'

In terror Anne fled away. Timmy growled and would have leapt at the strange old watchman, but George had her hand on his collar. Dick rubbed his head where the cinder had hit him.

'We're going,' he said soothingly to Sam. It was plain that the old fellow was a bit funny in the head. 'We didn't mean to trespass. You look after your spook-trains. We won't interfere with you!'

The boys and George turned away, and caught up with Anne. 'What did he mean?' she asked, scared. 'What are spook-trains? Trains that aren't real? Does he really see them at night?'

'He just imagines them,' said Julian. 'I expect being there all alone in that deserted old railway yard has made him think strange things. Don't worry, Anne. There are no

such things as spook-trains.'

'But he spoke as if there were,' said Anne, 'he really did. I'd hate to see a spook-train. Wouldn't you Ju?'

'No. I'd *love* to see one,' said Julian, and he turned to Dick. 'Wouldn't you, Dick? Shall we come one night and watch? Just to see?'

CHAPTER FIVE

Back at camp again

THE CHILDREN and Timmy left the deserted railway yard behind them and climbed up the heathery slope to find their way back to their camping place. The boys could not stop talking about Wooden-Leg Sam and the strange things he said.

'It's a funny business altogether,' said Julian. 'I wonder why that yard isn't used any more – and where that tunnel leads to – and if trains ever do run there.'

'I expect there's quite an ordinary explanation,' said Dick. 'It's just that Wooden-Leg Sam made it all seem so weird. If there had been a proper watchman we shouldn't have thought there was anything strange about it at all.'

'Perhaps the boy at the farm would know,' said Julian. 'We'll ask him tomorrow. I'm afraid there aren't any spook-trains really – but, gosh, I'd love to go and watch for one, if there were any.'

'I wish you wouldn't talk like that,' said Anne, unhappily. 'You know, it makes me feel as if you want another adventure. And I don't.'

'Well, there won't be any adventure, so don't worry,' said Dick, comfortingly. 'And, anyway, if there was an adventure you could always go and hold old Luffy's hand.

41

He wouldn't see an adventure if it was right under his nose. You'd be quite safe with him.'

'Look – who's that up there?' said George, seeing Timmy prick up his ears, and then hearing him give a little growl.

'Shepherd or something, I should think,' said Julian. He shouted out cheerfully. 'Good afternoon! Nice day it's been!'

The old man on the path just above them nodded his head. He was either a shepherd or farm labourer of some sort. He waited for them to come up.

'Have you seen any of my sheep down along there?' he asked them. 'They've got red crosses on them.'

'No. There aren't any down there,' said Julian. 'But there are some further along the hill. We've been down to the railway yard and we'd have seen any sheep on the slope below.'

'Don't you go down there,' said the old shepherd, his faded blue eyes looking into Julian's. 'That's a bad place, that is.'

'Well, we've been hearing about spook-trains!' said Julian, with a laugh. 'Is that what you mean?'

'Ay. There're trains that nobody knows of running out of that tunnel,' said the shepherd. 'Many's the time I've heard them when I've been up here at night with my sheep. That tunnel hasn't been used for thirty years – but the trains, they still come out of it, just as they used to.'

'How do you know? Have you seen them?' asked Julian, a cold shiver creeping down his spine quite suddenly.

'No. I've only heard them,' said the old man. 'Choo, choo, they go, and they jangle and clank. But they don't whistle any more. Old Wooden-Leg Sam reckons they're spook-trains, with nobody to drive them and nobody to tend them. Don't you go down to that place. It's bad and scary.'

Julian caught sight of Anne's scared face. He laughed loudly. 'What a tale! I don't believe in spook-trains – and neither do you, shepherd. Dick, have you got the tea in your bag? Let's find a nice place and have some sandwiches and cake. Will you join us, shepherd?'

'No, thank you kindly,' said the old man, moving off. 'I'll be after my sheep. Always wandering they are, and they keep me wandering, too. Good day, sir, and don't go down to that bad place.'

Julian found a good spot out of sight of 'that bad place', and they all sat down. 'All a lot of nonsense,' said Julian, who wanted Anne to feel happier again. 'We can easily ask the farmer's boy about it tomorrow. I expect it's all a silly tale made up by that old one-legged fellow, and passed on to the shepherd.'

'I expect so,' said Dick. 'You noticed that the shepherd had never actually *seen* the trains, Julian? Only heard them. Well, sound travels far at night, and I expect what he heard was simply the rumblings of the trains that go underground here. There's one going somewhere now! I can feel the ground trembling!'

They all could. It was a peculiar feeling. The rumbling stopped at last and they sat and ate their tea, watching Timmy scraping at a rabbit-hole and trying his hardest to get down it. He covered them with sandy soil as he burrowed, and nothing would stop him. He seemed to have gone completely deaf.

'Look here, if we don't get Timmy out of that hole now he'll be gone down so far that we'll have to drag him out by his tail,' said Julian, getting up. 'Timmy! TIM-MY! The rabbit's miles away. Come on out.'

It took both George and Julian to get him out. He was most indignant. He looked at them as if to say: '*Well*, what

44

spoil-sports! Almost got him and you drag me out!'

He shook himself, and bits of grit and sand flew out of his hair. He took a step towards the hole again, but George caught hold of his tail. 'No, Timmy. Home now!'

'He's looking for a spook-train,' said Dick, and that made everyone laugh, even Anne.

They set off back to the camping place, pleasantly tired, with Timmy following rather sulkily at their heels. When they at last got back they saw Mr Luffy sitting waiting for them. The blue smoke from his pipe curled up into the air.

'Hallo, hallo!' he said, and his brown eyes looked up at them from under his shaggy eyebrows. 'I was beginning to wonder if you'd got lost, Still, I suppose that dog of yours would always bring you back.'

Timmy wagged his tail politely. 'Woof,' he agreed, and went to drink out of the bucket of water. Anne stopped him just in time.

'No, Timmy! You're not to drink out of our washing-up water. There's yours, in the dish over there.'

Timmy went to his dish and lapped. He thought Anne was very fussy. Anne asked Mr Luffy if he would like any supper.

'We're not having a proper supper,' she said. 'We had tea so late. But I'll cook you something if you like, Mr Luffy.'

'Very kind of you. But I've had an enormous tea,' said Mr Luffy. 'I've brought up a fruit cake for you, from my

45

own larder. Shall we share it for supper? And I've got a bottle of lime juice, too, which will taste grand with some of the stream water.'

The boys went off to get some fresh stream water for drinking. Anne got out some plates and cut slices of the cake.

'Well,' said Mr Luffy. 'Had a nice walk?'

'Yes,' said Anne, 'except that we met a strange one-legged man who told us he saw spook-trains.'

Mr Luffy laughed. 'Well, well! He must be a cousin of a little girl I know who thought she was sitting on a volcano.'

Anne giggled. 'You're not to tease me. No, honestly, Mr Luffy, this old man was a watchman at a sort of old railway yard – not used now – and he said when the spook-trains came, he blew out his light and got under his bed so that they shouldn't get him.'

'Poor old fellow,' said Mr Luffy. 'I hope he didn't frighten you.'

'He did a bit,' said Anne. 'And he threw a cinder at Dick and hit him on the head. Tomorrow we're going to the farm to ask the boy there if he's heard of the spook-trains, too. We met an old shepherd who said he'd heard them but not seen them.'

'Well, well – it all sounds most interesting,' said Mr Luffy. 'But these exciting stories usually have a very tame explanation, you know. Now would you like to see what I found today? A very rare and interesting little beetle.'

He opened a small square tin and showed a shiny beetle to Anne. It had green feelers and a red fiery spot near its tail-end. It was a lovely little thing.

'Now that's much more exciting to me than half a dozen spook-trains,' he told Anne. 'Spook-trains won't keep me awake at night – but thinking of this little beetle-fellow here certainly will.'

'I don't very much like beetles,' said Anne. 'But this one certainly is pretty. Do you really like hunting about all day for insects, and watching them, Mr Luffy?'

'Yes, very much,' said Mr Luffy. 'Ah, here come the boys with the water. Now we'll hand the cake round, shall we? Where's George? Oh, there she is, changing her shoes.'

George had a blister, and she had been putting a strip of plaster on her heel. She came up when the boys arrived and the cake was handed round. They sat in a circle, munching, while the sun gradually went down in a blaze of red.

'Nice day tomorrow again,' said Julian. 'What shall we do?'

'We'll have to go to the farm first,' said Dick. 'The farmer's wife said she'd let us have some more bread if we turned up in the morning. And we could do with more eggs if we can get them. We took eight hard-boiled ones with us today and we've only one or two left. And who's eaten all the tomatoes, I'd like to know?'

'All of you,' said Anne at once. 'You're perfect pigs over the tomatoes.'

'I'm afraid I'm one of the pigs,' apologised Mr Luffy.

'I think you fried me six for my breakfast, Anne.'

'That's all right,' said Anne. 'You didn't have as many as the others, even so! We can easily get some more.'

It was pleasant sitting there, eating and talking, and drinking lime juice and stream water. They were all tired, and it was nice to think of the cosy sleeping-bags. Timmy lifted his head and gave a vast yawn, showing an enormous amount of teeth.

'Timmy! I could see right down to your tail then!' said George. 'Do shut your mouth up. You've made us all yawn.'

So he had. Even Mr Luffy was yawning. He got up. 'Well, I'm going to turn in,' he said. 'Good night. We'll make plans tomorrow morning. I'll bring up some breakfast for you, if you like. I've got some tins of sardines.'

'Oh, thanks,' said Anne. 'And there's some of this cake left. I hope you won't think that's too funny a breakfast, Mr Luffy – sardines and fruit cake?'

'Not a bit. It sounds a most sensible meal,' came Mr Luffy's voice from down the hillside. 'Good night!'

The children sat there a few minutes longer. The sun went right out of sight. The wind grew a little chilly. Timmy yawned enormously again.

'Come on,' said Julian. 'Time we turned in. Thank goodness Timmy didn't come into our tent and walk all over me last night. Good night, girls. It's going to be a heavenly night – but as I shall be asleep in about two shakes of a duck's tail, I shan't see much of it!'

The girls went into their tent. They were soon in their sleeping-bags. Just before they went to sleep Anne felt the slight shivering of the earth that meant a train was running underground somewhere. She could hear no rumbling sound. She fell asleep thinking of it.

The boys were not asleep. They, too, had felt the trembling of the earth beneath them, and it had reminded them of the old railway yard.

'Funny about those spook-trains, Dick,' said Julian, sleepily. 'Wonder if there *is* anything in it?'

'No. How could there be?' said Dick. 'All the same we'll go to the farm tomorrow and have a chat with that boy. He lives on the moors and he ought to know the truth.'

'The real truth is that Wooden Leg Sam is potty, and imagines all he says, and the old shepherd is ready to believe in anything strange,' said Julian.

'I expect you're right,' said Dick. 'Oh my goodness, what's that?'

A dark shape stood looking in at the tent-flap. It gave a little whine.

'Oh, it's you, Timmy. Would you mind *not* coming and pretending you're a spook-train or something?' said Dick. 'And if you dare to put so much as half a paw on my middle, I'll scare you down the hill with a roar like a man-eating tiger. Go away.'

Timmy put a paw on Julian. Julian yelled out to George. 'George! Call this dog of yours, will you? He's just about to turn himself round twenty times on my middle, and curl himself up for the night.'

There was no answer from George. Timmy, feeling that he was not wanted, disappeared. He went back to George and curled himself up on her feet. He put his nose down on his paws and slept.

'Spooky Timmy,' murmured Julian, re-arranging himself. 'Timmy spooky – no, I mean – oh dear, what do I mean?'

'Shut up,' said Dick. 'What with you and Timmy messing about, I can't get – to – sleep!' But he could and he did – almost before he had finished speaking. Silence fell on the little camp, and nobody noticed when the next train rumbled underground – not even Timmy!

CHAPTER SIX

Day at the farm

THE NEXT day the children were up very early, as early as Mr Luffy, and they all had breakfast together. Mr Luffy had a map of the moorlands, and he studied it carefully after breakfast.

'I think I'll go off for the whole day,' he said to Julian, who was sitting beside him. 'See that little valley marked here – Crowleg Vale – well, I have heard that there are some of the rarest beetles in Britain to be found there. I think I'll take my gear and go along. What are you four going to do?'

'Five,' said George at once. 'You've forgotten Timmy.'

'So I have. I beg his pardon,' said Mr Luffy, solemnly. 'Well – what are you going to do?'

'We'll go over to the farm and get more food,' said Julian. 'And ask that farm-boy if he's heard the tale of the spook-trains. And perhaps look round the farm and get to know the animals there. I always like a farm.'

'Right,' said Mr Luffy, beginning to light his pipe. 'Don't worry about me if I'm not back till dusk. When I'm bug-hunting I lose count of the time.'

'You're sure you won't get lost?' said Anne, anxiously.

51

She didn't really feel that Mr Luffy could take proper care of himself.

'Oh yes. My right ear always warns me if I'm losing my way,' said Mr Luffy. 'It waggles hard.'

He waggled it at Anne and she laughed. 'I wish you'd tell me how you do that,' she said. 'I'm sure you know. You can't think how thrilled the girls at school would be if I learnt that trick. They'd think it was super.'

Mr Luffy grinned and got up. 'Well, so long,' he said. 'I'm off before Anne makes me give her a lesson in ear-waggles.'

He went off down the slope to his own tent. George and Anne washed-up, while the boys tightened some tent ropes that had come loose, and generally tidied up.

'I suppose it's quite all right leaving everything unguarded like this,' said Anne, anxiously.

'Well, we did yesterday,' said Dick. 'And who's likely to come and take anything up here in this wild and lonely spot, I'd like to know? You don't imagine a spook-train will come along and bundle everything into its luggage-van, do you, Anne?'

Anne giggled. 'Don't be silly. I just wondered if we ought to leave Timmy on guard, that's all.'

'Leave Timmy!' said George, amazed. 'You don't really think I'd leave Timmy behind every time we go off anywhere, Anne? Don't be an idiot.'

'No, I didn't really think you would,' said Anne. 'Well,

I suppose nobody will come along here. Throw over that tea-cloth, George, if you've finished with it.'

Soon the tea-cloths were hanging over the gorse bushes to dry in the sun. Everything was put away neatly in the tents. Mr Luffy had called a loud goodbye and gone. Now the Five were ready to go off to the farm.

Anne took a basket, and gave one to Julian too. 'To bring back the food,' said she. 'Are you ready to go now?'

They set off over the heather, their knees brushing through the honeyed flowers, and sending scores of busy bees into the air. It was a lovely day again, and the children felt free and happy.

They came to the trim little farm. Men were at work in the fields, but Julian did not think they were very industrious. He looked about for the farm-boy.

The boy came out of a shed and whistled to them. 'Hallo! You come for some more eggs? I've collected quite a lot for you.'

He stared at Anne. 'You didn't come yesterday. What's your name?'

'Anne,' said Anne. 'What's yours?'

'Jock,' said the boy, with a grin. He was rather a nice boy, Anne thought, with straw-coloured hair, blue eyes, and rather a red face which looked very good-tempered.

'Where's your mother?' said Julian. 'Can we get some bread and other things from her today? We ate an awful lot of our food yesterday, and we want to stock up our larder again!'

'She's busy just now in the dairy,' said Jock. 'Are you in a hurry? Come and see my pups.'

They all walked off with him to a shed. In there, right at the end, was a big box lined with straw. A collie dog lay there with five lovely little puppies. She growled at Timmy fiercely, and he backed hurriedly out of the shed. He had met fierce mother-dogs before, and he didn't like them!

The four children exclaimed over the fat little puppies, and Anne took one out very gently. It cuddled into her arms and made funny little whining noises.

'I wish it was mine,' said Anne. 'I should call it Cuddle.'

'What a frightful name for a dog,' said George scornfully. 'Just the kind of silly name you *would* think of, Anne. Let me hold it. Are they all yours, Jock?'

'Yes,' said Jock, proudly. 'The mother's mine, you see. Her name's Biddy.'

Biddy pricked up her ears at her name and looked up at Jock out of bright, alert eyes. He fondled her silky head.

'I've had her for four years,' he said. 'When we were at Owl Farm, old Farmer Burrows gave her to me when she was eight weeks old.'

'Oh – were you at another farm before this one, then?' asked Anne. 'Have you always lived on a farm? Aren't you lucky!'

'I've only lived on two,' said Jock. 'Owl Farm and this one. Mum and I had to leave Owl Farm when Dad died, and we went to live in a town for a year. I hated that. I was glad when we came here.'

'But I thought your father was here!' said Dick, puzzled.

'That's my stepfather,' said Jock. 'He's no farmer, though!' He looked round and lowered his voice. 'He doesn't know much about farming. It's my mother that tells the men what to do. Still, he gives her plenty of money to do everything well, and we've got fine machinery and wagons and things. Like to see the dairy? It's slap up-to-date and Mum loves working in it.'

Jock took the four children to the shining, spotless dairy. His mother was at work there with a girl. She nodded and smiled at the children. 'Good morning! Hungry again? I'll pack you up plenty of food when I've finished in the dairy. Would you like to stay and have dinner with my Jock? He's lonely enough here in the holidays, with no other boy to keep him company.'

'Oh, *yes* – do let's!' cried Anne, in delight. 'I'd like that. Can we, Ju?'

'Yes. Thank you very much, Mrs – er – Mrs . . .' said Julian.

'I'm Mrs Andrews,' said Jock's mother. 'But Jock is Jock Robins – he's the son of my first husband, a farmer. Well, stay to dinner all of you, and I'll see if I can give you a meal that will keep you going for the rest of the day!'

This sounded good. The four children felt thrilled, and Timmy wagged his tail hard. He liked Mrs Andrews.

'Come on,' said Jock, joyfully. 'I'll take you all round the farm, into every corner. It's not very big, but we're going to make it the best little farm on the moorlands. My

56

stepfather doesn't seem to take much interest in the work of the farm, but he's jolly generous when it comes to handing out money to Mum to buy everything she wants.'

It certainly seemed to the children that the machinery on the farm was absolutely up-to-date. They examined the combine, they went into the little cowshed and admired the clean stone floor with white brick walls, they climbed into the red-painted wagons, and they wished they could try the two motor-tractors that stood side by side in a barn.

'You've got plenty of men here to work the farm,' said Julian. 'I shouldn't have thought there was enough for so many to do on this small place.'

'They're not good workers,' said Jock, his face creasing into frowns. 'Mum's always getting wild with them. They just don't know what to do. Dad gives her plenty of men to work the farm, but he always chooses the wrong ones! They don't seem to like farm-work, and they're always running off to the nearest town whenever they can. There's only one good fellow and he's old. See him over there? His name's Will.'

The children looked at Will. He was working in the little vegetable garden, an old fellow with a shrivelled face, a tiny nose and a pair of very blue eyes. They liked the look of him.

'Yes. He *looks* like a farm-worker,' said Julian. 'The others don't.'

'He won't work with them,' said Jock. 'He just says rude things to them, and calls them ninnies and idjits.'

'What's an idjit?' asked Anne.

'An idiot, silly,' said Dick. He walked up to old Will. 'Good morning,' he said. 'You're very busy. There's always a lot to do on a farm, isn't there?'

The old fellow looked at Dick out of his very blue eyes, and went on with his work. 'Plenty to do and plenty of folk to do it, and not much done,' he said, in a croaking kind of voice. 'Never thought I'd be put to work with ninnies and idjits. Not ninnies and idjits!'

'There! What did I tell you?' said Jock, with a grin. 'He's always calling the other men that, so we just have to let him work right away from them. Still, I must say he's about right – most of the fellows here don't know the first thing about work on a farm. I wish my stepfather would let us have a few proper workers instead of these fellows.'

'Where's your stepfather?' said Julian, thinking he must be rather peculiar to pour money into a little moorland farm like this, and yet choose the wrong kind of workers.

'He's away for the day,' said Jock. 'Thank goodness!' he added, with a sideways look at the others.

'Why? Don't you like him?' asked Dick.

'He's all right,' said Jock. 'But he's not a farmer, though he makes out he's always wanted to be – and what's more he doesn't like me one bit. I try to like him for Mum's sake. But I'm always glad when he's out of the way.'

'Your mother's nice,' said George.

'Oh, yes – Mum's grand,' said Jock. 'You don't know what it means to her to have a little farm of her own

58

again, and to be able to run it with the proper machinery and all.'

They came to a large barn. The door was locked. 'I told you what was in here before,' said Jock. 'Lorries! You can peek through that hole here at them. Don't know why my stepfather wanted to buy up so many, but I suppose he got them cheap – he loves to get things cheap and sell them dear! He did say they'd be useful on the farm, to take goods to the market.'

'Yes – you told us that when we were here yesterday,' said Dick. 'But you've got heaps of wagons for that!'

'Yes. I reckon they weren't bought for the farm at all, but for holding here till prices went high and he could make a lot of money,' said Jock, lowering his voice. 'I don't tell Mum that. So long as she gets what she wants for the farm, I'm going to hold my tongue.'

The children were very interested in all this. They wished they could see Mr Andrews. He must be a peculiar sort of fellow, they thought. Anne tried to imagine what he was like.

'Big and tall and dark and frowny,' she thought. 'Rather frightening and impatient, and he certainly won't like children. People like that never do.'

They spent a very pleasant morning poking about the little farm. They went back to see Biddy the collie and her pups. Timmy stood patiently outside the shed, with his tail down. He didn't like George to take so much interest in other dogs.

A bell rang loudly. 'Good! Dinner!' said Jock. 'We'd better wash. We're all filthy. Hope you feel hungry, because I guess Mum's got a super dinner for us.'

'I feel terribly hungry,' said Anne. 'It seems ages since we had breakfast. I've almost forgotten it!'

They all felt the same. They went into the farmhouse and were surprised to find a very nice little bathroom to wash in. Mrs Andrews was there, putting out a clean roller towel.

'Fine little bathroom, isn't it?' she said. 'My husband had it put in for me. First proper bathroom I've ever had!'

A glorious smell rose up from the kitchen downstairs. 'Come on!' said Jock, seizing the soap. 'Let's hurry. We'll be down in a minute, Mum!'

And they were. Nobody was going to dawdle over washing when a grand meal lay waiting for them downstairs!

CHAPTER SEVEN

Mr Andrews comes home

THEY ALL sat down to dinner. There was a big meat-pie, a cold ham, salad, potatoes in their jackets, and home-made pickles. It really was difficult to know what to choose.

'Have some of both,' said Mrs Andrews, cutting the meat-pie. 'Begin with the pie and go on with the ham. That's the best of living on a farm, you know – you do get plenty to eat.'

After the first course there were plums and thick cream, or jam tarts and the same cream. Everyone tucked in hungrily.

'I've never had such a lovely dinner in my life,' said Anne, at last. 'I wish I could eat some more but I can't. It was super, Mrs Andrews.'

'Smashing,' said Dick. That was his favourite word these holidays. 'Absolutely smashing.'

'Woof,' said Timmy, agreeing. He had had a fine plateful of meaty bones, biscuits and gravy, and he had licked up every crumb and every drop. Now he felt he would like to have a snooze in the sun and not do a thing for the rest of the day.

The children felt rather like that, too. Mrs Andrews handed them a chocolate each and sent them out of doors.

'You go and have a rest now,' she said. 'Talk to Jock. He doesn't get enough company of his own age in the holidays. You can stay on to tea, if you like.'

'Oh thanks,' said everyone, although they all felt that they wouldn't even be able to manage a biscuit. But it was so pleasant at the farm that they felt they would like to stay as long as they could.

'May we borrow one of Biddy's puppies to have with us?' asked Anne.

'If Biddy doesn't mind,' said Mrs Andrews, beginning to clear away. 'And if Timmy doesn't eat it up!'

'Timmy wouldn't dream of it!' said George at once. 'You go and get the puppy, Anne. We'll find a nice place in the sun.'

Anne went off to get the puppy. Biddy didn't seem to mind a bit. Anne cuddled the fat little thing against her, and went off to the others, feeling very happy. The boys had found a fine place against a haystack, and sat leaning against it, the sun shining down warmly on them.

'Those men of yours seem to take a jolly good lunch-hour off,' said Julian, not seeing any of them about.

Jock gave a snort. 'They're bone lazy. I'd sack the lot if I were my stepfather. Mum's told him how badly the men work, but he doesn't say a word to them. I've given up bothering. I don't pay their wages – if I did, I'd sack the whole lot!'

'Let's ask Jock about the spook-trains,' said George,

fonding Timmy's ears. 'It would be fun to talk about them.'

'Spook-trains? Whatever are they?' asked Jock, his eyes wide with surprise. 'Never heard of them!'

'Haven't you really?' asked Dick. 'Well, you don't live very far from them, Jock!'

'Tell me about them,' said Jock. 'Spook-trains – no, I've never heard of one of those.'

'Well, I'll tell you what we know,' said Julian. 'Actually we thought you'd be able to tell us much more about them than we know ourselves.'

He began to tell Jock about their visit to the deserted railway yard, and Wooden-Leg Sam, and his peculiar behaviour. Jock listened, enthralled.

'Coo! I wish I'd been with you. Let's all go there together, shall we?' he said. 'This was quite an adventure you had, wasn't it? You know, I've never had a single adventure in all my life, not even a little one. Have you?'

The four children looked at one another, and Timmy looked at George. Adventures! What didn't they know about them? They had had so many.

'Yes. We've had heaps of adventures – real ones – smashing ones,' said Dick. 'We've been down in dungeons, we've been lost in caves, we've found secret passages, we've looked for treasure – well, I can't tell you what we've done! It would take too long.'

'No, it wouldn't,' said Jock eagerly. 'You tell me. Go on. Did you all have the adventures? Little Anne, here, too?'

'Yes, all of us,' said George. 'And Timmy as well. He rescued us heaps of times from danger. Didn't you, Tim?'

'Woof, woof,' said Timmy, and thumped his tail against the hay.

They began to tell Jock about their many adventures. He was a very, very good listener. His eyes almost fell out of his head, and he went brick-red whenever they came to an exciting part.

'My word!' he said at last. 'I've never heard such things in my life before. Aren't you lucky? You just go about

64

having adventures all the time, don't you? I *say* – do you think you'll have one here, these hols?'

Julian laughed. 'No. Whatever kind of adventure would there be on these lonely moorlands? Why, you yourself have lived here for three years, and haven't even had a tiny adventure.'

Jock sighed. 'That's true. I haven't.' Then his eyes brightened again. 'But see here – what about those spook-trains you've been asking me about? Perhaps you'll have an adventure with those?'

'Oh, no, I don't want to,' said Anne, in a horrified voice. 'An adventure with spook-trains would be simply horrid.'

'I'd like to go down to that old railway yard with you and see Wooden Leg Sam,' said Jock longingly. 'Why, that would be a real adventure to me, you know – just talking to a funny old man like that, and wondering if he was suddenly going to throw cinders at us. Take me with you next time you go.'

'Well – I don't know that we meant to go again,' said Julian. 'There's really nothing much in his story except imagination – the old watchman's gone peculiar in the head through being alone there so much, guarding a yard where nothing and nobody ever comes. He's just remembering the trains that used to go in and out before the line was given up.'

'But the shepherd said the same as Sam,' said Jock. 'I *say* – what about going down there one night and watching for a spook-train!'

'NO!' said Anne, in horror.

'You needn't come,' said Jock. 'Just us three boys.'

'And me,' said George at once. 'I'm as good as any boy, and I'm not going to be left out. Timmy's coming, too.'

'Oh, please don't make these awful plans,' begged poor Anne. 'You'll *make* an adventure come, if you go on like this.'

Nobody took the least notice of her. Julian looked at Jock's excited face. 'Well,' he said, 'if we do go there again, we'll tell you. And if we think we'll go watching for spook-trains, we'll take you with us.'

Jock looked as if he could hug Julian. 'That would be terrific,' he said. 'Thanks a lot. Spook-trains! I *say*, just suppose we really did see one! Who'd be driving it? Where would it come from?'

'Out of the tunnel, Wooden-Leg Sam says,' said Dick. 'But I don't see how we'd spot it, except by the noise it made, because apparently the spook-trains only arrive in the dark of the night. Never in the daytime. We wouldn't *see* much, even if we were there.'

It was such an exciting subject to Jock that he persisted in talking about it all the afternoon. Anne got tired of listening, and went to sleep with Biddy's puppy in her arms. Timmy curled up by George and went to sleep too. He wanted to go for a walk, but he could see that there was no hope with all this talking going on.

It was tea-time before any of them had expected it. The bell rang, and Jock looked most surprised.

'Tea! Would you believe it? Well, I *have* had an exciting afternoon talking about all this. And look here, if you don't make up your minds to go spook-train hunting I'll jolly well go off by myself. If only I could have an adventure like the kind you've had, I'd be happy.'

They went in to tea, after waking Anne up with difficulty. She took the puppy back to Biddy, who received it gladly and licked it all over.

Julian was surprised to find that he was quite hungry again. 'Well,' he said, as he sat down at the table, 'I didn't imagine I'd feel hungry again for a week – but I do. What a marvellous tea, Mrs Andrews. Isn't Jock lucky to have meals like this always!'

There were home-made scones with new honey. There were slices of bread thickly spread with butter, and new-made cream cheese to go with it. There was sticky brown gingerbread, hot from the oven, and a big solid fruit cake that looked almost like a plum pudding when it was cut, it was so black.

'Oh dear! I wish now I hadn't had so much dinner,' sighed Anne. 'I don't feel hungry enough to eat a bit of everything and I would so like to!'

Mrs Andrews laughed. 'You eat what you can, and I'll give you some to take away, too,' she said. 'You can have some cream cheese, and the scones and honey – and some of the bread I made this morning. And maybe you'd like a slab of the gingerbread. I made plenty.'

'Oh, thanks,' said Julian. 'We'll be all right tomorrow

with all that. You're a marvellous cook, Mrs Andrews. I wish I lived on your farm.'

There was the sound of a car coming slowly up the rough track to the farmhouse, and Mrs Andrews looked up. 'That's Mr Andrews come back,' she said. 'My husband, you know, Jock's stepfather.'

Julian thought she looked a little worried. Perhaps Mr Andrews didn't like children and wouldn't be pleased to see them sitting round his table when he came home tired.

'Would you like us to go, Mrs Andrews?' he asked politely. 'Perhaps Mr Andrews would like a bit of peace for his meal when he comes in – and we're rather a crowd, aren't we?'

Jock's mother shook her head. 'No, you can stay. I'll get him a meal in the other room if he'd like it.'

Mr Andrews came in. He wasn't in the least like Anne or the others had imagined him to be. He was a short, dark little man, with a weak face and a nose much too big for it. He looked harassed and bad-tempered, and stopped short when he saw the five children.

'Hallo, dear,' said Mrs Andrews. 'Jock's got his friends here today. Would you like a bit of tea in your room? I can easily put a tray there.'

'Well,' said Mr Andrews, smiling a watery kind of smile, 'perhaps it would be best. I've had a worrying kind of day, and not much to eat.'

'I'll get you a tray of ham and pickles and bread,' said his wife. 'It won't take a minute. You go and wash.'

Mr Andrews went out. Anne was surprised that he seemed so small and looked rather stupid. She had imagined someone big and burly, strong and clever, who was always going about doing grand deals and making a lot of money. Well, he must be cleverer than he looked, to make enough money to give Mrs Andrews all she needed for her farm.

Mrs Andrews bustled about with this and that, laying a tray with a snow-white cloth, and plates of food. Mr Andrews could be heard in the bathroom, splashing as he washed. Then he came downstairs and put his head in at the door. 'My meal ready?' he asked. 'Well, Jock – had a good day?'

'Yes, thanks,' said Jock, as his stepfather took the tray from his mother and turned to go. 'We went all round the farm this morning – and we talked and talked this afternoon. And oh, I say – do you know anything about spook-trains, sir?'

Mr Andrews was just going out of the door. He turned in surprise. 'Spook-trains? What are you talking about?'

'Well, Julian says there's an old deserted railway yard a good way from here, and spook-trains are supposed to come out of the tunnel there in the dark of night,' said Jock. 'Have you heard of them?'

Mr Andrews stood stock still, his eyes on his step-son. He looked dismayed and shocked. Then he came back into the room and kicked the door shut behind him.

'I'll have my tea here after all,' he said. 'Well, to think

you've heard of those spook-trains! I've been careful not to mention them to your mother or to you, Jock, for fear of scaring you!'

'Gee!' said Dick. 'Are they really true then? They can't be.'

'You tell me all you know, and how you know about it,' said Mr Andrews, sitting down at the table with his tray. 'Go on. Don't miss out a thing. I want to hear everything.'

Julian hesitated. 'Oh – there's nothing really to tell, sir – just a lot of nonsense.'

'You tell it me!' almost shouted Mr Andrews. 'Then I'll tell *you* a few things. And I tell you, you won't go near that old railway yard again   no, that you won't!'

CHAPTER EIGHT

A lazy evening

THE FIVE children and Mrs Andrews stared in surprise at Mr Andrews, when he shouted at them. He repeated some of his words again.

'Go on! You tell me all you know. And then I'll tell *you*!'

Julian decided to tell, very shortly, what had happened at the old railway yard, and what Wooden-Leg Sam had said. He made the tale sound rather bald and dull. Mr Andrews listened to it with the greatest interest, never once taking his eyes off Julian.

Then he sat back and drank a whole cup of strong tea in one gulp. The children waited for him to speak, wondering what he had to say.

'Now,' he said, making his voice sound important and impressive, 'you listen to me. Don't any of you ever go down to that yard again. It's a bad place.'

'Why?' asked Julian. 'What do you mean – a bad place?'

'Things have happened there – years and years ago,' said Mr Andrews. 'Bad things. Accidents. It was all shut up after that and the tunnel wasn't used any more. See? Nobody was allowed to go there, and nobody did, because they were scared. They knew it was a bad place, where bad things happen.'

72

Anne felt frightened. 'But Mr Andrews – you don't mean there really are spook-trains, do you?' she asked, her face rather pale.

Mr Andrews pursed up his lips and nodded very solemnly indeed. 'That's just what I do mean. Spook-trains come and go. Nobody knows why. But it's bad luck to be there when they come. They might take you away, see?'

Julian laughed. 'Oh – not as bad as that, sir, surely! Anyway, you're frightening Anne, so let's change the subject. I don't believe in spook-trains.'

But Mr Andrews didn't seem to want to stop talking about the trains. 'Wooden-Leg Sam was right to hide himself when they come along,' he said. 'I don't know how he manages to stay on in a bad place like that. Never knowing when a train is going to come creeping out of that tunnel in the darkness.'

Julian was not going to have Anne frightened any more. He got up from the table and turned to Mrs Andrews.

'Thank you very much for a lovely day and lovely food!' he said. 'We must go now. Come along, Anne.'

'Wait a minute,' said Mr Andrews. 'I just want to warn you all very solemnly that you mustn't go down to that railway yard. You hear me, Jock? You might never come back. Old Wooden-Leg Sam's mad, and well he may be, with spook-trains coming along in the dead of night. It's a bad and dangerous place. You're not to go near it!'

73

'Well – thank you for the warning, sir,' said Julian, politely, suddenly disliking the small man with the big nose very much indeed. 'We'll be going. Goodbye, Mrs Andrews. Goodbye, Jock. Come along tomorrow and have a picnic with us, will you?'

'Oh, thanks! Yes, I will,' said Jock. 'But wait a minute – aren't you going to take any food with you?'

'Yes, of course they are,' said Mrs Andrews, getting up from her chair. She had been listening to the conversation with a look of puzzled wonder on her face. She went out into the scullery, where there was a big, cold larder. Julian followed her. He carried the two baskets.

'I'll give you plenty,' said Mrs Andrews, putting loaves, butter, and cream cheese into the baskets. 'I know what appetites you youngsters get. Now, don't you be too scared at what my husband's just been saying – I saw that little Anne was frightened. I've never heard of the spook-trains, and I've been here for three years. I don't reckon there's much in the tale, you know, for all my husband's so set on warning you not to go down to the yard.'

Julian said nothing. He thought that Mr Andrews had behaved rather oddly about the whole story. Was he one of the kind of people who believed in all sorts of silly things and got scared himself? He looked weak enough! Julian found himself wondering how a nice woman like Mrs Andrews could have married such a poor specimen of a man. Still, he was a generous fellow, judging by all Jock had said, and perhaps Jock's mother felt grateful to him for giving her the farm and the money to run it with. That must be it.

Julian thanked Mrs Andrews, and insisted on paying her, though she would have given him the food for nothing. She came into the kitchen with him and he saw that the others had already gone outside. Only Mr Andrews was left, eating ham and pickles.

'Goodbye, sir,' said Julian politely.

'Goodbye. And you remember what I've told you, boy,' said Mr Andrews. 'Bad luck comes to people who see the spook-trains – yes, terrible bad luck. You keep away from them.'

Julian gave a polite smile and went out. It was evening now and the sun was setting behind the moorland hills, though it still had a long way to go before it disappeared. He caught up with the others. Jock was with them.

'I'm just coming half-way with you,' said Jock. 'I say! My stepfather was pretty scary about those trains, wasn't he?'

'I felt pretty scary too, when he was warning us about them,' said Anne. 'I shan't go down to that yard again, ever. Will you, George?'

'If the boys did, I would,' said George, who didn't look very much as if she wanted to, all the same.

'*Are* you going to the yard again?' asked Jock, eagerly. 'I'm not scared. Not a bit. It would be an adventure to go and watch for a spook-train.'

'We might go,' said Julian. 'We'll take you with us, if we do. But the girls aren't to come.'

'Well, I like that!' said George angrily. 'As if you could leave me behind! When have I been scared of anything? I'm as brave as any of you.'

'Yes. I know. You can come as soon as we find out it's all a silly story,' said Julian.

'I shall come whenever you go,' flashed back George. 'Don't you dare to leave me out. I'll never speak to you again if you do.'

Jock looked most surprised at this sudden flare-up of temper from George. He didn't know how fierce she could be!

'I don't see why George shouldn't come,' he said. 'I bet she'd be every bit as good as a boy. I thought she was one when I first saw her.'

George gave him one of her sweetest smiles. He couldn't have said anything she liked better! But Julian would not change his mind.

'I mean what I say. The girls won't come if we do go, so that's that. For one thing, Anne certainly wouldn't want to come, and if George came without her she'd be left all alone up at the camp. She wouldn't like that.'

'She could have Mr Luffy's company,' said George, looking sulky again.

'Idiot! As if we'd want to tell Mr Luffy we were going off exploring deserted railway yards watched over by a mad, one-legged fellow who swears there are spook-trains!'

said Julian. 'He'd stop us going. You know what grown-ups are like. Or he'd come with us, which would be worse.'

'Yes. He'd see moths all the time, not spook-trains,' said Dick, with a grin.

'I'd better go back now,' said Jock. 'It's been a grand day. I'll come up tomorrow and picnic with you. Goodbye.'

They called goodbye to Jock, and went on their way to the camp. It was quite nice to see it again, waiting for them, the two tents flapping a little in the breeze. Anne pushed her way through the tent-flap, anxious to see that everything was untouched.

Inside the tent it was very hot. Anne decided to put the food they had brought under the bottom of the big gorse bush. It would be cooler there. She was soon busy about her little jobs. The boys went down to see if Mr Luffy was back, but he wasn't.

'Anne! We're going to bathe in the stream!' they called. 'We feel hot and dirty. Are you coming? George is coming too.'

'No, I won't come,' Anne called back. 'I've got lots of things to do.'

The boys grinned at one another. Anne did so enjoy 'playing house'. So they left her to it, and went to the stream, from which yells and howls and shrieks soon came. The water was colder than they expected, and nobody liked to lie down in it – but everyone was well and truly splashed, and the icy-cold drops falling on their hot bodies made them squeal and yell. Timmy didn't in the least mind the iciness of the water. He rolled over and over in it, enjoying himself.

'Look at him, showing off!' said Dick. 'Aha, Timmy, if I could bathe in a fur coat like you, I wouldn't mind the cold water either.'

'Woof,' said Timmy, and climbed up the shallow bank. He shook himself violently and thousands of icy-cold silvery drops flew from him and landed on the three shivering children. They yelled and chased him away.

It was a pleasant, lazy evening. Mr Luffy didn't appear at all. Anne got a light meal of bread and cream cheese and a piece of gingerbread. Nobody felt like facing another big meal that day. They lay in the heather and talked comfortably.

'This is the kind of holiday I like,' said Dick.

'So do I,' said Anne. 'Except for the spook-trains. That's spoilt it a bit for me.'

'Don't be silly, Anne,' said George. 'If they are not real it's just a silly story, and if they are real, well, it might be an adventure.'

There was a little silence. 'Are we going down to the yard again?' asked Dick lazily.

'Yes, I think so,' said Julian. 'I'm not going to be scared off it by weird warnings from Pa Andrews.'

'Then I vote we go one night and wait to see if a spook-train does come along,' said Dick.

A LAZY EVENING

'I shall come too,' said George.

'No, you won't,' said Julian. 'You'll stay with Anne.'

George said nothing, but everyone could feel mutiny in the air.

'Do we tell Mr Luffy, or don't we?' said Dick.

'You know we've said we wouldn't,' said Julian. He yawned. 'I'm getting sleepy. And the sun has gone, so it will soon be dark. I wonder where old Luffy is?'

'Do you think I'd better wait up and see if he wants something to eat?' said Anne, anxiously.

'No. Not unless you want to keep awake till midnight!' said Julian. 'He'll have got some food down in his tent. He'll be all right. I'm going to turn in. Coming, Dick?'

The boys were soon in their sleeping-bags. The girls lay in the heather for a little while longer, listening to the lonely-sounding cry of the curlews going home in the dusk. Then they, too, went into their own tent.

Once safely in their sleeping-bags, the two boys felt suddenly wide awake. They began to talk in low voices.

'Shall we take Jock down to see the yard in the daytime? Or shall we go one night and watch for the Train from Nowhere?' said Julian.

'I vote we go and watch at night,' said Dick. 'We'll never see a spook-train in the daytime. Wooden-Leg Sam is an interesting old chap, especially when he chucks cinders about – but I don't know that I like him enough to go and visit him again!'

'Well – if Jock badly wants to go and have a snoop round tomorrow morning when he comes, we'd better take him,' said Julian. 'We can always go one night, too, if we want to.'

'Right. We'll wait and see what Jock says,' said Dick. They talked a little longer and then felt sleepy. Dick was just dropping off when he heard something coming wriggling through the heather. A head was stuck through the opening of the tent.

'If you dare to come in, I'll smack your silly face,' said Dick, thinking it was Timmy. 'I know what you want, you perfect pest – you want to flop down on my tummy.

You just turn yourself round and go away! Do you hear?'

The head in the opening moved a little but didn't go away. Dick raised himself up on one elbow.

'Put one paw inside my tent and you'll be sent rolling down the hill!' he said. 'I love you very much in the daytime, but I'm not fond of you at night – not when I'm in a sleeping-bag anyway. Scoot!'

The head made a peculiar apologetic sound. Then it spoke. 'Er – you're awake, I see. Are all of you all right – the girls too? I'm only just back.'

'Gosh! It's Mr Luffy,' said Dick, filled with horror. 'I say, sir – I'm most awfully sorry – I thought you were Timmy, come to flop himself down on top of me, like he often does. So sorry, sir.'

'Don't mention it!' said the shadowy head with a chuckle. 'Glad you're all right. See you tomorrow!'

CHAPTER NINE

Night visitor

MR LUFFY slept very late the next morning and nobody liked
to disturb him. The girls yelled with laughter when they
heard how Dick had spoken to him the night before,
thinking he was Timmy the dog.

'He was very decent about it,' said Dick. 'Seemed to
think it was quite amusing. I hope he'll still think so this
morning!'

They were all sitting eating their breakfast – ham,
tomatoes, and the bread Mrs Andrews had given them the
day before. Timmy collected the bits as usual, and wondered
if George would let him have a lick of the cream cheese
she was now putting on her bread. Timmy loved cheese.
He looked at the lump in the dish and sighed all over
George. He could easily eat that in one mouthful! How he
wished he could.

'I wonder what time Jock will come up,' said George.
'If he came up pretty soon, we could go for a nice long
walk over the moors, and picnic somewhere. Jock ought to
know some fine walks.'

'Yes. We'll mess about till he comes, and then tell
him he's to be our guide and take us to the nicest walk
he knows,' said Anne. 'Oh, Timmy, you beast – you've

taken my nice lump of cream cheese right out of my fingers!'

'Well, you were waving it about under his nose, so what could you expect?' said George. 'He thought you were giving it to him.'

'Well, he shan't have any more. It's too precious,' said Anne. 'Oh, dear – I wish we didn't eat so much. We keep bringing in stacks of food, and it hardly lasts any time.'

'I bet Jock will bring some more,' said Dick. 'He's a sensible sort of fellow. Did you get a peep into that enormous larder of his mother's? It's like a great cave, goes right back into the wall, with dozens of stone shelves – and all filled with food. No wonder Jock's tubby.'

'Is he? I never noticed,' said Anne. 'Is that him whistling?'

It wasn't. It was a curlew, very high up. 'Too early for him yet,' said Julian. 'Shall we help you to clear up, Anne?'

'No. That's my job and George's,' said Anne firmly. 'You go down and see if Mr Luffy is awake. He can have a bit of ham and a few tomatoes, if he likes.'

They went down to Mr Luffy's tent. He was awake, sitting at the entrance, eating some kind of breakfast. He waved a sandwich at them.

'Hallo, there! I'm late this morning. I had a job getting back. I went much too far. Sorry I woke you up last night, Dick.'

'You didn't. I wasn't asleep,' said Dick, going rather red. 'Did you have a good day, Mr Luffy?'

'Bit disappointing. Didn't find quite all the creatures I'd hoped,' said Mr Luffy. 'What about you? Did you have a good day?'

'Fine,' said Dick, and described it. Mr Luffy seemed very interested in everything, even in Mr Andrews's rather frightening warning about the railway yard.

'Silly chap he sounds,' said Mr Luffy, shaking the crumbs off his front. 'All the same – I should keep away from the yard, if I were you. Stories don't get about for nothing, you know. No smoke without fire!'

'Why, sir – surely *you* don't believe there's anything spooky about the trains there?' said Dick, in surprise.

'Oh, no – I doubt if there *are* any trains,' said Mr Luffy. 'But when a place has got a bad name it's usually best to keep away from it.'

'I suppose so, sir,' said Dick and Julian together. Then they hastily changed the subject, afraid that Mr Luffy, like Mr Andrews, might also be going to forbid them to visit the railway yard. And the more they were warned about it and forbidden to go, the more they felt that they really must!

'Well, we must get back,' said Dick. 'We're expecting Jock – that's the boy at the farm – to come up for the day, and we thought we'd go out walking and take our food with us. Are you going out, too, sir?'

'Not today,' said Mr Luffy. 'My legs are tired and stiff with so much scrambling about yesterday, and I want to mount some of the specimens I found. Also I'd

like to meet your farm friend – what's his name –
Jock?'

'Yes, sir,' said Julian. 'Right. We'll bring him along as
soon as he comes, then off we'll go. You'll be left in peace
all day!'

But Jock didn't come. The children waited for him all
the morning and he didn't turn up. They held up their
lunch until they were too hungry to wait any longer, and
then they had it on the heather in front of their tents.

'Funny,' said Julian. 'He knows where the camp
is, because we pointed it out to him when he came
half-way home with us yesterday. Perhaps he'll come this
afternoon.'

But he didn't come in the afternoon either, nor did he
come after tea. Julian debated whether or not to go and see
what was up, but decided against it. There must be some
good reason why Jock hadn't come, and Mrs Andrews
wouldn't want them all visiting her two days running.

It was a disappointing day. They didn't like to leave the
tents and go for even a short stroll in case Jock came. Mr
Luffy was busy all day long with his specimens. He was
sorry Jock had disappointed them. 'He'll come tomorrow,'
he said. 'Have you got enough food? There's some in that
tin over there if you want it.'

'Oh, no thank you, sir,' said Julian. 'We've plenty really.
We're going to have a game of cards. Like to join us?'

'Yes, I think I will,' said Mr Luffy, getting up and
stretching himself. 'Can you play rummy?'

They could – and they beat poor Mr Luffy handsomely, because he couldn't play at all. He blamed his luck on his bad cards, but he enjoyed the game immensely. He said the only thing that really put him off was the way that Timmy stood behind him and breathed down his neck all the time.

'I kept feeling certain that Timmy thought he knew how to play my cards better than I could,' he complained. 'And whenever I did something wrong, he breathed down my neck harder than usual.'

Everyone laughed, and George privately thought that Timmy would probably play very much better than Mr Luffy if only he could hold the cards.

Jock didn't come at all. They put the cards away when they could no longer see them, and Mr Luffy announced that he was going to bed. 'It was very late when I got back last night,' he said. 'I really must have an early night.'

The others thought they would go to bed too. The thought of their cosy sleeping-bags was always a nice one when darkness came on.

The girls crept into their bags and Timmy flopped down on George. The boys were in their bags about the same time and Dick gave a loud yawn.

'Good night, Ju,' he said, and fell fast asleep. Julian was soon asleep too. In fact, everyone was sound asleep when Timmy gave a little growl. It was such a small growl that neither of the girls heard it, and certainly Dick and Julian didn't, away in their tent.

Timmy raised his head and listened intently. Then he

gave another small growl. He listened again. Finally he got up, shook himself, still without waking George, and stalked out of the tent, his ears cocked and his tail up. He had heard somebody or something, and although he thought it was all right, he was going to make sure.

Dick was sound asleep when he felt something brushing against the outside of his tent. He awoke at once and sat up. He looked at the tent opening. A shadow appeared there and looked in.

Was it Timmy? Was it Mr Luffy? He mustn't make a mistake this time. He waited for the shadow to speak. But it didn't! It just stayed there as if it were listening for some movement inside the tent. Dick didn't like it.

'Timmy!' he said at last, in a low voice.

Then the shadow spoke: 'Dick? Or is it Julian? It's Jock here. I've got Timmy beside me. Can I come in?'

'*Jock!*' said Dick, in surprise. 'Whatever have you come at this time of night for? And why didn't you come today? We waited ages for you.'

'Yes. I know I'm awfully sorry,' said Jock's voice, and the boy wriggled himself into the tent. Dick poked Julian awake.

'Julian! Here's Jock – and Timmy. Get off me, Timmy. Here, Jock, see if you can squeeze inside my sleeping-bag – there's room for us both, I think.'

'Oh, thanks,' said Jock, and squeezed inside with difficulty. 'How warm it is! I say, I'm terribly sorry I didn't come today – but my stepfather suddenly announced he wanted me to go somewhere with him for the whole day. Can't think why. He doesn't bother about me as a rule.'

'That was mean of him, seeing that he knew you were to come on a picnic with us,' said Julian. 'Was it something important?'

'No. Not at all,' said Jock. 'He drove off to Endersfield – that's about forty miles away – parked me in the public library there, saying he'd be back in a few minutes – and he didn't come back till past tea-time! I had some sandwiches with me, luckily. I felt pretty angry about it, I can tell you.'

'Never mind. Come tomorrow instead,' said Dick.

'I can't,' said Jock in despair. 'He's gone and arranged for me to meet the son of some friend of his – a boy called Cecil Dearlove – what a name! I'm to spend the day with this frightful boy. The worst of it is Mum's quite pleased about it. She never thinks my stepfather takes enough notice of me – good thing he doesn't, *I* think.'

'Oh blow – so you won't be able to come tomorrow either,' said Julian. 'Well – what about the next day?'

'It should be all right,' said Jock. 'But I've feeling I'll have dear love of a Cecil plonked on me for the day – to show him the cows and the puppies, dear pet! Ugh! When I could be with you four and Timmy.'

'It's bad luck,' said Julian. 'It really is.'

'I thought I'd better come and tell you,' said Jock. 'It's the first chance I've had, creeping up here tonight. I've brought some more food for you, by the way. I guessed you'd want some. I feel down in the dumps about that adventure – you know, going to see the railway yard. I was going to ask you to take me today.'

'Well – if you can't come tomorrow either – and perhaps not the next day – what about going one night?' said Dick. 'Would you like to come up tomorrow night, about this time? We won't tell the girls. We'll just go off by ourselves, we three boys – and watch!'

Jock was too thrilled to say a word. He let out a deep breath of joy. Dick laughed.

'Don't get too thrilled. We probably shan't see a thing. Bring a torch if you've got one. Come to our tent and jerk my toe. I'll probably be awake, but if I'm not, that'll wake me all right! And don't say a word to anyone of course.'

'Rather not,' said Jock, overjoyed. 'Well – I suppose I'd better be going. It was pretty weird coming over the moorland in the dark. There's no moon, and the stars don't give much light. I've left the food outside the tent. Better look out that Timmy doesn't get it.'

'Right. Thanks awfully,' said Julian. Jock got out of Dick's sleeping-bag and went backwards out of the tent, with Timmy obligingly licking his nose all the way. Jock then found the bag of food and rolled it in to Julian, who put it safely under the groundsheet.

'Good night,' said Jock, in a low voice, and they heard him scrambling over the heather. Timmy went with him, pleased at this unexpected visitor, and the chance of a midnight walk. Jock was glad to have the dog's company.

Timmy went right to the farm with him and then bounded back over the moorland to the camping place, longing to pounce on the rabbits he could smell here and there, but wanting to get back to George.

In the morning Anne was amazed to find the food in her 'larder' under the gorse bush. Julian had popped it there to surprise her. 'Look at this!' she cried, in astonishment. 'Meat-pies – more tomatoes – eggs, wherever did they come from?'

'Spook-train brought them in the night,' said Dick, with a grin.

'Volcano shot them up into the air,' said Mr Luffy, who was also there. Anne threw a tea-cloth at him.

'Tell me how it came here,' she demanded. 'I was worried about what to give you all for breakfast – and now there's more than we can possibly eat. Who put it there? George, do you know?'

But George didn't. She glanced at the smiling faces of the two boys. 'I bet Jock was here last night,' she said to them. 'Wasn't he?' And to herself she said: 'Yes – and somehow I think they've planned something together. You won't trick *me*, Dick and Julian. I'll be on the lookout from now on! Wherever you go, I go too!'

CHAPTER TEN

Hunt for a spook-train

THAT DAY passed pleasantly enough. The children, Timmy, and Mr Luffy all went off to a pool high up on the moorlands. It was called 'The Green Pool' because of its cucumber-green colour. Mr Luffy explained that some curious chemicals found there caused the water to look green.

'I hope we shan't come out looking green, too,' said Dick, getting into his bathing trunks. 'Are you going to bathe, Mr Luffy?'

Mr Luffy was. The children expected him to be a very poor swimmer and to splash about at the edge and do very little – but to their surprise he was magnificent in the water, and could swim faster even than Julian.

They had great fun, and when they were tired they came out to bask in the sun. The highroad ran alongside the green pool, and the children watched a herd of sheep being driven along, then a car or two came by, and finally a big army lorry. A boy sat beside the driver, and to the children's surprise he waved wildly at them.

'Who was that?' said Julian astonished. 'Surely he doesn't know us?'

George's sharp eye had seen who it was. 'It was Jock!

Sitting beside the driver. And, look, here comes his stepfather's fine new car. Jock's preferred to go with the lorry-driver instead of his stepfather! I don't blame him, either!'

The bright new car came by, driven by Mr Andrews. He didn't glance at the children by the wayside, but drove steadily on after the lorry.

'Going to market, I suppose,' said Dick, lying back again. 'Wonder what they're taking?'

'So do I,' said Mr Luffy. 'He must sell his farm produce at very high prices to be able to buy that fine car and all the machinery and gear you've told me about. Clever fellow Mr Andrews!'

'He doesn't look at all clever,' said Anne. 'He looks rather a weak, feeble sort of man, really, Mr Luffy. I can't even imagine him being clever enough to beat anyone down, or get the better of them.'

'Very interesting,' said Mr Luffy. 'Well, what about another dip before we have our dinner?'

It was a very nice day, and Mr Luffy was very good company. He could make fine jokes very solemnly indeed, and only the fact that his ear waggled violently showed the others that he too, was enjoying the joke. His right ear seemed to love to join in the joke, even if Mr Luffy's face was as solemn as Timmy's.

They arrived home at the camp about tea-time and Anne got a fine tea ready. They took it down to eat in front of Mr Luffy's tent. As the evening came on Julian and

Dick felt excitement rising in them. In the daytime neither of them really believed a word about the 'spook-trains', but as the sun sank and long shadows crept down the hills they felt pleasantly thrilled. Would they really see anything exciting that night?

It was a very dark night at first, because clouds lay across the sky and hid even the stars. The boys said good night to the girls and snuggled down into their sleeping-bags. They watched the sky through the tent opening.

Gradually the big clouds thinned out. A few stars appeared. The clouds thinned still more and fled away in rags. Soon the whole sky was bright with pin-points of light, and a hundred thousand stars looked down on the moorlands.

'We shall have a bit of starlight to see by,' whispered Julian. 'That's good. I don't want to stumble about over the heather and break my ankle in rabbit-holes in the pitch darkness. Nor do I want to use my torch on the way to the yard in case it's seen.'

'It's going to be fun!' Dick whispered back. 'I hope Jock comes. It will be maddening if he doesn't.'

He did come. There was a scrambling over the heather and once again a shadow appeared at the tent opening.

'Julian! Dick! I've come. Are you ready?'

It was Jock's voice, of course. Dick's thumb pressed the switch of his torch and for a moment its light fell on Jock's red, excited face, and then was switched off again.

'Hallo, Jock! So you were able to come,' said Dick. 'I

94

say, was that you in the lorry this morning, going by the green pool?'

'Yes. Did you see me? I saw you and waved like mad,' said Jock. 'I wanted to stop the lorry and get down and speak to you, but the driver's an awful bad-tempered sort of fellow. He wouldn't hear of stopping. Said my stepfather would be wild with him if he did. Did you see *him* – my stepfather, I mean? He was in his car behind.'

'Were you off to market or something?' asked Julian.

'I expect that's where the lorry was going,' said Jock. 'It was empty, so I suppose my stepfather was going to pick up something there. I came back in the car. The lorry was supposed to come later.'

'How did you like Cecil Dearlove?' asked Dick, grinning in the darkness.

'Awful! Worse than his name,' groaned Jock. 'Wanted me to play soldiers all the time! The frightful thing is I've got to have him at the farm for the day tomorrow. Another day wasted. What shall I do with him?'

'Roll him in the pig-sty,' suggested Dick. 'Or put him with Biddy's puppies and let him sleep there. Tell him to play soldiers with them.'

Jock chuckled. 'I wish I could. The worst of it is Mum is awfully pleased that my stepfather's got this Cecil boy for me to be friends with. Don't let's talk about it. Are you ready to start off?'

'Yes,' said Julian, and began to scramble quietly out of his bag. 'We didn't tell the girls. Anne doesn't want to come, and I don't want George to leave Anne by herself. Now, let's be very, very quiet till we're out of hearing.'

Dick got out of his bag too. The boys had not undressed that night, except for their coats, so all they had to do was to slip these on, and then crawl out of the tent.

'Which is the way – over there?' whispered Jock. Julian took his arm and guided him. He hoped he wouldn't lose his way in the starlit darkness. The moorland look so different at night!

'If we make for that hill you can dimly see over there against the starlit sky, we should be going in the right direction,' said Julian. So on they went, keeping towards the dark hill that rose up to the west.

It seemed very much farther to the railway yard at night than in the daytime. The three boys stumbled along, sometimes almost falling as their feet caught in tufts of heather. They were glad when they found some sort of path they could keep on.

'This is about where we met the shepherd,' said Dick, in a low voice. He didn't know why he spoke so quietly. He just felt as if he must. 'I'm sure we can't be very far off now.'

They went on for some way, and then Julian pulled Dick by the arm. 'Look,' he said. 'Down there, I believe that's the old yard. You can see the lines gleaming faintly here and there.'

They stood on the heathery slope above the old yard, straining their eyes. Soon they could make out dim shapes. Yes, it was the railway yard all right.

Jock clutched Julian's sleeve. 'Look – there's a light down there! Do you see it?'

The boys looked – and sure enough, down in the yard towards the other side of it, was a small yellow light. They stared at it.

'Oh – I think I know what it is,' said Dick, at last. 'It's the light in the watchman's little hut – old Wooden-Leg Sam's candle. Don't you think so, Ju?'

'Yes. You're right,' said Julian. 'I tell you what we'll do – we'll creep right down into the yard, and go over to the hut. We'll peep inside and see if old Sam is there. Then we'll hide somewhere about and wait for the spook-train to come!'

They crept down the slope. Their eyes had got used to the starlight by now, and they were beginning to see fairly well. They got right down to the yard, where their feet made a noise on some cinders there.

They stopped. 'Someone will hear us if we make a row like this,' whispered Julian.

'Who will?' whispered back Dick. 'There's no one here except old Sam in his hut!'

'How do you know there isn't?' said Julian. 'Good heavens, Jock, don't make such a row with your feet!'

They stood there, debating what was the best thing to do. 'We'd better walk right round the edge of the yard,' said Julian at last. 'As far as I remember, the grass has grown there. We'll walk on that.'

So they made their way to the edge of the yard. Sure

enough, there was grass there, and they walked on it without a sound. They went slowly and softly to where the light shone dimly in Sam's little hut.

The window was high and small. It was just about at the level of their heads, and the three boys cautiously eased themselves along to it and looked in.

Wooden-Leg Sam was there. He sat sprawled in a chair, smoking a pipe. He was reading a newspaper, squinting painfully as he did so. He obviously had not had his broken glasses mended yet. On a chair beside him was his wooden leg. He had unstrapped it, and there it lay.

'He's not expecting the spook-train tonight, or he wouldn't have taken off his wooden leg,' whispered Dick.

The candlelight flickered and shadows jumped about the tiny hut. It was a poor, ill-furnished little place, dirty and untidy. A cup without saucer or handle stood on the table, and a tin kettle boiled on a rusty stove.

Sam put down his paper and rubbed his eyes. He muttered something. The boys could not hear it, but they felt certain it was something about his broken glasses.

'Are there many lines in this yard?' whispered Jock, tired of looking in at old Sam. 'Where do they go to?'

'About half a mile or so up there is a tunnel,' said Julian, pointing past Jock. 'The lines come from there and run here, where they break up in many pairs – for shunting and so on, in the old days, I suppose, when this place was used.'

'Let's go up the lines to the tunnel,' said Jock. 'Come on. There's nothing to be seen here. Let's walk up to the tunnel.'

'All right,' said Julian. 'We may as well. I don't expect we'll see much up there either! I think these spook-trains are all a tall story of old Sam's!'

They left the little hut with its forlorn candlelight, and made their way round the yard again. Then they followed the single-track line away from the yard and up towards the tunnel. It didn't seem to matter walking on cinders now, and making a noise. They walked along, talking in low voices.

And then things began to happen! A far-off muffled noise came rumbling out of the tunnel, which was now so near that the boys could see its black mouth. Julian heard it first. He stood still and clutched Dick.

'I say! Listen! Can you hear that?'

The others listened. 'Yes,' said Dick. 'But it's only a train going through one of the underground tunnels – the noise is echoing out through this one.'

'It isn't. That noise is made by a train coming through this tunnel!' said Julian. The noise grew louder and louder. A clanking made itself heard too. The boys stepped off the lines and crouched together by the side, waiting, hardly daring to breathe.

Could it be the spook-train? They watched for the light of an engine-lamp to appear like a fiery eye in the tunnel. But none came. It was darker than night in there! But the noise came nearer and nearer and nearer. Could there be the noise of a train without a train? Julian's heart began to beat twice as fast, and Dick and Jock found themselves clutching one another without knowing it.

The noise grew thunderous, and then out from the tunnel came something long and black, with a dull glow in front that passed quickly and was gone. The noise deafened the boys, and then the clanking and rumbling grew less as the train, or whatever it was, passed by. The ground trembled and then was still.

'Well, there you are,' said Julian, in a rather trembly voice. 'The spook-train – without a light or a signal! Where's it gone? To the yard, do you think?'

'Shall we go and see?' asked Dick. 'I didn't see anyone in the cab, even in the glow of what must have been the fire there – but there must be *someone* driving it! I say, what a weird thing, isn't it? It *sounded* real enough, anyway.'

'We'll go to the yard,' said Jock, who, of the three, seemed the least affected. 'Come on.'

They made their way very slowly – and then Dick gave a sharp cry. 'Blow! I've twisted my ankle. Half a minute!'

He sank down to the ground in great pain. It was only a sharp twist, not a sprain, but for a few minutes Dick could do nothing but groan. The others dared not leave him. Julian knelt by him, offering to rub the ankle, but Dick wouldn't let him touch it. Jock stood by anxiously.

It took about twenty minutes for Dick's ankle to be strong enough for him to stand on again. With the help of the others he got to his feet and tested his ankle. 'It's all right, I think. I can walk on it – slowly. Now we'll go to the yard and see what's happening!'

But even as they started to walk slowly back, they heard a noise coming up the lines from the far-away yard, 'Rumble, rumble, rumble, jangle, clank!'

'It's coming back again!' said Julian. 'Stand still. Watch! It'll be going back into the tunnel!'

They stood still and watched and listened. Again the noise came nearer and grew thunderous. They saw the glow of what might be the fire in the cab, and then it passed. The train disappeared into the blackness of the tunnel mouth and they heard the echo of its rumblings for some time.

'Well, there you are! There *is* a spook-train!' said Julian, trying to laugh, though he felt a good deal shaken. 'It came and it went – where from or where to, nobody knows! But we've heard it and seen it, in the darkness of the night. And jolly creepy it was, too!'

CHAPTER ELEVEN

Mostly about Jock

THE THREE boys stood rather close together, glad to feel each other in the darkness. They couldn't believe that they had found what they had come looking for so doubtfully! What kind of a train was this that had come rumbling out of the tunnel so mysteriously, and then, after a pause at the yard, had gone just as mysteriously back again?

'If only I hadn't twisted my ankle, we could have followed the train down the lines to the yard, and have gone quite close to it there,' groaned Dick. 'What an ass I am, messing things up at the most exciting moment!'

'You couldn't help it,' said Jock. 'I *say*! We've seen the spook-train! I can hardly believe it. Does it go all by itself, with nobody to drive it? Is it a real train?'

'Judging by the noise it made, it's real all right,' said Julian. 'And it shot out smoke, too. All the same, it's jolly strange. I can't say I like it much.'

'Let's go and see what's happened to Wooden-Leg Sam,' said Dick. 'I bet he's under his bed!'

They made their way slowly back to the yard, Dick limping a little, though his ankle was practically all right again. When they came to the yard they looked towards Sam's hut. The light was there no longer.

'He's blown it out and got under the bed!' said Dick. 'Poor Sam! It really must be terrifying for him. Let's go and peep into his hut.'

They went over to it and tried to see in at the window. But there was nothing to be seen. The hut was in complete darkness. Then suddenly a little flare flashed out somewhere near the floor.

'Look – there's Sam! He's lighting a match,' said Julian. 'See – he's peeping out from under the bed. He looks scared stiff. Let's tap on the window and ask him if he's all right.'

But that was quite the wrong thing to do! As soon as Julian tapped sharply on the window, Sam gave an anguished yell and retired hurriedly under the bed again, his wavering match-light going out.

'It's come for to take me!' they heard him wailing. 'It's come for to take me! And me with my wooden leg off too.'

'We're only frightening the poor old fellow,' said Dick. 'Come on. Let's leave him. He'll have a fit or something if we call out to him. He honestly thinks the spook-train's come to get him.'

They wandered round the dark yard for a few minutes, but there was nothing to find out in the darkness. No more rumbling came to their ears. The spook-train was evidently not going to run again that night.

'Let's go back,' said Julian. 'That really was exciting! Honestly, my hair stood on end when that train came puffing out of the tunnel. Where on earth did it come from? And what's the reason for it?'

They gave it up, and began to walk back to the camp. They scrambled through the heather, tired but excited. 'Shall we tell the girls we've seen the train?' said Dick.

'No,' said Julian. 'It would only scare Anne, and George would be furious if she knew we'd gone without her. We'll wait and see if we discover anything more before we say anything, either to the girls or to old Luffy.'

'Right,' said Dick. 'You'll hold your tongue, too, won't you, Jock?'

'Course,' said Jock, scornfully. 'Who would I tell? My stepfather? Not likely! How furious he'd be if he knew we'd all pooh-poohed his warnings and gone down to see the spook-train after all!'

He suddenly felt something warm against his legs, and gave a startled cry: 'What's this? Get away!'

But the warm thing turned out to be Timmy, who had come to meet three boys. He pressed against each of them in turn and whined a little.

'He says, "Why didn't you take me with you?"' said Dick. 'Sorry, old thing, but we couldn't. George would never have spoken to us again if we'd taken you, and left her behind! How would you have liked spook-trains, Timmy? Would you have run into a corner somewhere and hidden?'

'Woof,' said Timmy, scornfully. As if he would be afraid of anything!

They reached their camping place and began to speak in whispers. 'Goodbye, Jock. Come up tomorrow if you can. Hope you don't have that Cecil boy to cope with!'

'Goodbye! See you soon,' whispered Jock, and disappeared into the darkness, with Timmy at his heels. Another chance of a midnight walk? Good, thought Timmy, just what he'd like! It was hot in the tent, and a scamper in the cool night air would be fine.

Timmy growled softly when they came near to Olly's Farm, and stood still, the hackles on his neck rising up a little. Jock put his hand on the dog's head and stopped.

'What's the matter, old boy? Burglars or something?'

He strained his eyes in the darkness. Big clouds now covered the stars and there was no light at all to see by. Jock made out a dim light in one of the barns. He crept over to it to see what it was. It went out as he came near, and then he heard the sound of footsteps, the quiet closing of the barn door, and the click of a padlock as it was locked.

Jock crept nearer – too near, for whoever it was must have heard him and swung round, lashing out with his arm. He caught Jock on the shoulder, and the boy over-balanced. He almost fell, and the man who had struck him clutched hold of him. A flash-light was put on and he blinked in the sudden light.

'It's you, Jock!' said an astonished voice, rough and impatient. 'What are you doing out here at this time of night?'

107

'Well, what are *you* doing?' demanded Jock, wriggling free. He switched on his own torch and let the light fall on the man who had caught him. It was Peters, one of the farm men, the one in whose lorry he had ridden that very day.

'What's it to do with you?' said Peters, angrily. 'I had a breakdown, and I've only just got back. Look here – you're fully dressed! Where have you been at this time of night? Did you hear me come in and get up to see what was happening?'

'You never know!' said Jock cheekily. He wasn't going to say anything that might make Peters suspicious of him. 'You just never know!'

'Is that Biddy?' said Peters, seeing a dark shadow slinking away. 'Do you mean to say you've been out with Biddy? What in the world have you been doing?'

Jock thanked his lucky stars that Peters hadn't spotted it was Timmy, not Biddy. He moved off without saying another word. Let Peters think what he liked! It was bad luck, though, that Peters had had a breakdown and come in late. If the man told his stepfather he'd seen Jock, fully dressed in the middle of the night, there'd be questions asked by both his mother and his stepfather, and Jock, who was a truthful boy, would find things very difficult to explain.

He scuttled off to bed, climbing up the pear-tree outside his window, and dropping quietly into his room. He opened his door softly to hear if anyone was awake in the house, but all was dark and silent.

'Blow Peters!' thought Jock. 'If he splits on me, I'm for it!'

He got into bed, pondered over the curious happenings of the night for a few minutes, and then slid into an uneasy sleep, in which spook-trains, Peters, and Timmy kept doing most peculiar things. He was glad to awake in the bright, sunny morning and find his mother shaking him.

'Get up, Jock! You're very late. Whatever's made you so sleepy? We're half-way through breakfast!'

Peters, apparently, didn't say anything to Jock's step-father about seeing Jock in the night. Jock was very thankful. He began to plan how to slip off to the others at the camp. He'd take them some food! That would be a fine excuse.

'Mum, can I take a basket of stuff to the campers?' he said, after breakfast. 'They must be running short now.'

'Well, that boy is coming,' said his mother. 'What's his name – Cecil something? Your stepfather says he's such a nice boy. You did enjoy your day with him yesterday, didn't you?'

Jock would have said quite a lot of uncomplimentary things about dear Cecil if his stepfather had not been there, sitting by the window reading the paper. As it was, he shrugged his shoulders and made a face, hoping that his mother would understand his feelings. She did.

'What time is Cecil coming?' she said. 'Perhaps there's time for you to run to the camp with a basket.'

'I don't want him running off up there,' said

110

Mr Andrews, suddenly butting into the conversation, and putting down his newspaper. 'Cecil may be here at any minute – and I know what Jock is! He'd start talking to those kids and forget all about coming back. Cecil's father is a great friend of mine, and Jock's got to be polite to him, and be here to welcome him. There's to be no running off to that camp today.'

Jock looked sulky. Why must his stepfather suddenly interfere in his plans like this? Rushing him off to the town, making him take Cecil for a friend! Just when some other children had come into his rather lonely life and livened it up, too! It was maddening.

'Perhaps I can go up to the camp myself with some food,' said his mother, comfortingly. 'Or maybe the children will come down for some.'

Jock was still sulky. He stalked out into the yard and went to look for Biddy. She was with her pups who were now trying to crawl round the shed after her. Jock hoped the campers would come to fetch food themselves that day. Then at least he would get a word with them.

Cecil arrived by car. He was about the same age as Jock, though he was small for twelve years old. He had curly hair which was too long, and his grey flannel suit was very, very clean and well-pressed.

'Hallo!' he called to Jock. 'I've come. What shall we play at? Soldiers?'

'No. American Indians,' said Jock, who had suddenly

remembered his old American Indian head-dress with masses of feathers round it, and a trail of them falling down the back. He rushed indoors, grinning. He changed into the whole suit, and put on his head-dress. He took his paint-box and hurriedly painted a pattern of red, blue and green on his face. He found his tomahawk and went downstairs. He would play at American Indians, and terrify that annoying boy!

Cecil was wandering round by himself. To his enormous horror, as he turned a corner, a most terrifying figure rose up from behind a wall, gave a horrible yell and pounced on him, waving what looked like a dangerous chopper.

Cecil turned and fled, howling loudly, with Jock leaping madly after him, whooping for all he was worth, and thoroughly enjoying himself. He had had to play at soldiers all the day before with dear Cecil. He didn't see why Cecil shouldn't play American Indians all day with him today!

Just at that moment, the four campers arrived to fetch food, with Timmy running beside them. They stopped in amazement at the sight of Cecil running like the wind, howling dismally, and a fully-dressed and painted American Indian leaping fiercely after him.

Jock saw them, did a comical war-dance all round them, much to Timmy's amazement, yelled dramatically, pretended to cut off Timmy's tail and then tore after the vanishing Cecil.

The children began to laugh helplessly. 'Oh dear!' said Anne, with tears of laughter in her eyes, 'that must be Cecil he's after. I suppose this is Jock's revenge for having to play soldiers all day with him yesterday. Look, there they go round the pig-sty. Poor Cecil. He really thinks he's going to be scalped!'

Cecil disappeared into the farm kitchen, sobbing, and Mrs Andrews ran to comfort him. Jock made off back to the others, grinning all over his war-painted face.

'Hallo,' he said. 'I'm just having a nice quiet time with dear Cecil. I'm so glad to see you. I wanted to come over, but my stepfather said I wasn't to – I must play with Cecil. Isn't he frightful?'

'Awful,' everyone agreed.

'I say, will your mother be furious with you for frightening Cecil like that? Perhaps we'd better not ask her for any food yet?' said Julian.

'Yes, you'd better wait a bit,' said Jock, leading them to the sunny side of the haystack they had rested by before. 'Hallo, Timmy! Did you get back all right last night?'

Jock had completely forgotten that the girls didn't know of the happenings of the night before. Both Anne and George at once pricked up their ears. Julian frowned at Jock, and Dick gave him a secret nudge.

'What's up?' said George, seeing all this by-play. 'What happened last night?'

'Oh, I just came up to have a little night-talk with the boys – and Timmy walked back with me,' said Jock, airily. 'Hope you didn't mind him coming, George.'

George flushed an angry red. 'You're keeping something from me,' she said to the boys. 'Yes, you are. I know you are. I believe you went off to the railway yard last night! Did you?'

There was an awkward silence. Julian shot an annoyed look at poor Jock, who could have kicked himself.

'Go on – tell me,' persisted George, an angry frown on her forehead. 'You beasts! You did go! And you never woke me up to go with you! Oh, I do think you're mean!'

'Did you see anything?' said Anne, her eyes going from

114

one boy to another. Each of the girls sensed that there had been some kind of adventure in the night.

'Well,' began Julian. And then there was an interruption. Cecil came round the haystack, his eyes red with crying. He glared at Jock.

'Your father wants you,' he said. 'You're to go at once. You're a beast, and I want to go home. Can't you hear your father yelling for you? He's got a stick – but I'm not sorry for you! I hope he whacks you hard!'

CHAPTER TWELVE

George loses her temper

JOCK MADE a face at Cecil and got up. He went slowly off round the haystack, and the others listened in silence for whacks and yells. But none came.

'He frightened me,' said Cecil, sitting down by the others.

'Poor icle ting,' said Dick at once.

'Darling baby,' said George.

'Mother's pet,' said Julian. Cecil glared at them all. He got up again, very red.

'If I didn't know my manners, I'd smack your faces,' he said, and marched off hurriedly, before his own could be smacked.

The four sat in silence. They were sorry for Jock. George was angry and sulky because she knew the others had gone off without her the night before. Anne was worried.

They all sat there for about ten minutes. Then round the haystack came Jock's mother, looking distressed. She carried a big basket of food.

The children all stood up politely. 'Good morning, Mrs Andrews,' said Julian.

'I'm sorry I can't ask you to stop today,' said

Mrs Andrews. 'But Jock has really behaved very foolishly. I wouldn't let Mr Andrews give him a hiding because it would only make Jock hate his stepfather, and that would never do. So I've sent him up to bed for the day. You won't be able to see him, I'm afraid. Here is some food for you to take. Oh, dear – I'm really very sorry about all this. I can't think what came over Jock to behave in such a way. It's not a bit like him.'

Cecil's face appeared round the haystack, looking rather smug. Julian grinned to himself.

'Would you like us to take Cecil for a nice long walk over the moors?' he said. 'We can climb hills and jump over streams and scramble through the heather. It would make such a nice day for him.'

Cecil's face immediately disappeared.

'Well,' said Mrs Andrews, 'that really would be very kind of you. Now that Jock's been sent upstairs for the day there's no one for Cecil to play with. But I'm afraid he's a bit of a mother's boy, you know. You'll have to go carefully with him. Cecil! Cecil! Where are you? Come and make friends with these children.'

But Cecil had gone. There was no answer at all. He didn't want to make friends with 'these children'. He knew better than that! Mrs Andrews went in search of him, but he had completely disappeared.

The four children were not at all surprised. Julian, Dick and Anne grinned at one another. George stood with her back to them, still sulky.

Mrs Andrews came back again, out of breath. 'I can't find him,' she said. 'Never mind. I'll find something for him to do when he appears again.'

'Yes. Perhaps you've got some beads for him to thread? Or a nice easy jigsaw puzzle to do?' said Julian, very politely. The others giggled. A smile appeared on Mrs Andrews's face.

'Bad boy!' she said. 'Oh dear – poor Jock. Well it's his own fault. Now goodbye, I must get on with my work.'

She ran off to the dairy. The children looked round the haystack. Mr Andrews was getting into his car. He would soon be gone. They waited a few minutes till they heard the car set off down the rough cart-track.

'That's Jock's bedroom – where the pear-tree is,' said Julian. 'Let's just have a word with him before we go. It's a shame.'

They went across the farmyard and stood under the pear-tree – all except George, who stayed behind the haystack with the food, frowning. Julian called up to the window above: 'Jock!'

A head came out, the face still painted terrifyingly in streaks and circles. 'Hallo! He didn't whack me. Mum wouldn't let him. All the same, I'd rather he had – it's awful being stuck up here this sunny day. Where's dear Cecil?'

'I don't know. Probably in the darkest corner of one of the barns,' said Julian. 'Jock, if things are difficult in the daytime, come up at night. We've got to see you somehow.'

'Right,' said Jock. 'How do I look? Like a real American Indian?'

'You look frightful,' grinned Julian. 'I wonder old Timmy knew you.'

'Where's George?' asked Jock.

'Sulking behind the haystack,' said Dick. 'We shall have an awful day with her now. You let the cat properly out of the bag, you idjit!'

'Yes. I'm a ninny and an idjit,' said Jock, and Anne giggled. 'Look – there's Cecil. You might tell him to beware of the bull, will you?'

'Is there a bull?' said Anne, looking alarmed.

'No. But that's no reason why he shouldn't beware of one,' grinned Jock. 'So long! Have a nice day!'

The three left him, and strolled over to Cecil, who had just appeared out of a dark little shed. He made a face at them, and stood ready to run to the dairy where Mrs Andrews was busy.

Julian suddenly clutched Dick and pointed behind Cecil. 'The bull! Beware of the bull!' he yelled suddenly.

Dick entered into the joke. 'The bull's loose! Look out! Beware of the bull!' he shouted.

Anne gave a shriek. It all sounded so real that, although she knew it was a joke, she felt half-scared. 'The bull!' she cried.

119

Cecil turned green. His legs shook. 'W-w-w-where is it?' he stammered.

'Look out behind you!' yelled Julian, pointing. Poor Cecil, convinced that a large bull was about to pounce on him from behind, gave an anguished cry and tore on tottering legs to the dairy. He threw himself against Mrs Andrews.

'Save me, save me! The bull's chasing me.'

'But there's no bull here,' said Mrs Andrews, in surprise. 'Really, Cecil! Was it a pig after you, or something?'

Helpless with laughter, the three children made their way back to George. They tried to tell her about the make-believe bull, but she turned away and wouldn't listen. Julian shrugged his shoulders. Best to leave George to herself when she was in one of her rages! She didn't lose her temper as often as she used to, but when she did she was very trying indeed.

They went back to the camp with the basket of food. Timmy followed soberly. He knew something was wrong with George and he was unhappy. His tail was down, and he looked miserable. George wouldn't even pat him.

When they got back to the camp, George flared up.

'How dare you go off without me when I told you I meant to come? Fancy taking Jock and not letting me go! I think you're absolute beasts. I never really thought you'd do a thing like that, you and Dick.'

'Don't be silly, George,' said Julian. 'I told you we

didn't mean to let you and Anne go. I'll tell you all that happened – and it's pretty thrilling!'

'What? Tell me quickly!' begged Anne, but George obstinately turned away her head as if she was not interested.

Julian began to relate all the curious happenings of the night. Anne listened breathlessly. George was listening too, though she pretended not to. She was very angry and very hurt.

'Well, there you are,' said Julian, when he had finished. 'If that's what people mean by spook-trains, there was one puffing in and out of that tunnel all right! I felt pretty scared, I can tell you. Sorry you weren't there too, George – but I didn't want to leave Anne alone.'

George was not accepting any apologies. She still looked furious.

'I suppose Timmy went with you,' she said. 'I think that was horrid of him – to go without waking me, when he knew I'd like to be with you on the adventure.'

'Oh, don't be so silly,' said Dick, in disgust. 'Fancy being angry with old Tim, too! You're making him miserable. And anyway, he *didn't* come with us. He just came to meet us when we got back, and then went off to keep Jock company on his way back to the farm.'

'Oh,' said George, and she reached out her hand to pat Timmy, who was filled with delight. 'At least Timmy was loyal to me then. That's something.'

There was a silence. Nobody ever knew quite how to

treat George when she was in one of her moods. It was really best to leave her to herself, but they couldn't very well go off and leave the camp just because George was there, cross and sulky.

Anne took hold of George's arm. She was miserable when George behaved like this. 'George,' she began, 'there's no need to be cross with me, too. *I* haven't done anything!'

'If you weren't such a little coward, too afraid to go with us, I'd have been able to go too,' said George unkindly, dragging her arm away.

Julian was disgusted. He saw Anne's hurt face and was angry with George.

'Shut up, George,' he said. 'You're being horrid, saying catty things like that! I'm astonished at you.'

George was ashamed of herself, but she was too proud to say so. She glared at Julian.

'And *I'm* astonished at *you*,' she said. 'After all the adventures we've had together, you try to keep me out of this one. But you *will* let me come next time, won't you, Julian?'

'What! After your frightful behaviour today?' said Julian, who could be just as obstinate as George when he wanted to. 'Certainly not. This is my adventure and Dick's – and perhaps Jock's. Not yours or Anne's.'

He got up and stalked down the hill with Dick. George sat pulling bits of heather off the stems, looking mutinous and angry. Anne blinked back tears. She hated this sort of thing. She got up to get dinner ready. Perhaps after a good meal they would all feel better.

Mr Luffy was sitting outside his tent, reading. He had already seen the children that morning. He looked up, smiling.

'Hallo! Come to talk to me?'

'Yes,' said Julian, an idea uncurling itself in his mind. 'Could I have a look at that map of yours, Mr Luffy? The big one you've got showing every mile of these moorlands?'

'Of course. It's in the tent somewhere,' said Mr Luffy.

The boys found it and opened it. Dick at once guessed why Julian wanted it. Mr Luffy went on reading.

'It shows the railways that run under the moorlands too, doesn't it?' said Julian. Mr Luffy nodded.

'Yes. There are quite a few lines. I suppose it was easier to tunnel under the moors from valley to valley rather than make a permanent way over the top of them. In any case, a railway over the moors would probably be completely snowed up in the winter-time.'

The boys bent their heads over the big map; it showed the railways as dotted lines when they went underground, but by long black lines when they appeared in the open air, in the various valleys.

They found exactly where they were. Then Julian's finger ran down the map a little and came to where a small line showed itself at the end of a dotted line.

He looked at Dick, who nodded. Yes – that showed

where the tunnel was, out of which the 'spook-train' had come, and the lines to the deserted yard. Julian's finger went back from the yard to the tunnel, where the dotted lines began. His finger traced the dotted lines a little way till they became whole lines again. That was where the train came out into another valley!

Then his finger showed where the tunnel that led from the yard appeared to join up with another one, that also ran for some distance before coming out into yet another valley. The boys looked at one another in silence.

125

Mr Luffy suddenly spotted a day-flying moth and got up to follow it. The boys took the chance of talking to one another.

'The spook-train either runs through its own tunnel to the valley beyond – or it turns off into this fork and runs along to the other valley,' said Julian, in a low voice. 'I tell you what we'll do, Dick. We'll get Mr Luffy to run us down to the nearest town to buy something – and we'll slip along to the station there and see if we can't make a few inquiries about these two tunnels. We may find out something.'

'Good idea,' said Dick, as Mr Luffy came back. 'I say, sir, are you very busy today? Could you possibly run us down to the nearest town after dinner?'

'Certainly, certainly,' said Mr Luffy, amiably. The boys looked at one another in delight. *Now* they might find out something! But they wouldn't take George with them. No – they would punish her for her bad temper by leaving her behind!

CHAPTER THIRTEEN

A thrilling plan

ANNE CALLED them to dinner. 'Come along!' she cried. 'I've got it all ready. Tell Mr Luffy there's plenty for him, too.'

Mr Luffy came along willingly. He thought Anne was a marvellous camp-housekeeper. He looked approvingly at the spread set out on a white cloth on the ground.

'Hm! Salad. Hard-boiled eggs. Slices of ham. And what's this – apple-pie! My goodness! Don't tell me you cooked that here, Anne.'

Anne laughed. 'No. All this came from the farm, of course. Except the lime juice and water.'

George ate with the others, but said hardly a word. She was brooding over her wrongs, and Mr Luffy looked at her several times, puzzled.

'Are you quite well, George?' he said, suddenly. George went red.

'Yes, thank you,' she said, and tried to be more herself, though she couldn't raise a smile at all. Mr Luffy watched her, and was relieved to see that she ate as much as the others. Probably had some sort of row, he guessed correctly. Well, it would blow over! He knew better than to interfere.

They finished lunch and drank all the lime juice. It was a hot day and they were very thirsty indeed. Timmy emptied all his dish of water and went and gazed longingly into the canvas bucket of washing-water. But he was too well-behaved to drink it, now that he knew he mustn't. Anne laughed, and poured some more water into his dish.

'Well,' said Mr Luffy, beginning to fill his old brown pipe, 'if anyone wants to come into town with me this afternoon, I'll be starting in fifteen minutes.'

'I'll come!' said Anne, at once. 'It won't take George and me long to wash-up these things. Will you come too, George?'

'No,' said George, and the boys heaved a sigh of relief. They had guessed she wouldn't want to come with them – but, if she'd known what they were going to try and find out, she would have come all right!

'I'm going for a walk with Timmy,' said George, when all the washing-up had been done.

'All right,' said Anne, who secretly thought that George would be much better left on her own to work off her ill-feelings that afternoon. 'See you later.'

George and Timmy set off. The others went with Mr Luffy to where his car was parked beside the great rock. They got in.

'Hi! The trailer's fastened to it,' called Julian. 'Wait a bit. Let me get out and undo it. We don't want to take an empty trailer bumping along behind us for miles.'

'Dear me. I always forget to undo the trailer,' said

Mr Luffy, vexed. 'The times I take it along without meaning to!'

The children winked at one another. Dear old Luffy! He was always doing things like that. No wonder his wife fussed round him like an old hen with one foolish chicken when he was at home.

They went off in the car, jolting over the rough road till they came to the smooth highway. They stopped in the centre of the town. Mr Luffy said he would meet them for tea at five o'clock at the hotel opposite the parking-place.

The three of them set off together, leaving Mr Luffy to go to the library and browse there. It seemed funny to be without George. Anne didn't much like it, and said so.

'Well, we don't like going off without George either,' said Julian. 'But honestly, she can't behave like that and get away with it. I thought she'd grown out of that sort of thing.'

'Well, you know how she adores an adventure,' said Anne. 'Oh dear – if I hadn't felt so scared you'd have taken me along, and George would have gone too. It's quite true what she said about me being a coward.'

'You're not,' said Dick. 'You can't help being scared of things sometimes – after all, you're the youngest of us – but being scared doesn't make you a coward. I've known you to be as brave as any of us when you've been scared stiff!'

'Where are we going?' asked Anne. The boys told her, and her eyes sparkled.

'Oh – are we going to find out where the spook-train comes from? It might come from one of two valleys then, judging from the map.'

'Yes. The tunnels aren't really very long ones,' said Julian. 'Not more than a mile, I should think. We thought we'd make some inquiries at the station and see if there's anyone who knows anything about the old railway yard and the tunnel beyond. We shan't say a word about the spook-train of course.'

They walked into the station. They went up to a railway plan and studied it. It didn't tell them much. Julian turned to a young porter who was wheeling some luggage along.

'I say! Could you help us? We're camping up on the moorlands, and we're quite near a deserted railway yard with lines that run into an old tunnel. Why isn't the yard used any more?'

'Don't know,' said the boy. 'You should ask old Tucky there – see him? He knows all the tunnels under the moors like the back of his hand. Worked in them all when he was a boy.'

'Thanks,' said Dick, pleased. They went over to where an old whiskered porter was sitting in the sun, enjoying a rest till the next train came in.

'Excuse me,' said Julian politely. 'I've been told that you know all about the moorland tunnels like the back of your hand. They must be very, very interesting.'

'My father and my grandfather built those tunnels,' said the old porter, looking up at the children out of small faded eyes that watered in the strong sunlight. 'And I've been guard on all the trains that ran through them.'

He mumbled a long string of names, going through all the list of tunnels in his mind. The children waited patiently till he had finished.

'There's a tunnel near where we're camping on the moorlands,' said Julian, getting a word in at last. 'We're not far from Olly's Farm. We came across an old deserted railway yard, with lines that led into a tunnel. Do you know it?'

'Oh yes, that's an old tunnel,' said Tucky, nodding his grey head, on which his porter's cap sat all crooked. 'Hasn't been used for many a long year. Nor the yard either. Wasn't enough traffic there, fur as I remember. They shut up the yard. Tunnel isn't used any more.'

The boys exchanged glances. So it wasn't used any more! Well, they knew better.

'The tunnel joins another, doesn't it?' said Julian. The porter, pleased at their interest in the old tunnels he knew so well, got up and went into an office behind. He came out with a dirty, much-used map, which he spread out on his knee. His black finger-nail pointed to a mark on the map.

'That's the yard see? It was called Olly's Yard, after the farm. There're the lines to the tunnel. Here's the tunnel. It runs right through to Kilty Vale – there it is. And here's where it used to join the tunnel to Roker's Vale. But that was bricked up years ago. Something happened there – the roof fell in, I think it was – and the company decided not to use the tunnel to Roker's Vale at all.'

The children listened with the utmost interest. Julian reasoned things out in his mind. If that spook-train came from anywhere then it must come from Kilty Vale, because that was the only place the lines went to now, since the way to Roker's Vale had been bricked up where the tunnels joined.

'I suppose no trains run through the tunnel from Kilty Vale to Olly's Yard now, then?' he said.

Tucky snorted. 'Didn't I tell you it hasn't been used for years? The yard at Kilty Vale's been turned into something else, though the lines are still there. There's been no engine through that tunnel since I was a young man.'

This was all very, very interesting. Julian thanked old Tucky so profusely that he wanted to tell the children everything all over again. He even gave them the old map.

'Oh, thanks,' said Julian, delighted to have it. He looked at the others. 'This'll be jolly useful!' he said, and they nodded.

They left the pleased old man and went out into the town. They found a little park and sat down on a seat. They were longing to discuss all that Tucky had told them.

'It's jolly strange,' said Dick. 'No trains run there now – the tunnel's not been used for ages – and Olly's Yard must have been derelict for years.'

'And yet, there appear to be trains that come and go!' said Julian.

'Then, they *must* be spook-trains,' said Anne, her eyes wide and puzzled. 'Julian, they must be, mustn't they?'

'Looks like it,' said Julian. 'It's most mysterious. I can't understand it.'

'Ju,' said Dick, suddenly. 'I know what we'll do! We'll wait one night again till we see the spook-train come out of the tunnel to the yard. Then one of us can sprint off to the *other* end of the tunnel – it's only about a mile long – and wait for it to come out the other side! Then we'll find out why a train still runs from Kilty Vale to Olly's Yard through that old tunnel.'

'Jolly good idea,' said Julian, thrilled. 'What about tonight? If Jock comes, he can go, too. If he doesn't, just you and I will go. *Not* George.'

They all felt excited. Anne wondered if she would be brave enough to go too, but she knew that when the night came she wouldn't feel half as brave as she did now! No, she wouldn't go. There was really no need for her to join in this adventure at present. It hadn't even turned out to be a proper one yet – it was only an unsolved mystery!

George hadn't come back from her walk when they reached the camp. They waited for her, and at last she appeared with Timmy, looking tired out.

'Sorry I was an ass this morning,' she said at once. 'I've walked my temper off! Don't know what came over me.'

'That's all right,' said Julian amiably. 'Forget it.'

They were all very glad that George had recovered her temper, for she was a very prickly person indeed when she was angry. She was rather subdued and said nothing at all about spook-trains or tunnels. So they said nothing either.

The night was fine and clear. Stars shone out brilliantly again in the sky. The children said good night to Mr Luffy at ten o'clock and got into their sleeping-bags. Julian and Dick did not mean to go exploring till midnight, so they lay and talked quietly.

About eleven o'clock they heard somebody moving cautiously outside. They wondered if it was Jock, but he did not call out to them. Who could it be?

Then Julian saw a familiar head outlined against the starlit sky. It was George. But what in the world was she doing? He couldn't make it out at all. Whatever it was she wasn't making any noise over it, and she obviously thought the boys were asleep. Julian gave a nice little snore or two just to let her go on thinking so.

At last she disappeared. Julian waited a few minutes and then put his head cautiously out of the tent opening. He felt about, and his fingers brushed against some string. He grinned to himself and got back into the tent.

'I've found out what George was doing,' he whispered. 'She's put string across the entrance of our tent, and I bet it runs to her tent and she's tied it to her big toe or something, so that if we go out without her she'll feel the pull of the string when we go through it and wake up and follow us!'

'Good old George,' chuckled Dick. 'Well, she'll be unlucky. We'll squeeze out under the sides of the tent!'

Which was what they did do at about a minute past twelve! They didn't disturb George's string at all. They were out on the heather and away down the slope while George was sleeping soundly in her tent beside Anne waiting for the pull on her toe which didn't come. Poor George!

A THRILLING PLAN

The boys arrived at the deserted railway yard and looked to see if Wooden-Leg Sam's candle was alight. It was. So the spook-train hadn't come along *that* night, yet.

They were just scrambling down to the yard when they heard the train coming. There was the same rumbling noise as before, muffled by the tunnel – and then out of the tunnel, again with no lamps, came the spook-train, clanking on its way to the yard!

'Quick, Dick! You sprint off to the tunnel opening and watch for the train to go back in again. And I'll find my way across the moor to the other end of the tunnel. There was a path marked on that old map, and I follow that!' Julian's words tumbled over each other in his excitement. 'I'll jolly well watch for the spook-train to complete its journey, and see if it vanishes into thin air or what!'

And off he went to find the path that led over the moors to the other end of the tunnel. He meant to see what happened at the other end if he had to run all the way!

CHAPTER FOURTEEN

Jock comes to camp

JULIAN FOUND the path quite by chance and went along it as fast as he could. He used his torch, for he did not think he would meet anyone out on such a lonely way at that time of night. The path was very much overgrown, but he could follow it fairly easily, even running at times.

'If that spook-train stops about twenty minutes in the yard again, as it did before, it will give me just about time to reach the other end of the tunnel,' panted Julian. 'I'll be at Kilty's Yard before it comes.'

It seemed a very long way. But at last the path led downwards, and some way below him Julian could see what might be a railway yard. Then he saw that big sheds were built there – or what looked like big sheds in the starlight.

He remembered what the old porter had said. Kilty's Yard was used for something else now – maybe the lines had been taken up. Maybe even the tunnel had been stopped up, too. He slipped quickly down the path and came into what had once been the old railway yard. Big buildings loomed up on every side. Julian thought they must be workshops of some kind. He switched his torch on and off very quickly, but the short flash had shown

138

him what he was looking for – two pairs of railway lines. They were old and rusty, but he knew they must lead to the tunnel.

He followed them closely, right up to the black mouth of the dark tunnel. He couldn't see inside at all. He switched his torch on and off quickly. Yes – the lines led right inside the tunnel. Julian stopped and wondered what to do.

'I'll sneak into the tunnel a little way and see if it's bricked up anywhere,' he thought. So in he went, walking between one pair of lines. He put on his torch, certain that no one would see its light and challenge him to say what he was doing out so late at night.

The tunnel stretched before him, a great yawning hole, disappearing into deep blackness. It was certainly not bricked up. Julian saw a little niche in the brickwork of the tunnel and decided to crouch in it. It was one of the niches made for workmen to stand in when trains went by in the old days.

Julian crouched down in the dirty old niche and waited. He glanced at the luminous face of his watch. He had been twenty minutes getting here. Maybe the train would be along in a few minutes. He would be very, very close to it! Julian couldn't help wishing that Dick was with him. It was so eerie waiting there in the dark for a mysterious train that apparently belonged to no one and came and went from nowhere to nowhere!

He waited and he waited. Once he thought he heard a

rumble far away down the tunnel, and he held his breath, feeling certain that the train was coming. But it didn't come. Julian waited for half an hour and still the train had not appeared. What had happened to it?

'I'll wait another ten minutes and then I'm going,' Julian decided. 'I've had about enough of hiding in a dark, dirty tunnel waiting for a train that doesn't come! Maybe it has decided to stay in Olly's Yard for the night.'

After ten minutes he gave it up. He left the tunnel, went into Kilty's Yard and then up the path to the moors. He hurried along it, eager to see if Dick was at the other end of the tunnel. Surely he would wait there till Julian came back!

Dick was there, tired and impatient. When he saw a quick flash from Julian's torch he answered it with his own. The two boys joined company thankfully.

'You *have* been ages!' said Dick, reproachfully. 'What happened? The spook-train went back into the tunnel ages and ages ago. It only stayed about twenty minutes in the yard again.'

'Went back into the tunnel!' exclaimed Julian. 'Did it really? Well, it never came out the other side! I waited for ages. I never even heard it – though I did hear a very faint rumble once, or thought I did.'

The boys fell silent, puzzled and mystified. What sort of a train was this that puffed out of a tunnel at dead of night, and went back again, but didn't appear out of the other end?

'I suppose the entrance to that second tunnel the porter told us about *is* really bricked up?' said Julian at last. 'If it wasn't, the train could go down there, of course.'

'Yes. That's the only solution, if the train's a real one and not a spook one,' agreed Dick. 'Well, we can't go exploring the tunnels now – let's wait and do it in the daytime. I've had enough tonight!'

Julian had had enough too. In silence the two boys went back to camp. They quite forgot the string in front of their tent, and scrambled right through it. They got into the sleeping-bags thankfully.

The string, fastened to George's big toe through a hole she had cut in her sleeping-bag, pulled hard, and George woke up with a jump. Timmy was awake, having heard the boys come back. He licked George when she sat up.

George had not undressed properly. She slipped quickly out of her bag and crawled out of her tent. Now she would catch the two boys going off secretly and follow them!

But there was no sign or sound of them anywhere around. She crawled silently to their tent. Both boys had fallen asleep immediately, tired out with their midnight trip. Julian snored a little, and Dick breathed so deeply that George could quite well hear him as she crouched outside, listening. She was very puzzled. Someone had pulled at her toe – so somebody must have scrambled through that string. After listening for a few minutes, she gave it up and went back to her tent.

In the morning, George was furious! Julian and Dick

141

related their night's adventure, and George could hardly believe that once again they had gone without her – and that they had managed to get away without disturbing the string! Dick saw George's face and couldn't help laughing.

'Sorry, old thing. We discovered your little trick and avoided it when we set out – but typically, we forgot all about it coming back. We must have given your toe a frightful tug. Did we? I suppose you *did* tie the other end of the string to your toe?'

George looked as if she could throw all the breakfast things at him. Fortunately for everyone Jock arrived at that moment. He didn't wear his usual beaming smile but seemed rather subdued.

'Hallo, Jock!' said Julian. 'Just in time for a spot of breakfast. Sit down and join us.'

'I can't,' said Jock. 'I've only a few minutes. Listen. Isn't it rotten – I'm to go away and stay with my stepfather's sister for two weeks! Two weeks! You'll be gone when I come back, won't you?'

'Yes. But, Jock, *why* have you got to go away?' said Dick, surprised. 'Has there been a row or something?'

'I don't know,' said Jock. 'Mum won't say, but she looks pretty miserable. My stepfather's in a frightful temper. It's my opinion they want me out of the way for some reason. I don't know this sister of my stepfather's very well – only met her once – but she's pretty awful.'

'Well, come over here and stay with us, if they want to

get rid of you,' said Julian, sorry for Jock. Jock's face brightened.

'I *say*, that's a fine idea!' he said.

'Smashing,' agreed Dick. 'Well, I don't see what's to stop you. If they want to get rid of you, it can't matter where you go for a fortnight. We'd love to have you.'

'Right. I'll come,' said Jock. 'I'll not say a word about it, though, to my stepfather. I'll let Mum into the secret. She was going to take me away today, but I'll just tell her I'm coming to you instead. I don't think she'll split on me, and I hope she'll square things with my step-aunt.'

Jock's face beamed again now. The others beamed back, even George, and Timmy wagged his tail. It would be nice to have Jock – and what a lot they had to tell him.

He went off to break the news to his mother, while the others washed up and cleared things away. George became sulky again when Jock was gone. She simply could not or would not realise that Julian meant what he said!

When they began to discuss everything that had happened the night before, George refused to listen. 'I'm not going to bother about your stupid spook-trains any more,' she said. 'You wouldn't let me join you when I wanted to, and now I shan't take any interest in the matter.'

And she walked off with Timmy, not saying where she was going.

'Well, let her go,' said Julian, exasperated and cross. 'What does she expect me to do? Climb down and say we'll let her come the next night we go?'

143

'We said we'd go in the daytime,' said Dick. 'She could come then, because if Anne doesn't want to come it won't matter leaving her here alone in the daytime.'

'You're right,' said Julian. 'Let's call her back and tell her.' But by that time George was out of hearing.

'She's taken sandwiches,' said Anne. 'She means to be gone all day. Isn't she an idiot?'

Jock came back after a time, with two rugs and an extra jersey and more food. 'I had hard work to persuade Mum,' he said. 'But she said yes at last. Though mind you, I'd have come anyhow! I'm not going to be shoved about by my stepfather just out of spite. I *say* – isn't this great! I never thought I'd be camping out with you. If there isn't room in your tent for me, Julian, I can sleep out on the heather.'

'There'll be room,' said Julian. 'Hallo, Mr Luffy! You've been out early!'

Mr Luffy came up and glanced at Jock. 'Ah, is this your friend from the farm? How do you do? Come to spend a few days with us? I see you have an armful of rugs!'

'Yes. Jock's coming to camp a bit with us,' said Julian. 'Look at all the food he's brought. Enough to stand a siege!'

'It is indeed,' said Mr Luffy. 'Well, I'm going to go through some of my specimens this morning. What are you going to do?'

'Oh, mess about till lunch-time,' said Julian. 'Then we might go for a walk.'

Mr Luffy went back to his tent and they could hear him whistling softly as he set to work. Suddenly Jock sat up straight and looked alarmed.

'What's the matter?' asked Dick. Then he heard what Jock had heard. A shrill whistle blown loudly by somebody some way off.

'That's my stepfather's whistle,' said Jock. 'He's whistling for me. Mum must have told him, or else he's found out I've come over here.'

'Quick – let's scoot away and hide,' said Anne. 'If you're not here he can't take you back! Come on! Maybe he'll get tired of looking for you, and go.'

Nobody could think of a better idea, and certainly nobody wanted to face a furious Mr Andrews. All four shot down the slope and made their way to where the heather was high and thick. They burrowed into it and lay still, hidden by some high bracken.

Mr Andrews's voice could soon be heard, shouting for Jock, but no Jock appeared. Mr Andrews came out by Mr Luffy's tent. Mr Luffy, surprised at the shouting, put his head out of his tent to see what it was all about. He didn't like the look of Mr Andrews at all.

'Where's Jock?' Mr Andrews demanded, scowling at him.

'I really do not know,' said Mr Luffy.

'He's got to come back,' said Mr Andrews, roughly. 'I won't have him hanging about here with those kids.'

'What's wrong with them?' inquired Mr Luffy. 'I

145

must say I find them very well-behaved and pleasant-mannered.'

Mr Andrews stared at Mr Luffy, and put him down as a silly, harmless old fellow who would probably help him to get Jock back if he went about it the right way.

'Now look here,' said Mr Andrews. 'I don't know who you are, but you must be a friend of the children's. And if so, then I'd better warn you they're running into danger. See?'

'Really? In what way?' asked Mr Luffy, mildly and disbelievingly.

'Well, there's bad and dangerous places about these moorlands,' said Mr Andrews. 'Very bad. I know them. And those children have been messing about in them. See? And if Jock comes here, he'll start messing about too, and I don't want him to get into any danger. It would break his mother's heart.'

'Quite,' said Mr Luffy.

'Well, will you talk to him and send him back?' said Mr Andrews. 'That railway yard now – that's a most dangerous place. And folks do say that there're spook-trains there. I wouldn't want Jock to be mixed up in anything of that sort.'

'Quite,' said Mr Luffy again, looking closely at Mr Andrews. 'You seem very concerned about this – er – railway yard.'

'Me? Oh, no,' said Mr Andrews. 'Never been near the horrible place. I wouldn't want to see spook-trains – make

146

me run a mile! It's just that I don't want Jock to get into danger. I'd be most obliged if you'd talk to him and send him home, when they all come back from wherever they are.'

'Quite,' said Mr Luffy again, most irritatingly. Mr Andrews gazed at Mr Luffy's bland face and suddenly wished he could smack it. 'Quite, quite, quite!' Gr-r-r-r-r-r!

He turned and went away. When he had gone for some time, and was a small speck in the distance, Mr Luffy called loudly.

'He's gone! Please send Jock here so that I can – er – address a few words to him.'

Four children appeared from their heathery hiding-place. Jock went over to Mr Luffy, looking mutinous.

'I just wanted to say,' said Mr Luffy, 'that I quite understand why you want to be away from your stepfather, and that I consider it's no business of mine where you go in order to get away from him!'

Jock grinned. 'Oh, thanks awfully,' he said. 'I thought you were going to send me back!' He rushed over to the others. 'It's all right,' he said. 'I'm going to stay, and, I say – what about going and exploring down that tunnel after lunch? We *might* find that spook-train then!'

'Good idea!' said Julian. 'We will! Poor old George – she'll miss that little adventure too!'

CHAPTER FIFTEEN

George has an adventure

GEORGE HAD gone off with one fixed idea in her mind. She was going to find out something about that mysterious tunnel! She thought she would walk over the moorlands to Kilty's Yard, and see what she could see there. Maybe she could walk right back through the tunnel itself!

She soon came to Olly's Yard. There it lay below her, with Wooden-Leg Sam pottering about. She went down to speak to him. He didn't see or hear her coming and jumped violently when she called to him.

He swung round, squinting at her fiercely. 'You clear off!' he shouted. 'I've been told to keep you children out of here, see? Do you want me to lose my job?'

'Who told you to keep us out?' asked George, puzzled as to who could have known they had been in the yard.

'*He* did, see?' said the old man. He rubbed his eyes, and then peered at George short-sightedly again. 'I've broken my glasses,' he said.

'Who's "he" – the person who told you to keep us out?' said George.

But the old watchman seemed to have one of his sudden strange changes of temper again. He bent down and picked up a large cinder. He was about to fling it at

149

George when Timmy gave a loud and menacing growl. Sam dropped his arm.

'You clear out,' he said. 'You don't want to get a poor old man like me into trouble, do you? You look a nice kind boy you do. You wouldn't get Wooden-Leg Sam into trouble, would you?'

George turned to go. She decided to take the path that led to the tunnel and peep inside. But when she got there there was nothing to see. She didn't feel that she wanted to walk all alone inside that dark mouth, so she took the path that Julian had taken the night before, over the top of the tunnel. But she left it half-way to look at a curious bump that jutted up from the heather just there.

She scraped away at the heather and found something hard beneath. She pulled at it but it would not give. Timmy, thinking she was obligingly digging for rabbits, came to help. He scrambled below the heather – and then he suddenly gave a bark of fright and disappeared!

George screamed: 'Timmy! What have you done? Where are you?'

To her enormous relief she heard Timmy's bark some way down. Where *could* he be? She called again, and once more Timmy barked.

George tugged at the tufts of heather, and then suddenly she saw what the curious mound was. It was a built-up vent-hole for the old tunnel – a place where the smoke came curling out in the days when trains ran there often. It had been barred across with iron, but the bars had rusted and fallen in, and heather had grown thickly over them.

'Oh, Timmy, you must have fallen down the vent,' said George, anxiously. 'But not very far down. Wait a bit and I'll see what I can do. If only the others were here to help!'

But they weren't, and George had to work all by herself to try and get down to the broken bars. It took her a very long time, but at last she had them exposed, and saw where Timmy had fallen down.

He kept giving short little barks, as if to say: 'It's all right. I can wait. I'm not hurt!'

George had to sit down and take a rest after her efforts. She was hungry, but she said to herself that she would *not*

eat till she had somehow got down to Timmy, and found out where he was. Soon she began her task again.

She climbed down through the fallen-in vent. It was very difficult, and she was terrified of the rusty old iron bars breaking off under her weight. But they didn't.

Once down in the vent she discovered steps made of great iron nails projecting out. Some of them had thin rungs across. There had evidently once been a ladder up to the top of the vent. Most of the rungs had gone, but the iron nails that supported them still stood in the brick walls of the old round vent. She heard Timmy give a little bark. He was quite near her now.

Cautiously she went down the great hole. Her foot touched Timmy. He had fallen on a collection of broken iron bars, which, caught in part of the old iron ladder, stuck out from it, and made a rough landing-place for the dog to fall on.

'Oh, Timmy,' said George, horrified. 'However am I going to get you out of here? This hole goes right down into the tunnel.'

She couldn't possibly pull Timmy up the hole. It was equally impossible to get him down. He could never climb down the iron ladder, especially as it had so many rungs missing.

George was in despair. 'Oh, Timmy! Why did I lose my temper and walk out on the others to do some exploring all by myself? Don't fall, Timmy. You'll break your legs if you do.'

Timmy had no intention of falling. He was frightened, but so far his curious landing-place felt firm. He kept quite still.

'Listen, Tim,' said George, at last. 'The only thing I can think of is to climb down round it somehow and see how far it is to the tunnel itself. There might even be someone there to help! No, that's silly. There can't be. But I might find an old rope – anything – that I could use to help you down with. Oh, dear, what a horrible nightmare!'

George gave Timmy a reassuring pat, and then began to feel about for the iron rungs with her feet. Further down they were all there, and it was easy to climb lower and lower. She was soon down in the tunnel itself. She had her torch with her and switched it on. Then she nearly gave a scream of horror.

Just near to her was a silent train! She could almost touch the engine. Was it – could it be – the spook-train itself? George stared at it, breathing fast.

It looked very, very old and out-of-date. It was smaller than the trains she was used to – the engine was smaller and so were the trucks. The funnel was longer and the wheels were different from those of ordinary trains. George stared at the silent train by the light of her torch, her mind in a muddle. She really didn't know *what* to think!

It *must* be the spook-train! It had come from this tunnel the night before, and had gone back again – and it hadn't run all the way through to Kilty's Yard, because Julian had watched for it, and it hadn't come out there. No – it

had run here, to the middle of the dark tunnel, and there it stood, waiting for night so that it might run again.

George shivered. The train belonged to years and years ago! Who drove it at night? Did anybody? Or did it run along without a driver, remembering its old days and old ways? No, that was silly. Trains didn't think or remember. George shook herself and remembered Timmy.

And just at that very moment, poor Timmy lost his foothold on the iron bars, and fell! He had stretched out to listen for George, his foot had slipped – and now he was hurtling down the vent! He gave a mournful howl.

He struck against part of the ladder and that stopped his headlong fall for a moment. But down he went again, scrabbling as he fell, trying to get hold of something to save himself.

George heard him howl and knew he was falling. She was so horror-stricken that she simply couldn't move. She stood there at the bottom of the vent like a statue, not even breathing.

Timmy fell with a thump beside her, and a groan was jerked out of him. In a trice George was down by him on her knees. 'Timmy! Are you hurt? Are you alive? Oh, Timmy, say something!'

'Woof,' said Timmy, and got up rather unsteadily on his four legs. He had fallen on a pile of the softest soot! The smoke of many, many years had sooted the walls of the vent, and the weather had sent it down to the bottom, until quite a pile had collected at one side. Timmy had fallen plump in the middle of it, and almost buried himself. He shook himself violently, and soot flew out all over George.

She didn't know or care. She hugged him, and her face and clothes grew as black as soot! She felt about and found the soft pile that had saved Timmy from being hurt.

'It's soot! I came down the other side of the vent, so I didn't know the soot was there. Oh, Timmy, what a bit of luck for you! I thought you'd be killed – or at least badly hurt,' said George.

He licked her sooty nose and didn't like the taste of it.

George stood up. She didn't like the idea of climbing up that horrid vent again – and, anyway, Timmy couldn't. The only thing to do was to walk out of the tunnel. She wouldn't have fancied walking through the tunnel before, in case she met the spook-train – but here it was, close beside her, and she had been so concerned about Timmy that she had quite forgotten it.

Timmy went over to the engine and smelt the wheels. Then he jumped up into the cab. Somehow the sight of Timmy doing that took away all George's fear. If Timmy could jump up into the spook-train, there couldn't be much for her to be afraid of!

She decided to examine the trucks. There were four of them, all covered trucks. Shining her torch, she climbed up into one of them, pulling Timmy up behind her. She expected to find it quite empty, unloaded many, many years ago by long-forgotten railwaymen.

But it was loaded with boxes! George was surprised. Why did a spook-train run about with boxes in it? She shone her torch on to one – and then quickly switched it out!

She had heard a noise in the tunnel. She crouched down in the truck, put her hand on Timmy's collar, and listened. Timmy listened, too, the hackles rising on his neck.

It was a clanging noise. Then there came a bang. Then a light shone out, and the tunnel was suddenly as bright as day!

The light came from a great lamp in the side of the tunnel. George peeped cautiously out through a crack in the truck. She saw that this place must be where the tunnel forked. One fork went on to Kilty's Yard – but surely the other fork was supposed to be bricked up? George followed the lines with her eyes. One set went on down the tunnel to Kilty's Yard, the other set ran straight into a great wall, which was built across the second tunnel, that once led to Roker's Yard.

'Yes – it *is* bricked up, just as the old porter told Julian,' said George to herself. And then she stared in the greatest amazement, clutching the side of the truck, hardly believing her eyes.

Part of the wall was opening before her! Before her very eyes, a great mass of it slid back in the centre of the wall – back and back – until a strange-shaped opening, about the size of the train itself, showed in the thick wall. George gasped. Whatever could be happening?

A man came through the opening. George felt sure she

had seen him before somewhere. He came up to the engine of the train and swung himself into the cab.

There were all sorts of sounds then from the cab. What was the man doing? Starting the fire to run the train? George did not dare to try and see. She was trembling now, and Timmy pressed himself against her to comfort her.

Then came another set of noises – steam noises. The man must be going to start the engine moving. Smoke came from the funnel. More noises, and some clanks and clangs.

It suddenly occurred to George that the man might be going to take the train through that little opening in the bricked-up wall. Then – supposing he shut the wall up again – George would be a prisoner! She would be in the truck, hidden behind that wall, and the wall would be closed so that she couldn't escape.

'I must get out before it's too late,' thought George, in a panic. 'I only hope the man doesn't see me!'

But just as she was about to try and get out, the engine gave a loud 'choo-choo', and began to move backwards! It ran down the lines a little way, then forward again, and this time its wheels were on the set of lines that led to the second tunnel, where the small opening now showed so clearly in the wall.

George didn't dare to get out of the moving train. So there she crouched as the engine steamed quickly to the hole in the wall that stretched right across the other tunnel. That hole just fitted it! It must have been made for it, thought George, as the train moved through it.

The train went right through and came out in another tunnel. Here there was a bright light, too. George peered out through the crack. There was more than a tunnel here! What looked like vast caves stretched away on each side of the tunnel, and men lounged about in them. Who on earth were they, and what were they doing with that old train?

There was a curious noise at the back of the train. The hole in the stout brick wall closed up once more! Now there was no way in or out. 'It's like the Open-Sesame trick in *Ali Baba and the Forty Thieves*,' thought George. 'And, like Ali Baba, I'm in the cave – and don't know the way to get myself out! Thank goodness Timmy is with me!'

The train was now at a standstill. Behind it was the thick wall – and then George saw that in front of it was a thick wall, too! This tunnel must be bricked up in two places – and in between was this extraordinary cavern, or whatever it was. George puzzled her head over the strange place, but couldn't make head or tail of it.

'Well! Whatever would the others say if they knew you and I were actually in the spook-train itself, tucked away in its hiding-place where nobody in the world can find it?' whispered George to Timmy. 'What are we to do, Timmy?'

Timmy wagged his tail cautiously. He didn't understand all this. He wanted to lie low for a bit and see how things turned out.

'We'll wait till the men have gone away, Timmy,' whispered George. 'That is, if they ever do! Then we'll get out and see if we can manage that Open-Sesame entrance and get away. We'd better tell Mr Luffy about all this. There's something very strange and very mysterious here – and we've fallen headlong into it!'

CHAPTER SIXTEEN

In the tunnel again

JOCK WAS really enjoying himself at the camp. He had a picnic lunch with the others, and ate as much as they did, looking very happy. Mr Luffy joined them, and Jock beamed at him, feeling that he was a real friend.

'Where's George?' asked Mr Luffy.

'Gone off by herself,' said Julian.

'Have you quarrelled, by any chance?' said Mr Luffy.

'A bit,' said Julian. 'We have to let George get over it by herself, Mr Luffy. She's like that.'

'Where's she gone?' said Mr Luffy, helping himself to a tomato. 'Why isn't she back to dinner?'

'She's taken hers with her,' said Anne. 'I feel a bit worried about her, somehow. I hope she's all right.'

Mr Luffy looked alarmed. 'I feel a bit worried myself,' he said. 'Still, she's got Timmy with her.'

'We're going off on a bit of exploring,' said Julian, when they had all finished eating. 'What are *you* going to do, Mr Luffy?'

'I think I'll come with you,' said Mr Luffy, unexpectedly. The children's hearts sank. They couldn't possibly go exploring for spook-trains in the tunnel if Mr Luffy was with them.

'Well – I don't think it will be very interesting for you, sir,' said Julian, rather feebly. However, Mr Luffy took the hint and realised he wasn't wanted that afternoon.

'Right,' he said. 'In that case I'll stay here and mess about.'

The children sighed with relief. Anne cleared up, with Jock helping her, and then they called goodbye to Mr Luffy and set off, taking their tea with them.

Jock was full of excitement. He was so pleased to be with the others, and he kept thinking of sleeping in the camp that night – what fun it would be! Good old Mr Luffy, taking his side like that. He bounded after the others joyfully as they went off to the old railway yard.

Wooden-Leg Sam was pottering about there as usual. They waved to him, but he didn't wave back. Instead he shook his fist at them and tried to bawl in his husky voice: 'You clear out! Trespassing, that's what you are. Don't you come down here or I'll chase you!'

'Well, we won't go down then,' said Dick, with a grin. 'Poor old man – thinking of chasing us with that wooden leg of his. We won't give him the chance. We'll just walk along here, climb down the lines and walk up them to the tunnel.'

Which is what they did, much to the rage of poor Sam. He yelled till his voice gave out, but they took no notice, and walked quickly up the lines. The mouth of the tunnel looked very round and black as they came near.

'Now we'll jolly well walk right through this tunnel and

see where that spook-train is that came out of it the other night,' said Julian. 'It didn't come out the other end, so it *must* be somewhere in the middle of the tunnel.'

'If it's a real spook-train, it might completely disappear,' said Anne, not liking the look of the dark tunnel at all. The others laughed.

'It won't have disappeared,' said Dick. 'We shall come across it somewhere, and we'll examine it thoroughly and try and find out exactly what it is, and why it comes and goes in such a mysterious manner.'

They walked into the black tunnel, and switched on their torches, which made little gleaming paths in front of them. They walked up the middle of one pair of lines, Julian in front keeping a sharp lookout for anything in the shape of a train!

The lines ran on and on. The children's voices sounded weird and echoing in the long tunnel. Anne kept close to Dick, and half wished she hadn't come. Then she remembered that George had called her a coward, and she put up her head, determined not to show that she was scared.

Jock talked almost without stopping. 'I've never done anything like this in my life. I call this a proper adventure, hunting for spook-trains in a dark tunnel. It makes me feel nice and shivery all over. I do hope we find the train. It simply *must* be here somewhere!'

They walked on and on and on. But there was no sign of any train. They came to where the tunnel forked into the second one, that used to run to Roker's Vale.

Julian flashed his torch on the enormous brick wall that stretched across the second tunnel.

'Yes, it's well and truly bricked up,' he said. 'So that only leaves this tunnel to explore. Come on.'

They went on again, little knowing that George and Timmy were behind that brick wall, hidden in a truck of the spook-train itself! They walked on and on down the lines, and found nothing interesting at all.

They saw a little round circle of bright light some way in front of them. 'See that?' said Julian. 'That must be the end of this tunnel – the opening that goes into Kilty's Yard. Well, if the train isn't between here and Kilty's Yard, it's gone!'

In silence they walked down the rest of the tunnel, and came out into the open air. Workshops were built all over Kilty's Yard. The entrance to the tunnel was weed-grown and neglected. Weeds grew even across the lines there.

'Well, no train has been out of this tunnel here for years,' said Julian, looking at the thick weeds. 'The wheels would have chopped the weeds to bits.'

'It's extraordinary,' said Dick, puzzled. 'We've been right through the tunnel and there's no train there at all, yet we know it goes in and out of it. What's happened to it?'

'It *is* a spook-train,' said Jock, his face red with excitement. 'Must be. It only exists at night, and then comes out on its lines, like it used to do years ago.'

'I don't like thinking that,' said Anne, troubled. 'It's a horrid thought.'

164

IN THE TUNNEL AGAIN

'What are we going to do now?' Julian asked. 'We seem to have come to a blank. No train, nothing to see, empty tunnel. What a dull end to an adventure.'

'Let's walk back all the way again,' said Jock – he wanted to squeeze as much out of this adventure as he could. 'I know we shan't see the train this time any more than we did the last time, but you never know!'

'I'm not coming through that tunnel again,' said Anne. 'I want to be out in the sun. I'll walk over the top of the tunnel, along the path there that Julian took the other night and you three can walk back, and meet me at the other end.'

'Right,' said Julian and the three boys disappeared into the dark tunnel. Anne ran up the path that led alongside the top of it. How good it was to be in the open air again! That horrid tunnel! She ran along cheerfully, glad to be out in the sun.

She got to the other end of the tunnel quite quickly, and sat down on the path above the yard to wait for the others. She looked for Wooden-Leg Sam. He was nowhere to be seen. Perhaps he was in his little hut.

She hadn't been there for more than two minutes when something surprising happened. A car came bumping slowly down the rough track to the yard! Anne sat up and watched. A man got out – and Anne's eyes almost fell out of her head. Why, it was – surely it was Mr Andrews, Jock's stepfather!

He went over to Sam's hut and threw open the door.

Anne could hear the sound of voices. Then she heard another noise – the sound of a heavy lorry coming. She saw it came cautiously down the steep, rough track. It ran into an old tumbledown shed and stayed there. Then three men came out and Anne stared at them. Where had she seen them before?

'Of course! They're the farm labourers at Jock's farm!' she thought. 'But what are they doing here? How very strange!'

Mr Andrews joined the men and, to Anne's dismay, they began to walk up the lines to the tunnel! Her heart almost stopped. Goodness, Julian, Dick and Jock were still in that tunnel, walking through it. They would bump right into Mr Andrews and his men – and then what would happen? Mr Andrews had warned them against going there, and had ordered Jock not to go.

Anne stared at the four men walking into the far-off mouth of the tunnel. What could she do? How could she warn the boys? She couldn't! She would just have to stay there and wait for them to come out – probably chased by a furious Mr Andrews and the other men. Oh dear, dear – if they were caught they would probably all get an awful telling off! What *could* she do?

'I can only wait,' thought poor Anne. 'There's nothing else to do. Oh, do come, Julian, Dick and Jock. I daren't do anything but wait for you.'

She waited and waited. It was now long past tea-time. Julian had the tea, so there was nothing for Anne to eat.

IN THE TUNNEL AGAIN

Nobody came out of the tunnel. Not a sound was heard. Anne at last decided to go down and ask Wooden-Leg Sam a few questions. So, rather afraid, the girl set off down to the yard.

Sam was in his hut, drinking cocoa, and looking very sour. Something had evidently gone wrong. When he saw Anne's shadow across the doorway he got up at once, shaking his fist.

'What, you children again! You went into that tunnel this afternoon, and so I went up and telephoned Mr Andrews to come and catch you all, poking your noses in all the time. How did you get out of that tunnel? Are the others with you? Didn't Mr Andrews catch you, eh?'

Anne listened to all this in horror. So old Sam had actually managed to telephone Mr Andrews, and tell tales on them – so that Jock's stepfather and his men had come to catch them. This was worse than ever.

'You come in here,' said Sam suddenly, and he darted his big arm at her. 'Come on. I don't know where the others are, but I'll get one of you!'

Anne gave a scream and ran away at top speed. Wooden-Leg Sam went after her for a few yards and then gave it up. He bent down and picked up a handful of cinders. A shower of them fell all round Anne, and made her run faster than ever.

She tore up the path to the heather, and was soon on the moors again, panting and sobbing. 'Oh, Julian! Oh, Dick!

IN THE TUNNEL AGAIN

What's happened to you? Oh, where's George? If only she would come home, she'd be brave enough to look for them, but I'm not. I must tell Mr Luffy. He'll know what to do!'

She ran on and on, her feet catching continually in the tufts of thick heather. She kept falling over and scrambling up again. She now had only one idea in her mind – to find Mr Luffy and tell him every single thing! Yes, she would tell him about the spook-trains and all. There was something strange and important about the whole thing now, and she wanted a grown-up's help.

She staggered on and on. 'Mr Luffy! Oh, Mr Luffy, where are you? MR LUFFY!'

But no Mr Luffy answered her. She came round the gorse bushes she thought were the ones sheltering the camp – but, alas, the camp was not there. Anne had lost her way!

'I'm lost,' said Anne, the tears running down her cheeks. 'But I mustn't get scared. I must try to find the right path now. Oh, dear, I'm quite lost! MR LUFFY!'

Poor Anne. She stumbled on blindly, hoping to come to the camp, calling every now and again. 'Mr Luffy. Can you hear me? MR LUFFFFFFFY!'

CHAPTER SEVENTEEN

An amazing find

IN THE meantime, what had happened to the three boys walking back through the tunnel? They had gone slowly along examining the lines to see if a train could have possibly run along them recently. Few weeds grew in the dark airless tunnel, so they could not tell by those.

But, when they came about half-way, Julian noticed an interesting thing. 'Look,' he said, flashing his torch on to the lines before and behind them. 'See that? The lines are black and rusty behind us now, but here this pair of lines is quite bright – as if they had been used a lot.'

He was right. Behind them stretched black and rusty lines, sometimes buckled in places – but in front of them, stretching to the mouth of the tunnel leading to Olly's Yard, the lines were bright, as if train-wheels had run along them.

'That's funny,' said Dick. 'Looks as if the spook-train ran only from here to Olly's Yard and back. But why? And where in the world is it now? It's vanished into thin air!'

Julian was as puzzled as Dick. Where *could* a train be if it was not in the tunnel? It had obviously run to the middle of the tunnel, and then stopped – but where had it gone now?

AN AMAZING FIND

'Let's go to the mouth of the tunnel and see if the lines are bright all the way,' said Julian at last. 'We can't discover much here – unless the train suddenly materialises in front of us!'

They went on down the tunnel, their torches flashing on the lines in front of them. They talked earnestly as they went. They didn't see four men waiting for them, four men who crouched in a little niche at the side of the tunnel, waiting there in the dark.

'Well,' said Julian, 'I think—' and then he stopped, because four dark figures suddenly pounced on the three boys and held them fast. Julian gave a shout and struggled, but the man who had hold of him was far too strong to escape from. Their torches were flung to the ground. Julian's broke, and the other two torches lay there, their beams shining on the feet of the struggling company.

It didn't take more than twenty seconds to make each boy a captive, his arms behind his back. Julian tried to kick, but his captor twisted his arm so fiercely that he groaned in pain and stopped his kicking.

'Look here! What's all this about?' demanded Dick. 'Who are you, and what do you think you're doing? We're only three boys exploring an old tunnel. What's the harm in that?'

'Take them all away,' said a voice that everyone recognised at once.

'Mr Andrews! Is it you?' cried Julian. 'Set us free. You

know us – the boys at the camp. And Jock's here too. What do you think you're doing?'

Mr Andrews didn't answer, but he gave poor Jock a box on the right ear that almost sent him to the ground.

Their captors turned them about, and led them roughly up the tunnel, towards the middle. Nobody had a torch so it was all done in the darkness and the three boys stumbled badly, though the men seemed sure-footed enough.

They came to a halt after a time. Mr Andrews left them and Julian heard him go off somewhere to the left. Then there came a curious noise – a bang, a clank, and then a sliding, grating sound. What could be happening? Julian strained his eyes in the darkness, but he could see nothing at all.

He didn't know that Mr Andrews was opening the bricked-up wall through which the train had gone. He didn't know that he and the others were being pushed out of the first tunnel into the other one, through the curious hole in the wall. The three boys were shoved along in the darkness, not daring to protest.

Now they were in the curious place between the two walls which were built right across the place where the second tunnel forked from the first one. The place where the spook-train stood in silence – the place where George was, still hidden in one of the trucks with Timmy! But nobody knew that, of course; not even Mr Andrews guessed that a girl and a dog were listening in a truck nearby!

He put on a torch and flashed it in the faces of the three boys, who, although they were not showing any fear, felt rather scared all the same. This was so weird and unexpected, and they had no idea where they were at all.

'You were warned not to go down to that yard,' said the voice of one of the men. 'You were told it was a bad and dangerous place. So it is. And you've got to suffer for not taking heed of the warning! You'll be tied up and left here till we've finished our business. Maybe that'll be three days, maybe it'll be three weeks!'

'Look here, you can't keep us prisoner for all that time!' said Julian, alarmed. 'Why, there will be search parties out for us all over the place! They will be sure to find us.'

'Oh, no they won't,' said the voice. 'Nobody will find you here. Now, Peters – tie 'em up!'

Peters tied the three boys up. They had their legs tied, and their arms too, and were set down roughly against a wall. Julian protested again.

'What are you doing this for? We're quite harmless. We don't know a thing about your business, whatever it is.'

'We're not taking any chances,' said the voice. It was not Mr Andrews's voice, but a firm, strong one, full of determination and a large amount of annoyance.

'What about Mum?' said Jock suddenly, to his stepfather. 'She'll be worried.'

'Well, let her be worried,' said the voice again, answering before Mr Andrews could say a word. 'It's your own fault. You were warned.'

AN AMAZING FIND

The feet of the four men moved away. Then there came the same noises again as the boys had heard before. They were made by the hole in the wall closing up, but the boys didn't know that. They couldn't imagine what they were. The noises stopped and there was dead silence. There was also pitch darkness. The three boys strained their ears, and felt sure that the men had gone.

'Well! The brutes! Whatever are they up to?' said Julian in a low voice, trying to loosen the ropes round his hands.

'They've got some secret to hide,' said Dick. 'Gosh, they've tied my feet so tightly that the rope is cutting into my flesh.'

'What's going to happen?' came Jock's scared voice. This adventure didn't seem quite so grand to him now.

'Sh!' said Julian suddenly. 'I can hear something!'

They all lay and listened. What was it they could hear?

'It's – it's a dog whining,' said Dick, suddenly.

It was. It was Timmy in the truck with George. He had heard the voices of the boys he knew, and he wanted to get to them. But George, not sure yet that the men had gone, still had her hand on his collar. Her heart beat for joy to think she was alone no longer. The three boys – and Anne, too, perhaps – were there, in the same strange place as she and Timmy were.

The boys listened hard. The whining came again. Then, George let go her hold of Timmy's collar, and he leapt headlong out of the truck. His feet pattered eagerly over the ground. He went straight to the boys in the darkness, and Julian felt a wet tongue licking his face. A warm body pressed against him, and a little bark told him who it was.

'Timmy! I say, Dick – it's Timmy!' cried Julian, in joy. 'Where did he come from? Timmy, is it really you?'

'Woof,' said Timmy, and licked Dick next and then Jock.

'Where's George then?' wondered Dick.

'Here,' said a voice, and out of the truck scrambled George, switching on her torch as she did so. She went over to the boys. 'Whatever's happened? How did you come here? Were you captured or something?'

'Yes,' said Julian. 'But, George – where are we? And what are *you* doing here too? It's like a peculiar dream!'

'I'll cut your ropes first, before I stop to explain anything,' said George, and she took out her sharp knife. In a few moments she had cut the boys' bonds, and they all sat up, rubbing their sore ankles and wrists, groaning.

'Thanks, George! Now I feel fine,' said Julian, getting up. 'Where *are* we? Gracious, is that an engine there? What's it doing here?'

'That, Julian, is the spook-train!' said George, with a laugh. 'Yes, it is, really.'

'But we walked all the way down the tunnel and out of the other end, without finding it,' said Julian puzzled. 'It's most mysterious.'

'Listen, Ju,' said George. 'You know where that second tunnel is bricked up, don't you? Well, there's a way in through the wall – a whole bit of it moves back in a sort

176

of Open-Sesame manner! The spook-train can run in through the hole, on the rails. Once it's beyond the wall it stops, and the hole is closed up again.'

George switched her torch round to show the astonished boys the wall through which they had come. Then she swung her torch to the big wall opposite. 'See that?' she said. 'There are *two* walls across this second tunnel, with a big space in between – where the spook-train hides! Clever, isn't it?'

'It would be, if I could see any sense in it,' said Julian. 'But I can't. Why should anyone mess about with a silly spook-train at night?'

'That's what we've got to find out,' said George. 'And now's our chance. Look, Julian – look at all the caves stretching out on either side of the tunnel here. They would make wonderful hiding-places!'

'What for?' said Dick. 'I can't make head or tail of this!'

George swung her torch on the three boys and then asked a sudden question: 'I say – where's Anne?'

'Anne! She didn't want to come back with us through the tunnel, so she ran over the moorlands to meet us at the other end, by Olly's Yard,' said Julian. 'She'll be worried stiff, won't she, when we don't turn up? I only hope she doesn't come wandering up the tunnel to meet us – she'll run into those men if she does.'

Everyone felt worried. Anne hated the tunnel and she would be very frightened if people pounced on her in the darkness. Julian turned to George.

'Swing your torch round and let's see these caves. There doesn't seem to be anyone here now. We could have a snoop round.'

George swung her torch round, and Julian saw vast and apparently fathomless caves stretching out on either side, cut out of the sides of the tunnel. Jock saw something else. By the light of the torch he caught sight of a switch on the wall. Perhaps it opened the hole in the wall.

He crossed to it and pulled it down. Immediately the place was flooded with a bright light. It was a light-switch he had found. They all blinked in the sudden glare.

'That's better,' said Julian, pleased. 'Good for you, Jock! Now we can see what we're doing.'

He looked at the spook-train standing silently near them on its rails. It certainly looked very old and forgotten – as if it belonged to the last century, not to this.

'It's quite a museum piece,' said Julian, with interest. 'So that's what we heard puffing in and out of the tunnel at night – old Spooky!'

'I hid in that truck there,' said George, pointing, and she told them her own adventure. The boys could hardly believe she had actually puffed into this secret place, hidden on the spook-train itself!

'Come on – now let's look at these caves,' said Dick. They went over to the nearest one. It was packed with crates and boxes of all kinds. Julian pulled one open and whistled.

'All black market stuff, I imagine. Look here – crates of tea, crates of whisky and brandy, boxes and boxes of stuff – goodness knows what! This is a real black market hiding-place!'

The boys explored a little further. The caves were piled high with valuable stuff, worth thousands of pounds.

'All stolen, I suppose,' said Dick. 'But what do they *do* with it? I mean – how do they dispose of it? They bring it here in the train, of course, and hide it – but they must have some way of getting rid of it.'

'Would they repack it on the train and run it back to the yard when they had enough lorries to take it away?' said Julian.

'No!' said Dick. 'Of course not. Let me see – they steal it, pile it on to lorries at night, take it somewhere temporarily . . .'

'Yes – to my mother's farm!' said Jock, in a scared voice. 'All those lorries there in the barn – that's what they're used for! And they come down to Olly's Yard at night and the stuff is loaded in secret on the old train that comes puffing out to meet them – and then it's taken back here and hidden!'

'Wheeeee-ew!' Julian whistled. 'You're right, Jock! That's just what happens. What a cunning plot – to use a perfectly honest little farm as a hiding-place, to stock the farm with black-market men for labourers – no wonder they are such bad workers – and to wait for dark nights to run the stuff down to the yard and load it on the train!'

'Your stepfather must make a lot of money at this game,' said Dick to Jock.

'Yes. That's why he can afford to pour money into the farm,' said Jock, miserably. 'Poor Mum. This will break her heart. All the same, I don't think my stepfather's the chief one in this. There's somebody behind him.'

'Yes,' said Julian, thinking of the mean little Mr Andrews, with his big nose and weak chin. 'There probably is. Now – I've thought of something else. If this stuff is got rid of in any other way except down the tunnel it came up, there must somewhere be a way out of these caves!'

'I believe you're right,' said George. 'And if there is – we'll find it! And what's more, we'll escape that way!'

'Come on!' said Julian, and he switched off the glaring light. 'Your torch will give enough light now. We'll try this cave first. Keep your eyes open, all of you!'

CHAPTER EIGHTEEN

A way of escape

THE FOUR children and Timmy went into the big cave. They made their way round piles of boxes, chests and crates, marvelling at the amount the men must have stolen from time to time.

'These aren't man-made caves,' said Julian. 'They're natural. I expect the roof did perhaps fall in where the two tunnels met, and the entrance between them was actually blocked up.'

'But were *two* walls built then?' said Dick.

'Oh, no. We can't guess how it was that this black market hiding-place came into existence,' said Julian, 'but it might perhaps have been known there were caves here – and when someone came prospecting along the tunnel one day, maybe they even found an old train buried under a roof-fall or something like that.'

'And resurrected it, and built another wall secretly for a hiding-place – and used the train for their own purposes!' said Dick. 'Made that secret entrance, too. How ingenious!'

'Or it's possible the place was built during the last war,' said Julian. 'Maybe secret experiments were carried on here – and given up afterwards. The place might have been discovered by the black marketeers then, and used in this clever way. We can't tell!'

They had wandered for a good way in the cave by now, without finding anything of interest beyond the boxes and chests of all kinds of goods. Then they came to where a pile was very neatly arranged, with numbers chalked on boxes that were built up one on top of another. Julian halted.

'Now this looks as if these boxes were about to be shifted off somewhere,' he said. 'All put in order and numbered. Surely the exit must be somewhere here?'

He took George's torch from her and flashed it all round. Then he found what he wanted. The beam of light shone steadily on a strong roughly-made wooden door, set in the wall of the cave. They went over to it in excitement.

'This is what we want!' said Julian. 'I bet this is the exit to some very lonely part of the moors, not far from a road that lorries can come along to collect any goods carried out of here! There are some very deserted roads over these moors, running in the middle of miles of lonely moorland.'

'It's a clever organisation,' said Dick. 'Lorries stored at an innocent farm, full of goods for hiding in the tunnel-caves at a convenient time. The train comes out in the dark to collect the goods, and takes them back here, till the hue and cry after the goods has died down. Then out they go through this door to the moorlands, down to the lorries which come to collect them and whisk them away to the black market!'

183

'I told you how I saw Peters late one night, locking up the barn, didn't I?' said Jock, excitedly. 'Well, he must have got the lorry full of stolen goods then – and the next night he loaded them on to the spook-train!'

'That's about it,' said Julian, who had been trying the door to see if he could open it. 'I say, this door's maddening. I can't make it budge an inch. There's no lock that I can see.'

They all shoved hard, but the door would not give at all. It was very stout and strong, though rough and unfinished. Panting and hot, the four of them at last gave it up.

'Do you know what I think?' said Dick. 'I think the beastly thing has got something jammed hard against it on the outside.'

'Sure to have, when you come to think of it,' said Julian. 'It will be well hidden too – heather and bracken and stuff all over it. Nobody would ever find it. I suppose the lorry-drivers come across from the road to open the door when they want to collect the goods. And shut it and jam it after them.'

'No way of escape there, then,' said George in disappointment.

''Fraid not,' said Julian. George gave a sigh.

'Tired, old thing?' Julian asked kindly. 'Or hungry?'

'Both,' said George.

'Well, we've got some food somewhere, haven't we?' said Julian. 'I remember one of the men slinging my bag in after me. We've not had what we brought for tea yet. What about having a meal now? We can't seem to escape at the moment.'

'Let's have it here,' said George. 'I simply can't go a step further!'

They sat down against a big crate. Dick undid his kitbag. There were sandwiches, cake and chocolate. The four of them ate thankfully, and wished they had something to wash down the food with. Julian kept wondering about Anne.

'I wonder what she did,' he said. 'She'd wait and wait, I suppose. Then she might go back to the camp. But she doesn't know the way very well, and she might get lost. Oh dear – I don't know which would be worse for Anne, being lost on the moor or a prisoner down here with us!'

'Perhaps she's neither,' said Jock, giving Timmy his last bit of sandwich. 'I must say I'm jolly glad to have Timmy. Honest, George, I couldn't believe it when I heard Tim whine, and then heard your voice, too. I thought I must be dreaming.'

They sat where they were for a little longer and then decided to go back to the tunnel where the train was. 'It's just possible we might find the switch that works the Open-Sesame bit,' said Julian. 'We ought to have looked before, really, but I didn't think of it.'

They went back to where the train stood silently on its pair of lines. It seemed such an ordinary old train now that the children couldn't imagine why they had ever thought it was strange and spooky.

They switched on the light again, then they looked about for any lever or handle that might perhaps open the hole in the wall. There didn't seem to be anything at all. They tried a few switches, but nothing happened.

Then George suddenly came across a big lever low down in the brick wall itself. She tried to move it and couldn't. She called Julian.

'Ju! Come here. I wonder if this has got anything to do with opening that hole.'

The three boys came over to George. Julian tried to swing the lever down. Nothing happened. He pulled it but it wouldn't move. Then he and Dick pushed it upwards with all their strength.

And hey presto, there came a bang from somewhere, as

something heavy shifted, and then a clanking as if machinery was at work. Then came the sliding, grating noise and a great piece of the brick wall moved slowly back, and then swung round sideways and stopped. The way of escape was open!

'Open Sesame!' said Dick, grandly, as the hole appeared.

'Better switch off the light here,' said Julian. 'If there's anyone still in the tunnel they might see the reflection of it on the tunnel-wall beyond, and wonder what it was.'

He stepped back and switched it off, and the place was in darkness again. George put on her torch, and its feeble beam lighted up the way of escape.

'Come on,' said Dick, impatiently, and they all crowded out of the hole. 'We'll make for Olly's Yard.' They began to make their way down the dark tunnel.

'Listen,' said Julian, in a low voice. 'We'd better not talk at all, and we'd better go as quietly as we can. We don't know who may be in or out of this tunnel this evening. We don't want to walk bang into somebody.'

So they said nothing at all, but kept close to one another in single file, walking at the side of the track.

They had not gone more than a quarter of a mile before Julian stopped suddenly. The others bumped into one another, and Timmy gave a little whine as somebody trod on his paw. George's hand went down to his collar at once.

The four of them and Timmy listened, hardly daring to

breathe. Somebody was coming up the tunnel towards them! They could see the pin-point of a torch, and hear the distant crunch of footsteps.

'Other way, quick!' whispered Julian, and they all turned. With Jock leading them now, they made their way as quickly and quietly as they could back to the place where the two tunnels met. They passed it and went on towards Kilty's Yard, hoping to get out that way.

But alas for their hopes, a lantern stood some way down the tunnel there, and they did not dare to go on. There might be nobody with the lantern – on the other hand there might. What were they to do?

'They'll see that hole in the wall is open!' suddenly said Dick. 'We left it open. They'll know we've escaped then. We're caught again! They'll come down to find us, and here we'll be!'

They stood still, pressed close together, Timmy growling a little in his throat. Then George remembered something!

'Julian! Dick! We could climb up that vent that I came down,' she whispered. 'The one poor old Timmy fell down. Have we time?'

'Where is the vent?' said Julian, urgently. 'Quick, find it.'

George tried to remember. Yes, it was on the other side of the tunnel – near the place where the two tunnels met. She must look for the pile of soot. How she hoped the little light from her torch would not be seen. Whoever was coming up from Olly's Yard must be almost there by now!

She found the pile of soot that Timmy had fallen into. 'Here it is,' she whispered. 'But, oh, Julian! How can we take Timmy?'

'We can't,' said Julian. 'We must hope he'll manage to hide and then slink out of the tunnel by himself. He's quite clever enough.'

He pushed George up the vent first and her feet found the first rungs. Then Jock went up, his nose almost on George's heels. Then Dick – and last of all, Julian. But before he managed to climb the first steps, something happened.

A bright glare filled the tunnel, as someone switched on

the light that hung there. Timmy slunk into the shadows and growled in his throat. Then there came a shout.

'Who's opened the hole in the wall? It's open! Who's there?'

It was Mr Andrews's voice. Then came another voice, angry and loud: 'Who's here? Who's opened this place?'

'Those kids can't have moved the lever,' said Mr Andrews. 'We bound them up tightly.'

The men, three of them, went quickly through the hole in the wall. Julian climbed up the first few rungs thankfully. Poor Timmy was left in the shadows at the bottom.

Out came the men at a run. 'They've gone! Their ropes are cut! How could they have escaped? We put Kit down one end of the tunnel and we've been walking up this end. Those kids must be about here somewhere.'

'Or hiding in the caves,' said another voice. 'Peters, go and look, while we hunt here.'

The men hunted everywhere. They had no idea that the vent was nearby in the wall. They did not see the dog that slunk by them like a shadow, keeping out of their way, and lying down whenever the light from a torch came near him.

George climbed steadily, feeling with her feet for the iron nails whenever she came to broken rungs. Then she came to a stop. Something was pressing on her head. What was it? She put up her hand to feel. It was the collection of broken iron bars that Timmy had fallen on that morning. He had dislodged some of them, and they had then fallen in such a way that they had lodged across the vent, all twined into each other. George could climb no higher. She tried to move the bars, but they were heavy and strong – besides, she was afraid she might bring the whole lot on top of her and the others. They might be badly injured then.

'What's up, George? Why don't you go on?' asked Jock, who was next.

'There's some iron bars across the vent – ones that must have fallen when Timmy fell,' said George. 'I can't go any higher! I daren't pull too hard at the bars.'

Jock passed the message to Dick, and he passed it down to Julian. The four of them came to a full-stop!

'Blow!' said Julian. 'I wish I'd gone up first. What are we to do now?'

What indeed? The four of them hung there in the darkness, hating the smell of the sooty old vent, miserably uncomfortable on the broken rungs and nails.

'How do you like adventures now, Jock?' asked Dick. 'I bet you wish you were in your own bed at home!'

'I don't!' said Jock. 'I wouldn't miss this for worlds! I always wanted an adventure – and I'm not grumbling at this one!'

CHAPTER NINETEEN

What an adventure!

AND NOW, what had happened to Anne? She had stumbled on and on for a long time, shouting to Mr Luffy. And outside his tent Mr Luffy sat, reading peacefully. But, as the evening came, and then darkness, he became very worried indeed about the five children.

He wondered what to do. It was hopeless for one man to search the moors. Half a dozen or more were needed for that! He decided to get his car and go over to Olly's Farm to get the men from there. So off he went.

But when he got there he found no one at home except Mrs Andrews and the little maid. Mrs Andrews looked bewildered and worried.

'What is the matter?' said Mr Luffy gently, as she came running out to the car, looking troubled.

'Oh, it's you, Mr Luffy,' she said, when he told her who he was. 'I didn't know who you were. Mr Luffy, something strange is happening. All the men have gone – and all the lorries, too. My husband has taken the car and nobody will tell me anything. I'm so worried.'

Mr Luffy decided not to add to her worries by telling her the children were missing. He just pretended he had come to collect some milk. 'Don't worry,' he said

192

comfortingly to Mrs Andrews. 'You'll find things are all right in the morning, I expect. I'll come and see you then. Now I must be off on an urgent matter.'

He went bumping along the road in his car, puzzled. He had known there was something funny about Olly's Farm, and he had puzzled his brains a good deal over Olly's Yard and the spook-trains. He hoped the children hadn't got mixed up in anything dangerous.

'I'd better go down and report to the police that they're missing,' he thought. 'After all, I'm more or less responsible for them. It's very worrying indeed.'

He told what he knew at the police station, and the sergeant, an intelligent man, at once mustered six men and a police car.

'Have to find those kids,' he said. 'And we'll have to look into this Olly's Farm business, sir, and these here spook-trains, whatever they may be. We've known there was something funny going on, but we couldn't put our finger on it. But we'll find the children first.'

They went quickly up to the moors and the six men began to fan out to search, with Mr Luffy at the head. And the first thing they found was Anne!

She was still stumbling along, crying for Mr Luffy, but in a very small, weak voice now. When she heard his voice calling her in the darkness she wept for joy.

'Oh, Mr Luffy! You must save the boys,' she begged him. 'They're in that tunnel – and they've been caught by

Mr Andrews and his men, I'm sure. They didn't come out and I waited and waited! Do come!'

'I've got some friends here who will certainly come and help,' said Mr Luffy gently. He called the men, and in a few words told them what Anne had said.

'In the tunnel?' said one of them. 'Where the spook-trains run? Well, come on, men, we'll go down there.'

'You stay behind, Anne,' said Mr Luffy. But she wouldn't. So he carried her as he followed the men who were making their way through the heather, down to Olly's Yard. They did not bother with Wooden-Leg Sam. They went straight to the tunnel and walked up it quietly. Mr

Luffy was a good way behind with Anne. She refused to stay with him in the yard.

'No,' she said, 'I'm not a coward. Really I'm not. I want to help to rescue the boys. I wish George was here. Where's George?'

Mr Luffy had no idea. Anne clung to his hand, scared but eager to prove that she was not a coward. Mr Luffy thought she was grand!

Meanwhile, Julian and the others had been in the vent for a good while, tired and uncomfortable. The men had searched in vain for them and were now looking closely into every niche at the sides of the tunnel.

And, of course, they found the vent! One of the men shone his light up it. It shone on to poor Julian's feet! The man gave a loud shout that almost made Julian fall off the rung he was standing on.

'Here they are! Up this vent. Who'd have thought it? Come on down or it'll be the worse for you!'

Julian didn't move. George pushed desperately at the iron bars above her head, but she could not move them. One of the men climbed up the vent and caught hold of Julian's foot.

He dragged so hard at it that the boy's foot was forced off the rung. Then the man dragged off the other foot, and Julian found himself hanging by his arms with the man tugging hard at his feet. He could hang on no longer. His tired arms gave way and he fell heavily down, landing half on the man and half on the pile of soot. Another man pounced on Julian at once, while the first climbed up the vent to find the next boy. Soon Dick felt his feet being tugged at, too.

'All right, all right. I'll come down!' he yelled, and climbed down. Then Jock climbed down, too. The men looked at them angrily.

'Giving us a chase like this! Who undid your ropes?' said Mr Andrews, roughly. One of the men put a hand on his arm and nodded up towards the vent. 'Someone else is coming down,' he said. 'We only tied up three boys, didn't we? Who's this, then?'

It was George, of course. She wasn't going to desert the three boys. Down she came, as black as night with soot.

'Another boy!' said the men. 'Where did he come from?'

'Any more up there?' asked Mr Andrews.

'Look and see,' said Julian, and got a box on the ears for his answer.

'Treat them rough now,' ordered Peters. 'Teach them a lesson, the little pests. Take them away.'

The children's hearts sank. The men caught hold of them roughly. Blow! Now they would be made prisoners again.

Suddenly a cry came from down the tunnel: 'Police! Run for it!'

The men dropped the children's arms at once and stood undecided. A man came tearing up the tunnel. 'I tell you the police are coming!' he gasped. 'Are you stone deaf? There's a whole crowd of them. Run for it! Somebody's split on us.'

WHAT AN ADVENTURE!

'Get along to Kilty's Yard!' shouted Peters. 'We can get cars there. Run for it!'

To the children's dismay, the men tore down the tunnel to Kilty's Yard. They would escape! They heard the sound of the men's feet as they ran along the line.

George found her voice. 'Timmy! Where are you? After them, Timmy! Stop them!'

A black shadow came streaking by out of the hole in the wall, where Timmy had been hiding and watching for a chance to come to George. He had heard her voice and obeyed. He raced after the men like a greyhound, his tongue hanging out, panting as he went.

These were the men who had ill-treated George and the others, were they? Aha, Timmy knew how to deal with people like that!

The policemen came running up, and Mr Luffy and Anne came up behind them.

'They've gone down there, with Timmy after them,' shouted George. The men looked at her and gasped. She was black all over. The others were filthy dirty too, with sooty-black faces in the light of the lamp that still shone down from the wall of the tunnel.

'George!' shrieked Anne in delight. 'Julian! Oh, are you all safe? I went back to tell Mr Luffy about you and I got lost. I'm so ashamed!'

'You've nothing to be ashamed of, Anne,' said Mr Luffy. 'You're a grand girl! Brave as a lion!'

From down the tunnel came shouts and yells and loud

barks. Timmy was at work! He had caught up with the men and launched himself on them one after another, bringing each one heavily to the ground. They were terrified to find a big animal growling and snapping all around them. Timmy held them at bay in the tunnel, not allowing them to go one step further, snapping at any man who dared to go near.

The police ran up. Timmy growled extra fiercely just to let the men know that it was quite impossible to get by him. In a trice each of the men was imprisoned by a pair of strong arms and they were being told to come quietly.

They didn't go quietly. For one thing Mr Andrews lost his nerve and howled dismally. Jock felt very ashamed of him.

'Shut up,' said a burly policeman. 'We know you're only the miserable little cat's-paw – taking money from the big men to hold your tongue and obey orders.'

Timmy barked as if to say, 'Yes, don't you dare call him a *dog's* paw! That would be too good a name for him!'

'Well, I don't think I ever in my life saw dirtier children,' said Mr Luffy. 'I vote we all go back to my car and I drive the lot of you over to Olly's Farm for a meal and a bath!'

So back they all went, tired, dirty, and also feeling very thrilled.

What a night! They told Anne all that had happened, and she told them her story, too. She almost fell asleep in the car as she talked, she was so tired.

Mrs Andrews was sensible and kind, though upset to hear that her husband had been taken off by the police. She got hot water for baths, and laid a meal for the hungry children.

'I wouldn't worry overmuch, Mrs Andrews,' said kindly Mr Luffy. 'That husband of yours needs a lesson, you know. This will probably keep him going straight in future. The farm is yours, and you can now hire proper farm-workers who will do what you want them to do. And I think Jock will be happier without a stepfather for the present.'

'You're right, Mr Luffy,' said Mrs Andrews, wiping her eyes quickly. 'Quite right. I'll let Jock help me with the farm, and get it going beautifully. To think that Mr Andrews was in with all those black marketeers! It's that friend of his, you know, who makes him do all this. He's so weak. He knew Jock was snooping about in that tunnel, and that's why he wanted him to go away – and kept making him have a boy here or go out with him. I knew there was something funny going on.'

'No wonder he was worried when Jock took it into his head to go and camp with our little lot,' said Mr Luffy.

'To think of that old yard and tunnel being used again!' said Mrs Andrews. 'And all those tales about spook-trains – and the way they hid that train, and hid all the stuff, too. Why, it's like a fairy tale isn't it!'

She ran to see if the water was hot for the baths. It was, and she went to call the children, who were in the big bedroom next door. She opened it and looked in. Then she called Mr Luffy upstairs.

He looked in at the door, too. The five, and Timmy, were lying on the floor in a heap, waiting for the bath-water. They hadn't liked to sit on chairs or beds, they were so dirty. And they had fallen asleep where they lay, their faces as black as a sweep's.

'Talk about black marketeers!' whispered Mrs Andrews. 'Anyone would think we'd got the whole lot of them here in the bedroom!'

They all woke up and went to have a bath one by one, and a good meal after that. Then back to camp with Mr Luffy, Jock with them, too.

It was glorious to snuggle down into the sleeping-bags. George called out to the three boys.

'Now, don't you dare to go off without me tonight, see?'

'The adventure is over,' called back Dick. 'How did you like it, Jock?'

'Like it?' said Jock, with a happy sigh. 'It was simply – smashing!'

Five Get
Into Trouble

CONTENTS

CHAPTER ONE

Five make a holiday plan

'REALLY, QUENTIN, you are *most* difficult to cope with!' said Aunt Fanny to her husband.

The four children sat at the table, eating breakfast, and looking very interested. What had Uncle Quentin done now? Julian winked at Dick, and Anne kicked George under the table. Would Uncle Quentin explode into a temper, as he sometimes did?

Uncle Quentin held a letter in his hand, which his wife had just given back to him after she had read it. It was the letter that was causing all the trouble. Uncle Quentin frowned – and then decided not to explode. Instead he spoke quite mildly.

'Well, Fanny dear – how can I possibly be expected to remember exactly when the children's holidays come, and if they are going to be here with us or with your sister? You know I have my scientific work to do – and very important it is too, at the moment. *I* can't remember when the children's schools break up or go back!'

'You could always ask *me*,' said Aunt Fanny, exasperated. 'Really, Quentin, have you forgotten how we discussed having Julian, Dick and Anne here these Easter holidays because they all enjoy Kirrin and the sea so much at this

207

time of the year? You said you would arrange to go off to your conferences *after* they had had their holidays – not in the very middle of them!'

'But they've broken up so late!' said Uncle Quentin. 'I didn't know they were going to do that.'

'Well, but you know Easter came late this year, so they broke up late,' said Aunt Fanny, with a sigh.

'Father wouldn't think of that,' said George. 'What's the matter, Mother? Does Father want to go away in the middle of our holidays, or what?'

'Yes,' said Aunt Fanny, and she stretched out her hand for the letter again. 'Let me see, he would have to go off in two days' time and I must certainly go with him. I can't possibly leave you children alone here, with nobody in the house. If Joanna were not ill it would be all right, but she won't be back for a week or two.'

Joanna was the cook. The children were all very fond of her, and had been sorry to find her missing when they had arrived for the holidays.

'We can look after ourselves,' said Dick. 'Anne is quite a good cook.'

'I can help too,' said George. Her real name was Georgina, but everyone called her George. Her mother smiled.

'Oh, George, last time you boiled an egg you left it in the saucepan till it boiled dry! I don't think the others would like your cooking very much.'

'It was just that I forgot the egg was there,' said George.

'I went to fetch the clock to time it, and on the way I remembered Timmy hadn't had his dinner, and . . .'

'Yes, we know all about that,' said her mother with a laugh. 'Timmy had his dinner, but your father had to go without his tea!'

'Woof,' said Timmy from under the table, hearing his name mentioned. He licked George's foot just to remind her he was there.

'Well, let's get back to the subject,' said Uncle Quentin, impatiently. 'I've got to go to these conferences, that's certain. I've to read some important papers there. You needn't come with me, Fanny – you can stay and look after the children.'

'Mother doesn't need to,' said George. 'We can do something we badly wanted to do, but thought we'd have to put off till the summer hols.'

'Oh *yes*,' said Anne, at once. 'So we could! Do let's!'

'Yes – I'd like that too,' said Dick.

'Well – *what* is it?' asked Aunt Fanny. 'I'm quite in the dark. If it's anything dangerous, I shall say no. So make up your minds about that!'

'When do we *ever* do anything dangerous?' cried George.

'Plenty of times,' said her mother. 'Now, what's this plan of yours?'

'It's nothing much,' said Julian. 'It's only that all our bikes happen to be in first-class order, Aunt Fanny, and you know you gave us two small tents for Christmas – so we just thought it would be great fun sometime to go off on our bikes, taking our tents with us and do a little exploring round the countryside.'

'It's grand weather now – we could have fine fun,' said Dick. 'After all, you must have meant us to use the tents, Aunt Fanny! Here's our chance!'

'I meant you to use them in the garden, or on the beach,' said Aunt Fanny. 'Last time you went camping you had Mr Luffy with you to look after you. I don't think I like the idea of you going off by yourselves with tents.'

'Oh, Fanny, if *Julian* can't look after the others he must be a pretty feeble specimen,' said her husband, sounding impatient. 'Let them go! I'd bank on Julian any time to keep the others in order and see they were all safe and sound.'

'Thanks, Uncle,' said Julian, who was not used to compliments from his uncle Quentin! He glanced round at the other children and grinned. 'Of course, it's easy to manage this little lot – though Anne sometimes is *very* difficult!'

Anne opened her mouth indignantly. She was the smallest and the only really manageable one. She caught Julian's grin – he was teasing her, of course. She grinned back. 'I promise to be easy to manage,' she said in an innocent voice to her uncle Quentin.

He looked surprised. 'Well, I must say I should have thought that George was the only difficult one to . . .' he began, but stopped when he saw his wife's warning frown. George *was* difficult, but it didn't make her any less difficult if that fact was pointed out!

'Quentin, you never know when Julian is pulling your leg or not, do you?' said his wife. 'Well – if you *really* think Julian can be put in charge – and we can let them go off on a cycling tour – with their new tents . . .'

'Hurray! It's settled then!' yelled George, and began to thump Dick on the back in joy. 'We'll go off tomorrow. We'll . . .'

'GEORGE! There's no need to shout and thump like that,' said her mother. 'You know your father doesn't like it – and now you've excited Timmy too. Lie down, Timmy – there he's off round the room like a mad thing!'

Uncle Quentin got up to go. He didn't like it when mealtimes turned into pandemonium. He almost fell over the excited Timmy, and disappeared thankfully out of the room. What a household it was when the four children and the dog were there!

'Oh, Aunt Fanny, can we really go off tomorrow?' asked Anne, her eyes shining. 'It *is* such lovely April weather – honestly it's as hot as July. We hardly need to take any thick clothes with us.'

'Well, if you think that, you won't go,' said Aunt Fanny, firmly. 'It may be hot and sunny today, but you can never trust April to be the same two days together. It may be pouring tomorrow, and snowing on the next day! I shall have to give you money, Julian, so that you can go to an hotel any night the weather is bad.'

The four children immediately made up their minds that the weather would never be too bad!

'Won't it be fun?' said Dick. 'We can choose our own sleeping-place every night and put our tents there. We can bike half the night if it's moonlight, and we want to!'

'Ooooh – biking in moonlight – I've never done that,' said Anne. 'It sounds super.'

'Well, it's a good thing there is something you want to do while we are away,' said Aunt Fanny. 'Dear me, I've been married all these years to Quentin, and still he makes this kind of muddle without my knowing! Well, well, we'd better get busy today, and decide what you're to take.'

Everything suddenly seemed very exciting. The four children rushed to do their morning jobs of making the beds and tidying their rooms, talking at the tops of their voices.

'Who would have thought we'd be off on our own tomorrow!' said Dick, pulling his sheets and blankets up in a heap together.

'Dick! *I'll* make your bed,' cried Anne, shocked to see it made in such a hurried way. 'You can't possibly make it like that!'

'Oh, *can't* I!' cried Dick. 'You just wait and see! And what's more I'm making Julian's like that too, so you clear off and do your own, Anne – tuck in every corner, smooth the pillow, pat the eiderdown – do what you like with your own bed, but leave me to make mine my own way! Wait till we're off on our biking tour – you won't want to bother about beds then – you'll roll up your sleeping-bag and that will be that!'

He finished his bed as he spoke, dragging on the cover all crooked, and stuffing his pyjamas under the pillow. Anne laughed and went to make her own. She was excited too. The days stretched before her, sunny, full of strange places, unknown woods, big and little hills, chattering streams, wayside picnics, biking in the moonlight – did

213

Dick really mean that? How wizard!

They were all very busy that day, packing up into rucksacks the things they would need, folding up the tents into as small a compass as possible to tie on to their carriers, ferreting in the larder for food to take, looking out the maps they would want.

Timmy knew they were going off somewhere, and, of course, felt certain he was going too, so he was as excited as they were, barking and thumping his tail, and generally getting into everyone's way all day long. But nobody minded. Timmy was one of them, one of the 'Five', he could do almost everything but speak – it was quite unthinkable to go anywhere without dear old Timmy.

'I suppose Timothy can keep up with you all right, when you bike for miles?' Aunt Fanny asked Julian.

'Goodness yes,' said Julian. 'He never minds how far we go. I hope you won't worry about us, Aunt Fanny. You know what a good guard Timmy is.'

'Yes, I know,' said his aunt. 'I wouldn't be letting you go off like this with such an easy mind if I didn't know Timmy would be with you! He's as good as any grown-up at looking after you!'

'Woof, woof,' agreed Timmy. George laughed. 'He says he's as good as *two* grown-ups, Mother!' she said, and Timmy thumped his big tail on the floor.

'Woof, woof, *woof*,' he said. Which meant, 'Not two – but *three*!'

214

CHAPTER TWO

Away on their own

THEY WERE all ready the next day. Everything was neatly packed and strapped to the bicycles, except for the rucksacks, which each child was to carry on his or her back. The baskets held a variety of food for that day, but when it had been eaten Julian was to buy what they needed.

'I suppose all their brakes are in order?' said Uncle Quentin, thinking he ought to take some interest in the proceedings, and remembering that when *he* was a boy and had a bicycle, the brakes would never work.

'Oh, Uncle Quentin, of course they're all right,' said Dick. 'We'd never dream of going out on our bikes if the brakes and things weren't in order. The Highway Code is very strict about things like that, you know – and so are we!'

Uncle Quentin looked as if he had never even heard of the Highway Code. It was quite likely he hadn't. He lived in a world of his own, a world of theories and figures and diagrams – and he was eager to get back to it! However, he waited politely for the children to make last-minute adjustments, and then they were ready.

'Goodbye, Aunt Fanny! I'm afraid we shan't be able to

write to you, as you won't be able to get in touch with us to let us know where you get fixed up. Never mind, enjoy yourselves,' said Julian.

'Goodbye, Mother! Don't worry about us – we'll be having a jolly good time!' called George.

'Goodbye, Aunt Fanny; goodbye, Uncle Quentin!'

'So long, Uncle! Aunt Fanny, we're off!'

And so they were, cycling down the lane that led away from Kirrin Cottage. Their aunt and uncle stood at the gate, waving till the little party had disappeared round the corner in the sunshine. Timmy was loping along beside George's bicycle, on his long, strong legs, overjoyed at the idea of a really good run.

'Well, we're off,' said Julian, as they rounded the corner. 'What a bit of luck, going off like this by ourselves. Good old Uncle Quentin! I'm glad he made that muddle.'

'Don't let's ride too many miles the first day – I always get so stiff if we do,' said Anne.

'We're not going to,' said Dick. 'Whenever you feel tired just say so – it doesn't matter where we stop!'

The morning was very warm. Soon the children began to feel wet with perspiration. They had sweaters on and they took them off, stuffing them in their baskets. George looked more like a boy than ever, with her short curly hair blown up by the wind. All of them wore shorts and thin jerseys except Julian, who had on jeans. He rolled up the sleeves of his jersey, and the others did the same.

They covered mile after mile, enjoying the sun and the

wind. Timmy galloped beside them, untiring, his long pink tongue hanging out. He ran on the grassy edge of the road when there was one. He really was a very sensible dog!

They stopped at a tiny village called Manlington-Tovey. It had only one general store, but it sold practically everything – or seemed to! 'Hope it sells ginger-beer!' said Julian. 'My tongue's hanging out like Timmy's!'

The little shop sold lemonade, orangeade, lime juice, grapefruit juice and ginger-beer. It was really difficult to choose which to have. It also sold ice-creams, and soon the children were sitting drinking ginger-beer and lime juice mixed, and eating delicious ices.

'Timmy must have an ice,' said George. 'He does so love them. Don't you, Timmy?'

'Woof,' said Timmy, and gulped his ice down in two big, gurgly licks.

'It's really a waste of ice-creams to give them to Timmy,' said Anne. 'He hardly has time to taste them, he gobbles them so. No, Timmy, get down. I'm going to finish up every single bit of mine, and there won't be even a lick for you!'

Timmy went off to drink from a bowl of water that the shopwoman had put down for him. He drank and he drank, then he flopped down, panting.

The children took a bottle of ginger-beer each with them when they went off again. They meant to have it with their lunch. Already they were beginning to think with pleasure of eating the sandwiches put up into neat packets for them.

Anne saw some cows pulling at the grass in a meadow as they passed. 'It must be awful to be a cow and eat nothing but tasteless grass,' she called to George. 'Think what a cow misses – never tastes an egg and lettuce sandwich, never eats a chocolate eclair, never has a boiled egg – and can't even drink a glass of ginger-beer! Poor cows!'

George laughed. 'You do think of silly things, Anne,' she said. 'Now you've made me want my lunch all the more – talking about egg sandwiches and ginger-beer! I know Mother made us egg sandwiches – and sardine ones too.'

'It's no good,' chimed in Dick, leading the way into a little copse, his bicycle wobbling dangerously, 'it's no good – we can't go another inch if you girls are going to jabber about food all the time. Julian, what about lunch?'

It was a lovely picnic, that first one in the copse. There were clumps of primroses all round, and from somewhere nearby came the sweet scent of hidden violets. A thrush was singing madly on a hazel tree, with two chaffinches calling 'pink-pink' every time he stopped.

'Band and decorations laid on,' said Julian, waving his hand towards the singing birds and the primroses. 'Very nice too. We just want a waiter to come and present us with a menu!'

A rabbit lolloped near, its big ears standing straight up inquiringly. 'Ah – the waiter!' said Julian, at once. 'What have you to offer us today, Bunny? A nice rabbit-pie?'

The rabbit scampered off at top speed. It had caught the

218

smell of Timmy nearby and was panic-stricken. The children laughed, because it seemed as if it was the mention of rabbit-pie that had sent it away. Timmy stared at the disappearing rabbit, but made no move to go after it.

'Well, *Timmy*! That's the first time you've ever let a rabbit go off on its own,' said Dick. 'You *must* be hot and tired. Got anything for him to eat, George?'

'Of course,' said George. 'I made his sandwiches myself.'

And so she had! She had bought sausage meat at the butcher's and had actually made Timmy twelve sandwiches with it, all neatly cut and packed.

The others laughed. George never minded taking trouble over Timmy. He wolfed his sandwiches eagerly, and thumped his tail hard on the mossy ground. They all sat and munched happily, perfectly contented to be together out in the open air, eating a wonderful lunch.

Anne gave a scream. 'George! Look what you're doing! You're eating one of Timmy's sandwiches!'

'Urhh!' said George. 'I thought it tasted a bit strong. I must have given Timmy one of mine and taken his instead. Sorry, Tim!'

'Woof,' said Tim politely, and accepted another of his sandwiches.

'At the rate he eats them he wouldn't really notice if he had twenty or fifty,' remarked Julian. 'He's had all his now, hasn't he? Well, look out, everybody – he'll be after ours. Aha – the band has struck up again!'

Everyone listened to the thrush. 'Mind how you go,' sang the thrush. 'Mind how you go! Mind how you do-it, do-it, do-it!'

'Sounds like a Safety First poster,' said Dick, and settled down with his head on a cushion of moss. 'All right, old bird – we'll mind how we go – but we're going to have a bit of a snooze now, so don't play the band too loudly!'

'It *would* be a good idea to have a bit of a rest,' said Julian, yawning. 'We've done pretty well, so far. We don't want to tire ourselves out the very first day. Get off my legs, Timmy – you're frightfully heavy with all those sandwiches inside you.'

Timmy removed himself. He went to George and flumped himself down beside her, licking her face. She pushed him away.

'Don't be so licky,' she said, sleepily, 'just be on guard like a good dog, and see that nobody comes along and steals our bikes.'

Timmy knew what 'on guard' meant, of course. He sat up straight when he heard the words, and looked carefully all round, sniffing as he did so. Anyone about? No. Not a sight, sound or smell of any stranger. Timmy lay down again, one ear cocked, and one eye very slightly open. George always thought it was marvellous the way he could be asleep with one ear and eye and awake with the others. She was about to say this to Dick and Julian when she saw that they were sound asleep.

She fell asleep too. Nobody came to disturb them. A

small robin hopped near inquisitively, and, with his head on one side, considered whether or not it would be a good thing to pull a few hairs out of Timmy's tail to line his new nest. The slit in Timmy's awake-eye widened a little – woe betide the robin if he tried any funny tricks on Timmy!

The robin flew off. The thrush sang a little more, and the rabbit came out again. Timmy's eye opened wide. The rabbit fled. Timmy gave a tiny snore. Was he awake or was he asleep? The rabbit wasn't going to wait and find out!

It was half past three when they all awoke one by one. Julian looked at his watch. 'It's almost tea-time!' he said, and Anne gave a little squeal.

'Oh no – why we've only just had lunch, and I'm still as full as can be!'

Julian grinned. 'It's all right. We'll go by our tummies for our meals, not by our watches, Anne. Come on, get up! We'll go without you if you don't.'

They wheeled their bicycles out of the primrose copse and mounted again. The breeze was lovely to feel on their faces. Anne gave a little groan.

'Oh dear – I feel a bit stiff already. Do you mean to go very many miles more, Ju?'

'No, not many,' said Julian. 'I thought we'd have tea somewhere when we feel like it and then do a bit of shopping for our supper and breakfast and then hunt about for a really good place to put up our tents for the night. I found a little lake on the map, and I thought we could have a swim in it if we can find it.'

This all sounded very good indeed. George felt she could cycle for miles if a swim in a lake was at the end of it.

'That's a very nice plan of yours,' she said, approvingly. 'Very nice indeed. I think our whole tour ought to be planned round lakes – so that we can always have a swim, night and morning!'

'Woof,' said Timmy, running beside George's bicycle. 'Woof!'

'Timmy agrees too,' said George, with a laugh. 'But oh dear – I don't believe he brought his bathing-towel!'

CHAPTER THREE

A lovely day – and a lovely night

THE FIVE of them had a lovely time that evening. They had tea about half past five, and then bought what they wanted for supper and breakfast. New rolls, anchovy paste, a big round jam-tart in a cardboard box, oranges, lime juice, a fat lettuce and some ham sandwiches – it seemed a very nice assortment indeed.

'Let's hope we don't eat it all for supper, and have no breakfast left,' said George, packing the sandwiches into her basket. 'Get down, Timmy. These sandwiches are not for you. I've bought you a whacking big bone – *that* will keep you busy for hours!'

'Well, don't let him have it when we settle down for the night,' said Anne. 'He makes such a row, crunching and munching. He'd keep me awake.'

'*Nothing* would keep *me* awake tonight,' said Dick. 'I believe I could sleep through an earthquake. I'm already thinking kindly of my sleeping-bag.'

'I don't think we need to put up our tents tonight,' said Julian, looking up at the perfectly clear sky. 'I'll ask someone what the weather forecast was on the radio at six. Honestly I think we could just snuggle into our sleeping-bags and have the sky for a roof.'

'How smashing!' said Anne. 'I'd love to lie and look at the stars.'

The weather forecast was good. 'Fine and clear and mild.'

'Good,' said Julian. 'That will save us a lot of trouble – we don't even need to unpack our tents. Come on – have we got everything now? Does anyone feel as if we ought to buy any more food?'

The baskets were all full. Nobody thought it advisable to try and get anything more into them.

'We could get lots more in if Timmy would only carry his own bones,' said Anne. 'Half my basket is crammed with enormous bones for him. Why can't you rig up something so that Timmy could carry his own food, George? I'm sure he's clever enough.'

'Yes, he's clever enough,' said George. 'But he's much too greedy, Anne. You know that. He'd stop and eat all his food at once if he had to carry it. Dogs seem to be able to eat anything at any time.'

'They're lucky,' said Dick. 'Wish I could. But I just *have* to pause between my meals!'

'Now for the lake,' said Julian, folding up the map which he had just been examining. 'It's only about five miles away. It's called the Green Pool, but it looks a good bit bigger than a pool. I could do with a bathe. I'm so hot and sticky.'

They came to the lake at about half past seven. It was in a lovely place, and had beside it a small hut which was obviously used in summer-time for bathers to change into bathing-suits. Now it was locked, and curtains were drawn across the windows.

'I suppose we can go in for a dip if we like?' said Dick rather doubtfully. 'We shan't be trespassing or anything, shall we?'

'No. It doesn't say anything about being private,' said Julian. 'The water won't be very warm, you know, because it's only mid-April! But after all, we're used to cold baths every morning, and I daresay the sun has taken the chill off the lake. Come on, let's get into bathing things.'

They changed behind the bushes and then ran down to the lake. The water was certainly very cold indeed. Anne skipped in and out, and wouldn't do any more than that.

George joined the boys in a swim, and they all came out glowing and laughing. 'Brrr, that was cold!' said Dick. 'Come on, let's have a sharp run. Look at Anne – dressed already. Timmy, where are you? *You* don't mind the cold water, do you?'

They all tore up and down the little paths by the Green Pool like mad things. Anne was getting the supper ready. The sun had disappeared now, and although the evening was still very mild the radiant warmth of the day had gone. Anne was glad of her sweater.

'Good old Anne,' said Dick, when at last he and the others joined her, dressed again, with their sweaters on for warmth. 'Look, she's got the food all ready. You're fantastic, Anne. I bet if we stayed here for more than one night Anne would have made some kind of larder, and have arranged a good place to wash everything – and be looking for somewhere to keep her dusters and broom!'

'You're so *silly*, Dick,' said Anne. 'You ought to be glad I like messing about with the food and getting it ready for you. Oh, TIMMY! Shoo! Get away! Look at him, he's shaken millions and millions of drops of lakewater all over the food. You ought to have dried him, George. You know how he shakes himself after a swim.'

'Sorry,' said George. 'Tim, say you're sorry. Why must you be so *violent* about everything? If I shook myself like that my ears and fingers would fly off into the air!'

It was a lovely meal, sitting there in the evening light, watching the first stars come out in the sky. The children and Timmy were all tired but happy. This was the beginning of their trip and beginnings were always lovely – the days stretched out before you endlessly, and somehow you felt certain that the sun would shine every single day!

They were not long in snuggling into their sleeping-bags when they had finished the meal. They had set them all together in a row, so that they could talk if they wanted to. Timmy was thrilled. He walked solemnly across the whole lot, and was greeted with squeals and threats.

'Timmy! How dare you! When I've had such a big supper too!'

'TIMMY! You brute! You put all your great big feet down on me at once!'

'George, you *really* might stop Timmy from walking all over us like that! I only hope he's not going to do it all night long.'

Timmy looked surprised at the shouts. He settled down beside George, after a vain attempt to get into her sleeping-bag with her. George turned her face away from his licks.

'Oh, Timmy, I do love you but I wish you wouldn't make my face so wet. Julian, look at that glorious star – like a little round lamp. What is it?'

'It's not a star really – it's Venus, one of the planets,' said Julian, sleepily. 'But it's called the Evening Star. Fancy you not knowing that, George. Don't they teach you anything at your school?'

George tried to kick Julian through her sleeping-bag, but she couldn't. She gave it up and yawned so loudly that she set all the others yawning too.

Anne fell asleep first. She was the smallest and was more easily tired with long walks and rides than the others, though she always kept up with them valiantly. George gazed unblinkingly at the bright evening star for a minute and then fell asleep suddenly. Julian and Dick talked quietly for a few minutes. Timmy was quite silent. He was tired out with his miles and miles of running.

Nobody stirred at all that night, not even Timmy. He took no notice of a horde of rabbits who played not far off. He hardly pricked an ear when an owl hooted nearby. He didn't even stir when a beetle ran over his head.

But if George had woken and spoken his name Timmy would have been wide awake at once, standing over George and licking her, whining gently! George was the centre of his world, night and day.

The next day was fair and bright. It was lovely to wake up and feel the warm sun on their cheeks, and hear a thrush singing his heart out. 'It might be the very same thrush,' thought Dick, drowsily. 'He's saying, "Mind how you do-it, do-it, do-it!" just like the other one did.'

Anne sat up cautiously. She wondered if she should get up and have breakfast ready for the others – or would they want a bathe first?

Julian sat up next and yawned as he wriggled himself half out of his sleeping-bag. He grinned at Anne.

'Hallo,' he said. 'Had a good night? I feel fine this morning!'

'I feel rather stiff,' said Anne. 'But it will soon wear off. Hallo, George – you awake?'

George grunted and snuggled down farther in her sleeping-bag. Timmy pawed at her, whining. He wanted her to get up and go for a run with him.

Shut up, Timmy,' said George from the depth of her bag. 'I'm asleep!'

'I'm going for a bathe,' said Julian. 'Anyone else coming?'

'I won't,' said Anne. 'It will be too cold for me this morning. George doesn't seem to want to, either. You two boys go by yourselves. I'll have breakfast ready for you when you come back. Sorry I shan't be able to have anything hot for you to drink – but we didn't bring a kettle or anything like that.'

Julian and Dick went off to the Green Pool, still looking sleepy. Anne got out of her sleeping-bag and dressed quickly. She decided to go down to the pool with her sponge and flannel and wake herself up properly with the cold water. George was still in her sleeping-bag.

The two boys were almost at the pool. Ah, now they could see it between the trees, shining a bright emerald green. It looked very inviting indeed.

They suddenly saw a bicycle standing beside a tree. They looked at it in astonishment. It wasn't one of theirs. It must belong to someone else.

Then they heard splashings from the pool, and they hurried down to it. Was someone else bathing?

A boy was in the pool, his golden head shining wet and smooth in the morning sun. He was swimming powerfully across the pool, leaving long ripples behind him as he went. He suddenly saw Dick and Julian, and swam over to them.

'Hallo,' he said, wading out of the water. 'You come for a swim too? Nice pool of mine, isn't it?'

'What do you mean? It isn't really your pool, is it?' said Julian.

'Well, it belongs to my father, Thurlow Kent,' said the boy.

Both Julian and Dick had heard of Thurlow Kent, one of the richest men in the country. Julian looked doubtfully at the boy.

'If it's a private pool we won't use it,' he said.

'Oh come on!' cried the boy, and splashed cold water all over them. 'Race you to the other side!'

And off all three of them went, cleaving the green waters with their strong brown arms – what a fine beginning to a sunny day!

CHAPTER FOUR

Richard

ANNE WAS astonished to find three boys in the Green Pool instead of two. She stood by the water with her sponge and flannel, staring. Who was the third boy?

The three came back to the side of the pool where Anne stood. She looked at the strange boy shyly. He was not much older than she was, and not as big as Julian or Dick, but he was sturdily made, and had laughing blue eyes she liked. He smoothed back his dripping hair.

'This your sister?' he said to Julian and Dick. 'Hallo there!'

'Hallo,' said Anne and smiled. 'What's your name?'

'Richard,' he said. 'Richard Kent. What's yours?'

'Anne,' said Anne. 'We're on a biking tour.'

The boys had had no time to introduce themselves. They were still panting from their swim.

'I'm Julian and he's Dick, my brother,' said Julian, out of breath. 'I say – I hope we're not trespassing on your land as well as on your water!'

Richard grinned. 'Well, you are as a matter of fact. But I give you free permission! You can borrow my pool and my land as much as you like!'

'Oh thanks,' said Anne. 'I suppose it's your father's

232

property? It didn't say "Private" or anything, so we didn't know. Would you like to come and have breakfast with us? If you'll dress with the others they'll bring you to where we camped last night.'

She sponged her face and washed her hands in the pool, hearing the boys chattering behind the bushes where they had left their clothes. Then she sped back to their sleeping-place, meaning to tidy up the bags they had slept in, and put out breakfast neatly. But George was still fast asleep in her bag, her head showing at the top with its mass of short curls that made her look like a boy.

'George! Do wake up. Somebody's coming to breakfast,' said Anne, shaking her.

George shrugged away crossly, not believing her. It was just a trick to make her get up and help with the breakfast! Anne left her. All right – let her be found in her sleeping-bag if she liked!

She began to unpack the food and set it out neatly. What a good thing they had brought two extra bottles of lime juice. Now they could offer Richard one.

The three boys came up, their wet hair plastered down. Richard spotted George in the bag as Timmy came over to meet him. He fondled Timmy who, smelling that other dogs had been round Richard at home, sniffed him over with great interest.

'Who's that still asleep?' asked Richard.

'That's George,' said Anne. 'Too sleepy to wake up! Come on – I've got breakfast ready. Would you like to

233

start off with rolls and anchovy and lettuce? And there's lime juice if you want it.'

George heard Richard's voice as he sat talking with the others and was astonished. Who was that? She sat up, blinking, her hair tousled and short. Richard honestly thought she was a boy. She looked like one and she was called George!

'Top of the morning to you, George,' he said. 'Hope I'm not eating your share of the breakfast.'

'Who are you?' demanded George. The boys told her.

'I live about three miles away,' said the boy. 'I biked over here this morning for a swim. I say – that reminds me – I'd better bring my bike up here and put it where I can see it. I've had two stolen already through not having them under my eye.'

He shot off to get his bike. George took the opportunity of getting out of her sleeping-bag and rushed off to dress. She was back before Richard was, eating her breakfast. He wheeled his bicycle as he came.

'Got it all right,' he said, and flung it down beside him. 'Don't want to have to tell my father this one's gone, like the others. He's pretty fierce.'

'My father's a bit fierce too,' said George.

'Does he whip you?' asked Richard, giving Timmy a nice little titbit of roll and anchovy paste.

'Of course not,' said George. 'He's just got a temper, that's all.'

'Mine's got tempers and rages and furies, and if anyone

234

offends him or does him a wrong he's like an elephant – never forgets,' said Richard. 'He's made plenty of enemies in his lifetime. Sometimes he's had his life threatened, and he's had to take a bodyguard about with him.'

This all sounded extremely thrilling. Dick half-wished he had a father like that. It would be nice to talk to the other boys at school about his father's 'bodyguard'.

'What's his bodyguard like?' asked Anne, full of curiosity.

'Oh, they vary. But they're all big hefty fellows – they look like ruffians, and probably are,' said Richard, enjoying the interest the others were taking in him. 'One he had last year was awful – he had the thickest lips you ever saw, and such a big nose that when you saw him sideways you really thought he'd put a false one on just for fun.'

'Gracious!' said Anne. 'He sounds horrible. Has your father still got him?'

'No. He did something that annoyed Dad – I don't know what – and after a perfectly furious row my father chucked him out,' said Richard. 'That was the end of *him*. Jolly good thing too. I hated him. He used to kick the dogs around terribly.'

'*Oh!* What a beast!' said George, horrified. She put her arm round Timmy as if she was afraid somebody might suddenly kick him around too.

Julian and Dick wondered whether to believe all this. They came to the conclusion that the tales Richard told were very much exaggerated, and they listened with amusement, but not with such horror as the two girls, who hung on every word that Richard said.

'Where's your father now?' said Anne. 'Has he got a special bodyguard this very moment?'

'Rather! He's in America this week, but he's flying home soon – plus bodyguard,' said Richard, drinking the last of his lime juice from the bottle. 'Ummm, that's good. I say, aren't you lucky to be allowed to go off alone like this on your bikes and sleep where you like? My mother never will let *me* – she's always afraid something will happen to me.'

'Perhaps you'd better have a bodyguard too,' suggested Julian, slyly.

'I'd soon give him the slip,' said Richard. 'As a matter of fact I *have* got a kind of a bodyguard.'

'Who? Where?' asked Anne, looking all round as if she expected some enormous ruffian suddenly to appear.

'Well – he's supposed to be my holiday tutor,' said Richard, tickling Timmy round the ears. 'He's called Lomax and he's pretty awful. I'm supposed to tell him every time I go out – just as if I was a kid like Anne here.'

Anne was indignant. 'I don't have to tell anybody when I want to go off on my own,' she said.

'Actually I don't think we'd be allowed to rush off completely on our own unless we had old Timmy,' said Dick, honestly. 'He's better than any ruffianly bodyguard or holiday tutor. I wonder *you* don't have a dog.'

'Oh, I've got about five,' said Richard, airily.

'What are their names?' asked George, disbelievingly.

'Er – Bunter, Biscuit, Brownie, Bones – and er – Bonzo,' said Richard, with a grin.

'Silly names,' said George, scornfully. 'Fancy calling a dog *Biscuit*. You must be cracked.'

'You shut up,' said Richard, with a sudden scowl. 'I don't stand people telling me I'm cracked.'

'Well, you'll have to stand *me* telling you,' said George. 'I do think it's cracked to call a dog, a nice, decent dog, by a name like *Biscuit*!'

'I'll fight you then,' said Richard, surprisingly, and stood up. 'Come on – you stand up.'

237

George leapt to her feet. Julian shot out a hand and pulled her down again.

'None of that,' he said to Richard. 'You ought to be ashamed of yourself.'

'Why?' flared out Richard, whose face had gone very red. Evidently he and his father shared the same fierceness of temper!

'Well, you don't fight *girls*,' said Julian, scornfully. 'Or do you? Correct me if I'm wrong.'

Richard stared at him in amazement. 'What do you mean?' he said. 'Girls? Of course I don't fight girls. No decent boy hits a girl – but it's this boy here I want to fight – what do you call him? – George.'

To his great surprise Julian, Dick and Anne roared with laughter. Timmy barked madly too, pleased at the sudden ending of the quarrel. Only George looked mutinous and cross.

'What's up now?' asked Richard, aggressively. 'What's all the fun and games about?'

'Richard, George isn't a boy – she's a *girl*,' explained Dick at last. 'My goodness – she was just about to accept your challenge and fight you, too – two fierce little fox-terriers having a scrap!'

Richard's mouth fell open in even greater astonishment. He blushed redder than ever. He looked sheepishly at George.

'Are you *really* a girl?' he said. 'You behave so like a boy – and you look like one too. Sorry, George. Is your name *really* George?'

'No, Georgina,' said George, thawing a little at Richard's awkward apology, and pleased that he had honestly thought her a boy. She did so badly want to be a boy and not a girl.

'Good thing I *didn't* fight you,' said Richard, fervently. 'I should have knocked you flat!'

'Well, I like *that*!' said George, flaring up all over again. Julian pushed her back with his hand.

'Now, shut up, you two, and don't behave like idiots. Where's the map? It's time we had a squint at it and decided what we are going to do for today – how far we're going to ride, and where we're making for by the evening.'

Fortunately George and Richard both gave in with a good grace. Soon all six heads – Timmy's too – were bent over the map. Julian made his decision.

'We'll make for Middlecombe Woods – see, there they are on the map. That's decided then – it'll be a jolly nice ride.'

It might be a nice ride – but it was going to be something very much more than that!

CHAPTER FIVE

Six instead of five

'LOOK HERE,' said Richard, when they had tidied up everything, buried their bits of litter, and looked to see that no one had got a puncture in a tyre. 'Look here, I've got an aunt who lives in the direction of those woods – if I can get my mother to say I can come with you, will you let me? I can go and see my aunt on the way, then.'

Julian looked at Richard doubtfully. He wasn't very sure if Richard really *would* go and ask permission.

'Well – if you aren't too long about it,' he said. 'Of course we don't mind you coming with us. We can drop you at your aunt's on the way.'

'I'll go straight off now and ask my mother,' said Richard, eagerly, and he ran for his bicycle. 'I'll meet you at Croker's Corner – you saw it on the map. That will save time, because then I shan't have to come back here – it's not much farther than my home.'

'Right,' said Julian. 'I've got to adjust my brakes, and that will take ten minutes or so. You'll have time to go home and ask permission, and join us later. We'll wait for you; at least we'll wait for ten minutes, at Croker's Corner. If you don't turn up we'll know you didn't get permission. Tell your mother we'll have you safely at your aunt's.'

SIX INSTEAD OF FIVE

Richard shot off on his bicycle, looking excited. Anne began to clear up, and George helped her. Timmy got in everyone's way, sniffing about for dropped crumbs.

'Anyone would think he was half-starved!' said Anne. 'He had a lot more breakfast than I had. Timmy, if you walk through my legs again I'll tie you up!'

Julian adjusted his brakes with Dick's help. In about fifteen minutes they were ready to set off. They had planned where to stop to buy food for their lunch, and although the journey to Middlecombe Woods was a longer trip than they had made the day before, they felt able to cope with more miles on the second day. Timmy was eager to set off too. He was a big dog, and enjoyed all the exercise he was getting

'It'll take a bit of your fat off,' said Dick to Timmy. 'We don't like fat dogs, you know. They waddle and they puff.'

'Dick! Timmy's *never* been fat!' said George, indignantly, and then stopped as she saw Dick's grin. He was pulling her leg as usual. She kicked herself. Why did she always rise like that, when Dick teased her through Timmy? She gave him a friendly punch.

They all mounted their bicycles. Timmy ran ahead, pleased. They came to a lane and rode down it, avoiding the ruts. They came out into a road. It was not a main road, for the children didn't like those; they were too full of traffic and dust. They liked the shady lanes or the country roads where they met only a few carts or a farmer's car.

241

'Now, don't let's miss Croker's Corner,' said Julian. 'It should be along this way somewhere, according to the map. George, if you get into ruts like that you'll be thrown off.'

'All right, I know that!' said George. 'I only got into one because Timmy swerved across my wheel. He's after a rabbit or something. Timmy! Don't get left behind, you idiot.'

Timmy bounded reluctantly after the little party. Exercise was wonderful, but it did mean leaving a lot of marvellous wayside smells unsniffed at. It was a dreadful waste of smells, Timmy thought.

They came to Croker's Corner sooner than they thought. The signpost proclaimed the name – and there, leaning against the post, sitting on his bicycle was Richard, beaming at them.

'You've been jolly quick, getting back home and then on to here,' said Julian. 'What did your mother say?'

'She didn't mind a bit so long as I was with *you*,' said Richard. 'I can go to my aunt's for the night, she said.'

'Haven't you brought pyjamas or anything with you?' asked Dick.

'There are always spare ones at my aunt's,' explained Richard. 'Hurray – it will be marvellous to be out on my own all day with you – no Mr Lomax to bother me with this and that. Come on!'

They all cycled on together. Richard would keep trying to ride three abreast, and Julian had to warn him that

242

cyclists were not allowed to do that. 'I don't care!' sang Richard, who seemed in very high spirits. 'Who is there to stop us, anyway?'

'*I* shall stop you,' said Julian, and Richard ceased grinning at once. Julian could sound very stern when he liked. Dick winked at George, and she winked back. They had both come to the conclusion that Richard was very spoilt and liked his own way. Well, he wouldn't get it if he came up against old Julian!

They stopped at eleven for ice-creams and drinks. Richard seemed to have a lot of money. He insisted on buying ice-creams for all of them, even Timmy.

Once again they bought food for their lunch – new bread, farmhouse butter, cream cheese, crisp lettuce, fat red radishes and a bunch of spring onions. Richard bought a magnificent chocolate cake he saw in a first-class cake-shop.

'Gracious! That must have cost you a fortune!' said Anne. 'How are we going to carry it?'

'Woof,' said Timmy longingly.

'No, I certainly shan't let *you* carry it,' said Anne. 'Oh dear, we'll have to cut it in half, I think, and two people can share the carrying. It's such an enormous cake.'

On they went again, getting into the real country now, with villages few and far between. A farm here and there showed up on the hillsides, with cows and sheep and fowls. It was a peaceful, quiet scene, with the sun spilling down over everything, and the blue April sky above, patched with great white cotton-wool clouds.

243

'This is grand,' said Richard. 'I say, doesn't Timmy *ever* get tired? He's panting like anything now.'

'Yes, I think we ought to find somewhere for our lunch,' said Julian, looking at his watch. 'We've done a very good run this morning. Of course a lot of the way has been downhill. This afternoon we'll probably be slower, because we'll be getting into hilly country.'

They found a spot to picnic in. They chose the sunny side of a hedge, looking downhill into a small valley. Sheep and lambs were in the field they sat in. The lambs were very inquisitive, and one came right up to Anne and bleated.

'Do you want a bit of my bread?' asked Anne, and held it out to the lamb. Timmy watched indignantly. Fancy handing out food to those silly little creatures! He growled a little, and George shushed him.

Soon all the lambs were crowding round, quite unafraid, and one even tried to put its little front legs up on to George's shoulders! That was too much for Timmy! He gave such a sudden, fierce growl that all the lambs shot off at once.

'Oh, don't be so jealous, Timmy,' said George. 'Take this sandwich and behave yourself. Now you've frightened away the lambs, and they won't come back.'

They all ate the food and then drank their lime juice and ginger-beer. The sun was very hot. Soon they would all be burnt brown – and it was only April. How marvellous! Julian thought lazily that they were really lucky to have such weather – it would be awful to have to bike along all day in the pouring rain.

Once again the children snoozed in the afternoon sun, Richard too, and the little lambs skipped nearer and nearer. One actually leapt on to Julian as he slept, and he sat upright with a jerk. 'Timmy!' he began, 'if you leap on me again like that I'll . . .'

But it wasn't Timmy, it was a lamb! Julian laughed to himself. He sat for a few minutes and watched the little white creatures playing 'I'm king of the castle' with an old coop, then he lay down again.

'Are we anywhere near your aunt's house?' Julian asked Richard, when they once more mounted their bicycles.

'If we're anywhere near Great Giddings, we shall soon

be there,' said Richard, riding without holding his handlebars and almost ending up in the ditch. 'I didn't notice it on the map.'

Julian tried to remember. 'Yes, we should be at Great Giddings round about tea-time, say five o'clock or thereabouts. We'll leave you at your aunt's house for tea if you like.'

'Oh no, thank you,' said Richard, quickly. 'I'd much rather have tea with *you*. I *do* wish I could come on this tour with you. I suppose I couldn't possibly? You could telephone my mother.'

'Don't be an ass,' said Julian. 'You can have tea with us if you like but we drop you at your aunt's as arranged, see? No nonsense about that.'

They came to Great Giddings at about ten past five. Although it was called Great it was really very small. There was a little tea-place that said 'Home-made cakes and jams', so they went there for tea.

The woman who kept it was a plump, cheerful soul, fond of children. She guessed she would make very little out of the tea she served to five healthy children – but that didn't matter! She set to work to cut three big plates of well-buttered slices of bread, put out apricot jam, raspberry, and strawberry, and a selection of home-made buns that made the children's mouths water.

She knew Richard quite well, because he had sometimes been to her cottage with his aunt.

'I suppose you'll be going to stay with her tonight?' she

said to Richard, and he nodded, his mouth full of ginger cake. It was a lovely tea. Anne felt as if she wouldn't be able to eat any supper at all that night! Even Timmy seemed to have satisfied his enormous appetite.

'I think we ought to pay you double price for our gorgeous tea,' said Julian, but the woman wouldn't hear of it. No, no – it was lovely to see them all enjoying her cakes; she didn't want double price!

'Some people are so *awfully* nice and generous,' said Anne, as they mounted their bicycles to ride off again. 'You just can't help liking them. I do hope I can cook like that when I grow up.'

'If you do, Julian and I will always live with you and not dream of getting married!' said Dick, promptly, and they all laughed.

'Now for Richard's aunt,' said Julian. 'Do you know where the house is, Richard?'

'Yes, that's it over there,' said Richard, and rode up to a gate. 'Well, thanks awfully for your company. I hope I'll see you again soon! I have a feeling I shall! Goodbye!'

He rode up the drive and disappeared. 'What a sudden goodbye!' said George, puzzled. 'Isn't he *odd*?'

CHAPTER SIX

Odd happenings

THEY ALL thought it really was a little odd to disappear so suddenly like that, with just a casual goodbye. Julian wondered if he ought to have gone with him and delivered him safely on the door-step.

'Don't be an ass, Julian,' said Dick, scornfully. 'What *do* you think can happen to him from the front gate to the front door!'

'Nothing, of course. It's just that I don't trust that young fellow,' said Julian. 'You know I really wasn't sure he had asked his mother if he could come with us, to tell you the truth.'

'I thought that too,' said Anne. 'He did get to Croker's Corner so very quickly, didn't he? And he had quite a long way to go really, and he had to find his mother, and talk to her, and all that.'

'Yes, I've half a mind to pop up to the aunt's house and see if she expected him,' said Julian. But on second thoughts he didn't go. He would feel so silly if the aunt was there with Richard, and all was well – they would think that he and the others ought to be asked in.

So, after debating the matter for a few minutes they all rode off again. They wanted to get to Middlecombe

Woods fairly soon, because there were no villages between Great Giddings and Middlecombe, so they would have to find the woods and then go on to find a farmhouse somewhere to buy food for supper and breakfast. They hadn't been able to buy any in the shops at Great Giddings because it was early closing day, and they hadn't liked to ask the tea shop woman to sell them anything. They felt they had taken quite enough of her food already!

They came to Middlecombe Woods, and found a very fine place to camp in for the night. It was in a little dell, set with primroses and violets, a perfectly hidden place, secure from all prying eyes, and surely unknown even to tramps.

'This is glorious,' said Anne. 'We must be miles away from anywhere: I hope we can find some farmhouse or something that will sell us food, though! I know we don't feel hungry now, but we shall!'

'I think I've got a puncture, blow it,' said Dick, looking at his back tyre. 'It's a slow one, fortunately. But I think I won't risk coming along to look for farmhouses till I've mended it.'

'Right,' said Julian. 'And Anne needn't come either. She looks a bit tired. George and I will go. We won't take our bikes. It's easier to walk through the woods. We may be an hour or so, but don't worry, Timmy will know the way back all right, so we shan't lose you!'

Julian and George set off on foot, with Timmy following. Timmy too was tired, but nothing would have made him stay behind with Anne and Dick. He must go with his beloved George!

Anne put her bicycle carefully into the middle of a bush. You never knew when a tramp might be about, watching to steal something! It didn't matter when Timmy was there, because he would growl if a tramp came within a mile of them. Dick called out that he would mend his puncture now. He had found the hole already, where a small nail had gone in.

She sat near to Dick, watching him. She was glad to rest. She wondered if the others had found a farmhouse yet.

Dick worked steadily at mending the puncture. They had been there together about half an hour when they heard sounds.

Dick lifted his head and listened. 'Can you hear something?' he said to Anne. She nodded.

'Yes. Somebody's shouting. I wonder why!'

They both listened again. Then they distinctly heard yells. 'Help! Julian! Where are you? Help!'

They shot to their feet. Who was calling Julian for help? It wasn't George's voice. The yells grew louder, to panic-stricken shrieks.

'JULIAN! Dick!'

'Why, it must be Richard,' said Dick, amazed. 'What in the world does he want? What's happened?'

Anne was pale. She didn't like sudden happenings like this. 'Shall we – shall we go and find him?' she said.

There was a crashing not far off, as if somebody was making his way through the undergrowth. It was rather dark among the trees, and Anne and Dick could see nothing at first. Dick yelled loudly.

'Hey! Is that you, Richard! We're here!'

The crashing noise redoubled. 'I'm coming!' squealed Richard. 'Wait for me, wait for me!'

They waited. Soon they saw Richard coming, stumbling as fast as he could between the trees. 'Here we are,' called Dick. 'Whatever's the matter?'

Richard staggered towards them. He looked frightened

out of his life. 'They're after me,' he panted. 'You must save me. I want Timmy. He'll bite them.'

'*Who*'s after you?' asked Dick, amazed.

'Where's Timmy? Where's Julian?' cried Richard, looking round in despair.

'They've gone to a farmhouse to get some food,' said Dick. 'They'll be back soon, Richard. Whatever's the *matter*? Are you mad? You look awful.'

The boy took no notice of the questions. 'Where has Julian gone? I want Timmy. Tell me the way they went. I can't stay here. They'll catch me!'

'They went along there,' said Dick, showing Richard the path. 'You can just see the tracks of their feet. Richard, whatever is . . . ?'

But Richard was gone! He fled down the path at top speed, calling at the top of his voice, 'Julian! Timmy!'

Anne and Dick stared at one another in surprise. What had happened to Richard? Why wasn't he at his aunt's house? He must be mad!

'It's no good going after him,' said Dick. 'We shall only lose the way and not be able to find this place again – and the others will miss us and go hunting and get lost too! What *is* the matter with Richard?'

'He kept saying somebody was after him – *they* were after him!' said Anne. 'He's got some bee in his bonnet about something.'

'Bats in the belfry,' said Dick. 'Mad, dippy, daft! Well, he'll give Julian and George a shock when he runs into

252

them – if he does! The odds are he will miss them altogether.'

'I'm going to climb this tree and see if I can see anything of Richard or the others,' said Anne. 'It's tall, and it's easy to climb. You finish mending your puncture. I should just love to know what happens to Richard.'

Dick went back to his bicycle, puzzled. Anne climbed the tree. She climbed well, and was soon at the top. She gazed out over the countryside. There was an expanse of fields on one side, and woods stretched away on the other. She looked over the darkening fields, trying to see if a farmhouse was anywhere near. But she could see nothing.

Dick was just finishing his puncture when he heard another noise in the woods. Was it that idiot of a Richard coming back? He listened.

The noise came nearer. It wasn't a crashing noise, like Richard had made. It was a stealthy noise as if people were gradually closing in. Dick didn't much like it. Who was coming? Or perhaps – *what* was coming? Was it some wild animal – perhaps a badger and its mate? The boy stood listening.

A silence came. No more movements. No more rustling. Had he imagined it all? He wished Anne and the others were near him. It was eerie, standing there in the darkening wood, waiting and watching.

He decided that he had imagined it all. He thought it would be a very good idea if he turned on his bicycle lamp, then the light would soon dispel his silly ideas! He fumbled about for it on the front of his handlebars. He switched it on and a very comforting little glow at once spread a circle of light in the little dell.

Dick was just about to call up to Anne to tell her his absurd fears when the noises came again! There was absolutely no mistake about them this time.

A brilliant light suddenly pierced through the trees and fell on Dick. He blinked.

'Ah, so there you are, you little misery!' said a harsh voice, and someone came striding over to the dell. Somebody else followed behind.

'What do you mean?' asked Dick, amazed. He could not see who the men were because of the brilliant torch-light in his eyes.

'We've been chasing you for miles, haven't we? And you thought you'd get away. But we'd got you all the time!' said the voice.

'I don't understand this,' said Dick, putting on a bold voice. 'Who are you?'

'You know very well who we are,' said the voice. 'Didn't you run away screaming as soon as you saw Rooky? He went one way after you, and we went another – and we soon got you, didn't we? Now, you come along with us, my pretty!'

All this explained one thing clearly to Dick – that it was Richard they had been after, for some reason or other – and they thought *he* was Richard!

'I'm not the boy you're looking for,' he said. 'You'll get

into trouble if you touch *me*!'

'What's your name, then?' asked the first man.

Dick told him.

'Oh, so you're Dick – and isn't Dick short for Richard? You can't fool us with that baby-talk,' said the first man. 'You're the Richard we want, all right. Richard Kent, see?'

'I'm *not* Richard Kent!' shouted Dick, as he felt the man's hand clutching his arm suddenly. 'You take your hands off me. You wait till the police hear of this!'

'They *won't* hear of it,' said the man. 'They won't hear anything at all! Come on – and don't struggle or shout or you'll be sorry. Once you're at Owl's Dene we'll deal properly with you!'

Anne was sitting absolutely petrified up in the tree. She couldn't move or speak. She tried to call to poor Dick, but her tongue wouldn't say a word. She had to sit there and hear her brother being dragged away by two strange ruffians. She almost fell out of the tree in fright, and she heard him shouting and yelling when he was dragged away. She could hear the sound of crashing for a long time.

She began to cry. She didn't dare to climb down because she was trembling so much she was afraid she would lose her hold and fall.

She must wait for George and Julian to come back. Suppose they didn't? Suppose they had been caught too? She would be all by herself in the tree all night long. Anne sobbed up in the tree-top, holding on tightly.

The stars came out above her head, and she saw the very bright one again.

And then she heard the sound of footsteps and voices. She stiffened up in the tree. Who was it this time? Oh let it be Julian and George and Timmy; let it be Julian, George and Timmy!

CHAPTER SEVEN

Richard tells an alarming tale

JULIAN AND George had managed to find a little farmhouse tucked away in a hollow. A trio of dogs set up a terrific barking as they drew near. Timmy growled and the hair rose up on his neck. George put her hand on his collar.

'I won't go any nearer with Timmy,' she said. 'I don't want him to be set on by three dogs at once!'

So Julian went down to the farmhouse by himself. The dogs made such a noise and looked so fierce that he paused in the farmyard. He was not in the least afraid of dogs, but these looked most unpleasant, especially one big mongrel whose teeth were bared in a very threatening manner.

A voice called out to him. 'Clear off, you! We don't want no strangers here. When strangers come our eggs and hens go too!'

'Good evening,' called Julian, politely. 'We are four children camping out in the woods for the night. Could you let us have any food? I'll pay well for it.'

There was a pause. The man pulled his head in at the window he was shouting from, and was evidently speaking to someone inside.

He stuck it out again. 'I told you, we don't hold with strangers here, never did. We've only got plain bread and butter, and we can give you some hard-boiled eggs and milk and a bit of ham. That's all.'

'That'll do fine,' called Julian, cheerily. 'Just what we'd like. Shall I come and get it?'

'Not unless you want to be torn to pieces by those dogs,' came back the voice. 'You wait there. I'll be out when the eggs are done.'

'Blow,' said Julian, walking back to George. 'That means we'll have to kick our heels here for a while. What an unpleasant fellow! I don't think much of his place, do you?'

George agreed with him. It was ill-kept, the barn was falling to bits, rusty bits of machinery lay here and there in the thick grass. The three dogs kept up a continual barking and howling, but they did not come any nearer. George still kept her hand firmly on Timmy. He was bristling all over!

'What a lonely place to live in,' said Julian. 'No house within miles, I should think. No telephone. I wonder what they'd do if somebody was ill or had an accident and needed help.'

'I hope they'll hurry up with that food,' said George, getting impatient. 'It'll be dark soon. I'm getting hungry too.'

At last somebody came out of the tumbledown farmhouse. It was a bearded man, stooping and old, with long untidy hair and a pronounced limp. He had a grim and ugly face. Neither Julian nor George liked him.

'Here you are,' he said, waving his three dogs away behind him. 'Get back, you!' He aimed a kick at the nearest dog, and it yelped with pain.

'Oh don't!' said George. 'You hurt him.'

'He's my dog, isn't he?' said the man, angrily. 'You mind your own business!' He kicked out at another dog and scowled at George.

'What about the food?' said Julian, holding out his hand, anxious to be gone before trouble came between Timmy and the other dogs. 'George, take Timmy back a bit. He's upsetting the dogs.'

'Well, I like that!' said George. 'It's those other dogs that are upsetting *him*!'

She dragged Timmy back a few yards, and he stood there with all his hackles up on his neck, growling in a horrible way.

Julian took the food which was done up carelessly in old brown paper. 'Thanks,' he said. 'How much?'

'Five pounds,' said the old man, surprisingly.

'Don't be silly,' said Julian. He looked quickly at the food. 'I'll give you a pound for it, and that's more than it's worth. There's hardly any ham.'

'I said five pounds,' said the man, sullenly. Julian looked at him. 'He must be mad!' he thought. He held out the food to the ugly old fellow.

'Well, take it back,' he said. 'I haven't got five pounds

to give you for food. A pound is the most I can spare. Good night.'

The old man pushed the food back, and held out his other hand in silence. Julian fished in his pocket and brought out a pound coin. He placed it in the man's dirty hand, wondering why on earth the fellow had asked him for such a ridiculous sum before. The man put the money in his pocket.

'Clear off,' he said, suddenly, in a growling voice. 'We don't want strangers here, stealing our goods. I'll set my dogs on you if you come again!'

Julian turned to go, half-afraid that the extraordinary old man *would* set his dogs on him. The fellow stood there in the half-dark, yelling abuse at Julian and George as they made their way out of the farmyard.

'Well! We'll never go *there* again!' said George, furious at their treatment. 'He's mad as a hatter.'

'Yes. And I don't much fancy his food, either,' said Julian. 'Still, it's all we'll get tonight!'

They followed Timmy back to the woods. They were glad they had him, because otherwise they might have missed the way. But Timmy knew it. Once he had been along a certain route Timmy always knew it again. He ran on now, sniffing here and there, occasionally waiting for the others to catch him up.

Then he stiffened and growled softly. George put her hand on his collar. Somebody must be coming.

Somebody *was* coming! It was Richard on his way to

find them. He was still shouting and yelling, and the noise he made had already come to Timmy's sharp ears. It soon came to Julian's, and George's too, as they stood there waiting.

'Julian! Where are you? Where's Timmy? I want Timmy! They're after me, I tell you; they're after me.'

'Listen – it sounds like *Richard*,' said Julian, startled. 'What in the world is he doing here? – and yelling like that too! Come on, we must find out. Something's happened. I hope Dick and Anne are all right.'

They ran up the path as fast as they could in the twilight. Soon they met Richard, who had now stopped shouting, and was stumbling along, half-sobbing.

'Richard! What's up?' cried Julian. Richard ran to him and flung himself against him. Timmy did not go to him, but stood there in surprise. George stared through the twilight, puzzled. What in the world had happened?

'Julian! Oh, Julian! I'm scared stiff,' panted Richard, hanging on to Julian's arm.

'Pull yourself together,' said Julian, in the calm voice that had made a good effect on Richard. 'I bet you're just making a silly fuss. What's happened? Did you find your aunt was out or something? And come racing after us?'

'My aunt's away,' said Richard, speaking in a calmer voice. 'She . . .'

'*Away!*' said Julian, in surprise. 'But didn't your mother know that when she said you could . . . ?'

'I didn't ask my mother's permission to come,' cried

Richard. 'I didn't even go back home when you thought I did! I just biked straight to Croker's Corner and waited for you. I wanted to come with you, you see and I knew my mother wouldn't let me.'

This was said with a great air of bravado. Julian was disgusted.

'I'm ashamed of you,' he said. 'Telling us lies like that!'

'I didn't know my aunt was away,' said Richard, all his sudden cockiness gone when he heard Julian's scornful voice. 'I thought she'd be there and I was going to tell her to telephone my mother and say I'd gone for a trip with *you*. Then I thought I'd come biking after you and – and . . .'

'And tell us your aunt was away, and could you come with us?' finished Julian, still scornfully. 'A deceitful and ridiculous plan. I'd have sent you back at once; you might have known that.'

'Yes, I know. But I might have had a whole night camping out with you,' said Richard, in a small voice. 'I've never done things like that. I . . .'

'What I want to know is, what were you scared of when you came rushing along, yelling and crying,' said Julian, impatiently.

'Oh, Julian – it was horrible,' said Richard, and he suddenly clutched Julian's arm again. 'You see, I biked down back to my aunt's gate and out into the lane and I was just going along the way to Middlecombe Woods when a car met me. And I saw who was in the car!'

263

'Well, *who*?' said Julian, feeling as if he could shake Richard.

'It was – it was Rooky!' said Richard, in a trembling voice.

'Who's he?' said Julian, and George gave an impatient click. Would Richard never tell his story properly?

'Don't you remember? I told you about him. He was the fellow with thick lips and a huge nose that my father had for a bodyguard last year and he chucked him out,' said Richard. 'He always swore he'd have his revenge on my father – and on me too because I told tales about him to Dad and it was because of that he was sacked. So when I caught sight of him in the car I was terrified!'

'I *see*,' said Julian, seeing light. 'What happened then?'

'Rooky recognised me, and turned the car round and chased me on my bike,' said Richard, beginning to tremble again as he remembered that alarming ride. 'I pedalled for all I was worth and when I got to Middlecombe Woods I rode into the path there, hoping the car couldn't follow. It couldn't, of course – but the men leapt out – there were three of them, two I didn't know – and they chased me on foot. I pedalled and pedalled, and then I ran into a tree or something and fell off. I chucked my bike into a bush, and ran into the thick undergrowth to hide.'

'Go on,' said Julian, as Richard paused. 'What next?'

'The men split up then – Rooky went one way to find me, and the other two went another way. I waited till I thought they were gone, then I crept out and tore down the path again, hoping to find you. I wanted Timmy, you see, I thought he'd go for the men.'

Timmy growled. He certainly would have gone for them!

'Two of the men must have been hiding, waiting to hear me start up again,' went on Richard. 'And as soon as I began to run, they chased after me. I put them off the trail, though – I dodged and hid and hid and dodged – and then I came to Dick! He was mending a puncture. But you weren't with him – and it was you and Timmy I wanted – I knew the men would soon be catching me up, you see, so I tore on and on – and at last I found you. I've never been so glad in my life.'

It was a most extraordinary story – but Julian hardly paused to think about it. An alarming thought had come into his head. What about Dick and Anne? What would have happened to them if the men had suddenly come across them?

'Quick!' he said to George. 'We must get back to the others! Hurry!'

CHAPTER EIGHT

What's the best thing to do?

STUMBLING THROUGH the dark wood, Julian and George hurried as best they could. Timmy hurried too, knowing that something was worrying both his friends. Richard followed behind, half-crying again. He really had been very much afraid.

They came at last to the little dell where they had planned to spend the night. It was quite dark. Julian called loudly:

'Dick! Anne! Where are you?'

George had made her way to where she had hidden her bicycle. She fumbled for the lamp and switched it on. She took it off and flashed it round the dell. There was Dick's bicycle, with the puncture repair outfit on the ground beside it – but no Dick, and no Anne! What had happened?

'Anne!' yelled Julian, in alarm. 'Dick! Come here! We're back!'

And then a small trembling voice came down from the tree-top overhead.

'Oh, Julian! Oh Julian! I'm here.'

'It's Anne!' yelled Julian, his heart leaping in relief. 'Anne, where are you?'

'Up in this tree,' called back Anne, in a stronger voice. 'Oh, Ju, I've been so frightened, I didn't dare climb down in case I fell. Dick . . .'

'Where *is* Dick?' demanded Julian.

A sob came down to him. 'Two horrible men came – and they've taken him away. They thought he was Richard!'

Anne's voice became a wail. Julian felt that he must get her down from the tree so that she could be with them and be comforted. He spoke to George.

'Shine that lamp up here. I'm going up to fetch Anne.'

George silently shone the light of the lamp on the tree. Julian went up like a cat. He came to Anne who was still clinging tightly to a branch.

'Anne, I'll help you down. Come on, now – you can't

267

fall. I'm just below you. I'll guide your feet to the right branches.'

Anne was only too glad to be helped down. She was cold and miserable, and she longed to be with the others. Slowly she came down, with Julian's help, and he lifted her to the ground.

She clung to him, and he put his arm round his young sister. 'It's all right, Anne. I'm with you now. And here's George too – and old Timmy.'

'Who's *that*?' said Anne, suddenly seeing Richard in the shadows.

'Only Richard. He's behaved badly,' said Julian, grimly. 'It's all because of him and his idiotic behaviour that this has happened. Now, tell us slowly and carefully about Dick and the two men, Anne.'

Anne told him, not missing out anything at all. Timmy stood near her, licking her hand all the time. That was very comforting indeed! Timmy always knew when anyone was in trouble. Anne felt very much better when she had Julian's arm round her, and Timmy's tongue licking her!

'It's quite clear what's happened,' said Julian, when Anne had finished her alarming tale. 'This man Rooky recognised Richard, and he and the other two came after him, seeing a chance to kidnap him, and so get even with his father. Rooky was the only one who knew Richard, and he wasn't the man who caught Dick. The *others* got him – and they didn't know he wasn't Richard – and of course, hearing that his name was Dick they jumped to the conclusion that he was Richard – because Dick is short for Richard.'

'But Dick *told* them he wasn't Richard Kent,' said Anne, earnestly.

'Of course, but they thought he wasn't telling the truth,' said Julian. 'And they've taken him off. What did you say was the name of the place they were going to?'

'It sounded like Owl's Dene,' said Anne. 'Can we go there, Julian? If you told the men Dick was Dick and not Richard, they'd let him go, wouldn't they?'

'Oh yes,' said Julian. 'In any case, as soon as that fellow Rooky sets eyes on him he'll know there's a mistake been made. I think we can get old Dick away all right.'

A voice came out of the shadows nearby. 'What about *me*? Will you take me home first? *I* don't want to run into Rooky again.'

'I'm certainly not going to waste time taking *you* home,' said Julian, coldly. 'If it hadn't been for you and your tomfoolery we wouldn't have run into this trouble. You'll have to come with us. I'm going to find Dick first.'

'But I *can't* come with you – I'm afraid of Rooky!' wailed Richard.

'Well, stay here then,' said Julian, determined to teach Richard a lesson.

That was even worse. Richard howled loudly. 'Don't leave me here! Don't!'

'Now look here, if you come with us, you can always be dropped at a house somewhere, or at a police station and get yourself taken home somehow,' said Julian, exasperated. 'You're old enough to look after yourself. I'm fed up with you.'

Anne was sorry for Richard, although he had brought all this trouble on them. She knew how dreadful it was to feel really frightened. She put out a hand and touched him kindly.

'Richard! Don't be a baby. Julian will see that you're all right. He's just feeling cross with you now, but he'll soon get over it.'

'Don't you be too sure about that!' said Julian to Anne, pretending to be sterner than he really felt. 'What Richard wants is a jolly good hiding. He's untruthful and deceitful and an absolute baby!'

'Give me another chance,' almost wept poor Richard, who had never in his life been spoken to like this before. He tried to hate Julian for saying such things to him – but oddly enough he couldn't. He only respected and admired him all the more.

Julian said no more to Richard. He really thought the boy was too feeble for words. It was a nuisance that they had him with them. He would be no help at all – simply a tiresome nuisance.

'What are we going to do, Julian?' asked George, who had been very silent. She was fond of Dick, and was very worried about him. Where was Owl's Dene? How could they possibly find it in the night? And what about those awful men? How would they treat Julian if he demanded Dick back at once? Julian was fearless and straightforward – but the men wouldn't like him any the better for that.

'Well now, what *are* we going to do?' repeated Julian, and he fell silent.

'It's no good going back to that farm, and asking for help, is it?' said George, after a pause.

'Not a bit of good,' said Julian, at once. 'That old man wouldn't help anyone! And there's no telephone laid on, as we saw. No, that farm's no good. What a pity!'

'Where's the map?' said George, a sudden idea coming into her head. 'Would Owl's Dene be named on it, do you think?'

'Not if it's a house,' said Julian. 'Only places are named there. You'd want a frightfully big map to show every house.'

'Well, anyway – let's look at the map and see if it shows any more farms or villages,' said George, who felt as if she must *do* something, even if it was only looking at a map. Julian produced the map and unfolded it. He and the girls bent over it, by the light of the bicycle lamp, and Richard peered over their shoulders. Even Timmy tried to look, forcing his head under their arms.

'Get away, Tim,' said Julian. 'Look, here's where we are – Middlecombe Woods – see? My word, we *are* in a lonely spot! There isn't a village for miles!'

Certainly no village was marked. The countryside was shown, hilly and wooded, with a stream here and there,

271

and third-class roads now and again – but no village, no church, no bridge even was marked anywhere.

Anne gave a sudden exclamation and pointed to the contour of a hill on the map. 'Look, see what that hill's called?'

'Owl's Hill,' read out Julian. 'Yes, I see what you're getting at, Anne. If a house was built on that hill it might be called Owl's Dene, because of the name of the hill. What's more, a building *is* marked there! It hasn't a name, of course. It might be a farmhouse, an old ruin – or a big house of some kind.'

'*I* think it's very likely that's where Owl's Dene is,' said George. 'I bet it's that very house. Let's take our bikes and go.'

A huge sigh from Richard attracted their attention. '*Now* what's the matter with you?' said Julian.

'Nothing. I'm hungry, that's all,' said Richard.

The others suddenly realised that they too were hungry. In fact, *terribly* hungry! It was a long, long time since tea.

Julian remembered the food he and George had brought from the farm. Should they have it now or should they eat some on their way to Owl's Hill?

'Better eat as we go,' said Julian. 'Every minute we waste means a minute of worry for Dick.'

'I wonder what they'd do with him, if Rooky sees him and says he's not me, not the boy they want,' said Richard, suddenly.

'Set him free, I should think,' said George. 'Ruffians like

that would probably turn him loose in a deserted countryside and not care tuppence if he found his way home or not. We've absolutely *got* to find out what's happened – whether he's at Owl's Dene, or been set free, or what.'

'I can't come with you,' suddenly wailed Richard.

'Why?' demanded Julian.

'Because I haven't got my bike,' said Richard, dolefully. 'I chucked it away, you remember – and goodness knows where it is. I'd never find it again.'

'He can have Dick's,' said Anne. 'There it is, over there – with the puncture mended too.'

'Oh yes,' said Richard, relieved. 'For one frightful moment I thought I'd have to be left behind.'

Julian secretly wished he could be left behind. Richard was more trouble than he was worth!

'Yes, you can take Dick's bike,' he said. 'But no idiotic behaviour with it, mind – no riding without handlebars, or any tricks like that. It's Dick's bike, not yours.'

Richard said nothing. Julian was always ticking him off. He supposed he deserved it – but it wasn't at all pleasant. He pulled at Dick's bike, and found the lamp was missing. Dick, of course, had taken it off. He hunted round for it and found it on the ground. Dick had let it fall, and the switch had turned itself off when the lamp hit the ground. When Richard pressed the switch down the lamp came on again. Good!

'Now, come on,' said Julian, fetching his bicycle too. 'I'll hand out food to eat as we go. We must try to find our way to Owl's Hill as quick as ever we can!'

273

CHAPTER NINE

Moonlight adventure

THE FOUR of them rode carefully down the rough, woodland path. They were glad when they came out into a lane. Julian stopped for a moment to take his bearings.

'Now, according to the map, we ought to go to the right here then take the left at the fork some way down, and then circle a hill by the road at the bottom, and then ride a mile or two in a little valley till we come to the foot of Owl's Hill.'

'If we meet anyone we could ask them about Owl's Dene,' said Anne, hopefully.

'We shan't meet anyone out at night in this district!' said Julian. 'For one thing it's far from any village, and there will be no farmer, no policeman, no traveller for miles! We can't hope to meet anyone.'

The moon was up, and the sky cleared as they rode down the lane. It was soon as bright as day!

'We could switch off our lamps and save the batteries,' said Julian. 'We can see quite well now we're out of the woods and in the moonlight. Rather weird, isn't it?'

'I always think moonlight's strange, because although it shines so brightly on everything, you can never see much *colour* anywhere,' said Anne. She switched off her lamp too. She glanced down at Timmy.

'Switch off your head-lamps, Timmy!' she said, which made Richard give a sudden giggle. Julian smiled. It was nice to hear Anne being cheerful again.

'Timmy's eyes *are* rather like head-lamps, aren't they?' said Richard. 'I say – what about that food, Julian?'

'Right,' said Julian, and he fished in his basket. But it was very difficult to get it out with one hand, and try to hand it to the others.

'Better stop for a few minutes, after all,' he said at last. 'I've already dropped a hard-boiled egg, I think! Come on let's stack our bikes by the side of the road for three minutes, and gulp down something just to satisfy us for now.'

Richard was only too pleased. The girls were so hungry that they too thought it a good idea. They leapt off their bicycles in the moonlit road and went to the little copse at the side. It was a pine-copse, and the ground below was littered with dry brown pine-needles.

'Let's squat here for a minute or two,' said Julian. 'I say, what's that over there?'

Everyone looked. 'It's a tumbledown hut or something,' said George, and she went nearer to see. 'Yes, that's all – some old cottage fallen to bits. There's only part of the walls left. Rather an eerie little place.'

They went to sit down under the pine-trees. Julian shared out the food. Timmy got his bit too, though not so much as he would have liked! They sat there in the pine shadows, munching hungrily as fast as they could.

'I say, can anyone hear what I hear?' said Julian, raising his head. 'It sounds like a car!'

They all listened. Julian was right. A car *was* purring quietly through the countryside! What a bit of luck!

'If only it comes this way!' said Julian. 'We could stop it and ask it for help. It could take us to the nearest police station at any rate!'

They left their food in the little copse and went to the roadside. They could see no headlights shining anywhere, but they could still hear the noise of the car.

'Very quiet engine,' said Julian. 'Probably a powerful car. It hasn't got its headlights on because of the bright moonlight.'

'It's coming nearer,' said George. 'It's coming down this lane. Yes – it is!'

So it was. The noise of the engine came nearer, and nearer. The children got ready to leap out into the road to stop the car.

And then the noise of the engine died away suddenly. The moon shone down on a big streamlined car that had stopped a little way down the lane. It had no lights at all, not even side-lights. Julian put out his hand to stop the others from rushing into the road and shouting.

'Wait,' he said. 'This is just a bit strange!'

They waited, keeping in the shadows. The car had stopped not far from the tumbledown hut. A door opened

on the off-side. A man got out and rushed across the road
to the shadow of the hedge there. He seemed to be carrying
a bundle of some kind.

A low whistle sounded. The call of an owl came back.
'An answering signal!' thought Julian, intensely curious
about all this. 'I wonder what's happening?'

'Keep absolutely quiet,' he breathed to the others.
'George, look after Timmy – don't let him growl.'

But Timmy knew when he had to be quiet. He didn't
even give a whine. He stood like a statue, ears pricked,
eyes watching the lane.

Nothing happened for a while. Julian moved very
cautiously to the shelter of another tree, from where he
could see better.

He could see the tumbledown shack. He saw a shadow moving towards it from some trees beyond. He saw a man waiting – the man from the car probably. Who were they? What in the world could they be doing here at this time of night?

The man from the trees came at last to the man from the car. There was a rapid interchange of words, but Julian could not hear what they were. He was sure that the men had no idea at all that he and the other children were near. He cautiously crept to yet another tree, and peered from the shadows to try and see what was happening.

'Don't be long,' he heard one man say. 'Don't bring your things to the car. Stuff them down the well.'

Julian could not see properly what the man was doing, but he thought he must be changing his clothes. Yes, now he was putting on the others – probably from the bundle the first man had brought from the car. Julian was more and more curious. What a funny business! Who was the second man? A refugee? A spy?

The man who had changed his clothes now picked up his discarded ones and went to the back of the shack. He came back without them, and followed the first man across the lane to the waiting car.

Even before the door had closed, the engine was purring, and the car was away! It passed by the pine-copse where the children were watching, and they all shrank back as it raced by. Before it had gone very far it was travelling very fast indeed.

Julian joined the others. 'Well, what do you make of all that?' he said. 'Funny business, isn't it? I watched a man changing his clothes – goodness knows why. He's left them somewhere at the back of the shack – down a well, I think I heard them say. Shall we see?'

'Yes, let's,' said George, puzzled. 'I say, did you see the number on the car? I only managed to spot the letters – KMF.'

'I saw the numbers,' said Anne. '102. And it was a black Bentley.'

'Yes. Black Bentley, KMF 102,' said Richard. 'Up to some funny business, I'll be bound!'

They made their way to the ruined shack, and pushed through overgrown weeds and bushes into the backyard. There was a broken-down well there, most of its brick work missing.

It was covered by an old wooden lid. Julian removed it. It was still heavy, though rotten with age. He peered down the well, but there was nothing at all to be seen. It was far too deep to see to the bottom by the light of a bicycle lamp.

'Not much to be seen *there*,' said Julian, replacing the lid. 'I expect it *was* his clothes he threw down. Wonder why he changed them?'

'Do you think he could be an escaped prisoner?' said Anne, suddenly. 'He'd have to change his prison clothes, wouldn't he? – that would be the most important thing for him to do. Is there a prison near here?'

Nobody knew. 'Don't remember noticing one on the

map,' said Julian. 'No, somehow I don't think the man was an escaped prisoner – more likely a spy dropped down in this desolate countryside, and supplied with clothes – or perhaps a deserter from the army. That's even *more* likely!'

'Well, whatever he is I don't like it and I'm jolly glad the car's gone with the prisoner or deserter or spy,' said Anne. 'What a curious thing that we should just be nearby when this happened! The men would never, never guess there were four children and a dog watching just a few yards away.'

'Lucky for us they *didn't* know,' said Julian. 'They wouldn't have been at all pleased! Now, come on, we've wasted enough time. Let's get back to our food. I hope Timmy hasn't eaten it all. We left it on the ground.'

Timmy hadn't eaten even a crumb. He was sitting patiently by the food, occasionally sniffing at it. All that bread and ham and eggs waiting there and nobody to eat it!

'Good dog,' said George. 'You're very, very trustworthy, Timmy. You shall have a big bit of bread and ham for your reward.'

Timmy gulped it down in one mouthful, but there was no more for him to have. The others only just had enough for themselves, and ate every crumb. They rose to their feet in a very few minutes and went to get their bicycles.

'Now for Owl's Hill again,' said Julian. 'And let's hope we don't come across any more peculiar happenings tonight. We've had quite enough.'

CHAPTER TEN

Owl's Dene on Owl's Hill

OFF THEY went again, cycling fast in the brilliant moonlight. Even when the moon went behind a cloud it was still light enough to ride without lights. They rode for what seemed like miles, and then came to a steep hill.

'Is this Owl's Hill?' said Anne, as they dismounted to walk up it. It was too steep to ride.

'Yes,' said Julian. 'At least, I think so – unless we've come quite wrong. But I don't think we have. Now the thing is, shall we find Owl's Dene at the top or not? And how shall we know it *is* Owl's Dene!'

'We could ring the bell and ask,' said Anne.

Julian laughed. That was so like Anne. 'Maybe we'll have to do that!' he said. 'But we'll scout round a bit first.'

They pushed their bicycles up the steep road. Hedges bordered each side, and fields lay beyond. There were no animals in them that the children could see – no horses, sheep or cows.

'Look!' said Anne, suddenly. 'I can see a building – at least, I'm sure I can see chimneys!'

They looked where she pointed. Yes, certainly they were chimneys – tall, brick chimneys that looked old.

'Looks like an Elizabethan mansion, with chimneys like

that,' said Julian. He paused and took a good look. 'It must be a big place. We ought to come to a drive or something soon.'

They pushed on with their bicycles. Gradually the house came into view. It was more like a mansion, and in the moonlight it looked old, rather grand and very beautiful.

'There are the gates,' said Julian, thankfully. He was tired of pushing his bicycle up the hill. 'They're shut. Hope they're not locked!'

As they drew near to the great, wrought-iron gates, they slowly opened. The children paused in surprise. Why were they opening? Not for them, that was certain!

Then they heard the sound of a car in the distance. Of course, that was what the gates were opening for. The car, however, was not coming up the hill – it was coming down the drive on the other side of the gates.

'Get out of sight, quickly,' said Julian. 'We don't want to be seen yet.'

They crouched down in the ditch with their bicycles as a car came slowly out of the open gates. Julian gave an exclamation and nudged George.

'See that? It's the black Bentley again – KMF 102!'

'How mysterious!' said George, surprised. 'What's it doing rushing about the country at night and picking up stray men! Taking them to this place too. I wonder if it *is* Owl's Dene.'

The car went by and disappeared round a bend in the

hill. The children came out of the ditch with Timmy and their bicycles.

'Let's walk cautiously up to the gates,' said Julian. 'They're still open. Funny how they opened when the car came. I never saw anyone by them!'

They walked boldly up to the open gates.

'Look!' said Julian, pointing up to the great brick posts from which the gates were hung. They all looked, and exclaimed at the name shining there.

'Well! So it *is* Owl's Dene, after all!'

'There's the name in brass letters – Owl's Dene! We've found it!'

'Come on,' said Julian, wheeling his bicycle through the gateway. 'We'll go in and snoop round. We might be lucky enough to find old Dick somewhere about.'

They all went through the gates – and then Anne clutched Julian in fright. She pointed silently behind them.

The gates were closing again! But nobody was there to shut them. They closed silently and smoothly all by themselves. There was something very weird about that.

'Who's shutting them?' whispered Anne, in a scared voice.

'I think it must be done by machinery,' whispered back Julian. 'Probably worked from the house. Let's go back and see if we can find any machinery that works them.'

They left their bicycles by the side of the drive and walked back to the gates. Julian looked for a handle or latch to open them. But there was none.

He pulled at the gates. They did not budge. It was quite impossible to open them. They had been shut and locked by some kind of machinery, and nothing and nobody could open them but that special machinery.

'Blow!' said Julian, and he sounded so angry that the others looked at him in surprise.

'Well, don't you see? – we're locked in! We're as much prisoners here as Dick is, if he's here too. We can't get out through the gates, and if you take a look you'll see a high wall running round the property from the gates – and I don't mind betting it goes the *whole* way round. We can't get out even if we want to.'

They went back thoughtfully to their bicycles. 'Better wheel them a little way into the trees and leave them,' said Julian. 'They hinder us too much now. We'll leave them and go snooping quietly round the house. Hope there are no dogs.'

They left their bicycles well hidden among the trees at the side of the wide drive. The drive was not at all well-kept. It was mossy and weeds grew all over it. It was bare only where the wheels of cars had passed.

'Shall we walk up the drive or keep to the side?' asked George.

'Keep to the side,' said Julian. 'We should easily be seen in the moonlight, walking up the drive.'

So they kept to the side, in the shadows of the trees. They followed the curves of the long drive until the house itself came into sight.

It really was very big indeed. It was built in the shape of the letter E with the middle stroke missing. There was a courtyard in front, overgrown with weeds. A low wall, about knee high, ran round the courtyard.

There was a light in a room on the top floor, and another one on the ground floor. Otherwise from that side the house was dark.

'Let's walk quietly round it,' said Julian, in a low voice. 'Goodness – what's that?'

It was a weird and terrible screech that made them all jump in alarm. Anne clutched Julian in fright.

They stood and listened.

Something came down silently and brushed George's hair. She almost screamed, but before she could, that terrible screech came again, and she put out her hand to quieten Timmy, who was amazed and scared.

'What is it, Ju!' whispered George. 'Something touched me then. Before I could see what it was it was gone.'

'Listen, it's all right,' whispered back Julian. 'It's only an owl – a screech-owl!'

'Good gracious – so it was,' breathed back George, in great relief. 'What an ass I was not to think of it. It's a barn-owl – a screech-owl out hunting. Anne, were you scared?'

'I should just think I was!' said Anne, letting go her hold on Julian's arm.

'So was I,' said Richard, whose teeth were still chattering with fear. 'I nearly ran for my life! I would have too, if I could have got my legs to work – but they were glued to the ground!'

The owl screeched again, a little farther away, and another one answered it. A third one screeched, and the night was really made hideous with the unearthly calls.

'I'd rather have a brown owl any day, calling To-whooo-oo-oo,' said George. 'That's a nice noise. But this screeching is frightful.'

'No wonder it's called Owl's Hill,' said Julian. 'Perhaps it's always been a haunt of the screech-owls.'

The four children and Timmy began to walk quietly round the house, keeping to the shadows as much as they could. Everywhere was dark at the back except two long windows. They were leaded windows, and curtains were pulled across them. Julian tried to see through the cracks.

He found a place where two curtains didn't quite meet. He put his eye to the crack and looked in.

'It's the kitchen,' he told the others. 'An enormous place – lit with one big oil-lamp. All the rest of the room is in shadow. There's a great fire-place at the end, with a few logs burning in it.'

'Anyone there?' asked George, trying to see through the crack too. Julian moved aside and let her take her turn.

'No one that I can see,' he said. George gave an exclamation as she looked, and Julian pushed her aside to look in again.

He saw a man walking into the room – a funny, dwarf-like fellow, with a hunched back that seemed to force his head on one side. He had a very evil face. Behind him came a woman – thin, drab and the picture of misery.

The man flung himself into a chair and began to fill a pipe. The woman took a kettle off the fire and went to fill hot-water bottles in a corner.

'She must be the cook,' thought Julian. 'What a misery she looks! I wonder what the man is – man-of-all-work, I suppose. What an evil face he's got!'

The woman spoke timidly to the man in the chair. Julian, of course, could not hear a word from outside the window. The man answered her roughly, banging on the arm of the chair as he spoke.

The woman seemed to be pleading with him about something. The man flew into a rage, picked up a poker and threatened the woman with it. Julian watched in horror. Poor woman! No wonder she looked miserable if that was the sort of thing that kept happening.

However, the man did nothing with the poker except brandish it in temper, and he soon replaced it, and settled down in his chair again. The woman said no more at all, but went on filling the bottles. Julian wondered who they were for.

He told the others what he had seen. They didn't like it at all. If the people in the kitchen behaved like that whatever would those in the other part of the house be like?

They left the kitchen windows and went on round the house. They came to a lower room, lit inside. But there the curtains were tightly drawn, and there was no crack to look through.

They looked up to the one room high up that was lit. Surely Dick must be there? Perhaps he was locked up in the attic, all by himself? How they wished they knew!

Dared they throw up a stone? They wondered if they should try. There didn't seem any way at all of getting into the house. The front door was well and truly shut. There was a side door also tightly shut and locked, because they had tried it. Not a single window seemed to be open.

'I think I *will* throw up a stone,' said Julian at last. 'I feel sure Dick's up there, if he has been taken here – and you're certain you heard the men say "Owl's Dene", aren't you, Anne?'

'Quite certain,' said Anne. 'Do throw a stone, Julian. I'm getting so worried about poor Dick.'

Julian felt about on the ground for a stone. He found one embedded in the moss that was everywhere. He balanced it in his hand. Then up went the stone, but fell just short of the window. Julian got another. Up it went – and hit the glass of the window with a sharp crack. Somebody came to the pane at once.

Was it Dick? Everyone strained their eyes to see – but the window was too far up. Julian threw up another stone, and that hit the window too.

'I think it *is* Dick,' said Anne. 'Oh dear – no it isn't after all. Can't *you* see, Julian?'

But the person at the window, whoever he was, had now disappeared. The children felt a bit uncomfortable. Suppose it hadn't been Dick? Suppose it had been someone else who had now disappeared from the room to go and look for them?

'Let's get away from this part of the house,' whispered Julian. 'Get round to the other side.'

They made their way round quietly – and Richard suddenly pulled at Julian's arm. 'Look!' he said. 'There's a window open! Can't we get in there?'

CHAPTER ELEVEN

Trapped!

JULIAN LOOKED at the casement window. The moonlight shone on it. It certainly was a little ajar. 'How did we miss that when we went round before?' he wondered. He hesitated a little. Should they try to get in or not? Wouldn't it be better to rap on the back door and get that miserable-looking woman to answer it and tell them what they wanted to know?

On the other hand there was that evil-looking hunchback there. Julian didn't like the look of him at all. No, on the whole it might be better to creep in at the window, see if it was Dick upstairs, set him free, and then all escape through the same open window. Nobody would know. The bird would have flown, and everything would be all right.

Julian went to the window. He put a leg up and there he was astride the window. He held out a hand to Anne. 'Come on, I'll give you a hand,' he said, and pulled her up beside him. He lifted her down on the floor inside.

Then George came, and then Richard. George was just leaning out to encourage Timmy to jump in through the window too, when something happened!

A powerful torchlight went on, and its beam shone right across the room into the dazzled eyes of the four children! They stood there, blinking in alarm. What was this?

Then Anne heard the voice of one of the men who had captured Dick. 'Well, well, well – a crowd of young burglars!'

The voice changed suddenly to anger. 'How *dare* you break in here! I'll hand you over to the police.'

From outside Timmy growled fiercely. He jumped up at the window and almost succeeded in leaping through. The man grasped what was happening at once, and went to the open window. He shut it with a bang. Now Timmy couldn't get in!

'Let my dog in!' said George, angrily, and stupidly tried to open the window again. The man brought his torch down sharply on her hand and she cried out in pain.

'That's what happens to boys who go against my wishes,' said the man, whilst poor George nursed her bruised hand.

'Look here,' began Julian, fiercely, 'what do you think you're doing? We're not burglars – and what's more we'd be very, very glad if you'd hand us over to the police!'

'Oh, you would, would you?' said the man. He went to the door of the room and yelled out in a tremendous voice: 'Aggie! AGGIE! Bring a lamp here at once.'

There was an answering shout from the kitchen, and almost immediately the light of a lamp appeared shining down the passage outside. It grew brighter, and the miserable-looking woman came in with a big oil-lamp. She stared in amazement at the little group of children. She seemed about to say something when the man gave her a rough push.

'Get out. And keep your mouth shut. Do you hear me?'

The woman scuttled out like a frightened hen. The man looked round at the children in the light of the lamp. The room was very barely furnished and appeared to be a sitting-room of some kind.

'So you don't mind being given up to the police?' said the man. 'That's very interesting. You think they'd approve of you breaking into my house?'

'I tell you, we *didn't* break in,' said Julian, determined to get that clear, at any rate. 'We came here because we had reason to believe that you've got my brother locked up somewhere in this house – and it's all a mistake. You've got the wrong boy.'

Richard didn't like this at all. He was terribly afraid of being locked up in place of Dick! He kept behind the others as much as possible.

The man looked hard at Julian. He seemed to be thinking. 'We haven't a boy here at all,' he said at last. 'I really don't know what you mean. You don't suggest that I go about the countryside picking boys up and making them prisoners, do you?'

'I don't know what you do,' said Julian. 'All I know is this – you captured Dick, my brother, this evening in Middlecombe Woods, thinking he was Richard Kent –

well, he's not, he's my brother Dick. And if you don't set him free at once, I'll tell the police what we know.'

'And dear me – *how* do you know all this?' asked the man. 'Were you there when he was captured, as you call it?'

'One of us was,' said Julian bluntly. 'In the tree overhead. That's how we know.'

There was a silence. The man took out a cigarette and lighted it. 'Well, you're quite mistaken,' he said. 'We've no boy held prisoner here. The thing is ridiculous. Now it's very, very late – would you like to bed down here for the night and get off in the morning? I don't like to send a parcel of kids out into the middle of the night. There's no telephone here, or I'd ring your home.'

Julian hesitated. He felt certain Dick was in the house. If he said he would stay for the night he might be able to find out if Dick was really there or not. He could quite well see that the man didn't want them tearing off to the police. There was something at Owl's Dene that was secret and sinister.

'We'll stay,' he said at last. 'Our people are away – they won't worry.'

He had forgotten about Richard for the moment. His people certainly *would* worry! Still, there was nothing to do about it. The first thing was to find Dick. Surely the men would be mad to hold him a prisoner once they were certain he wasn't the boy. Perhaps Rooky, the ruffian who knew Richard, hadn't yet arrived – hadn't seen Dick? That must be the reason that this man wanted them to stay the night. Of course, he'd wait till Rooky came, and when Rooky said, 'No, he's not the boy we want!' they'd let Dick go. They'd have to!

The man called for Aggie again. She came at once.

'These kids are lost,' said the man to her. 'I've said I'll put them up for the night. Get one of the rooms ready – just put down mattresses and blankets, that's all. Give them some food if they want it.'

Aggie was evidently tremendously astonished. Julian guessed that she was not used to this man being kind to lost children. He shouted at her.

'Well, don't stand dithering there. Get on with the job. Take these kids with you.'

Aggie beckoned to the four children. George hung back. 'What about my dog?' she said. 'He's still outside, whining. I can't go to bed without him.'

'You'll have to,' said the man, roughly. 'I won't have him in the house at any price, and that's flat.'

'He'll attack anyone he meets,' said George.

'He won't meet anyone out there,' said the man. 'By the way, how did you get in through the gates?'

'A car came out just as we got there and we slipped in before the gates closed,' said Julian. 'How do the gates shut? By machinery?'

'Mind your own business,' said the man, and went down the passage in the opposite direction.

'Pleasant, kindly fellow,' said Julian to George.

'Oh, a sweet nature,' answered George. The woman stared at them both in surprise. She didn't seem to realise that they meant the opposite to what they said! She led the way upstairs.

She came to a big room with a carpet on the floor, a small bed in a corner, and one or two chairs. There was no other furniture.

'I'll get some mattresses and put them down for you,' she said.

'I'll help you,' offered Julian, thinking it would be a good idea to see round a bit.

'All right,' said the woman. 'You others stay here.'

She went off with Julian. They went to a cupboard and the woman tugged at two big mattresses. Julian helped her. She seemed rather touched by his help.

'Well, thank you,' she said. 'They're pretty heavy.'

'Don't expect you have many children here, to stay, do you?' asked Julian.

'Well, it's funny that you should come just after . . .' the woman began. Then she stopped and bit her lip, looking anxiously up and down the passage.

'Just after what?' asked Julian. 'Just after the other boy came, do you mean?'

'Sh!' said the woman, looking scared to death. 'Whatever do you know about *that*? You shouldn't have said that. Mr Perton will skin me alive if he knew you'd said that. He'd be sure I'd told you. Forget about it.'

'That's the boy who's locked up in one of the attics at

the top of the house, isn't it?' said Julian, helping her to
carry one of the mattresses to the big bedroom. She dropped
her end in the greatest alarm.

'Now! Do you want to get me into terrible trouble –
and yourselves too? Do you want Mr Perton to tell old
Hunchy to whip you all? You don't know that man!
He's wicked.'

'When's Rooky coming?' asked Julian, bent on
astonishing the woman, hoping to scare her into one
admission after another. This was too much for her
altogether. She stood there shaking at the knees, staring at
Julian as if she couldn't believe her ears.

'What do you know about Rooky?' she whispered. 'Is he coming here? Don't tell me he's coming here!'

'Why? Don't you like him?' asked Julian. He put a hand on her shoulder. 'Why are you so frightened and upset? What's the matter? Tell me. I might be able to help you.'

'Rooky's bad,' said the woman. 'I thought he was in prison. Don't tell me he's out again. Don't tell me he's coming here.'

She was so frightened that she wouldn't say a word more. She began to cry, and Julian hadn't the heart to press her with any more questions. In silence he helped her to drag the mattresses into the other room.

'I'll get you some food,' said the poor woman, sniffing miserably. 'You'll find blankets in that cupboard over there if you want to lie down.'

She disappeared. Julian told the others in whispers what he had been able to find out. 'We'll see if we can find Dick as soon as things are quiet in the house,' he said. 'This is a bad house – a house of secrets, of strange comings and goings. I shall slip out of our room and see what I can find out later on. I think that man – Mr Perton is his name – is really waiting for Rooky to come and see if Dick is Richard or not. When he finds he isn't I've no doubt he'll set him free – and us too.'

'What about *me*?' said Richard. 'Once he sees me, I'm done for. I'm the boy he wants. He hates my father and he hates me too. He'll kidnap me, take me somewhere, and ask an enormous ransom for me, just to punish us!'

TRAPPED!

'Well, we must do something to prevent him seeing you,' said Julian. 'But I don't see why he *should* see you – it's only Dick he'll want to see. He won't be interested in what he thinks are Dick's brothers and sisters! Now for goodness' sake don't start to howl again, or honestly I'll give you up to Rooky myself! You really are a frightful little coward – haven't you any courage at all!'

'All this has come about because of your silly lies and deceit,' said George, quite fiercely. 'It's all because of you that our trip is spoilt, that Dick's locked up and poor Timmy's outside without me.'

Richard looked quite taken aback. He shrank into a corner and didn't say another word. He was very miserable. Nobody liked him, nobody believed him, nobody trusted him. Richard felt very, very small indeed.

CHAPTER TWELVE

Julian looks round

THE WOMAN brought them some food. It was only bread and butter and jam, with some hot coffee to drink. The four children were not really hungry, but they were very thirsty, and they drank the coffee eagerly.

George opened the window and called softly down to Timmy. 'Tim! Here's something for you!'

Timmy was down there all right, watching and waiting. He knew where George was. He had howled and whined for some time, but now he was quiet.

George was quite determined to get him indoors if she could. She gave him all her bread and jam, dropping it down bit by bit, and listening to him wolfing it up. Anyway, old Timmy would know she was thinking of him!

'Listen,' said Julian, coming in from the passage outside, where he had stood listening for a while. 'I think it would be a good idea if we put out this light, and settled down on the mattresses. But I shall make up a lump on mine to look like me, so that if anyones comes they'll think I'm there on the mattress. But I shan't be.'

'Where will you be, then?' asked Anne. 'Don't leave us!'

'I shall be hiding outside in that cupboard,' said Julian. 'I've a sort of feeling that our pleasant host, Mr Perton,

300

will come along presently to lock us in – and I've no intention of being locked in! I think he'll flash a torch into the room, see that we're all four safely asleep on the mattresses, and then quietly lock the door. Well, *I* shall be able to unlock it when I come back from the cupboard outside and we shan't be prisoners at all!'

'Oh, that really is a good idea,' said Anne, cuddling herself up in a blanket. 'You'd better go and get into the cupboard now, Julian, before we're locked up for the night!'

Julian blew out the lamp. He tiptoed to the door and opened it. He left it ajar. He went into the passage and fumbled his way to where he knew the cupboard should be. Ah, there it was. He pulled the handle and the door opened silently. He slipped inside and left the door open just a crack, so that he would be able to see if anyone came along the wide passage.

He waited there about twenty minutes. The cupboard smelt musty, and it was very boring standing there doing absolutely nothing.

Then, through the crack in the door, he suddenly noticed that a light was coming. Ah, somebody was about!

He peered through the crack. He saw Mr Perton coming quietly along the corridor with a little oil-lamp held in his hand. He went to the door of the children's bedroom and pushed it a little. Julian watched him, hardly daring to breathe.

Would he notice that the figure on one of the mattresses

was only a lump made of a blanket rolled up and covered by another blanket? Julian fervently hoped that he wouldn't. All his plans would be spoilt if so.

Mr Perton held the lamp high in his hand and looked cautiously into the room. He saw four huddled-up shapes lying on the mattresses – four children – he thought.

They were obviously asleep. Softly, Mr Perton closed the door, and just as softly locked it. Julian watched anxiously to see if he pocketed the key or not. No – he hadn't! He had left it in the lock. Oh good!

The man went away again, treading softly. He did not go downstairs, but disappeared into a room some way down on the right. Julian heard the door shut with a click. Then he heard another click. The man evidently believed in locking himself in. Perhaps he didn't trust his other comrade, wherever he was – or Hunchy or the woman.

Julian waited a while and then crept out of the cupboard. He stole up to Mr Perton's room and looked through the keyhole to see if the room was in darkness or not. It was! Was Mr Perton snoring? Not that Julian could hear.

However Julian was not going to wait till he heard Mr Perton snore. He was going to find Dick – and he was pretty certain that the first place to look was in that attic upstairs!

'I bet Mr Perton was up there with Dick and heard me throwing stones at the window,' thought Julian. 'Then he slipped down and opened that window to trap us into getting in there, and we fell neatly into the trap! He must have been waiting inside the room for us. I don't like Mr Perton – too full of bright ideas!'

He was half-way up the flight of stairs that led to the attics now – going very carefully and slowly, afraid of making the stairs creak loudly. They did creak – and at every creak poor Julian stopped and listened to see if anyone had heard!

There was a long passage at the top turning at both ends into the side-wings. Julian stood still and debated – now which way ought he to go? Where exactly was that lit window? It was somewhere along this long passage, he was certain. Well, he'd go along the doors and see if a light shone out through the keyhole, or under the door anywhere.

Door after door was ajar. Julian peeped round each, making out bare dark attics, or box-rooms with rubbish in. Then he came to a door that was closed. He peered through the keyhole. No light came from inside the room.

Julian knocked gently. A voice came at once – Dick's voice. 'Who's there?'

'Sh! It's me – Julian,' whispered Julian. 'Are you all right, Dick?'

There came the creak of a bed, then the pattering of feet across a bare floor. Dick's voice came through the door, muffled and cautious.

'Julian! How did you get here? This is marvellous! Can you unlock the door and let me out?'

Julian had already felt for a key – but there was none. Mr Perton had taken *that* key, at any rate!

'No. The key's gone,' he said. 'Dick, what did they do to you?'

'Nothing much. They dragged me off to the car and shoved me in,' said Dick, through the door. 'The man called Rooky wasn't there. The others waited for him for some time, then drove off. They thought he might have gone off to see someone they meant to visit. So I haven't seen him. He's coming tomorrow morning. What a shock for him when he finds I'm not Richard!'

'Richard's here too,' whispered Julian. 'I wish he wasn't

– because if Rooky happens to see him he'll be kidnapped, I'm sure! The only hope is that Rooky will only see *you* – and as the other men think we're all one family, they may let us all go. Did you come straight here in the car, Dick?'

'Yes,' said Dick. 'The gates opened like magic when we got here, but I couldn't see anybody. I was shoved up here and locked in. One of the men came to tell me all the things Rooky was going to do to me when he saw me – and then he suddenly went downstairs and hasn't come back again.'

'Oh, I bet that was when we chucked stones up at your window,' said Julian at once. 'Didn't you hear them?'

'Yes, so that was the crack I heard! The man with me went across to the window at once and he must have seen you. Now, what about *you*, Ju? How on earth did you get here? Are you all really here? I suppose that was Timmy I heard howling outside.'

Julian quickly told him all his tale from the time he and George had met the howling Richard to the moment he had slipped up the stairs to find Dick.

There was a silence when he had finished his tale. Then Dick's voice came through the crack.

'Not much good making any plans, Julian. If things go all right, we'll be out of here by the morning, when Rooky finds I'm not the boy he wants. If things go wrong at least we're all together, and we can make plans then. I wonder what his mother will think when Richard doesn't get home tonight.'

'Probably think he's gone off to the aunt's,' said Julian.

'I should think he's a very unreliable person. Blow him! It was all because of him we got into this fix.

'I expect the men will have some cock-and-bull story tomorrow morning, about why they got hold of you, when they find you're not Richard,' went on Julian. 'They'll probably say you threw stones at their car or something, and they took you in hand – or found you hurt and brought you here to help you! Anyway, whatever they say, we won't make much fuss about it. We'll go quietly – and then we'll get things moving! I don't know what's going on here, but it's something fishy. The police ought to look into it, I'm certain.'

'Listen, that's Timmy again,' said Dick. 'Howling like anything for George, I suppose. You'd better go, Julian, in case he wakes up one of the men and they come out and find you here. Good night. I'm awfully glad you're near! Thanks awfully for coming to find me.'

'Good night,' said Julian, and went back along the corridor, walking over the patches of moonlight, looking fearfully into the dark shadows in case Mr Perton or somebody else was waiting for him!

But nobody was about. Timmy's howling died down. There was a deep silence in the house. Julian went down the stairs to the floor on which the bedroom was where the others lay asleep. He paused outside it. Should he do any further exploring? It really was such a chance!

He decided that he would. Mr Perton was fast asleep, he hoped. He thought probably Hunchy and the woman had gone to bed too. He wondered where the other man was, who had brought Dick to Owl's Dene. He hadn't seen him at all. Perhaps he had gone out in that black Bentley they had seen going out of the gate.

Julian went down to the ground floor. A brilliant thought had just occurred to him. Couldn't he undo the front door and get the others down, and send them out, free? He himself couldn't escape, because it would mean leaving Dick alone.

Then he gave up the idea. 'No,' he thought. 'For one thing George and Anne would refuse to go without me – and even if they agreed to get out of the front door, and go down the drive to the gates, how would they undo them? They're worked by some machinery from the house.'

So his brilliant idea came to nothing. He decided to look into all the rooms on the ground floor. He looked into the kitchen first. The fire was almost out. The moonlight came through the cracks of the curtains and lit up the dark silent room. Hunchy and the woman had evidently retired somewhere.

There was nothing of interest in the kitchen. Julian went into the room opposite. It was a dining-room, with a long polished table, candlesticks on the walls and mantelpiece, and the remains of a wood fire. Nothing of interest there either.

The boy went into another room. Was it a workroom, or what? There was a radio there, and a big desk. There was a stand with a curious instrument of some kind that had a stout wheel-like handle. Julian suddenly wondered if it would open the gates! Yes, that was what it was for. He saw a label attached to it. Left Gate. Right Gate. Both Gates.

'That's what it is – the machinery for opening either or both of the gates. If only I could get Dick out of that room I'd get us all out of this place in no time!' said Julian. He twisted the handle – what would happen?

CHAPTER THIRTEEN

Strange secret

A CURIOUS groaning, whining noise began, as some kind of
strong machinery was set working. Julian hurriedly turned
the handle back. If it was going to make all that noise, he
wasn't going to try his hand at opening the gates! It would
bring Mr Perton out of his room in a rush!

'Most ingenious, whatever it is,' thought the boy,
examining it as well as he could in the moonlight that
streamed through the window. He looked round the room
again. A noise came to his ears and he stood still.

'It's somebody snoring,' he thought. 'I'd better not mess
about here any more! Where are they sleeping? Somewhere
not far from here, that's certain.'

He tiptoed cautiously into the next room and looked
inside it. It was a lounge, but there was nobody there at
all. He couldn't hear the snoring there either.

He was puzzled. There didn't seem to be any other room
nearby where people could sleep. He went back to the
workroom or study. Yes, now he could hear that noise
again – and it *was* somebody snoring! Somebody quite
near – and yet not near enough to hear properly, or to see.
Most peculiar.

Julian walked softly round the room, trying to find a

309

place where the snoring sounded loudest of all. Yes, by this bookcase that reached to the ceiling. That was where the snoring sounded most of all. Was there a room behind this wall, next to the workroom? Julian went out to investigate. But there was no room behind the study at all – only the wall of the corridor, as far as he could see. It was more and more mysterious.

He went back to the study again, and over to the bookcase. Yes, there it was again. *Somebody* was asleep and snoring not far off – but WHERE?

Julian began to examine the bookcase. It was full of books jammed tightly together – novels, biographies, reference books – all higgledy-piggledy. He removed some from a shelf and examined the bookcase behind. It was of solid wood.

He put back the books and examined the big bookcase again. It was a very solid affair. Julian looked carefully at the books, shining in the moonlight. One shelf of books looked different from the others – less tidy – the books not so jammed together. Why should just one shelf be different?

Julian quietly took the books from that shelf. Behind them was the solid wood again. Julian put his hand at the back and felt about. A knob was hidden in a corner. A knob! Whatever was that there for?

Cautiously Julian turned the knob this way and that. Nothing happened. Then he pressed it. Still nothing happened. He pulled it – and it slid out a good six inches.

Then the whole of the back of that particular shelf slid quietly downwards, and left an opening big enough for somebody to squeeze through! Julian held his breath. A sliding panel! What was behind it?

A dim flickering light came from the space behind. Julian waited till his eyes were used to it after the bright moonlight. He was trembling with excitement. The snoring now sounded so loud that Julian felt as if the snorer must be almost within hand's reach!

Then gradually he made out a tiny room, with a small narrow bed, a table and a shelf on which a few articles could dimly be made out. A candle was burning in a corner. On the bed was the snorer. Julian could not see what he was like, except that he looked big and burly as he lay there, snoring peacefully.

'What a find!' thought Julian. 'A secret hiding-place – a place to hide all kinds of people, I suppose, who have enough money to pay for such a safe hole. This fellow ought to have been warned not to snore! He gave himself away.'

The boy did not dare to stay there any longer, looking into that curious secret room. It must be built in a space between the wall of the study and the wall of the corridor – probably a very old hiding-place made when the house was built.

Julian felt for the knob. He pushed it back into place, and the panel slid up again, as noiselessly as before. It was evidently kept in good working order!

The snoring was muffled again now. Julian replaced the books, hoping that they were more or less as he had found them.

He felt very thrilled. He had found one of the secrets of Owl's Dene, at any rate. The police would be *very* interested to hear about that secret hole – and perhaps they would be even more interested to hear about the person inside it!

It was absolutely essential now that he and the others should escape. Would it be all right if he went without Dick? No, if the men suspected any dirty work on his part – discovered that he knew of the secret hole, for instance – they might harm Dick. Regretfully Julian decided that there must be no escape for him unless everyone, including Dick, could come too.

He didn't explore any more. He suddenly felt very tired indeed and crept softly upstairs. He felt as if he simply must lie down and think. He was too tired to do anything else.

He went to the bedroom. The key was still in the lock outside. He went into the room and shut the door. Mr Perton would find the door unlocked the next morning, but probably he would think he hadn't turned the key properly. Julian lay down on the mattress beside Richard. All the others were fast asleep.

He meant to think out all his problems – but no sooner had he closed his eyes than he was fast asleep. He didn't hear Timmy howling outside once more. He didn't hear the screech-owl that made the night hideous on the hill. He didn't see the moon slide down the sky.

It was not Mr Perton who awoke the children next morning, but the woman. She came into the room and called to them.

'If you want breakfast you'd better come down and have it!'

They all sat up in a hurry, wondering where in the world they were. 'Hallo!' said Julian, blinking sleepily. 'Breakfast, did you say? It sounds good. Is there anywhere we can wash?'

'You can wash down in the kitchen,' said the woman, sullenly. 'I'm not cleaning any bathroom up after you!'

'Leave the door unlocked for us to get out!' said Julian, innocently. 'Mr Perton locked it last night.'

'So he said,' answered the woman, 'but he *hadn't* locked it! It wasn't locked when I tried the door this morning. Aha! You didn't know that, did you? You'd have been wandering all over the house, I suppose, if you'd guessed that.'

'Probably we should,' agreed Julian, winking at the others. They knew that he had meant to go and find Dick in the night, and snoop round a bit – but they didn't know all he had discovered. He hadn't had the heart to wake them and tell them the night before.

'Don't you be too long,' said the woman, and went out of the door, leaving it open.

'I hope she's taken some breakfast up to poor old Dick,'

313

said Julian, in a low voice. The others came close to him.

'Ju, did you find Dick last night?' whispered Anne. He nodded. Then, very quickly and quietly he told them all he had discovered – where Dick was, and then how he had heard the snoring, and discovered the secret panel, the hidden room, and the man who slept so soundly there, not knowing that Julian had seen him.

'Julian! How thrilling!' said George. 'Whoever would have thought of all that?'

'Oh yes, and I discovered the machinery that opens the gates too,' said Julian. It's in the same room. But come on, if we don't go down to the kitchen that woman will be after us again. I hope Hunchy won't be there, I don't like him.'

Hunchy, however, *was* there, finishing his breakfast at a small table. He scowled at the children, but they took absolutely no notice of him.

'You've been a long time,' grumbled the woman. 'There's the sink over there, if you want to wash, and I've put a towel out for you. You look pretty dirty, all of you.'

'We are,' said Julian, cheerfully. 'We could have done with a bath last night – but we didn't exactly get much of a welcome, you know.'

When they had washed they went to a big scrubbed table. There was no cloth on it. The woman had put out some bread and butter and some boiled eggs and a jug of steaming hot cocoa. They all sat down and began to help themselves. Julian talked cheerfully, winking at the others to make them do the same. He wasn't going to let the hunchback think they were scared or worried in any way.

'Shut up, you,' said Hunchy, suddenly. Julian took no notice. He went on talking, and George backed him up valiantly, though Anne and Richard were too scared, after hearing the hunchback's furious voice.

'Did you hear what I said?' suddenly yelled Hunchy, and got up from the little table where he had been sitting. 'Hold your tongues, all of you! Coming into my kitchen and making all that row! Hold your tongues!'

Julian rose too. 'I don't take orders from you, whoever you are,' he said, and he sounded just like a grown-up. 'You hold your tongue – or else be civil.'

'Oh, don't talk to him like that, don't,' begged the woman, anxiously. 'He's got such a temper – he'll take a stick to you!'

'I'd take a stick to *him* – except that I don't hit fellows smaller than myself,' said Julian.

What would have happened if Mr Perton hadn't appeared in the kitchen at that moment nobody knew! He stalked in and glared round, sensing that there was a row going on.

'You losing your temper again, Hunchy?' he said. 'Keep it till it's needed. I'll ask you to produce it sometime today possibly – if these kids don't behave themselves!' He looked round at the children with a grim expression. Then he glanced at the woman.

'Rooky's coming soon,' he told her. 'And one or two others. Get a meal – a good one. Keep these children in here, Hunchy, and keep an eye on them. I may want them later.'

He went out. The woman was trembling. 'Rooky's coming,' she half-whispered to Hunchy.

'Get on with your work, woman,' said the dwarf. 'Go out and get the vegetables in yourself – I've got to keep an eye on these kids.'

The poor woman scuttled about. Anne was sorry for her. She went over to her. 'Shall I clear away and wash up for you?' she asked. 'You're going to be busy and I've nothing to do.'

'We'll all help,' said Julian. The woman gave him an astonished and grateful glance. It was plain that she was not used to good manners or politeness of any sort.

'Yah!' said Hunchy, sneeringly. 'You won't get round *me* with your smarmy ways!'

Nobody took the slightest notice of him. All the children began to clear away the breakfast things, and Anne and George stacked them in the sink, and began to wash them.

'Yah!' said Hunchy again.

'And yah to you,' said Julian, pleasantly, which made the others laugh, and Hunchy scowl till his eyes disappeared under his brows!

CHAPTER FOURTEEN

Rooky is very angry

ABOUT AN hour later there was a curious grinding, groaning noise that turned to a whining. Richard, Anne and George jumped violently. But Julian knew what it was.

'The gates are being opened,' he told them, and they remembered how he had described the machinery that opened the gates – the curious wheel-like handle, labelled 'Left Gate. Right Gate. Both Gates'.

'How do *you* know that?' asked Hunchy at once, surprised and suspicious.

'Oh, I'm a good guesser,' replied Julian airily. 'Correct me if I'm wrong, but I couldn't help thinking the gates were being opened, and I'm guessing it's Rooky that's coming through them!'

'You're so sharp you'll cut yourself one day,' grumbled Hunchy, going to the door.

'So my mother told me when I was two years old,' said Julian, and the others giggled. If there was any answering back to be done, Julian could always do it!

They all went to the window. George opened it. Timmy was there, sitting just outside. George had begged the woman to let him in, but she wouldn't. She had thrown him some scraps, and told George there was a pond he could drink from, but beyond that she wouldn't go.

'Timmy,' called George, as she heard the sound of a car purring quietly up the drive, 'Timmy, stay there. Don't move!'

She was afraid that Timmy might perhaps run round to the front door, and go for anyone who jumped out of the car. Timmy looked up at her inquiringly. He was puzzled about this whole affair. Why wasn't he allowed inside the house with George? He knew there were some people who didn't welcome dogs into their houses – but George never went to those houses. It was a puzzle to him, too, to understand why she didn't come out to him.

Still, she was there, leaning out of the window; he could hear her voice; he could even lick her hand if he stood up on his hind legs against the wall.

'You shut that window and come inside,' said Hunchy, maliciously. He took quite a pleasure in seeing that George was upset at being separated from Timmy.

'Here comes the car,' said Julian. They all looked at it – and then glanced at each other. KMF 102 – of course!

The black Bentley swept by the kitchen windows and up to the front door. Three men got out. Richard crouched back, his face going pale.

Julian glanced round at him raising his eyebrows, mutely asking him if he recognised one of the men as Rooky. Richard nodded miserably. He was very frightened now.

The whining, groaning noise came again. The gates were being shut. Voices came from the hall, then the men went into one of the rooms, and there was the sound of a door being shut.

Julian wondered if he could slip out of the room unnoticed and go up to see if Dick was all right. He sidled to the door, thinking that Hunchy was engrossed in cleaning an array of dirty shoes. But his grating voice sounded at once.

'Where you going? If you don't obey orders I'll tell Mr Perton – and won't you be sorry!'

'There's quite a lot of people in this house going to be sorry for themselves soon,' said Julian, in an irritatingly cheerful voice. 'You be careful, Hunchy.'

Hunchy lost his temper suddenly and threw the shoe-brush he was using straight at Julian. Julian caught it deftly and threw it up on the high mantelpiece.

'Thanks,' he said. 'Like to throw another?'

'Oh don't,' said the woman, beseechingly. 'You don't know what he's like when he's in a real temper. Don't!'

The door of the room that the men had gone into opened, and somebody went upstairs. 'To fetch Dick,' thought Julian at once. He stood and listened.

Hunchy got another shoe-brush and went on polishing, muttering angrily under his breath. The woman went on preparing some food. The others listened with Julian. They too guessed that the man had gone to fetch Dick to show him to Rooky.

Footsteps came down the stairs again – two lots this time. Yes, Dick must be with the man, they could hear his voice.

'Let go my arm! I can come without being dragged!' they heard him say indignantly. Good old Dick! He wasn't going to be dragged about without making a strong protest.

He was taken into the room where the other three men were waiting. Then a loud voice was heard.

'He's not the boy! Fools, you've got the wrong boy!'

Hunchy and the woman heard the words too. They gaped at one another. Something had gone wrong. They went to the door and stood there silently. The children just stood behind them. Julian edged Richard away very gradually.

'Rub some soot over your hair,' he whispered. 'Make it as black as you can, Richard. If the men come out here to see us, they're not likely to recognise you so easily if your hair's black. Go on, quick, while the others aren't paying attention.'

Julian was pointing to the inside of the grate, where black soot hung. Richard put his trembling hands into it and covered them with it. Then he rubbed the soot over his yellow hair.

'More,' whispered Julian. 'Much more! Go on. I'll stand in front of you so that the others can't see what you're doing.'

Richard rubbed soot even more wildly over his hair.

Julian nodded. Yes, it looked black enough now. Richard looked quite different. Julian hoped Anne and George would be sensible enough not to exclaim when they saw him.

There was evidently some sharp argument going on in the room off the hall. Voices were raised, but not many words could be made out from where the children stood at the kitchen door. Dick's voice could be heard too. It suddenly sounded quite clearly.

'I TOLD you you'd made a mistake. Now you just let me go, see!'

Hunchy suddenly pushed everyone roughly away from the door – except poor Richard who was standing over in a dark corner, shaking with fright!

'They're coming,' he hissed. 'Get away from the door.'

Everyone obeyed. Hunchy took up a shoe-brush again, the woman went to peel potatoes, the children turned over the pages of some old magazines they had found.

Footsteps came to the kitchen door. It was flung open. Mr Perton was there – and behind him another man. No mistaking who *he* was!

Thick-lipped, with an enormous nose – yes, he was the ruffian Rooky, once bodyguard to Richard's father, the man who hated Richard because he had told tales on him and who had been sent off in disgrace by the boy's father.

Richard cowered back in his corner, hiding behind the others. Anne and George had given him astonished stares when they had noticed his hair, but neither of them had said a word. Hunchy and the woman didn't seem to have noticed any change in him.

Dick was with the two men. He waved to the others. Julian grinned. Good old Dick!

Rooky glanced at all four children. His eyes rested for a moment on Richard, and then glanced away. He hadn't recognised him!

'Well, Mr Perton,' said Julian. 'I'm glad to see you've got my brother down from the room you locked him up in last night. I imagine that means he can come with us now. Why you brought him here as you did, and made him a prisoner last night I can't imagine.'

'Now look here,' said Mr Perton, in quite a different voice from the one he had used to them before. 'Now look here, quite frankly we made a mistake. You don't need to know why or how – that's none of your business. This isn't the boy we wanted.'

'We *told* you he was our brother,' said Anne.

'Quite,' said Mr Perton, politely. 'I am sorry I disbelieved you. These things happen. Now, we want to make you all a handsome present for any inconvenience you have suffered – er – ten pounds for you to spend on ice-creams and so on. You can go whenever you like.'

'And don't try and tell any fairy stories to anyone,' said Rooky suddenly, in a threatening voice. 'See? We made a mistake – but we're not having it talked about. If you say anything silly, we shall say that we found this boy lost in the woods, took pity on him and brought him here for the night – and that you kids were – found trespassing in the grounds. You understand?'

'I understand perfectly,' said Julian, in a cool rather scornful voice. 'Well, I take it we can all go now, then?'

'Yes,' said Mr Perton. He put his hand into his pocket and took out some pound coins. He handed two to each of the children. They glanced at Julian to see if they were to take them or not. Not one of them felt willing to accept Mr Perton's money. But they knew they must take them if Julian did.

Julian accepted the two coins handed to him, and pocketed them without a word of thanks. The others did the same. Richard kept his head down well all the time, hoping that the two men would not notice how his knees were shaking. He was really terrified of Rooky.

'Now clear out,' said Rooky when the ten pounds had been divided. 'Forget all this – or you'll be very sorry.'

He opened the door that led into the garden. The children trooped out silently, Richard well in their midst. Timmy was waiting for them. He gave a loud bark of welcome and flung himself on George, fawning on her, licking every bit of her he could reach. He looked back at the kitchen door and gave a questioning growl as if to say, 'Do you want me to go for anyone in there?'

'No,' said George. 'You come with us, Timmy. We'll get out of here as quickly as we can.'

'Give me your pound coins, quick,' said Julian in a low voice, when they had rounded a corner and were out of sight of the windows. They all handed them to him wonderingly. What was he going to do with them?

The woman had come out to watch them go. Julian beckoned to her. She came hesitatingly down the garden. 'For you,' said Julian, putting the coins into her hand. 'We don't want them.'

The woman took them, amazed. Her eyes filled with tears. 'Why, it's a fortune – no, no, you take them back. You're kind, though – so kind.'

ROOKY IS VERY ANGRY

Julian turned away, leaving the astonished and delighted woman standing staring after them. He hurried after the others.

'That was a very, very good idea of yours,' said Anne, warmly, and the others agreed. All of them had been sorry for the poor woman.

'Come on,' said Julian. 'We don't want to miss the opening of the gates! Listen, can you hear the groaning noise back at the house. Somebody has set the machinery working that opens the gates. Thank goodness we're free – and Richard too. That *was* a bit of luck!'

'Yes, I was so scared Rooky would recognise me, even though my hair was sooted black,' said Richard, who was now looking much more cheerful. 'Oh look, we can see the end of the drive now, and the gates are wide open. We're free!'

'We'll get our bikes,' said Julian. 'I know where we left them. You can ride on my crossbar, Richard, because we're a bike short. Dick must have his bike back now – you remember you borrowed it? Look, here they are.'

They mounted their bicycles and began to cycle down the drive – and then Anne gave a scream.

'Julian! Look, look – the gates are closing again. Quick, quick – we'll be left inside!'

Everyone saw in horror that the gates were actually closing, very slowly. They pedalled as fast as they could – but it was no use. By the time they got there the two great gates were fast shut. No amount of shaking would open them. And just as they were so very nearly out!

CHAPTER FIFTEEN

Prisoners

THEY ALL flung themselves down on the grass verge and groaned.

'What have they done that for, just as we were going out?' said Dick. 'Was it a mistake, do you think? I mean – did they think we'd had time to go out, or what?'

'Well, if it was a mistake, it's easy to put right,' said Julian. 'I'll just cycle back to the house and tell them they shut the gates too soon.'

'Yes, you do that,' said George. 'We'll wait here.'

But before Julian could even mount his bicycle there came the sound of the car purring down the long drive. All the children jumped to their feet. Richard ran behind a bush in panic. He was terrified of having to face Rooky again.

The car drew up by the children and stopped. 'Yes, they're still here,' said Mr Perton's voice, as he got out of the car. Rooky got out too. They came over to the children.

Rooky ran his eyes over them. 'Where's that other boy?' he asked quickly.

'I can't imagine,' said Julian, coolly. 'Dear me, I wonder if he had time to cycle out of the gateway. Why did you shut the gates so soon, Mr Perton?'

Rooky had caught sight of Richard's shivering figure behind the bush. He strode over to him and yanked him out. He looked at him closely. Then he pulled him over to Mr Perton.

'Yes, I thought so – *this* is the boy we want! He's sooted his hair or something, and that's why I didn't recognise him. But when he'd gone I felt sure there was something familiar about him – that's why I wanted another look.' He shook poor Richard like a dog shaking a rat.

'Well, what do you want to do about it?' asked Mr Perton, rather gloomily.

'Hold him, of course,' said Rooky. 'I'll get back at his father now – he'll have to pay a very large sum of money for his horrible son! That'll be useful, won't it? And I can pay this kid out for some of the lies he told his father about me. Nasty little rat.'

He shook Richard again. Julian stepped forward, white and furious.

'Now you stop that,' he said. 'Let the boy go. Haven't you done enough already – keeping my brother locked up for nothing – holding us all for the night – and now you talk about kidnapping! Haven't you just come out of prison? Do you want to go back there?'

Rooky dropped Richard and lunged out at Julian. With a snarl Timmy flung himself between them and bit the man's hand. Rooky let out a howl of rage and nursed his injured hand. He yelled at Julian.

'Call that dog to heel. Do you hear?'

'I'll call him to heel all right – if you talk sense,' said Julian, still white with rage. 'You're going to let us all go, here and now. Go back and open these gates.'

Timmy growled terrifyingly, and both Rooky and Mr Perton took some hurried steps backwards. Rooky picked up a very big stone.

'If you dare to throw that I'll set my dog on you again!' shouted George, in sudden fear. Mr Perton knocked the stone out of Rooky's hand.

'Don't be a fool,' he said. 'That dog could make mincemeat of us – great ugly brute. Look at his teeth. For goodness' sake let the kids go, Rooky.'

'Not till we've finished our plans,' said Rooky fiercely, still nursing his hand. 'Keep them all prisoners here! We shan't be long before our jobs are done. And what's more I'm going to take that little rat there off with me when I go! Ha! I'll teach him a few things – and his father too.'

Timmy growled again. He was straining at George's hand. She had him firmly by the collar. Richard trembled when he heard Rooky's threats about him. Tears ran down his face.

'Yes, you can howl all you like,' said Rooky, scowling at him. 'You wait till I get you! Miserable little coward, you never did have any spunk, you just ran round telling tales and misbehaving yourself whenever you could.'

'Look, Rooky, you'd better come up to the house and have that hand seen to,' said Mr Perton. 'It's bleeding badly. You ought to wash it and put some stuff on it – you know a dog's bite is dangerous. Come on. You can deal with these kids afterwards.'

Rooky allowed himself to be led back to the car. He shook his unhurt fist at the children as they watched silently.

'Interfering brats! Little . . .'

But the rest of his pleasant words were lost in the purring of the car's engine. Mr Perton backed a little, turned the car, and it disappeared up the drive. The five children sat themselves down on the grass verge. Richard began to sob out loud.

'Do shut up, Richard,' said George. 'Rooky was right when he said you were a little coward, with no spunk. So you are. Anne's much pluckier than you are. I wish to goodness we had never met you.'

Richard rubbed his hands over his eyes. They were sooty, and made his face look most peculiar with streaks of black soot mixed with his tears. He looked very woebegone indeed.

'I'm sorry,' he sniffed. 'I know you don't believe me – but I really am. I've always been a bit of a coward – I can't help it.'

'Yes you can,' said Julian, scornfully. 'Anybody can help being a coward. Cowardice is just thinking of your own miserable skin instead of somebody else's. Why, even little Anne is more worried about us than she is about herself – and that makes her brave. She couldn't be a coward if she tried.'

This was a completely new idea to Richard. He tried to wipe his face dry. 'I'll try to be like you,' he said, in a muffled voice. 'You're all so decent. I've never had friends like you before. Honestly, I won't let you down again.'

'Well, we'll see,' said Julian, doubtfully. 'It would certainly be a surprise if you turned into a hero all of a sudden – a very *nice* surprise, of course – but in the meantime it would be a help if you stopped howling for a bit and let us talk.'

Richard subsided. He really looked very peculiar with his soot-streaked face. Julian turned to the others.

'This is maddening!' he said. 'Just as we so nearly got out. I suppose they'll shut us up in some room and keep us there till they've finished whatever this "job" is. I imagine the "job" consists of getting that hidden fellow away in safety – the one I saw in the secret room.'

'Won't Richard's parents report his disappearance to the police?' said George, fondling Timmy, who wouldn't stop licking her now he had got her again.

'Yes, they will. But what good will that do? The police won't have the faintest notion where he is,' said Julian. 'Nobody knows where we are, either, come to that, but Aunt Fanny won't worry yet, because she knows we're off on a cycling tour, and wouldn't be writing to her anyway.'

'Do you think those men will really take me off with them when they go?' asked Richard.

'Well, we'll hope we shall have managed to escape

before that,' said Julian, not liking to say yes, certainly Richard would be whisked away!

'How *can* we escape?' asked Anne. 'We'd never get over those high walls. And I don't expect anyone ever comes by here – right at the top of this deserted hill. No tradesman would ever call.'

'What about the postman?' asked Dick.

'They probably arrange to fetch their post each day,' said Julian. 'I don't expect they want anyone coming here at all. Or, there may be a letter-box outside the gate. I never thought of that!'

They went to see. But although they craned their necks to see each side, there didn't seem to be any letter-box at all for the postman to slip letters in. So the faint hope that had risen in their minds, that they might catch the postman and give him a message, vanished at once.

'Hallo, here's the woman – Aggie, or whatever her name is,' said George, suddenly, as Timmy growled. They all turned their heads. Aggie was coming down the drive in a hurry – could she be going out? Would the gates open for her?

Their hopes died as she came near. 'Oh, there you are! I've come with a message. You can do one of two things – you can stay out in the grounds all day, and not put foot into the house at all – or you can come into the house and be locked up in one of the rooms.'

She looked round cautiously and lowered her voice. 'I'm sorry you didn't get out; right down upset I am. It's bad enough for an old woman like me, being cooped up here with Hunchy, but it's not right to keep children in this place. You're nice children too.'

'Thanks,' said Julian. 'Now, seeing that you think we're so nice – tell us, is there any way we can get out besides going through these gates?'

'No. No way at all,' said the woman. 'It's like a prison, once those gates are shut. Nobody's allowed in, and you're only allowed out if it suits Mr Perton and the others. So don't try to escape – it's hopeless.'

Nobody said anything to that. Aggie glanced over her shoulder as if she feared somebody might be listening – Hunchy perhaps – and went on in a low voice.

'Mr Perton said I wasn't to give you much food. And he said Hunchy's to put down food for the dog with poison in it, so don't you let him eat any but what I give you myself.'

'The brute,' cried George, and she held Timmy close against her. 'Did you hear that, Timmy? It's a pity you didn't bite Mr Perton too!'

'Sh!' said the woman, afraid. 'I didn't mean to tell you all this, you know that – but you're kind, and you gave me all that money. Right down nice you are. Now, you listen to me – you'd better say you'd rather keep out here in the grounds, because if you're locked up I wouldn't dare to bring you much food in case Rooky came in and saw it. But if you stay out here it's easier. I can give you plenty.'

'Thank you very much,' said Julian, and the others nodded too. 'In any case we'd rather be out here. I suppose Mr Perton is afraid we'd stumble on some of his strange secrets in the house if we had the free run there! All right, tell him we'll be in the grounds. What about our food? How shall we manage about that? We don't want to get you into trouble, but we're very hungry for our meals, and we really could do with a good dinner today.'

'I'll manage it for you,' said Aggie, and she actually smiled. 'But mind what I say now – don't you let that dog eat anything Hunchy puts down for him! It'll be poisoned.'

A voice shouted from the house. Aggie jerked her head up and listened. 'That's Hunchy,' she said. 'I must go.'

She hurried back up the drive. 'Well, well, well,' said Julian, 'so they thought they'd poison old Timmy, did they? They'll have to think again, old fellow, won't they?'

'Woof,' said Timmy, gravely, and didn't even wag his tail!

CHAPTER SIXTEEN

Aggie – and Hunchy

'I FEEL as if I want some exercise,' said George, when Aggie had gone. 'Let's explore the grounds. You never know what we might find!'

They got up, glad of something to do to take their minds off their surprising problems. Really, who would have thought yesterday, when they were happily cycling along sunny country roads, that they would be held prisoner like this today? You just never knew what would happen. It made life exciting, of course, but it did spoil a cycling tour!

They found absolutely nothing of interest in the grounds except a couple of cows, a large number of hens, and a brood of young ducklings. Evidently even the milkman didn't need to call at Owl's Dene! It was quite self-contained.

'I expect that black Bentley goes down each day to some town or other, to collect letters, and to buy meat, or fish,' said George. 'Otherwise Owl's Dene could keep itself going for months on end if necessary without any contact with the outside world. I expect they've got stacks and stacks of tinned food.'

'It's weird to find a place like this, tucked away on a deserted hill, forgotten by everyone – guarding goodness

338

knows what secrets,' said Dick. 'I'd love to know who that man was you saw in the secret room, Julian – the snorer!'

'Someone who doesn't want to be seen even by Hunchy or Aggie,' said Julian. 'Someone the police would dearly love to see, I expect!'

'I *wish* we could get out of here,' said George, longingly. 'I hate the place. It's got such a nasty "feel" about it. And I hate the thought of somebody trying to poison Timmy.'

'Don't worry, he won't be poisoned,' said Dick. 'We won't let him be. He can have half *our* food, can't you, Timmy, old fellow?'

Timmy agreed. He woofed and wagged his tail. He wouldn't leave George's side that morning, but stuck to her like a leech.

'Well, we've been all round the grounds and there's nothing much to see,' said Julian, when they had come back near the house. 'I suppose Hunchy sees to the milking and feeds the poultry and brings in the vegetables. Aggie has to manage the house. I say – look – there's Hunchy now. He's putting down food for Timmy!'

Hunchy was making signs to them. 'Here's the dog's dinner!' he yelled.

'Don't say a word, George,' said Julian in a low voice. 'We'll pretend to let Timmy eat it, but we'll really throw it away somewhere – and he'll be frightfully astonished when Timmy is still all-alive-o tomorrow morning!'

Hunchy disappeared in the direction of the cowshed, carrying a pail. Anne gave a little giggle.

'I know what we'll pretend! We'll pretend that Timmy ate half and didn't like the rest so we gave it to the hens and ducks!'

'And Hunchy will be frightfully upset because he'll think they'll die and he'll get into a row,' said George. 'Serve him right! Come on, let's get the food now.'

She ran to pick up the big bowl of food. Timmy sniffed at it and turned away. It was obvious that he wouldn't have fancied it much even if George had allowed him to have it. Timmy was a very sensible dog.

'Quick, get that spade, Ju, and dig a hole before Hunchy comes back,' said George, and Julian set to work grinning. It didn't take him more than a minute to dig a large hole in the soft earth of a bed. George emptied all the food into the hole, wiped the bowl round with a handful of leaves and watched Julian filling in the earth. Now no animals could get at the poisoned food.

'Let's go to the hen-run now, and when we see Hunchy we'll wave to him,' said Julian. 'He'll ask us what we've been doing. Come on. He deserves to have a shock.'

They went to the hen-house, and stood looking through the wire surrounding the hen-run. As Hunchy came along they turned and waved to him. George pretended to scrape some scraps out of the dog's bowl into the run. Hunchy stared hard. Then he ran towards her, shouting.

'Don't do that, don't do that!'

'What's the matter?' asked George, innocently, pretending to push some scraps through the wire. 'Can't I give the hens some scraps?'

'Is that the bowl I put the dog's food down in?' asked Hunchy, sharply.

'Yes,' said George.

'And he didn't eat all the food – so you're giving it to my hens!' shouted Hunchy in a rage, and snatched the bowl out of George's hands. She pretended to be very angry.

'Don't! Why shouldn't your hens have scraps from the dog's bowl? The food you gave Timmy looked very nice – can't the hens have some?'

Hunchy looked into the hen-run with a groan. The hens were pecking about near the children for all the world as if they were eating something just thrown to them. Hunchy felt sure they would all be dead by the next day – and then, what trouble he would get into!

He glared at George. 'Idiot of a boy! Giving my hens that food! You deserve a good whipping.'

He thought George was a boy, of course. The others looked on with interest. It served Hunchy right to get into a panic over his hens, after trying to poison dear old Timmy.

Hunchy didn't seem to know what to do. Eventually he took a stiff brush from a nearby shed and went into the hen-run. He had evidently decided to sweep the whole place in case any poisoned bits of food were still left about. He swept laboriously and the children watched him, pleased that he should punish himself in this way.

'I've never seen anyone bother to sweep a hen-run before,' said Dick, in a loud and interested voice.

'Nor have I,' said George at once. 'He must be very anxious to bring his hens up properly.'

'It's jolly hard work, I should think,' said Julian. 'Glad I haven't got to do it. Pity to sweep up all the bits of food, though. An awful waste.'

Everyone agreed heartily to this.

'Funny he should be so upset about my giving the hens any scraps of the food he put down for Timmy,' said George. 'I mean, it seems a bit *suspicious*.'

'It does rather,' agreed Dick. 'But then perhaps he's a suspicious character.'

Hunchy could hear all this quite plainly. The children meant him to, of course. He stopped his sweeping and scowled evilly at them.

'Clear off, you little pests,' he said, and raised his broom as if to rush at the children with it.

'He looks like an angry hen,' said Anne, joining in.

'He's just going to cluck,' put in Richard, and the others laughed. Hunchy ran to open the gate of the hen-run, red with anger.

'Of course, it's just struck me – he *might* have put poison into Timmy's bowl of food,' said Julian, loudly.

'That's why he's so upset about his hens. Dear, dear, how true the old proverb is – he that digs a pit shall fall into it himself!'

The mention of poison stopped Hunchy's rush at once. He flung the broom into the shed, and made off for the house without another word.

'Well, we gave him a bit more than he bargained for,' said Julian.

'And you needn't worry, hens,' said Anne, putting her face to the wire-netting of the run. 'You're not poisoned – and we wouldn't *dream* of harming you!'

'Aggie's calling us,' said Richard. 'Look, perhaps she's got some food for us.'

'I hope so,' said Dick. 'I'm getting very hungry. It's funny that grown-ups never seem to get as hungry as children. I do pity them.'

'Why? Do you *like* being hungry?' said Anne as they walked over to the house.

'Yes, if I know there's a good meal in the offing,' said Dick. 'Otherwise it wouldn't be at all funny. Oh goodness – is this all that Aggie has provided?'

On the window-sill was a loaf of stale-looking bread and a piece of very hard yellow cheese. Nothing else at all. Hunchy was there, grinning.

'Aggie says that's your dinner,' he said, and sat himself down at the table to spoon out enormous helpings of a very savoury stew.

'A little revenge for our behaviour by the hen-run,'

murmured Julian softly. 'Well, well, I thought better than this of Aggie. I wonder where she is.'

She came out of the kitchen door at that moment, carrying a washing-basket that appeared to be full of clothes. 'I'll just hang these out, Hunchy, and I'll be back,' she called to him. She turned to the children and gave them a broad wink.

'There's your dinner on the window-sill,' she said. 'Get it and take it somewhere to eat. Hunchy and I don't want you round the kitchen.'

She suddenly smiled and nodded her head down towards the washing-basket. The children understood immediately. Their real dinner was in there!

They snatched the bread and cheese from the sill and followed her. She set down the basket under a tree, where it was well-hidden from the house. A clothes-line stretched there. 'I'll be out afterwards to hang my washing,' she said, and with another smile that changed her whole face, she went back to the house.

'Good old Aggie,' said Julian, lifting up the top cloth in the basket. 'My word, just look here!'

CHAPTER SEVENTEEN

Julian has a bright idea

AGGIE HAD managed to pack knives, forks, spoons, plates and mugs into the bottom of the basket. There were two big bottles of milk. There was a large meat-pie with delicious-looking pastry on top, and a collection of buns, biscuits and oranges. There were also some home-made sweets. Aggie had certainly been very generous!

All the things were quickly whipped out of the basket. The children carried them behind the bushes, sat down and proceeded to eat a first-rate dinner. Timmy got his share of the meat-pie and biscuits. He also gobbled up a large part of the hard yellow cheese.

'Now, we'd better rinse everything under that garden tap over there, and then pack them neatly into the bottom of the basket again,' said Julian. 'We don't want to get Aggie into any sort of trouble for her kindness.'

The dishes were soon rinsed and packed back into the basket. The clothes were drawn over them – nothing could be seen!

Aggie came outside to them in about half an hour. The children went to her and spoke in low voices.

'Thanks, Aggie, that was super!'

'You *are* a brick. We did enjoy it!'

346

'I bet Hunchy didn't enjoy his dinner as much as *we* did!'

'Sh!' said Aggie, half-pleased and half-scared. 'You never know when Hunchy's listening. He's got ears like a hare! Listen, I'll be coming out to get the eggs from the hen-run at tea-time. I'll have a basket with me for the eggs – and I shall have your tea in it. I'll leave your tea in the hen-house when I get the eggs. You can fetch it when I've gone.'

'You're a wonder, Aggie!' said Julian, admiringly. 'You really are.'

Aggie looked pleased. It was plain that nobody had said a kind or admiring word to her for years and years. She was a poor, miserable, scared old woman – but she was quite enjoying this little secret. She was pleased at getting the better of Hunchy too. Perhaps she felt it was some slight revenge for all the years he had ill-treated her.

She hung out some of the clothes in the basket, left one in to cover the dinner things, and then went back into the house.

'Poor old thing,' said Dick. 'What a life!'

'Yes, *I* shouldn't like to be cooped up here for years and years with ruffians like Perton and Rooky,' said Julian.

'It looks as if we shall be if we don't hurry up and think of some plan of escape,' said Dick.

'Yes. We'd better think hard again,' said Julian. 'Come over to those trees there. We can sit on the grass under them and talk without being overheard anywhere.'

'Look, Hunchy is polishing the black Bentley,' said

347

George. 'I'll just pass near him with Timmy, and let Timmy growl. He'll see Timmy's all alive and kicking then.'

So she took Timmy near the Bentley, and of course he growled horribly when he came upon Hunchy. Hunchy promptly got into the car and shut the door. George grinned.

'Hallo!' she said. 'Going off for a ride? Can Timmy and I come with you?'

She made as if she was going to open the door, and Hunchy yelled loudly: 'Don't you let that dog in here! I've seen Rooky's hand – one finger's very bad indeed. I don't want that dog going for *me*.'

'Do take me for a ride with you, Hunchy,' persisted George. 'Timmy loves cars.'

'Go away,' said Hunchy, hanging on to the door handle for dear life. 'I've got to get this car cleaned up for Mr Perton this evening. You let me get out and finish the job.'

George laughed and went off to join the others.

'Well, he can see Timmy's all-alive-o,' said Dick, with a grin. 'Good thing too. We'd find ourselves in a much bigger fix if we hadn't got old Timmy to protect us.'

They went over to the clump of trees and sat down.

'What was it that Hunchy said about the car?' asked Julian. George told him. Julian looked thoughtful. Anne knew that look – it meant that Julian was thinking of a plan! She prodded him.

'Ju! You've got a plan, haven't you? What is it?'

'Well, I'm only just wondering about something,' said Julian, slowly. 'That car – and the fact that Mr Perton is going out in it tonight – which means he will go out through those gates . . .'

'What of it?' said Dick. 'Thinking of going with him?'

'Well, yes, I was,' said Julian, surprisingly. 'You see, if he's not going till dark, I think I could probably get into the boot and hide there till the car stops somewhere, and then I could open the boot, get out, and go off for help!'

Everyone looked at him in silence. Anne's eyes gleamed. 'Oh, Julian! It's a brilliant plan.'

'It sounds jolly good,' said Dick.

'The only thing is I don't like being left here without Julian,' said Anne, suddenly feeling scared. 'Everything's all right if Julian's here.'

'*I* could go,' said Dick.

'Or I could,' said George, 'only there wouldn't be room for Timmy too.'

'The boot looks pretty big from outside,' said Julian. 'I wish I could take Anne with me. Then I'd know she was safe. You others would be all right so long as you had Timmy.'

They discussed the matter thoroughly. They dropped it towards tea-time when they saw Aggie coming out with a basket to collect the eggs. She made a sign to them not to come over to her. Possibly someone was watching. They stayed where they were, and watched her go into the hen-house. She remained there a short time, and then came out with a basketful of new-laid eggs. She walked to the house without looking at the children again.

'I'll go and see if she's left anything in the hen-house,' said Dick, and went over to it. He soon appeared again, grinning. His pockets bulged!

Aggie had left about two dozen potted-meat sandwiches, a big slab of cherry cake and a bottle of milk. The children went under the bushes and Dick unloaded his pockets. 'She even left a bone for old Tim,' he said.

'I suppose it's all right,' said George doubtfully. Julian smelt it.

'Perfectly fresh,' he said. 'No poison here at all! Anyway, Aggie wouldn't play a dirty trick like that. Come on, let's tuck in.'

They were very bored after tea, so Julian arranged some races and some jumping competitions. Timmy, of course, would have won them all if he had been counted as a proper competitor. But he wasn't. He went in for everything, though, and barked so excitedly that Mr Perton came to a window and yelled to him to stop.

'Sorry!' yelled back George. 'Timmy's so full of beans today, you see!'

'Mr Perton will be wondering why,' said Julian, with a grin. 'He'll be rowing Hunchy for not getting on with the poison job.'

When it began to grow dark the children went cautiously to the car. Hunchy had finished working on it. Quietly

Julian opened the boot and looked inside. He gave an exclamation of disappointment.

'It's only a small one! I can't get in there, I'm afraid. Nor can you, Dick.'

'I'll go then,' said Anne, in a small voice.

'Certainly not,' said Julian.

'Well – *I'll* go,' said Richard, surprisingly. 'I could just about squash in there.'

'*You!*' said Dick. 'You'd be scared stiff.'

Richard was silent for a moment. 'Yes, I should,' he admitted. 'But I'm still ready to go. I'll do my very best if you'd like me to try. After all, it's me or nobody. You won't let Anne go and there's not enough room for George and Timmy and not enough for either you or Julian, Dick.'

Everyone was astonished. It didn't seem a bit like Richard to offer to do an unselfish or courageous action. Julian felt very doubtful.

'Well, this is a serious thing, you know, Richard,' he said. 'I mean, if you're going to do it, you've got to do it properly – go right through with it, not get frightened in the middle and begin howling, so that the men hear you and examine the boot.'

'I know,' said Richard. 'I think I can do it all right. I do wish you'd trust me a bit.'

'I can't understand your offering to do a difficult thing like that,' said Julian. 'It doesn't seem a bit like you – you've not shown yourself to be at all plucky *so* far!'

351

'Julian, I think *I* understand,' said Anne suddenly, and she pulled at her brother's sleeve. 'He's thinking of *our* skins this time, not of his own – or at least he's trying to. Let's give him a chance to show he's got a bit of courage.'

'I only just want a chance,' said Richard in a small voice.

'All right,' said Julian. 'You shall have it. It'll be a very pleasant surprise if you take your chance and do something helpful!'

'Tell me exactly what I've got to do,' said Richard, trying to keep his voice from trembling.

'Well, once you're in the boot we'll have to shut you in. Goodness knows how long you'll have to wait there in the dark,' said Julian. 'I warn you it will be jolly stuffy and uncomfortable. When the car goes off it will be more uncomfortable still.'

'Poor Richard,' said Anne.

'As soon as the car stops anywhere and you hear the men get out, wait a minute to give them time to get out of sight and hearing – and then scramble out of the boot yourself and go straight to the nearest police station,' said Julian. 'Tell your story *quickly*, give this address – Owl's Dene, Owl's Hill, some miles from Middlecombe Woods – and the police will do the rest. Got all that?'

'Yes,' said Richard.

'Do you still want to go, now you know what you're in for?' asked Dick.

'Yes,' said Richard again. He was surprised by a warm hug from Anne.

'Richard, you're nice – and I didn't think you were!' said Anne.

He then got a thump on the back from Julian. 'Well, Richard, pull this off and you'll wipe out all the silly things you've done! Now, what about getting into the boot immediately? We don't know when the men will be coming out.'

'Yes. I'll get in now,' said Richard, feeling remarkably brave after Anne's hug and Julian's thump. Julian opened the boot. He examined the inside of the boot-cover. 'I don't believe Richard could open it from the inside,' he said. 'No, he couldn't. We mustn't close it tight, then – I'll have to wedge it a bit open with a stick or something. That will give him a little air, and he'll be able to push the boot open when he wants to. Where's a stick?'

Dick found one. Richard got into the boot and curled himself up. There wasn't very much room even for him! He looked extremely cramped. Julian shut the boot and wedged it with a stick so that there was a crack of half an inch all round.

Dick gave him a sharp nudge. 'Quick, someone's coming!'

CHAPTER EIGHTEEN

Hunt for Richard!

MR PERTON could be seen standing at the front door, outlined in the light from the lamp in the hall. He was talking to Rooky, who, apparently, was not going out. It seemed as if only Mr Perton was leaving in the car.

'Good luck, Richard,' Julian whispered, as he and the others melted into the shadows on the other side of the drive. They stood there in the darkness, watching Mr Perton walk over to the car. He got in and slammed the door. Thank goodness he hadn't wanted to put anything in the boot!

The engine started up and the car purred away down the drive. At the same time there came the grating sound of the gate machinery being used.

'Gates are opening for him,' muttered Dick. They heard the car go right down the drive and out of the gateway without stopping. It hooted as it went, evidently a signal to the house. The gates had been opened just at the right moment. They were now being shut, judging by the grinding noise going on.

The front door closed. The children stood in silence for a minute or two, thinking of Richard shut up in the boot.

'I'd never have thought it of him,' said George.

'No, but you just simply never know what is in anybody,' said Julian thoughtfully. 'I suppose even the worst coward, the most despicable crook, the most dishonest rogue *can* find some good thing in himself if he wants to badly enough.'

'Yes, it's the "wanting-to" that must be so rare, though,' said Dick. 'Look, there's Aggie at the kitchen door. She's calling us in.'

They went to her. 'You can come in now,' she said. 'I can't give you much supper, I'm afraid, because Hunchy will be here – but I'll put some cake up in your room, under the blankets.'

They went into the kitchen. It was pleasant with a log-fire and the mellow light from an oil-lamp. Hunchy was at the far end doing something with a rag and polish. He gave the children one of his familiar scowls. 'Take that dog out and leave him out,' he ordered.

'No,' said George.

'Then I'll tell Rooky,' said Hunchy. Neither he nor Aggie seemed to notice that there were only four children, not five.

'Well, if Rooky comes here I've no doubt Timmy will bite his other hand,' said George. 'Anyway, won't he be surprised to find Timmy still alive and kicking?'

Nothing more was said about Timmy. Aggie silently put the remains of a plum-pie on the table. 'There's your supper,' she said.

355

There was a very small piece each. As they were finishing, Hunchy went out. Aggie spoke in a whisper.

'I heard the radio at six o'clock. There was a police message about one of you – called Richard. His mother reported him missing and the police put it out on the radio.'

'Did they really?' said Dick. 'I say, they'll soon be here then!'

'But do they know where you are?' asked Aggie, surprised. Dick shook his head.

'Not yet – but I expect we'll soon be traced here.'

Aggie looked doubtful. 'Nobody's ever been traced here yet – nor ever will be, it's my belief. The police did come once, looking for somebody, and Mr Perton let them in, all polite-like. They hunted everywhere for the person they said they wanted, but they couldn't find him.'

Julian nudged Dick. He thought *he* knew where the police might have found him – in the little secret room behind that sliding panel.

'Funny thing,' said Julian. 'I haven't seen a telephone here. Don't they have one?'

'No,' said Aggie. 'No phone, no gas, no electricity, no water laid on, no nothing. Only just secrets and signs and comings and goings and threats and . . .'

She broke off as Hunchy came back, and went to the big fire-place, where a kettle was slung over the burning logs. Hunchy looked around at the children.

'Rooky wants the one of you that's called Richard,' he

said, with a horrible smile. 'Says he wants to teach him a few lessons.'

All the four felt extremely thankful that Richard was not there. They felt sure he wouldn't have liked the lessons that Rooky wanted to teach him.

They looked round at one another and then all round the room. 'Richard? Where *is* Richard?'

'What do you mean – where's Richard?' said Hunchy, in a snarling voice that made Timmy growl. 'One of you is Richard – that's all I know.'

'Why – there were five children – now there's only four!'

said Aggie, in sudden astonishment. 'I've only just noticed. Is Richard the missing one?'

'Dear me, *where's* Richard gone?' said Julian, pretending to be surprised. He called him. 'Richard! Hey, Richard, where are you?'

Hunchy looked angry. 'Now, none of your tricks. One of you is Richard. Which one?'

'Not one of us is,' answered Dick. 'Gracious, where *can* Richard be? Do you suppose we've left him in the grounds, Ju?'

'Must have,' said Julian. He went to the kitchen window and swung it wide open. 'RICHARD!' he roared. 'You're wanted, RICHARD!'

But no Richard answered or appeared, of course. He was miles away in the boot of the black Bentley!

There came the sound of angry footsteps in the hall and the kitchen door was flung open. Rooky stood there, scowling, his hand done up in a big bandage. With a delighted bark Timmy leapt forward. George caught him just in time.

'That dog! Didn't I say he was to be poisoned?' shouted Rooky, furiously. 'Why haven't you brought that boy to me, Hunchy?'

Hunchy looked afraid. 'He doesn't seem to be here,' he answered sullenly. 'Unless one of these here children is him, sir.'

Rooky glanced over them. 'No, he's not one of them. Where is Richard?' he demanded of Julian.

'I've just been yelling for him,' said Julian, with an air of amazement. 'Funny thing. He was out in the grounds all day with us, and now we're indoors, he just isn't here. Shall I go and hunt in the grounds?'

'I'll shout for him again,' said Dick, going to the window. 'RICHARD!'

'Shut up!' said Rooky. '*I'll* go and find him. Where's my torch? Get it, Aggie. And when I find him, he'll be sorry for himself, very, very sorry!'

'I'll come too,' said Hunchy. 'You go one way and I'll go another.'

'Get Ben and Fred too,' ordered Rooky. Hunchy departed to fetch Ben and Fred, whoever they were. The children supposed they must be the other men who had arrived with Rooky the night before.

Rooky went out of the kitchen door with his powerful torch. Anne shivered. She was very, very glad that Richard couldn't be found, however hard the men looked for him. Soon there came the sound of other voices in the grounds, as the four men separated into two parties, and began to search every yard.

'Where is he, the poor boy?' whispered Aggie.

'I don't know,' said Julian, truthfully. He wasn't going to give any secrets away to Aggie, even though she seemed really friendly to them.

She went out of the room and the children clustered together, speaking in low voices.

'I *say*, what a blessing it was Richard that went off in

the Bentley and not one of *us*,' whispered George.

'My word, yes – I didn't like the look on Rooky's face when he came into the kitchen just now,' said Julian.

'Well, Richard's got a little reward for trying to be brave,' said Anne. 'He's missed some ill-treatment from Rooky!'

Julian glanced at a clock in the kitchen. 'Look, it's almost nine. There's a radio on that shelf. Let's put it on and see if there's a message about Richard.'

He switched it on and twiddled the knob till he got the right station. After a minute or two of news, there came the message they wanted to hear.

'Missing from home since Wednesday, Richard Thurlow Kent, a boy of twelve, well-built, fair hair, blue eyes, wearing grey shorts and grey jersey. Probably on a bicycle.'

So the message went on, ending with a police telephone number that could be called. There was of course no message about Julian and the others. They were relieved. 'That means that Mother won't be worrying,' said George. 'But it also means that unless Richard can get help nobody can possibly find out we're here – if we're not missed we can't be searched for, and I don't really want to be here much longer.'

Nobody did, of course. All their hopes were now on Richard. He seemed rather a broken reed to rely on – but you never knew! He just might be successful in escaping unseen from the boot and getting to a police station.

After about an hour Rooky and the others came in, all in a furious temper. Rooky turned on Julian.

'What's happened to that boy? You must know.'

'Gr-r-r-r-r,' said Timmy at once. Rooky beckoned to Julian to come into the hall. He shut the kitchen door and shouted at Julian again.

'Well, you heard what I said – where's that boy?'

'Isn't he out in the grounds?' said Julian, putting on a very perturbed look. 'Good gracious, what *can* have happened to him? I assure you he was with us all day. Aggie will tell you that – and Hunchy too.'

'They've already told me,' said Rooky. 'He's not in the grounds. We've gone over every inch. Where is he?'

'Well, would he be somewhere in the house, then?' suggested Julian, innocently.

'How can he be?' raged Rooky. 'The front door's been closed and locked all day except when Perton went out. And Hunchy and Aggie swear he didn't come into the kitchen.'

'It's an absolute mystery,' said Julian. 'Shall I hunt all over the house? The others can help me. Maybe the dog will smell him out.'

'I'm not having that dog out of the kitchen,' said Rooky. 'Or any of *you*, either! I believe that boy's about somewhere, laughing up his sleeve at us all – and I believe you know where he is too!'

'I don't,' said Julian. 'And that's the truth.'

'When I *do* find him, I'll ... I'll ...' Rooky broke off, quite unable to think of anything bad enough to do to poor Richard.

He went to join the others, still muttering. Julian went thankfully back to the kitchen. He was very glad Richard was well out of the way. It was pure chance that he had gone – but what a very good thing! Where was Richard now? What was he doing? Was he still in the boot of the car? How Julian wished he knew!

CHAPTER NINETEEN

Richard has his own adventure

RICHARD HAD been having a much too exciting time. He had gone with the car, of course, crouching in the boot at the back, with a box of tools digging into him, and a can of petrol smelling horribly nearby, making him feel sick.

Through the gates went the car, and down the hill. It went at a good pace, and once stopped very suddenly. It had gone round a corner and almost collided with a stationary lorry, so that Mr Peiton had put the brake on in a hurry. Poor Richard was terrified. He bumped his head hard on the back of the boot and gave a groan.

He sat curled up, feeling sick and scared. He began to wish he had not tried to be a hero and get help. Being any kind of a hero was difficult – but this was a dreadful way of being heroic.

The car went on for some miles; Richard had no idea where it was going. At first he heard no other traffic at all – then he heard the sound of many wheels on the road, and knew he must be getting near a town. Once they must have gone by a railway station or railway line because Richard could distinctly hear the noise of a train, and then a loud hooting.

363

RICHARD HAS HIS OWN ADVENTURE

The car stopped at last. Richard listened intently. Was it stopping just for traffic lights – or was Mr Perton getting out? If so, that was his chance to escape!

He heard the car door slam. Ah, Mr Perton was out of the car then. Richard pressed hard at the cover of the boot. Julian had wedged it rather tightly, but it gave at last, and the lid of the boot opened. It fell back with rather a noise.

Richard looked out cautiously. He was in a dark street. A few people were walking on the pavement opposite. A lamp-post was some way away. Could he get out now – or would Mr Perton be about and see him?

He stretched out a leg to slide from the boot and jump to the ground – but he had been huddled up in an awkward position for so long that he was too stiff to move. Cramp caught him and he felt miserably uncomfortable as he tried to straighten himself out.

Instead of jumping out and taking to his heels at once, poor Richard had to go very slowly indeed. His legs and arms would *not* move quickly. He sat for a half-minute on the open boot-lid, trying to make up his mind to jump down.

And then he heard Mr Perton's voice! He was running down the steps of the house outside which he had parked the car. Richard was horrified. It hadn't dawned on him that he would come back so quickly.

He tried to jump from the boot-cover, and fell sprawling to the ground. Mr Perton heard him, and, thinking someone was trying to steal something from his car he rushed up to the boot.

Richard scrambled up just in time to get away from his outstretched hand. He ran to the other side of the road as fast as he could, hoping that his stiff, cramped legs wouldn't let him down. Mr Perton tore after him.

'Hey, you, stop! What are you doing in my car?' shouted Mr Perton. Richard dodged a passer-by and tore on, panic-stricken. He mustn't be caught; he mustn't be caught!

Mr Perton caught up with him just under the lamp-post. He grabbed Richard's collar and swung him round roughly. 'You let me go!' yelled Richard, and kicked Mr Perton's ankles so hard that he almost fell over.

Mr Perton recognised him! 'Good gracious – it's you!' he cried. 'The boy Rooky wants! What are you doing here? How did you . . . ?'

But with a last despairing struggle, Richard was off again, leaving his coat in Mr Perton's hands! His legs were feeling better now, and he could run faster.

He tore round the corner, colliding with another boy. He was off and away before the boy could even call out. Mr Perton also tore round the corner and collided with the same boy – who, however, was a bit quicker than before, and clutched Mr Perton by the coat, in a real rage at being so nearly knocked over again.

By the time Mr Perton had got himself free from the angry boy, Richard was out of sight. Mr Perton raced to the corner of the road, and looked up and down the poorly lit road. He gave an exclamation of anger.

'Lost him! Little pest – how did he get here? Could he have been at the back of the car? Ah, surely that's him over there!'

It was. Richard had hidden in a garden, but was now being driven out by the barking of a dog. In despair he tore out of the gate and began running again. Mr Perton tore after him.

Round another corner, panting hard. Round yet another, hoping that no passer-by would clutch at him and stop him. Poor Richard! He didn't feel at all heroic, and didn't enjoy it a bit either.

He stumbled round the next corner and came into the main street of the town – and there, opposite, was a lamp that had a very welcome word shining on the glass.

POLICE

Thankfully Richard stumbled up the steps and pushed open the police station door. He almost fell inside. There was a kind of waiting-room there with a policeman sitting at a table. He looked up in astonishment as Richard came in in such a hurry.

'Now then, what's all this?' he asked the boy.

Richard looked fearfully back at the door, expecting Mr Perton to come in at any moment. But he didn't. The door remained shut. Mr Perton was not going to visit any police station if he could help it – especially with Richard pouring out a most peculiar story!

Richard was panting so much that he couldn't say a word at first. Then it all came out. The policeman listened in amazement, and very soon stopped Richard's tale, and called a big burly man in, who proved to be a most important police inspector.

He made Richard tell his tale slowly and as clearly as he could. The boy was now feeling much better – in fact he was feeling quite proud of himself! To think he'd done it – escaped in the boot of the car, got out, managed to get away from Mr Perton, and arrive safely at the police station. Marvellous!

'Where's this Owl's Dene?' demanded the Inspector, and the constable nearby answered.

'Must be that old place on Owl's Hill, sir. You remember we once went there on some kind of police business, but it seemed to be all right. Run by a hunch-back and his sister for some man who is often away abroad – Perton, I think the name was.'

'That's right!' cried Richard. 'It was Mr Perton's car I came here in – a black Bentley.'

'Know the number?' said the Inspector, sharply.

'KMF 102,' said Richard at once.

'Good lad,' said the Inspector. He picked up a telephone and gave a few curt instructions for a police car to try to trace the Bentley immediately.

'So you're Richard Thurlow Kent,' he said. 'Your

mother is very upset and anxious about you. I'll see that she is telephoned straight away. You'd better be taken home now in a police car.'

'Oh but, sir, can't I go with you to Owl's Dene when you drive up there?' said Richard, deeply disappointed. 'You'll be going there, won't you? – because of all the others – Anne, Dick, George and Julian.'

'We'll be going all right,' said the Inspector, grimly. 'But you won't be with us. You've had enough adventures. You can go home and go to bed. You've done well to escape and come here. Quite the hero!'

Richard couldn't help feeling pleased – but how he wished he could race off to Owl's Dene with the police. What a marvellous thing it would be to march in with them and show Julian how well he had managed his part of the affair! Perhaps Julian would think better of him then.

The Inspector, however, was not having any boys in the cars that were to go to Owl's Dene, and Richard was taken off by the young constable, and told to wait till a car came to take him home.

The telephone rang, and the Inspector answered it. 'No trace of the Bentley? Right. Thanks.'

He spoke to the young constable. 'Didn't think they'd get him. He's probably raced back to Owl's Dene to warn the others.'

'We'll get there soon after!' said the constable with a grin. 'Our Wolseley's pretty well as fast as a Bentley!'

Mr Perton had indeed raced off, as soon as he saw Richard stumbling up the police station steps. He had gone back to his car at top speed, jumped in, slammed the door and raced away as fast as he could, feeling certain that the police would be on the look-out for KMF 102 immediately.

He tore dangerously round the corners, and hooted madly, making everyone leap out of the way. He was soon out in the country, and there he put on terrific speed, his powerful headlights picking out the dark country lanes for half a mile ahead.

As he came to the hill on which Owl's Dene stood, he hooted loudly. He wanted the gates opened quickly! Just as he got up to them they opened. Someone had heard his hooting signal – good! He raced up the drive and stopped at the front door. It opened as he jumped out. Rooky stood there, and two other men with him, all looking anxious.

'What's up, Perton? Why are you back so quickly?' called Rooky. 'Anything wrong?'

Mr Perton ran up the steps, shut the door and faced the three men in the hall.

'Do you know what's happened? That boy, Richard Kent, was in the car when I went out! See? Hidden in the back or in the boot, or somewhere! Didn't you miss him?'

'Yes,' said Rooky. 'Of course we missed him. Did you let him get away, Perton?'

'Well, seeing that I didn't know he was in hiding, and

had to leave the car to go in and see Ted, it was easy for him to get away!' said Mr Perton. 'He ran like a hare. I nearly grabbed him once, but he wriggled out of his coat. And as he ended up finally in the police station I decided to give up the chase and come back to warn you.'

'The police will be out here then, before you can say Jack Robinson,' shouted Rooky. 'You're a fool, Perton – you ought to have got that boy. There's our ransom gone west – and I was so glad to be able to get my hands on the little brute.'

'It's no good crying over spilt milk,' said Perton. 'What about Weston? Suppose the police find *him*. They're looking for him all right – the papers have been full of only two things the last couple of days – Disappearance of Richard Thurlow Kent and Escape from Prison of Solomon Weston! And we're mixed up with both these. Do you want to be shoved back into prison again, Rooky? You've only just come out, you know. What are we going to do?'

'We must think,' said Rooky, in a panic-stricken voice. 'Come in this room here. We must *think*.'

CHAPTER TWENTY

The secret room

THE FOUR children had heard the car come racing up the drive, and had heard Mr Perton's arrival. Julian went to the kitchen door, eager to find out what he could. If Mr Perton was back, then either Richard had played his part well, and had escaped – or he had been discovered, and had been brought back.

He heard every word of the excited talk out in the hall. Good, good good! – Richard had got away – and was even now telling his tale to the police. It surely wouldn't be very long before the police arrived at Owl's Dene then – and what surprising things they would find there!

He tiptoed out into the hall when he heard the men go into the room nearby. What were their plans! He hoped they would not vent their rage on him or the others. It was true they had Timmy, but in a real emergency Rooky would probably think nothing of shooting the dog straightaway.

Julian didn't at all like what he heard from the room where the men talked over their plans.

'I'm going to bang all those kids' heads together as hard as I can, to start with,' growled Rooky. 'That big boy – what's his name? – Julian or something – must have planned Richard Kent's escape – I'll give him a real good thrashing, the interfering little beast.'

'What about the sparklers, Rooky?' said another man's voice. 'We'd better put them in a safe hiding-place before the police arrive. We'll have to hurry.'

'Oh, it'll be some time before they find they can't open that gate,' said Rooky. 'And it'll take a little more time before they climb that wall. We'll have time to put the sparklers into the room with Weston. If *he's* safe there, they'll be safe too.'

'Sparklers!' thought Julian, excited. 'Those are diamonds – so they've got a haul of diamonds hidden somewhere. Whatever next?'

'Get them,' ordered Mr Perton. 'Take them to the secret room – and be quick about it, Rooky. The police may be here at any minute now.'

'We'll spin some tale about that kid Richard and his friends,' said the voice of a fourth man. 'We'll say they were caught trespassing, the lot of them, and kept here as a little punishment. Actually, if there's time, I think it would be best to let the rest of them go. After all – they don't *know* anything. They can't give away any secrets.'

Rooky didn't want to let them go. He had grim plans for them, but the others argued him over. 'All right,' he said sullenly. 'Let them go, then – if there's time! You take them down to the gate, Perton, and shove them out before the police arrive. They'll probably set off thankfully and get lost in the dark. So much the better.'

'You get the sparklers then, and see to them,' said Mr Perton, and Julian heard him getting up from his chair. The boy darted back to the kitchen.

It looked as if there would be nothing for it but to let themselves be led down to the gates and shoved out, and Julian decided that if that happened they would wait at the gateway till the police arrived. They wouldn't get lost in the dark, as Rooky hoped!

Mr Perton came into the kitchen. His eyes swept over the four children. Timmy growled.

'So you made a little plan, did you, and hid Richard in the car?' he said. 'Well, for that we're going to turn you all out into the night and you'll probably lose yourselves for days in the deserted countryside round here and I hope you do!'

374

Nobody said anything. Mr Perton aimed a blow at Julian, who ducked. Timmy sprang at the man, but George had hold of his collar, and he just missed snapping Mr Perton's arm in two!

'If that dog had stayed here a day longer I'd have shot him,' said Mr Perton, fiercely. 'Come on, all of you, get a move on.'

'Goodbye, Aggie,' said Anne. Aggie and Hunchy watched them go out of the kitchen door into the dark garden. Aggie looked very scared indeed. Hunchy spat after them and said something rude.

But, when they were half-way down the drive, there came the sound of cars roaring at top speed up the hill to the gates of Owl's Dene! Two cars, fast and powerful, with brilliant headlights. Police cars, without a doubt! Mr Perton stopped. Then he shoved the children roughly back towards the house. It was too late to set them free and hope they would lose themselves.

'You look out for Rooky,' he said to them. 'He goes mad when he's frightened – and he's going to be frightened now, with the police hammering at the gates!'

Julian and the others cautiously edged into the kitchen. They weren't going to risk meeting Rooky if they could help it. Nobody was there at all, not even Hunchy or Aggie. Mr Perton went through to the hall.

'Have you put those sparklers away?' he called, and a voice answered him: 'Yes. Weston's got them with him. They're OK. Did you get the kids out in time?'

'No – and the police are at the gates already,' growled Mr Perton.

A howl came from someone – probably Rooky. 'The police – already! If I had that kid Richard here I'd skin him alive. Wait till I've burnt a few letters I don't want found – then I'll go and get hold of the other kids. I'm going to put somebody through it for this, and I don't care who.'

'Don't be foolish, Rooky,' said Mr Perton's voice. 'Do you want to get yourself into trouble again through your violent temper? Leave the kids alone.'

Julian listened to all this and felt very uneasy indeed. He ought to hide the others. Even Timmy would be no protection if Rooky had a gun. But where could he hide them?

'Rooky will search the whole house from top to bottom if he loses his temper much more, and really makes up his mind to revenge himself on us,' thought Julian. 'What a pity there isn't another secret room – we could hide there and be safe!'

But even if there was one he didn't know of it. He heard Rooky go upstairs with the others. Now, if he and the other children were going to hide somewhere in safety, this was their chance. But WHERE could they hide?

An idea came to Julian – was it a brilliant one, or wasn't it? He couldn't make up his mind at first. Then he decided that brilliant or not they had got to try it.

He spoke to the others. 'We've got to hide. Rooky isn't safe when he's in a temper.'

'Where shall we hide?' said Anne, fearfully.

'In the secret room!' said Julian. They all gaped at him in amazement.

'But – but somebody else is already hidden there – you told us you saw him last night,' said George at last.

'I know. That can't be helped. He's the last person to give us away, if we share his hiding-place – he wouldn't want to be found himself!' said Julian. 'It will be a frightful squash, because the secret room is very, very small – but it's the safest place I can think of.'

'Timmy will have to come too,' said George firmly. Julian nodded.

'Of course. We may need him to protect us against the hidden man!' he said. 'He may be pretty wild at us all invading his hiding-place. We don't want to have him calling Rooky. We'll be all right once we're in the room, because Timmy will keep him quiet. And once we're in he won't call out because we'll tell him the police are here!'

'Fine,' said Dick. 'Let's go. Is the coast clear?'

'Yes. They're all upstairs for some reason or other,' said Julian. 'Probably destroying things they don't want found. Come on.'

Hunchy and Aggie were still not to be seen. They had probably heard what the scare was about and were hidden away themselves! Julian led the way quietly to the little study.

They stared at the big, solid wooden bookcase that

stretched from floor to ceiling. Julian went quickly to one shelf and emptied out the books. He felt for the knob.

There it was! He pulled it out, and the back panel of the shelf slid noiselessly downwards, leaving the large hole there, like a window into the secret room.

The children gasped. How strange! How very extraordinary! They blinked through the hole and saw the small room behind, lit by a little candle. They saw the hidden man too – and he saw them! He looked at them in the very greatest astonishment.

'Who are you?' he said, in a threatening voice. 'Who told you to open the panel? Where're Rooky and Perton?'

'We're coming through to join you,' said Julian quietly. 'Don't make a noise.'

He shoved George up first. She slid through the narrow opening sideways and landed feet-first on the floor. Timmy followed immediately, pushed through by Julian.

The man was up on his feet now, angry and surprised. He was a big burly fellow, with very small close-set eyes and a cruel mouth.

'Now, look here,' he began in a loud voice. 'I won't have this. Where's Perton? Hey, Per . . .'

'If you say another word I'll set my dog on you,' said George, at a sign from Julian. Timmy growled so ferociously that the man shrank back at once.

'I – I . . .' he began. Timmy growled again and bared all his magnificent teeth in a snarl. The man climbed up on the narrow bed and subsided, looking astonished and furious. Dick went through the opening next, then Anne. By that time the small room was uncomfortably crowded.

'I say,' said Julian, suddenly remembering something, 'I shall have to stay outside the room – because the books have got to be put back, otherwise Rooky will notice the shelf is empty and guess we're hiding in the secret room. Then we'll be at his mercy.'

'Oh, Ju, you must come in with us,' said Anne, frightened.

'I can't, Anne. I must shut the panel and put the books back,' said Julian. 'I can't risk your being discovered till the police have safely caught that madman Rooky! I shall be all right, don't you worry.'

'The police?' whispered the man in the secret room, his eyes almost falling out of his head. 'Are the police here?'

'At the gates,' answered Julian. 'So keep quiet if you don't want them on top of you at once!'

He pushed the knob. The panel slid back into place without a sound. Julian replaced the books on the shelf as fast as he could. Then he darted out of the study, so that the men would not even guess what he had been up to. He was very thankful that Rooky had kept away long enough for him to carry out his plan.

Where should he hide himself? How long would it take the police to get over the wall, or break down the great gates? Surely they would soon be here?

There came the sound of footsteps running down the

379

stairs. It was Rooky. He caught sight of Julian at once. 'Ah – there you are! Where are the others? I'll show you what . . .'

Rooky carried a whip in his hand and looked quite crazy. Julian was afraid. He darted back into the study and locked the door. Rooky began to hammer at it. Then such a crash came on the door that Julian guessed he was smashing it down with one of the hall chairs. The door would be down in a moment!

CHAPTER TWENTY-ONE

A very exciting finish!

JULIAN WAS a courageous boy, but just at that minute he felt very scared indeed. And what must the children hidden in the secret room beyond be thinking? Poor Anne must be feeling terrified at Rooky's shouts and the crashing on the door.

And then a really marvellous idea came to Julian. Why, oh why hadn't he thought of it before? He could open the gates himself for the police to come in! He knew how to do it – and there was the wheel nearby in the corner, that set the gate machinery working! Once he had the gates open it would not be more than a few minutes, surely, before the police were hammering at the front door.

Julian ran to the wheel-like handle. He turned it strongly. A grinding, whining noise came at once, as the machinery went into action.

Rooky was still crashing at the door with the heavy chair. Already he had broken in one panel of it. But when he suddenly heard the groaning of the machinery that opened the gates, he stopped in panic. The gates were being opened! The police would soon be there – he would be caught!

He forgot the beautiful stories he had arranged to tell,

forgot the plans that he and the others had made, forgot everything except that he must hide. He flung down the chair and fled.

Julian sat down in the nearest chair, his heart beating as if he had just been running a race. The gates were open – Rooky had fled – the police would soon be there! And, even as he sat thinking this, there came the sound of powerful cars roaring up the wide drive. Then the engines stopped, and car doors were thrown open.

Someone began to hammer at the front door. 'Open in the name of the law!' cried a loud voice, and then came another hammering.

Nobody opened the door. Julian unlocked the half-broken door of the study he was in, and peered cautiously into the hall. No one seemed to be about.

He raced to the front door, pulled back the bolts, and undid the heavy chain, afraid each moment that some of the men would come to punch him away. But they didn't.

The door was pushed open by the police, who swarmed in immediately. There were eight of them, and they looked surprised to see a boy there.

'Which boy's this?' said the Inspector.

'Julian, sir,' said Julian. 'I'm glad you've come. Things were getting pretty hot.'

'Where are the men?' asked the Inspector, walking right in.

'I don't know,' said Julian.

'Find them,' ordered the Inspector, and his men fanned

out up the hall. But before they could go into any room, a cool voice called to them from the end of the corridor.

'May I ask what all this is?'

It was Mr Perton, looking as calm as could be, smoking a cigarette. He stood at the door of his sitting-room, seeming quite unperturbed. 'Since when has a man's house been broken into for no reason at all?'

'Where are the rest of you?' demanded the Inspector.

'In here, Inspector,' drawled Mr Perton. 'We were having a little conference, and heard the hammering at the door. Apparently you got in somehow. I'm afraid you'll get into trouble for this.'

The Inspector advanced to the room where Mr Perton stood. He glanced into it.

'Aha – our friend Rooky, I see,' he said, genially. 'Only a day or two out of prison, Rooky, and you're mixed up in trouble again. Where's Weston?'

'I don't know what you mean,' said Rooky, sullenly. 'How should I know where he is? He was in prison last time I knew anything about him.'

'Yes. But he escaped,' said the Inspector. 'Somebody helped him, Rooky. Somebody planned his escape for him – friends of yours – and somebody knows where the diamonds are that he stole and hid. I've a guess that you're going to share them with him in return for getting your friends to help him. Where is Weston, Rooky?'

'I tell you I don't *know*,' repeated Rooky. 'Not here, if that's what you're getting at. You can search the whole house from top to bottom, if you like. Perton won't mind. Will you, Perton? Look for the sparklers, too, if you want to. I don't know anything about them.'

'Perton, we've suspected you for a long time,' said the Inspector, turning to Mr Perton, who was still calmly smoking his cigarette. 'We think you're at the bottom of all these prison escapes – that's why you bought this lonely old house, isn't it? – so that you could work from it undisturbed? You arrange the escapes, you arrange for a change of clothes, you arrange for a safe hiding-place till the man can get out of the country.'

'Utter nonsense,' said Mr Perton.

'And you only help criminals who have been known to do a clever robbery and hide the stuff before they're caught,' went on the Inspector, in a grim voice. 'So you know you'll make plenty of profit on your deals, Perton. Weston is here all right – and so are the diamonds. Where are they?'

'They're not here,' said Perton. 'You're at liberty to look and see. You won't get anything out of *me*, Inspector. I'm innocent.'

Julian had listened to all this in amazement. Why, they had fallen into the very middle of a nest of thieves and rogues! Well, *he* knew where Weston was – and the diamonds too! He stepped forward.

'Tell your story later, son,' said the Inspector. 'We've things to do now.'

'Well, sir, I can save you a lot of time,' said Julian. 'I

know where the hidden prisoner is – and the diamonds too!'

Rooky leapt to his feet with a howl. Mr Perton looked at Julian hard. The other men glanced uneasily at one another.

'You don't know anything!' shouted Rooky. 'You only came here yesterday.'

The Inspector regarded Julian gravely. He liked this boy with the quiet manners and honest eyes.

'Do you mean what you say?' he asked.

'Oh yes,' said Julian. 'Come with me, sir.'

He turned and went out of the room. Everyone crowded after him – police, Rooky and the others, but three of the policemen quietly placed themselves at the back.

Julian led them to the study. Rooky's face went purple, but Perton gave him a sharp nudge and he said nothing. Julian went to the bookcase and swept a whole shelf of books out at once.

Rooky gave a terrific yell and leapt at Julian. 'Stop that! What are you doing?'

Two policemen were on the infuriated Rooky at once. They dragged him back. Julian pulled out the knob and the panel slid noiselessly downwards, leaving a wide space in the wall behind.

From the secret room four faces gazed out – the faces of three children – and a man. Timmy was there too, but he was on the floor. For a few moments nobody said a single word. The ones in the hidden room were so surprised to see such a crowd of policemen looking in at them – and the ones in the study were filled with amazement to see so many children in the tiny room!

'WELL!' said the Inspector. 'Well, I'm blessed! And if that isn't Weston himself, large as life and twice as natural!'

Rooky began to struggle with the policemen. He seemed absolutely infuriated with Julian.

'That boy!' he muttered. 'Let me get at him. That boy!'

'Got the diamonds there, Weston?' asked the Inspector, cheerfully. 'May as well hand them over.' Weston was very pale indeed. He made no move at all. Dick reached under the narrow bed and pulled out a bag. 'Here they are,' he said, with a grin. 'Jolly good lot they feel – heavy as anything! Can we come out now, Ju?'

All three were helped out by policemen. Weston was handcuffed before he was brought out. Rooky found that he also had handcuffs on all of a sudden, and to Mr Perton's angry surprise he heard a click at his own wrists too!

'A very, very nice little haul,' said the Inspector, in his most genial voice, as he looked inside the bag. 'What happened to your prison clothes, Weston? That's a nice suit you've got on – but you weren't wearing that when you left prison.'

'I can tell you where they are,' said Julian, remembering. Everyone stared in amazement, except George and Anne, who also knew, of course.

'They're stuffed down a well belonging to an old

tumbledown shack in a lane between here and Middle-combe Woods,' said Julian. 'I could easily find it for you any time.'

Mr Perton stared at Julian as if he couldn't believe his ears. 'How do you know that?' he asked roughly. 'You can't know a thing like that!'

'I do know it,' said Julian. 'And what's more you took him a new suit of clothes, and arrived at the shack in your black Bentley, didn't you – KMF 102? I saw it.'

'That's got you, Perton,' said the Inspector, with a pleased smile. 'That's put you on the spot, hasn't it? Good boy, this – notices a whole lot of interesting things. I shouldn't be surprised if he joins the police force some day. We could do with people like him!'

Perton spat out his cigarette and stamped on it viciously, as if he wished he was stamping on Julian. Those children! If that idiot Rooky hadn't spotted Richard Kent and gone after him, none of this would have happened. Weston would have been safely hidden, the diamonds sold, Weston could have been sent abroad, and he, Perton, would have made a fortune. Now a pack of children had spoilt everything.

'Any other people in the house?' the Inspector asked Julian. 'You appear to be the one who knows more than anybody else, my boy – so perhaps you can tell me that.'

'Yes – Aggie and Hunchy,' said Julian, promptly. 'But don't be hard on Aggie, sir – she was awfully good to us, and she's terrified of Hunchy.'

'We'll remember what you say,' promised the Inspector. 'Search the house, men. Bring along Aggie and Hunchy too. We'll want them for witnesses, anyway. Leave two men on guard here. The rest of us will go.'

It needed the black Bentley as well as the two police cars to take everyone down the drive and on to the next town! The children's bicycles had to be left behind, as they could not be got on the cars anywhere. As it was, it was a terrific squash.

'You going home tonight?' the Inspector asked Julian. 'We'll run you back. What about your parents? Won't they be worried by all this?'

'They're away,' explained Julian. 'And we were on a cycling tour So they don't know. There's really nowhere we can go for the night.'

But there was! There was a message awaiting the Inspector to say that Mrs Thurlow Kent would be very pleased indeed if Julian and the others would spend the night with Richard. She wanted to hear about their extraordinary adventures.

'Right,' said Julian. 'That settles that. We'll go there – and anyway, I want to bang old Richard on the back. He turned out quite a hero after all!'

'You'll have to stay around for a few days,' said the Inspector. 'We'll want you, I expect – you've a very fine tale to tell, and you've been a great help.'

'We'll stay around then,' said Julian. 'And if you could manage to have our bikes collected, sir, I'd be very grateful.'

Richard was at the front door to meet them all, although by now it was very late indeed. He was dressed in clean clothes and looked very spruce beside the dirty, bedraggled company of children that he went to greet.

'I wish I'd been in at the last!' he cried. 'I was sent off home, and I was wild. Mother – and Dad – here are the children I went off with.'

Mr Thurlow Kent had just come back from America. He shook hands with all of them. 'Come along in,' he said. 'We've got a fine spread for you – you must be ravenous!'

'Tell me what happened, tell me at once,' demanded Richard.

'We simply *must* have a bath first,' protested Julian. 'We're filthy.'

'Well, you can tell me while you're having a bath,' said Richard. 'I can't wait to hear!'

It was lovely to have hot baths and to be given clean clothes. George was solemnly handed out shorts like the boys, and the others grinned to see that both Mr and Mrs Kent thought she was a boy. George, of course, grinned too, and didn't say a word.

'I was very angry with Richard when I heard what he had done,' said Mr Kent, when they were all sitting at table, eating hungrily. 'I'm ashamed of him.'

Richard looked downcast at once. He gazed beseechingly at Julian.

'Yes – Richard made a fool of himself,' said Julian. 'And landed us all into trouble. He wants taking in hand, sir.'

A VERY EXCITING FINISH!

Richard looked even more downcast. He went very red, and looked at the table-cloth.

'But,' said Julian, 'he more than made up for his silliness, sir – he offered to squash himself into the boot of the car, and escape that way, and go and warn the police. That took some doing, believe me! I think quite a bit of Richard now!'

He leant over and gave the boy a pat on the back. Dick and the others followed it up with thumps, and Timmy woofed in his deepest voice.

Richard was now red with pleasure. 'Thanks,' he said, awkwardly. 'I'll remember this.'

'See you do, my boy!' said his father. 'It might all have ended very differently!'

'But it didn't,' said Anne happily. 'It ended like this. We can all breathe again!'

'Till the next time,' said Dick, with a grin. 'What do *you* say, Timmy, old boy?'

'Woof,' said Timmy, of course, and thumped his tail on the floor. 'WOOF!'

Five Fall
Into Adventure

CONTENTS

CHAPTER ONE

At Kirrin Cottage again

GEORGINA WAS at the station to meet her three cousins. Timmy her dog was with her, his long tail wagging eagerly. He knew quite well they had come to meet Julian, Dick and Anne, and he was glad. It was much more fun when the Five were all together.

'Here comes the train, Timmy!' said George. Nobody called her Georgina, because she wouldn't answer if they did. She looked like a boy with her short curly hair and her jeans and open-necked shirt. Her face was covered with freckles, and her legs and arms were as brown as a traveller's.

There was the far-off rumble of a train, and as it came nearer, a short warning hoot. Timmy whined and wagged his tail. He didn't like trains, but he wanted this one to come.

Nearer and nearer it came, slowing down as it reached Kirrin station. Long before it came to the little platform three heads appeared out of one of the windows, and three hands waved wildly. George waved back, her face one big smile.

The door swung open almost before the train stopped. Out came a big boy, and helped down a small girl. Then came another boy, not quite so tall as the first one, with a bag in each hand. He dragged a third bag out, and then George and Timmy were on him.

'Julian! Dick! Anne! Your train's late; we thought you were never coming!'

'Hallo, George! Here we are at last. Get down, Timmy, don't eat me.'

'Hallo, George! Oh, Timmy, you darling – you're just as licky as ever!'

'Woof,' said Timmy joyfully, and bounded all round like a mad thing, getting into everybody's way.

'Any trunk or anything?' asked George. 'Only those three bags?'

'Well, we haven't come for long this time, worse luck,' said Dick. 'Only a fortnight! Still, it's better than nothing.'

'You shouldn't have gone off to France all those six weeks,' said George, half-jealously. 'I suppose you've gone all French now.'

Dick laughed, waved his hands in the air and went off into a stream of quick French that sounded just like gibberish to George. French was not one of her strong subjects.

'Shut up,' she said, giving him a friendly shove. 'You're just the same old idiot. Oh, I'm so glad you've come. It's been lonely and dull at Kirrin without you.'

A porter came up with a barrow. Dick turned to him, waved his hands again, and addressed the astonished man in fluent French. But the porter knew Dick quite well.

'Go on with you,' he said. 'Argy-bargying in double-Dutch like that. Do you want me to wheel these up to Kirrin Cottage for you?'

'Yes, please,' said Anne. 'Stop it, Dick. It isn't funny when you go on so long.'

'Oh, let him go on,' said George, and she linked her

arms in Anne's and Dick's. 'It's lovely to have you again. Mother's looking forward to seeing you all.'

'I bet Uncle Quentin isn't,' said Julian, as they went along the little platform, Timmy capering round them.

'Father's in quite a good temper,' said George. 'You know he's been to America with Mother, lecturing and hearing other scientists lecturing too. Mother says everyone made a great fuss of him, and he liked it.'

George's father was a brilliant scientist, well-known all over the world. But he was rather a difficult man at home, impatient, hot-tempered and forgetful. The children were fond of him, but held him in great respect. They all heaved a sigh of relief when he went away for a few days, for then they could make as much noise as they liked, tear up and down the stairs, play silly jokes and generally be as mad as they pleased.

'Will Uncle Quentin be at home all the time we're staying with you?' asked Anne. She was really rather afraid of her hot-tempered uncle.

'No,' said George. 'Mother and Father are going away for a tour in Spain – so we'll be on our own.'

'Wizard!' said Dick. 'We can wear our bathing costumes all day long then if we want to.'

'And Timmy can come in at meal-times without being sent out whenever he moves,' said George. 'He's been sent out every single meal-time this week, just because he snapped at the flies that came near him. Father goes absolutely mad if Timmy suddenly snaps at a fly.'

'Shame!' said Anne, and patted Timmy's rough-haired back. 'You can snap at every single fly you like, Timmy, when we're on our own.'

'Woof,' said Timmy, gratefully.

'There won't be time for any adventure these hols,' said Dick, regretfully, as they walked down the lane to Kirrin Cottage. Red poppies danced along the way, and in the distance the sea shone as blue as cornflowers. 'Only two weeks – and back we go to school! Well, let's hope the weather keeps fine. I want to bathe six times a day!'

Soon they were all sitting round the tea-table at Kirrin Cottage, and their Aunt Fanny was handing round plates of her nicest scones and tea-cake. She was very pleased to see her nephews and niece again.

'Now George will be happy,' she said, smiling at the hungry four. 'She's been going about like a bear with a sore head the last week or two. Have another scone, Dick? Take two while you're about it.'

'Good idea,' said Dick, and helped himself. 'Nobody makes scones and cakes like you do, Aunt Fanny. Where's Uncle Quentin?'

'In his study,' said his aunt. 'He knows it's tea-time, and he's heard the bell, but I expect he's buried in something or other. I'll have to fetch him in a minute. I honestly believe he'd go without food all day long if I didn't go and drag him into the dining-room!'

'Here he is,' said Julian, hearing the familiar impatient footsteps coming down the hall to the dining-room. The

401

door was flung open. Uncle Quentin stood there, a newspaper in his hand, scowling. He didn't appear to see the children at all.

'Look here, Fanny!' he shouted. 'See what they've put in this paper – the very thing I gave orders was NOT to be put in! The dolts! the idiots! The . . .'

'Quentin! Whatever's the matter?' said his wife. 'Look – here are the children – they've just arrived.'

But Uncle Quentin simply didn't see any of the four children at all. He went on glaring at the paper. He rapped at it with his hand.

'*Now* we'll get the place full of reporters wanting to see me, and wanting to know all about my new ideas!' he said, beginning to shout. 'See what they've said! "This eminent scientist conducts all his experiments and works out all his ideas at his home, Kirrin Cottage. Here are his stack of notebooks, to which are now added two more – fruits of his visit to America, and here at his cottage are his amazing diagrams," and so on and so on.

'I tell you, Fanny, we'll have hordes of reporters down.'

'No, we shan't, dear,' said his wife. 'And, anyway, we are soon off to Spain. Do sit down and have some tea. And look, can't you say a word to welcome Julian, Dick and Anne?'

Uncle Quentin grunted and sat down. 'I didn't know they were coming,' he said, and helped himself to a scone. 'You might have told me, Fanny.'

'I told you three times yesterday and twice today,' said his wife.

Anne suddenly squeezed her uncle's arm. She was sitting next to him. 'You're just the same as ever, Uncle Quentin,' she said. 'You never, never remember we're coming! Shall we go away again?'

Her uncle looked down at her and smiled. His temper never lasted very long. He grinned at Julian and Dick. 'Well, here you are again!' he said. 'Do you think you can hold the fort for me while I'm away with your aunt?'

'You bet!' said all three together.

'We'll keep everyone at bay!' said Julian. 'With Timmy's help. I'll put up a notice: "*Beware, very fierce dog*".'

'Woof,' said Timmy, sounding delighted. He thumped

his tail on the floor. A fly came by his nose and he snapped at it. Uncle Quentin frowned.

'Have another scone, Father?' said George hurriedly. 'When are you and Mother going to Spain?'

'Tomorrow,' said her mother firmly. 'Now, don't look like that, Quentin. You know perfectly well it's been arranged for weeks, and you *need* a holiday, and if we don't go tomorrow all our arrangements will be upset.'

'Well, you might have *warned* me it was tomorrow,' said her husband, looking indignant. 'I mean – I've all my notebooks to check and put away, and . . .'

'Quentin, I've told you heaps of times that we leave on September the third,' said his wife, still more firmly. '*I* want a holiday, too. The four children will be quite all right here with Timmy – they'll love being on their own. Julian is almost grown-up now and he can cope with anything that turns up.'

Timmy snapped twice at a fly, and Uncle Quentin jumped. 'If that dog does that again,' he began, but his wife interrupted him at once.

'There, you see! You're as touchy and nervy as can be, Quentin, dear. It will do you good to get away – and the children will have a lovely two weeks on their own. Nothing can possibly happen, so make up your mind to leave tomorrow with an easy mind!'

Nothing can possibly happen? Aunt Fanny was wrong of course. *Anything* could happen when the Five were left on their own!

404

CHAPTER TWO

A meeting on the beach

IT REALLY was very difficult to get Uncle Quentin off the next day. He was shut up in his study until the last possible moment, sorting out his precious notebooks. The taxi arrived and hooted outside the gate. Aunt Fanny, who had been ready for a long time, went and rapped at the study door.

'Quentin! Unlock the door! You really must come. We shall miss the plane if we don't go now.'

'Just one minute!' shouted back her husband. Aunt Fanny looked at the four children in despair.

'That's the fourth time he's called out "Just one minute",' said George. The telephone shrilled out just then, and she picked up the receiver.

'Yes,' she said. 'No, I'm afraid you can't see him. He's off to Spain, and nobody will know where he is for the next two weeks. What's that? Wait a minute – I'll ask my mother.'

'Who is it?' said her mother.

'It's the *Daily Clarion*,' said George. 'They want to send a reporter down to interview Daddy. I told them he was going to Spain – and they said could they publish that?'

'Of course,' said her mother, thankfully. 'Once that's in

405

the papers nobody will ring up and worry you. Say, yes, George.'

George said yes, the taxi hooted more loudly than ever, and Timmy barked madly at the hooting. The study door was flung open and Uncle Quentin stood in the doorway, looking as black as thunder.

'Why can't I have a little peace and quiet when I'm doing important work?' he began. But his wife made a dart at him and dragged him down the hall. She put his hat in one hand, and would have put his stick into the other if he hadn't been carrying a heavy despatch case.

'You're not doing important work, you're off on a holiday,' she said. 'Oh, Quentin, you're worse than ever! What's that case in your hand? Surely you are not taking work away with you?'

The taxi hooted again, and Timmy woofed just behind Uncle Quentin. He jumped violently, and the telephone rang loudly.

'That's another reporter coming down to see you, Father,' said George. 'Better go quickly!'

Whether that bit of news really did make Uncle Quentin decide at last to go, nobody knew – but in two seconds he was sitting in the taxi, still clutching his despatch case, telling the taxi-driver exactly what he thought of people who kept hooting their horns.

'Goodbye, dears,' called Aunt Fanny, thankfully. 'Don't get into mischief. We're off at last.'

The taxi disappeared down the lane. 'Poor Mother!'

said George. 'It's always like this when they go for a holiday. Well, there's one thing certain – I shall NEVER marry a scientist.'

Everyone heaved a sigh of relief at the thought that Uncle Quentin was gone. When he was over-worked he really was impossible.

'Still, you simply have to make excuses for anyone with a brain like his,' said Julian. 'Whenever our science master at school speaks of him, he almost holds his breath with awe. Worst of it is, he expects *me* to be brilliant because I've got a brilliant uncle.'

'Yes. It's difficult to live up to clever relations,' said Dick. 'Well – we're on our own, except for Joanna. Good old Joanna! I bet she'll give us some smashing meals.'

'Let's go and see if she's got anything we can have now,' said George. 'I'm hungry.'

'So am I,' said Dick. They marched down the hall into the kitchen, calling for Joanna.

'Now, you don't need to tell me what you've come for,' said Joanna, the smiling, good-tempered cook. 'And I don't need to tell you this – the larder's locked.'

'Oh, Joanna – what a mean thing to do!' said Dick.

'Mean or not, it's the only thing to do when all four of you are around, to say nothing of that great hungry dog,' said Joanna, rolling out some pastry vigorously. 'Why, last holidays I left a meat pie and half a tongue and a cherry tart and trifle sitting on the shelves for the next

407

day's meals – and when I came back from my half-day's outing there wasn't a thing to be seen.'

'Well, we thought you'd left them there for our supper,' said Julian, sounding quite hurt.

'All right – but you won't get the chance of thinking anything like that again,' said Joanna, firmly. 'That larder door's going to be kept locked. Maybe I'll unlock it sometimes and hand you out a snack or two – but I'm the one that's going to unlock it, not you.'

The four drifted out of the kitchen again, disappointed. Timmy followed at their heels. 'Let's go down and have a bathe,' said Dick. 'If I'm going to have six bathes a day, I'd better hurry up and have my first one.'

'I'll get some ripe plums,' said Anne. 'We can take those down with us. And I expect the ice-cream man will come along to the beach too. We shan't starve! And we'd better wear our shirts and jeans over our bathing costumes, so we don't catch too much sun.'

Soon they were all down on the sand. They found a good place and scraped out comfortable holes to sit in. Timmy scraped his own.

'I can't imagine why Timmy bothers to scrape one,' said George. 'Because he always squeezes into mine sooner or later. Don't you, Timmy?'

Timmy wagged his tail, and scraped so violently that they were all covered with sand. 'Pooh!' said Anne, spitting sand out of her mouth. 'Stop it, Timmy. As fast as I scrape my hole, you fill it up!'

A MEETING ON THE BEACH

Timmy paused to give her a lick, and then scraped again, making a very deep hole indeed. He lay down in it, panting, his mouth looking as if he were smiling.

'He's smiling again,' said Anne. 'I never knew a dog that smiled like Timmy. Timmy, it's nice to have you again.'

'Woof,' said Timmy, politely, meaning that it was nice to have Anne and the others back again, too. He wagged his tail and sent a shower of sand over Dick.

They all wriggled down comfortably into their soft warm holes. 'We'll eat the plums first and then we'll have a bathe,' said Dick. 'Chuck me one, Anne.'

Two people came slowly along the beach. Dick looked at them out of half-closed eyes. A boy and a man – and what a ragamuffin the boy looked! He wore torn dirty jeans and a filthy jersey.

The man looked even worse. He slouched as he came, and dragged one foot. He had a straggly moustache and mean, clever little eyes that raked the beach up and down. The two were walking at the high-water mark and were obviously looking for anything that might have been cast up by the tide. The boy already had an old box, one wet shoe and some wood under his arm.

'What a pair!' said Dick to Julian. 'I hope they don't come near us. I feel as if I can smell them from here.'

The two walked along the beach and then back. Then, to the children's horror, they made a bee-line for where they were lying in their sandy holes, and sat down close beside them. Timmy growled.

The boy took no notice of Timmy's growling. But the man looked uneasy.

'Come on – let's have a bathe,' said Julian, annoyed at the way the two had sat down so close to them. After all, there was practically the whole of the beach to choose from – why come and sit almost on top of somebody else?

When they came back from their bathe the man had gone, but the boy was still there – and he had actually sat himself down in George's hole.

'Get out,' said George, shortly, her temper rising at once. 'That's my hole, and you jolly well know it.'

'Finders keepers,' said the boy, in a curious sing-song voice. 'It's my hole now.'

George bent down and pulled the boy roughly out of the hole. He was up in a trice, his fists clenched. George clenched hers, too.

Dick came up at a run. 'Now, George – if there's any fighting to be done, I'll do it,' he said. He turned to the scowling boy. 'Clear off! We don't want you here!'

The boy hit out with his right fist and caught Dick unexpectedly on the jawbone. Dick looked astounded. He hit out, too, and sent the tousle-headed boy flying.

'Yah, coward!' said the boy, holding his chin tenderly. 'Hitting someone smaller than yourself! I'll fight that first boy, but I won't fight *you*.'

'You can't fight him,' said Dick. 'He's a girl. You can't fight girls – and girls oughtn't to fight, anyway.'

'Says you!' said the dirty little ragamuffin, standing up

and doubling his fists again. 'Well, you look here – *I'm* a girl, too – so I can fight her all right, can't I?'

George and the ragamuffin stood scowling at one another, each with fists clenched. They looked so astonishingly alike, with their short, curly hair, brown freckled faces and fierce expressions that Julian suddenly roared with laughter. He pushed them firmly apart.

'Fighting's forbidden!' he said. He turned to the ragamuffin. 'Clear off!' he ordered. 'Do you hear me? Go on – off with you!'

The girl stared at him. Then she suddenly burst into tears and ran off howling.

'*She's* a girl all right,' said Dick, grinning at the howls. 'She's got some spunk though, facing up to me like that. Well, that's the last we'll see of *her*!'

But he was wrong. It wasn't!

CHAPTER THREE

Face at the window

THE FIVE curled up in their holes once more. Dick felt his jawbone. 'That ragamuffin of a girl gave me a good bang,' he said, half-admiringly. 'Little demon, isn't she! A bit of a live wire!'

'I can't see why Julian wouldn't let me have a go at her,' said George sulkily. 'It was my hole she sat in – she *meant* to be annoying! How dare she?'

'You can't go about fighting,' said Dick. 'Don't be an ass, George. I know you make out you're as tough as a boy, and you dress like a boy and climb trees – but it's really time you gave up thinking you're a boy.'

This sort of speech didn't please George at all. 'Well, anyway, I don't burst into howls if I'm beaten,' she said, turning her back on Dick.

'No, you don't,' agreed Dick. 'You've got as much spunk as any boy – much more than that other kid had. I'm sorry I sent her flying now. It's the first time I've ever hit a girl, and I hope it'll be the last.'

'I'm jolly glad you hit her,' said George. 'She's a nasty little beast. If I see her again I'll tell her what I think of her.'

'No, you won't,' said Dick. 'Not if I'm there, anyway. She had her punishment when I sent her flying.'

412

'Do shut up arguing, you two,' said Anne, and sent a shower of sand over them. 'George, don't go into one of your moods, for goodness' sake – we don't want to waste a single day of this two weeks.'

'Here's the ice-cream man,' said Julian, sitting up and feeling for the waterproof pocket in the belt of his bathing trunks. 'Let's have one each.'

'Woof,' said Timmy, and thumped his tail on the sand.

'Yes, all right – one for you, too,' said Dick. 'Though what sense there is in giving *you* one, I don't know. One lick, one swallow, and it's gone. It might be a fly for all you taste of it.'

Timmy gulped his ice-cream down at once and then went into George's hole, squeezing beside her, hoping for a lick of her ice, too. But she pushed him away.

'No, Timmy. Ice-cream's wasted on you! You can't even have a lick of mine. And do get back into your hole – you're making me frightfully hot.'

Timmy obligingly got out and went into Anne's hole. She gave him a little bit of her ice-cream. He sat panting beside her, looking longingly at the rest of the ice. 'You're melting it with your hot breath,' said Anne. 'Go into Julian's hole now!'

The five of them had a thoroughly lazy morning. As none of them had a watch they went in far too early for lunch, and were shooed out again by Joanna.

'How you can come in at ten past twelve for a one

o'clock lunch, I don't know!' she scolded. 'I haven't even finished the housework yet.'

'Well – it *felt* like one o'clock,' said Anne, disappointed to find there was so long to wait. Still, when lunch-time came, Joanna really did them well.

'Cold ham and tongue – cold baked beans – beetroot – crisp lettuce straight from the garden – heaps of tomatoes – cucumber – hard-boiled egg!' recited Anne in glee.

'Just the kind of meal I like,' said Dick, sitting down. 'What's for pudding?'

'There it is on the sideboard,' said Anne. 'Wobbly blancmange, fresh fruit salad and jelly. I'm glad I'm hungry.'

'Now, don't you give Timmy any of that ham and tongue,' Joanna warned George. 'I've got a fine bone for him. Coming, Timmy?'

Timmy knew the word 'bone' very well indeed. He trotted after Joanna at once, his feet sounding loudly in the hall. They heard Joanna talking kindly to him in the kitchen as she found him his bone.

'Good old Joanna,' said Dick. 'She's like Timmy – her bark is worse than her bite.'

'Timmy's got a good bite, though,' said George, helping herself to three tomatoes at once. 'And his bite came in useful heaps of times for us.'

They ate steadily, thinking of some of the hair-raising adventures they had had, when Timmy and his bite had certainly come in very useful. Timmy came in after a while, licking his lips.

'Nothing doing, old chap,' said Dick, looking at the empty dishes on the table. 'Don't tell me you've chomped up that bone already!'

Timmy had. He lay down under the table, and put his nose on his paws. He was happy. He had had a good meal, and he was with the people he loved best. He put his head as near George's feet as he could.

'Your whiskers are tickling me,' she said, and screwed up her bare toes. 'Pass the tomatoes, someone.'

'You *can't* manage any more tomatoes, surely!' said Anne. 'You've had five already.'

'They're out of my own garden,' said George, 'so I can eat as many as I like.'

After lunch they lazed on the beach till it was time for a bathe again. It was a happy day for all of them – warm, lazy, with plenty of running and romping about.

George looked out for the ragamuffin girl, but she didn't appear again. George was half sorry. She would have liked a battle of words with her, even if she couldn't have a fight!

They were all very tired when they went to bed that night. Julian yawned so loudly when Joanna came in with a jug of hot cocoa and some biscuits that she offered to lock up the house for him.

'Oh, no, thank you, Joanna,' said Julian at once. 'That's the man's job, you know, locking up the house. You can trust me all right. I'll see to every window and every door.'

'Right, Julian,' said Joanna, and bustled away to wind up the kitchen clock, rake out the fire, and go up to bed. The children went up, too, Timmy, as usual, at George's heels. Julian was left downstairs to lock up.

He was a very responsible boy. Joanna knew that he wouldn't leave a single window unfastened. She heard him trying to shut the little window in the pantry, and she called down:

'Julian! It's swollen or something, and won't shut properly. You needn't bother about it, it's too small for anyone to get into!'

'Right!' said Julian, thankfully, and went upstairs. He yawned a terrific yawn again, and set Dick off, too, as soon as he came into the bedroom they both shared. The girls, undressing in the next room, laughed to hear them.

'*You* wouldn't hear a burglar in the middle of the night, Julian and Dick!' called Anne. 'You'll sleep like logs!'

'Old Timmy can listen out for burglars,' said Julian, cleaning his teeth vigorously. 'That's his job, not mine. Isn't it, Timmy?'

'Woof,' said Timmy, clambering on to George's bed. He always slept curled up in the crook of her knees. Her mother had given up trying to insist that George didn't have Timmy on her bed at night. As George said, even if *she* agreed to that, Timmy wouldn't!

Nobody stayed awake for more than five seconds. Nobody even said anything in bed, except for a sleepy

416

good-night. Timmy gave a little grunt and settled down, too, his head on George's feet. It was heavy, but she liked it there. She put out a hand and stroked Timmy gently. He licked one of her feet through the bed-clothes. He loved George more than anyone in the world.

It was dark outside that night. Thick clouds had come up and put out all the stars. There was no sound to be heard but the wind in the trees and the distant surge of the sea – and both sounded so much the same that it was hard to tell the difference.

Not another sound – not even an owl hooting to its mate, or the sound of a hedgehog pattering in the ditch.

Then why did Timmy wake up? Why did he open first one eye and then another? Why did he prick up his ears and lie there, listening? He didn't even lift his head at first. He simply lay listening in the darkness.

He lifted his head cautiously at last. He slid off the bed as quietly as a cat. He padded across the room and out of the door. Down the stairs he went, and into the hall, where his claws rattled on the tiled floor. But nobody heard him. Everyone in the house was fast asleep.

Timmy stood and listened in the hall. He knew he had heard something. Could it have been a rat somewhere? Timmy lifted his nose and sniffed.

And then he stiffened from head to tail, and stood as if turned into stone. Something was climbing up the wall of the house. Scrape, scrape, scrape – rustle, rustle! Would a rat dare to do that?

Upstairs, in her bed, Anne didn't know why she suddenly woke up just then, but she did. She was thirsty, and she thought she would get a drink of water. She felt for her torch, and switched it on.

The light fell on the window first, and Anne saw something that gave her a terrible shock. She screamed loudly, and dropped her torch in fright. George woke up at once. Timmy came bounding up the stairs.

'Julian!' wailed Anne. 'Come quickly. I saw a face at the window, a horrible, dreadful face looking in at me!'

418

George rushed to the window, switching on her torch as she did so. There was nothing there. Timmy went with her. He sniffed at the open window and growled.

'Listen – I can hear someone running quickly down the path,' said Julian, who now appeared with Dick. 'Come on, Timmy – downstairs with you and after them!'

And down they all went – Anne too. They flung the front door wide and Timmy sped out, barking loudly. A face at the window? He'd soon find out who it belonged to!

CHAPTER FOUR

The next day

THE FOUR children waited at the open front door, listening to Timmy's angry, excited barking. Anne was trembling, and Julian put his arm round her comfortingly.

'What was this dreadful face like?' he asked her. Anne shivered in his arm.

'I didn't see very much,' she said. 'You see, I just switched on my torch, and the beam was directed on the window nearby – and it lit up the face for a second. It had nasty gleaming eyes – oh, I *was* frightened!'

'Then did it disappear?' asked Julian.

'I don't know,' said Anne. 'I was so frightened that I dropped my torch and the light went out. Then George woke up and rushed to the window.'

'Where on earth was Timmy?' said Dick, feeling suddenly surprised that Timmy hadn't awakened them all by barking. Surely he must have heard the owner of the face climbing up to the window?

'I don't know. He came rushing into the bedroom when I screamed,' said Anne. 'Perhaps he *had* heard a noise and had gone down to see what it was.'

'That's about it,' said Julian. 'Never mind, Anne. It was a tramp, I expect. He found all the doors and windows downstairs fastened – and shinned up the ivy to see if he could enter by way of a bedroom. Timmy will get him, that's certain.'

But Timmy didn't get him. He came back after a time, with his tail down, and a puzzled look in his eyes. 'Couldn't you find him, Timmy?' said George, anxiously.

'Woof,' said Timmy, mournfully, his tail still down. George felt him. He was wet through.

'Goodness! Where have you been to get so wet?' she said, in surprise. 'Feel him, Dick.'

Dick felt him, and so did the others. 'He's been in the sea,' said Julian. 'That's why he's wet. I guess the burglar, or whatever he was, must have sprinted down to the beach, when he knew Timmy was after him and jumped into a boat! It was his only chance of getting away.'

'And Timmy must have swum after him till he couldn't keep up any more,' said George. 'Poor old Tim. So you lost him, did you?'

Timmy wagged his tail a little. He looked very down-hearted indeed. To think he had heard noises and thought it was a rat – and now, whoever it was had got away from him. Timmy felt ashamed.

Julian shut and bolted the front door. He put up the chain, too. 'I don't think the Face will come back again in a hurry,' he said. 'Now he knows there's a big dog here he'll keep away. I don't think we need worry any more.'

They all went back to bed again. Julian didn't go to sleep for some time. Although he had told the others not to worry, he felt worried himself. He was sorry that Anne had been frightened, and somehow the boldness of the burglar in climbing up to a bedroom worried him, too. He must have been determined to get in somehow.

Joanna, the cook, slept through all the disturbance. Julian wouldn't wake her. 'No,' he said, 'don't tell her anything about it. She'd want to send telegrams to Uncle Quentin or something.'

So Joanna knew nothing about the night's happenings, and they heard her cheerfully humming in the kitchen the next morning as she cooked bacon and eggs and tomatoes for their breakfast.

Anne was rather ashamed of herself when she woke up and remembered the fuss she had made. The Face was rather dim in her memory now. She half wondered if she had dreamt it all. She asked Julian if he thought she might have had a bad dream.

'Quite likely,' said Julian, cheerfully, very glad that Anne should think this. 'More than likely! I wouldn't worry about it any more, if I were you.'

He didn't tell Anne that he had examined the thickly-growing ivy outside the window, and had found clear traces of the night-climber. Part of the sturdy clinging ivy-stem had come away from the wall, and beneath the window were strewn broken-off ivy leaves. Julian showed them to Dick.

'There *was* somebody,' he said. 'What a nerve he had, climbing right up to the window like that. A real cat-burglar!'

THE NEXT DAY

There were no footprints to be seen anywhere in the garden. Julian didn't expect to find any, for the ground was dry and hard.

The day was very fine and warm again. 'I vote we do what we did yesterday – go off to the beach and bathe,' said Dick. 'We might take a picnic lunch if Joanna will give us one.'

'I'll help her to make it up for us,' said Anne, and she and George went off to beg for sandwiches and buns. Soon they were busy wrapping up a colossal lunch.

'Do for twelve, I should think!' said Joanna, with a laugh. 'Here's a bottle of home-made lemonade, too. You can take as many ripe plums as you like as well. I shan't prepare any supper for you tonight – you'll not need it after this lunch.'

George and Anne looked at her in alarm. No *supper*! Then they caught the twinkle in her eye and laughed.

'We'll make all the beds and do our rooms before we go,' said Anne. 'And is there anything you want from the village?'

'No, not today. You hurry up with your jobs and get along to the beach,' said Joanna. 'I'll be quite glad of a peaceful day to myself. I shall turn out the larder and the hall cupboards and the scullery, and enjoy myself in peace!'

Anne seemed quite to have forgotten her fright of the night before as they went down to the beach that day, chattering and laughing together. Even if she *had* thought

423

about it, something soon happened that swept everything else from her mind.

The little ragamuffin girl was down on the beach again! She was alone. Her dreadful old father, or whatever he was, was not there.

George saw the girl first and scowled. Julian saw the scowl and then the girl, and made up his mind at once. He led the others firmly to where rocks jutted up from the beach, surrounded by limpid rock-pools.

'We'll be here today,' he said. 'It's so hot we'll be glad of the shade from the rocks. What about just here?'

'It's all right,' said George, half sulky and half amused at Julian for being so firm about things. 'Don't worry. I'm not having anything more to do with that smelly girl.'

'I'm glad to hear it,' said Julian. They had now turned a corner, and were out of sight of the girl. Big rocks ran in an upwards direction behind them, and jutted up all around them. Julian sat down in a lovely little corner, with rocks protecting them from the sun and the wind.

'Let's have a read before we bathe,' said Dick. 'I've got a mystery story here. I simply MUST find out who the thief is.'

He settled himself comfortably. Anne went to look for sea anemones in the pool. She liked the petal-like creatures that looked so like plants and weren't. She liked feeding them with bits of biscuit, seeing their 'petals' close over the fragments and draw them quickly inside.

George lay back and stroked Timmy. Julian began to

sketch the rocks around, and the little pools. It was all very peaceful indeed.

Suddenly something landed on George's middle and made her jump. She sat up, and so did Timmy.

'What was that?' said George indignantly. 'Did you throw something at me, Dick?'

'No,' said Dick, his eyes glued to his book.

Something else hit George on the back of the neck, and she put her hand up with an exclamation. 'What's happening? Who's throwing things?'

She looked to see what had hit her. Lying on the sand was a small roundish thing. George picked it up. 'Why – it's a damson stone,' she said. And 'Ping'! Another one hit her on the shoulder. She leapt up in a rage.

She could see nobody at all. She waited for another damson stone to appear, but none did.

'I just wish I could draw your face, George,' said Julian, with a grin. 'I never saw such a frown in my life. Ooch!'

The 'ooch!' was nothing to do with George's frown; it was caused by another damson stone that caught Julian neatly behind the ear. He leapt to his feet too. A helpless giggle came from behind a rock some way behind and above them. George was up on the ledge in a second.

Behind one of the rocks sat the ragamuffin girl. Her pockets were full of damsons, some of them spilling out as she rolled on the rocks, laughing. She sat up when she saw George, and grinned.

'What do you mean, throwing those stones at us?' demanded George.

'I wasn't throwing them,' said the girl.

'Don't tell lies,' said George scornfully. 'You know you were.'

'I wasn't. I was just spitting them,' said the awful girl.
'Watch!' She slipped a stone into her mouth, took a deep
breath and then spat out the stone. It flew straight at George
and hit her sharply and squarely on the nose. George
looked so extremely surprised that Dick and Julian roared
with laughter.

'Bet I can spit stones farther than any of you,' said the
ragamuffin. 'Have some of my damsons and see.'

'Right!' said Dick promptly. 'If you win I'll buy you an
ice-cream. If I do, you can clear off from here and not
bother us any more. See?'

'Yes,' said the girl, and her eyes gleamed and danced.
'But I shall win!'

CHAPTER FIVE

Ragamuffin Jo

GEORGE WAS most astonished at Dick. How very shocking to see who could spit damson stones out the farthest.

'It's all right,' said Julian to her in a low voice. 'You know how good Dick is at that sort of game. He'll win – and we'll send the girl scooting off, well and truly beaten.'

'I think you're horrible, Dick,' said George, in a loud voice. 'Horrible!'

'Who used to spit cherry-stones out and try and beat me last year?' said Dick at once. 'Don't be so high-and-mighty, George.'

Anne came slowly back from her pool, wondering why the others were up on the rocks. Damson stones began to rain round her. She stopped in astonishment. Surely – surely it couldn't be the others doing that? A stone hit her on her bare arm, and she squealed.

The ragamuffin girl won handsomely. She managed to get her stones at least three feet farther than Dick. She lay back, laughing, her teeth gleaming very white indeed.

'You owe me an ice-cream,' she said, in her sing-song voice. Julian wondered if she was Welsh. Dick looked at her, marvelling that she managed to get her stones so far.

'I'll buy you the ice-cream, don't worry,' he said.

'Nobody's ever beaten me before like that, not even Stevens, a boy at school with a most enormous mouth.'

'I do think you really are dreadful,' said Anne. 'Go and buy her the ice-cream and tell her to go home.'

'I'm going to eat it here,' said the girl, and she suddenly looked exactly as mulish and obstinate as George did when she wanted something she didn't think she would get.

'You look like George now!' said Dick, and immediately wished he hadn't. George glared at him, furious.

'What! That nasty, rude tangly-haired girl like *me*!' stormed George. 'Pooh! I can't bear to go near her.'

'Shut up,' said Dick, shortly. The girl looked surprised.

'What does she mean?' she asked Dick. 'Am I nasty? You're as *rude* as I am, anyway.'

'There's an ice-cream man,' said Julian, afraid that the hot-tempered George would fly at the girl and slap her. He whistled to the man, who came to the edge of the rocks and handed out six ice-creams.

'Here you are,' said Julian, handing one to the girl. 'You eat that up and go.'

They all sat and ate ice-creams, George still scowling. Timmy gulped his at once as usual. 'Look – he's had all his,' marvelled the girl. 'I call that a waste. Here, boy – have a bit of mine!'

To George's annoyance, Timmy licked up the bit of ice-cream thrown to him by the girl. How *could* Timmy accept anything from her?

Dick couldn't help being amused by this odd, bold little girl, with her tangled short hair and sharp darting eyes. He suddenly saw something that made him feel uncomfortable.

On her chin the girl had a big black bruise. 'I say,' said Dick, '*I* didn't give you that bruise yesterday, did I?'

'What bruise? Oh, this one on my chin?' said the girl, touching it. 'Yes, that's where you hit me when you sent me flying. *I* don't mind. I've had plenty worse ones from my dad.'

'I'm sorry I hit you,' said Dick, awkwardly. 'I am honestly. What's your name?'

'Jo,' said the girl.

'But that's a *boy's* name,' said Dick.

'So's George. But you said she was a girl,' said Jo, licking the last bits of ice-cream from her fingers.

'Yes, but George is short for Georgina,' said Anne. 'What's Jo short for?'

'Don't know,' said Jo. 'I never heard. All I know is I'm a girl and my name is Jo.'

'It's probably short for Josephine,' said Julian. They all stared at the possible Josephine. The short name of Jo certainly suited her – but not the long and pretty name of Josephine.

'It's really strange,' said Anne, at last, 'but Jo *is* awfully like you, George – same short curly hair – only Jo's is terribly messy and tangly – same freckles, dozens of them – same turned-up nose . . .'

430

'Same way of sticking her chin up in the air, same scowl, same glare!' said Dick. George put on her fiercest glare at these remarks, which she didn't like at all.

'Well, all I can say is I hope I haven't her layers of dirt and her sm—' she began, angrily. But Dick stopped her.

'She's probably not got any soap or hair-brush or anything. She'd be all right cleaned up. Don't be unkind, George.'

George turned her back. How *could* Dick stick up for that awful girl? 'Isn't she ever going?' she said. 'Or is she going to park herself on us all day long?'

'I'll go when I want to,' said Jo, and put on a scowl, so exactly like George's that Julian and Dick laughed in surprise. Jo laughed, too, but George clenched her fists furiously. Anne looked on in distress. She wished Jo would go, then everything would be all right again.

'I like that dog,' said Jo, suddenly, and she leaned over to where Timmy lay beside George. She patted him with a hand that was like a little brown paw. George swung round.

'Don't touch my dog!' she said. '*He* doesn't like you, either!'

'Oh, but he does,' said Jo, surprisingly. 'All dogs like *me*. So do cats. I can make your dog come to me as easy as anything.'

'Try!' said George, scornfully. 'He won't go to *you*! Will you, Tim?'

Jo didn't move. She began to make a peculiar little

whining noise down in her throat, like a forlorn puppy. Timmy pricked up his ears at once. He looked inquiringly at Jo. Jo stopped making the noise and held out her hand.

Timmy looked at it and turned away – but when he heard the whining again he got up, listening. He stared intently at Jo. Was this a kind of god-girl, that she could so well speak his language?

Jo flung herself on her face and went on with the small, whining noises that sounded as if she were a small dog in pain or sorrow. Timmy walked over to her and sat down, his head on one side, puzzled. Then he suddenly bent down and licked the girl's half-hidden face. She sat up at once and put her arms round Timmy's neck.

'Come here, Timmy,' said George, jealously. Timmy shook off the brown arms that held him and walked over to George at once.

Jo laughed.

'See? I made him come to me and give me one of his best licks! I can do that to any dog.'

'How can you?' asked Dick, in wonder. He had never seen Timmy make friends before with anyone who was disliked by George.

'I don't know, really,' said Jo, pushing back her hair again, as she sat up. 'I reckon it's in the family. My mother was in a circus, and she trained dogs for the ring. We had dozens – lovely they were. I loved them all.'

'Where is your mother?' asked Julian. 'Is she still in the circus?'

'No. She died,' said Jo. 'And I left the circus with my dad. We've got a caravan. Dad was an acrobat till he hurt his foot.'

The four children remembered how the man had dragged his foot as he walked. They looked silently at dirty little Jo. What a strange life she must have led!

'She's dirty, she's probably very good at telling lies and thieving, but she's got pluck,' thought Julian. 'Still, I'll be glad when she goes.'

'I wish I hadn't given her that awful bruise,' thought Dick. 'I wonder what she'd be like cleaned up and brushed? She looks as if a little kindness would do her good.'

'I'm sorry for her, but I don't much like her,' thought Anne.

'I don't believe a word she says!' thought George angrily. 'Not one word! She's a humbug. And I'm *ashamed* of Timmy for going to her. I feel very cross with him.'

'Where's your father?' said Julian at last.

'Gone off somewhere to meet somebody,' said Jo vaguely. 'I'm glad. He was in one of his tempers this morning. I went and hid under the caravan.'

There was a silence. 'Can I stay with you today till my dad comes back?' said Jo suddenly, in her sing-song voice. 'I'll wash myself if you like. I'm all alone today.'

'No. We don't want you,' said George, feeling as if she really couldn't bear Jo any longer. 'Do we, Anne?'

Anne didn't like hurting anyone. She hesitated. 'Well,' said at last, 'perhaps Jo *had* better go.'

434

'Yes,' said Julian. 'It's time you scooted off now, Jo. You've had a long time with us.'

Jo looked at Dick with mournful eyes, and touched the bruise on her chin as if it hurt her. Dick felt most uncomfortable again. He looked round at the others.

'Don't you think she could stay and share our picnic?' he said. 'After all – she can't *help* being dirty and – and . . .'

'It's all right,' said Jo, suddenly scrambling up. 'I'm going! There's my dad!'

They saw the man in the distance, dragging his foot as he walked. He caught sight of Jo and gave a shrill and piercing whistle. Jo made a face at them all, an impudent, ugly, insolent face.

'I don't like you!' she said. Then she pointed at Dick. 'I only like *him* – he's nice. Yah to the rest of you!'

And off she went like a hare over the sand, her bare feet hardly touching the ground.

'What an extraordinary girl!' said Julian. 'I don't feel we've seen the last of her yet!'

CHAPTER SIX

What happened in the night?

THAT NIGHT Anne began to look rather scared as darkness fell. She was remembering the Face at the Window!

'It won't come again, Ju, will it?' she said to her big brother half a dozen times.

'No, Anne. But if you like I'll come and lie down on George's bed instead of George tonight, and stay with you all night long,' said Julian.

Anne considered this and then shook her head. 'No. I think I'd almost rather have George and Timmy. I mean – George and I – and even you – might be scared of Faces, but Timmy wouldn't. He'd simply leap at them.'

'You're quite right,' said Julian. 'He would. All right then, I won't keep you company – but you'll see, nothing whatever will happen tonight. Anyway, if you like, we'll all close our bedroom windows and fasten them, even if we are too hot for anything – then we'll know nobody can possibly get in.'

So that night Julian not only closed all the doors and windows downstairs as he had done the night before (except the tiny pantry window that wouldn't shut), but he also shut and fastened all the ones upstairs.

'What about Joanna's window?' asked Anne.

WHAT HAPPENED IN THE NIGHT?

'She *always* sleeps with it shut, summer and winter,' said Julian, with a grin. 'Country folk often do. They think the night air's dangerous. Now, you've nothing at all to worry about, silly.'

So Anne went to bed with her mind at rest. George drew the curtains across their window so that even if the Face came again they wouldn't be able to see it!

'Let Timmy out for me, Julian, will you?' called George. 'Anne doesn't want me to leave her, even to take old Timmy out for his last walk. Just open the door and let him out. He'll come in when he's ready.'

'Right!' called Julian, and opened the front door. Timmy trotted out, tail wagging. He loved his last sniff round. He liked to smell the trail of the hedgehog who was out on his night-rounds; he liked to put his nose down a rabbit-hole and listen to stirrings down below; and he loved to follow the meanderings of rats and mice round by the thick hedges.

'Isn't Timmy in yet?' called George from the top of the stairs. 'Do call him, Ju. I want to go to bed. Anne's half-asleep already.'

'He'll be in in a moment,' said Julian, who wanted to finish his book. 'Don't fuss.'

But no Timmy appeared even when he had finished his book. Julian went to the door and whistled. He listened for Timmy to come. Then, hearing nothing, he whistled once more.

This time he heard the sound of pattering footsteps

coming up the path to the door. 'Oh there you are, Tim,' said Julian. 'What have you been up to? Chasing rabbits or something?'

Timmy wagged his tail feebly. He didn't jump up at Julian as he usually did. 'You look as if you've been up to some mischief, Tim,' said Julian. 'Go on – up to bed with you – and mind you bark if you hear the smallest sound in the night.'

'Woof,' said Timmy, in rather a subdued voice, and went upstairs. He climbed on to George's bed and sighed heavily.

'What a sigh!' said George. 'And what have you been eating, Timmy? Pooh – you've dug up some frightful old bone, I know you have. I've a good mind to push you off my bed. I suppose you suddenly remembered one you buried months ago. Pooh!'

Timmy wouldn't be pushed off the bed. He settled down to sleep, his nose on George's feet as usual. He snored a little, and woke George in about half an hour.

'Shut up, Timmy,' she said, pushing him with her feet. Anne woke up, alarmed.

'What is it, George?' she whispered, her heart thumping.

'Nothing. Only Timmy snoring. Hark at him. He won't stop,' said George, irritated. 'Wake up, Timmy, and stop snoring.'

Timmy moved sleepily and settled down again. He stopped snoring and George and Anne fell sound asleep. Julian woke once, thinking he heard something fall

– but hearing Timmy gently snoring again through the open doors of the two rooms, he lay down, his mind at rest.

If the noise had *really* been a noise Timmy would have heard it, no doubt about that. George always said that Timmy slept with one ear open.

Julian heard nothing more till Joanna went downstairs at seven o'clock. He heard her go into the kitchen and do something to the kitchen grate. He turned over and fell asleep again.

He was wakened suddenly twenty minutes later by loud screams from downstairs. He sat up and then leapt out of bed at once. He rushed downstairs. Dick followed him

'Look at this! The master's study – turned upside down – those drawers ransacked! The safe's open, too. Mercy me, who's been here in the night – with all the doors locked and bolted, too!' Joanna wailed loudly and wrung her hands as she gazed at the untidy room.

'I say!' said Dick, horrified. 'Someone's been searching for something pretty thoroughly! Even got the safe open – and wrenched the drawer out.'

'How did he get in?' said Julian, feeling bewildered. He went round the house, looking at doors and windows. Except for the kitchen door, which Joanna said she had unlocked and unbolted herself as soon as she came down, not a window or door had been touched. All were fastened securely.

439

Anne came down, looking scared. 'What's the matter?' she said. But Julian brushed her aside. How did that burglar get in? That was what he wanted to know. Through one of the *upstairs* windows, he supposed – one that somebody had opened last night after he had fastened it. Perhaps in the girls' room?

But no – not one window was open. All were fastened securely, including Joanna's. Then a thought struck him as he looked into George's room. Why hadn't Timmy barked? After all, there must have been quite a bit of noise, however quiet the thief had been. He had himself heard something and had awakened. Why hadn't Timmy, then?

George was trying to pull Timmy off the bed. 'Ju, Ju! There's something wrong with Timmy. He won't wake up!' she cried. 'He's breathing so heavily, too – just listen to him! And what's the matter downstairs? What's happened?'

Julian told her shortly while he examined Timmy. 'Somebody got in last night – your father's study's in the most awful mess – absolutely ransacked from top to bottom, safe and all. Goodness knows how the fellow got in to do it.'

'How awful!' said George, looking very pale. 'And now something's wrong with Tim. He didn't wake up last night when the burglar came – he's ill, Julian!'

'No, he's not. He's been doped,' said Julian, pulling back Timmy's eyelids. 'So *that's* why he was so long outside last night! Somebody gave him some meat or something with dope in – some kind of drug. And he ate it, and slept so soundly that he never heard a thing – and isn't even awake yet.'

441

'Oh, Julian – will he be all right?' asked George anxiously, stroking Timmy's motionless body. 'But how *could* he take any food from a stranger in the night?'

'Maybe he picked it up – the burglar may have flung it down hoping that Timmy would eat it,' said Julian. 'Now I understand why he looked so sheepish when he came in. He didn't even jump up and lick me.'

'Oh, dear – Timmy, do, do wake up,' begged poor George, and she shook the big dog gently. He groaned a little and snuggled down again.

'Leave him,' said Julian. 'He'll be all right. He's not poisoned, only drugged. Come down and see the damage!'

George was horrified at the state of her father's study. 'They were after his two special books of American notes, I'm sure they were,' she said. 'Father said that any other country in the world would be glad to have those. Whatever are we to do?'

'Better get in the police,' said Julian, gravely. 'We can't manage this sort of thing ourselves. And do you know your father's address in Spain?'

'No,' wailed George. 'He and Mother said they were going to have a *real* holiday this time – no letters to be forwarded, and no address left till they had been settled somewhere for a few days. Then they'd telegraph it.'

'Well, we'll certainly have to get the police in, then,' said Julian, looking rather white and stern. George glanced at him. He seemed suddenly very grown-up indeed. She watched him go out of the room. He went into the hall and rang up the police station. Joanna was very relieved.

'Yes, get in the police, that's what we ought to do,' she said. 'There's that nice Constable Wilkins, and that other one with the red face, what's he called – Mr Donaldson. I'll be making some coffee for them when they come.'

She cheered up considerably at the thought of handing out cups of her good hot coffee to two interested policemen, who would ask her plenty of questions that she would be only too delighted to answer. She bustled off to the kitchen.

The four children stared silently at the ruins of the study. What a mess! Could it ever be cleared up? Nobody would know what was gone till Uncle Quentin came back. How furious he would be.

'I hope nothing very important has been taken,' said Dick. 'It looks as if somebody knew there was something valuable here, and meant to get it!'

'And has probably got it,' said Julian. 'Hallo – that must be the police! Come on – I can see it will be a long time before we get out breakfast this morning!'

CHAPTER SEVEN

Policemen in the house

THE POLICE were very, very thorough. The children got tired of them long before lunch-time. Joanna didn't. She made them cups of coffee and put some of her home-made buns on a plate and sent Anne to pick up ripe plums. She felt proud to think that it was she who had discovered the ransacked study.

There were two policemen. One was a sergeant, rather solemn and very correct. He interviewed each of the children and asked them exactly the same questions. The other man went over the study bit by bit, very thoroughly indeed.

'Looking for finger-prints, I suppose,' said Anne. 'Oh dear – when can we go and bathe?'

The thing that puzzled everyone, the police included, was – how did the thief or thieves get in? Both policemen went round the house, slowly and deliberately trying every door and window still locked or fastened. They stood and looked at the pantry window for some time.

'Got in there, I suppose,' said one of them.

'Must have been as small as a monkey then,' said the other. He turned to Anne, who was the smallest of the four children. 'Could you squeeze through there, Missy, do you think?'

'No,' said Anne. 'But I'll try if you like.' So she tried – but she stuck fast before she got even half-way through, and Julian had to pull hard to get her down again.

'Have you any idea what has been stolen?' the sergeant asked Julian, who seemed extraordinarily grown-up that morning.

'No, sergeant – none of us has,' said Julian. 'Not even George here, who knows her father's work better than any of us. The only thing we know is that my uncle went to America to lecture a short time ago – and he brought back

445

two notebooks, full of valuable diagrams and notes. He did say that other countries might be very glad to get hold of those. I expect they were in that safe.'

'Well – they'll certainly be gone then,' said the sergeant, shutting his own fat notebook with a snap. 'Pity when people leave such things in an ordinary safe and then go off without leaving an address. Can't we possibly get in touch with him? This may be terribly important.'

'I know,' said Julian, looking worried. 'We shall have an address in a day or two – but I honestly don't see how we can get in touch before then.'

'Right,' said the sergeant. 'Well – we'll go now – but we'll bring back a photographer with us after lunch to photograph the room – then your cook can tidy it up. I know she's longing to.'

'Coming back *again!*' said Anne, when the two men had solemnly walked down the path, mounted very solid-looking bicycles, and gone sailing down the lane. 'Good gracious! Have we got to answer questions all over again?'

'Well, we'll go down to the beach and take a boat and go rowing,' said Julian, with a laugh. 'We'll be out of reach then. I don't see that we can give them any more help. I must say it's all very peculiar – I wish to goodness I knew how the thief got in.'

George had been very quiet and subdued all the morning. She had worried about Timmy, fearing that he had been poisoned, and not merely drugged, as Julian had said. But Timmy was now quite recovered, except that he seemed a bit sleepy still, and not inclined to gambol round in his usual ridiculous way. He looked extremely sheepish, too.

'I can't think why Timmy looks like that,' said George, puzzled. 'He usually only puts that look on when he's done something he's ashamed of – or got into mischief. He couldn't possibly know, could he, that whatever he picked up and ate last night was something he shouldn't eat?'

'No,' said Dick. 'He's sensible though, I think, not to touch poisoned meat – but he couldn't know if some harmless sleeping powder had been put into anything. It might have no smell and no taste. Perhaps he's just ashamed of being so sleepy!'

'If only he'd been awake!' groaned George. 'He would have heard any noise downstairs at once – and he'd have barked and woken us all, and flown downstairs himself to attack whoever was there! Why, oh why didn't I take him out myself last night as I usually do?'

'It was a chapter of accidents,' said Julian. 'You didn't take him out, so he was alone – and it happened that someone was waiting there with drugged food – which he either found or took from the thief . . .'

'*No,*' said George. 'Timmy would never, never take anything from someone he didn't know. I've always taught him that.'

'Well, he got it somehow – and slept through the very night he should have been awake,' said Julian. 'What I'm so afraid of, George, is that the thieves have got your

447

father's two American notebooks. They seem to have left most of the stuff – piles and piles of books of all kinds, filled with your father's tiny handwriting.'

Joanna came in to say lunch was ready. She told the children that the policemen had eaten every one of her home-made buns. She still felt important and excited, and was longing to get out to the village and tell everyone the news.

'You'd better stay in and give the policemen a good tea,' said Julian. 'They're coming back with a photographer.'

'Then I'd better do another baking,' said Joanna, pleased.

'Yes. Make one of your chocolate cakes,' said Anne.

'Oh, do you think they'd like one?' said Joanna.

'Not for *them*, Joanna – for us, of course!' said George. 'Don't waste one of your marvellous chocolate cakes on policemen. Can you make us up a picnic tea? We're fed up with being indoors – we're going out in a boat.'

Joanna packed them a good tea after they had had their lunch and they all set off before the police came back. Timmy was much less sleepy now and did a little caper round them as they walked to the beach. George brightened up at once.

'He's getting better,' she said. 'Timmy, I simply shan't let you out of my sight now! If anyone's going to dope you again they'll have to do it under my very nose.'

They had a lovely time out in George's boat. They went half-way to Kirrin Island and bathed from the boat, diving in and having swimming races till they were tired out.

448

Timmy joined them, though he couldn't swim nearly as fast as they could.

'He doesn't really *swim*,' said Anne. 'He just tries to *run* through the water. I wish he'd let me ride on his back like a sea-dog – but he always slips away under me when I try.'

They got back about six o'clock to find that the policemen had eaten the whole of the chocolate cake that Joanna had made, besides an extraordinary amount of scones and buns.

Also the study was not tidied up, and a man had come to mend the safe. Everything was safely back there, though the police had told Joanna that if there was anything of real value it should be handed to them till George's father came back.

'But we don't know which of all those papers are valuable!' said Julian. 'Well – we'll have to wait till Uncle Quentin cables us – and that may not be for days. Anyway, I don't expect we'll be worried by the thief again – he's got what he wanted.'

The exciting happenings of the day had made them all tired except Julian. 'I'm off to bed,' said Dick, about nine o'clock. 'Anne, why don't you go? You look exhausted.'

'Yes, I will,' said Anne. 'Coming, George?'

'I'm going to take Timmy out for his last walk,' said George. 'I shall never let him go out alone at night again. Come on, Timmy. If you want to go to bed I'll lock up the front door, Ju.'

'Right,' said Julian. 'I'll go up in a minute. I don't fancy staying down here by myself tonight. I'll fasten everything and lock up, except the front door. Don't forget to put up the chain, too, George – though I'm pretty certain we don't need to expect any more burglaries!'

'Or faces at the window,' said Anne, at once.

'No,' said Julian. 'There won't be any more of those either. Good-night, Anne – sleep well!'

Anne and Dick went upstairs. Julian finished the paper he was reading, and then got up to go round the house and lock up. Joanna was already upstairs, dreaming of policemen eating her chocolate cakes.

George went out with Timmy. He ran eagerly to the gate and then set off down the lane for his usual night walk with George. At a gate in the lane he suddenly stood still and growled as if he saw something unusual.

'Silly, Timmy!' said George, coming up. 'It's only somebody camping in a caravan! Haven't you seen a caravan before? Stop growling!'

They went on, Timmy sniffing into every rat-hole and rabbit-hole, enjoying himself thoroughly. George was enjoying the walk, too. She didn't hurry – Julian could always go up to bed if he didn't want to wait.

Julian did go up to bed. He left the front door ajar, and went yawning upstairs, suddenly feeling sleepy. He got into bed quietly and quickly seeing that Dick was already asleep. He lay awake listening for George. When he was half asleep, he heard the front door shut.

'There she is,' he thought, and turned over to go to sleep.

But it wasn't George. Her bed was empty all that night, and nobody knew, not even Anne. George and Timmy didn't come back!

CHAPTER EIGHT

Where can George be?

ANNE WOKE up in the night, feeling thirsty. She whispered across the room:

'George! Are you awake?'

There was no answer, so, very cautiously and quietly Anne got herself a drink from the decanter on the washstand. George was sometimes cross if she was awakened in the middle of the night. Anne got back into bed, not guessing that George hadn't answered because she wasn't there!

She fell asleep and didn't wake till she heard Dick's voice. 'Hey, you two – get up; it's a quarter to eight. We're going for a bathe!'

Anne sat up, yawning. Her eyes went to George's bed. It was empty. More than that, it was all neat and tidy, as if it had just been made!

'*Well!*' said Anne in astonishment. 'George is up already, and has even made her bed. She *might* have woken me, and I could have gone out with her. It's such a lovely day. I suppose she's taken Timmy for an early morning walk, like she sometimes does.'

Anne slipped into her bathing costume and ran to join the boys. They went downstairs together, their bare feet padding on the carpet.

WHERE CAN GEORGE BE?

'George has gone out already,' said Anne. 'I expect she woke early and took Timmy; I never even heard her!'

Julian was now at the front door. 'Yes,' he said. 'The door isn't locked or bolted – George must have slipped down, undone it and then just pulled the door softly to. How very considerate of her! Last time she went out early she banged the door so hard that she woke everyone in the house!'

'She may have gone fishing in her boat,' said Dick. 'She said yesterday she'd like to some early morning when the tide was right. She'll probably arrive complete with stacks of fish for Joanna to cook.'

They looked out to sea when they got to the beach. There was a boat far out on the water with what looked like two people in it, fishing.

'I bet that's George and Timmy,' said Dick. He yelled and waved his hands, but the boat was too far away, and nobody waved back. The three of them plunged into the cold waves. Brrrr-rrr-rrr!

'Lovely!' said Anne, when they came out again, the drops of sea-water running down their bodies and glistening in the early morning sun. 'Let's have a run now.'

They chased one another up and down the beach, and then, glowing and very hungry, went back to breakfast.

'Where's George?' asked Joanna, as she brought in their breakfast. 'I see her bed's made and all – what's come over her?'

'I think she's out fishing with Timmy,' said Dick. 'She was up and about long before we were.'

'I never heard her go,' said Joanna. 'She must have been very quiet. There you are now – there's a fine breakfast for you – sausages and tomatoes and fried eggs!'

'O-o-o-o-h, lovely,' said Anne. 'And you've done the sausages just how I like them, Joanna – all bursting their skins. Do you think we'd better eat George's too? She's still out in the boat. She may not be back for ages.'

'Well, then you'd better eat her share,' said Joanna. 'I've no doubt she took something out of the larder before she went. Pity I didn't lock it last night, as usual!'

They finished George's share between them and then started on toast and marmalade. After that Anne went to help Joanna make the beds and dust and mop. Julian and Dick went off to the village to do the morning's shopping at the grocer's.

Nobody worried about George at all. Julian and Dick came back from their shopping and saw the little boat still out on the sea.

'George will be absolutely starving by the time she comes back,' said Julian. 'Perhaps she's got one of her moods on and wants to be alone. She was awfully upset about Timmy being drugged.'

They met the ragamuffin Jo. She was walking along the beach, collecting wood, and she looked sullen and dirtier than ever.

'Hallo, Jo!' called Dick. She looked up and came

454

towards them without a smile. She looked as if she had been crying. Her small brown face was streaked where the tears had run through the dirt.

'Hallo!' she said, looking at Dick. She looked so miserable that Dick felt touched.

'What's the matter, kid?' he said, kindly.

Tears trickled down Jo's face as she heard the kindness in his voice. She rubbed them away and smudged her face more than ever.

'Nothing,' she said. 'Where's Anne?'

'Anne's at home, and George is out in that boat with Timmy fishing,' said Dick, pointing out to sea.

'Oh!' said Jo, and turned away to go on with her collecting of wood. Dick went after her.

'Hey!' he said. 'Don't go off like that. You just tell me what's wrong with you this morning.'

He caught hold of Jo and swung her round to face him. He looked closely at her and saw that she now had two bruises on her face – one going yellow, that he had given her when he had sent her flying two or three days before – and a new one, dark purple.

'Where did you get *that* bruise?' he said, touching it lightly.

'That was my dad,' said Jo. 'He's gone off and left me – taken the caravan and all! I wanted to go, too; but he wouldn't let me into the caravan. And when I hammered at the door, he came out and pushed me down the steps. That's when I got this bruise – and I've got another on my leg, too.'

Dick and Julian listened in horror. What kind of a life was this that Jo had to live? The boys sat down on the beach, and Dick pulled Jo down between them.

'But surely your father is coming back?' asked Julian. 'Is the caravan your only home?'

'Yes,' said Jo. 'I've never had another home. We've always lived in a caravan. Mum did, too, when she was alive. Things were better then. But this is the first time Dad's gone off without me.'

'But – how are you going to live?' asked Dick.

'Dad said Jake would give me money to buy food,' said Jo. 'But only if I do what he tells me. I don't like Jake. He's mean.'

'Who's Jake?' asked Julian, most astonished at all this.

'Jake's a traveller fellow. He knows my father,' said Jo. 'He's always turning up for a day or two, and going away again. If I wait about here, he'll come and give me five pence or so, I expect.'

'What will he tell you to do?' said Dick, puzzled. 'It all seems very strange and horrible to me. You're only a kid.'

'Oh, he may tell me to go poaching with him or – or – well, there's things we do that folks like you don't,' said Jo, suddenly realising that Dick and Julian would not at all approve of some of the things she did. 'I hope he gives me some money today, though. I haven't got any at all, and I'm hungry.'

Dick and Julian looked at one another. To think that in

these days there should be a forlorn waif like Jo, going in fear of others, and often hungry and lonely.

Dick put his hand in the shopping basket and pulled out a packet of chocolate and some biscuits. 'Here you are,' he said. 'Tuck into these – and if you'd like to go to the kitchen door some time today and ask Joanna, our cook, for a meal, she'll give you one. I'll tell her about you.'

'Folks don't like me at kitchen doors,' said Jo, cramming biscuits into her mouth. 'They're afraid I'll steal something.' She glanced up at Dick. 'And I do,' she said.

'You shouldn't do that,' said Dick.

'Well, wouldn't you, if you were so hungry you couldn't even bear to look at a baker's cart?' said Jo.

'No – I don't think so. At least, I hope not,' said Dick, wondering what he really would feel like if he were starving. 'Where's this Jake fellow?'

'I don't know. Somewhere about,' said Jo. 'He'll find me when he wants me. I've got to stay on the beach, Dad said. So I couldn't come to your house, anyway. I daren't leave here.'

The boys got up to go, worried about this little ragamuffin. But what could they do? Nothing, except feed her and give her money. Dick had slipped five pence into her hand, and she had pocketed it without a word, her eyes gleaming.

George was still not home by lunch-time; and now Julian for the first time began to feel anxious. He slipped out to the beach to see if the boat was still at sea. It was just pulling in – and with a sinking heart Julian saw that it was not George and Timmy who were in it, but two boys.

He went to look for George's boat – and there it was, high up on the boat-beach with many others. George had not been out in it at all!

He ran back to Kirrin Cottage and told the others. They were at once as anxious as he was. What *could* have become of George?

'We'll wait till tea-time,' said Julian. 'Then if she's not back we'll really have to do something about it – tell the police, I should think. But she *has* sometimes gone off for the day before, so we'll just wait a bit longer.'

Tea-time came – but no George, and no Timmy. Then they heard someone pattering up the garden path – was it Timmy? They leant out of the window to see.

'It's Jo,' said Dick, in disappointment. 'She's got a note or something. Whatever does *she* want?'

CHAPTER NINE

An extraordinary message – and a plan

JULIAN OPENED the front door. Jo silently gave him a plain envelope. Julian tore it open, not knowing what in the least to expect. Jo turned to go – but Julian put out his hand and caught hold of her firmly, whilst he read the note in complete amazement.

'Dick!' he called. 'Hold on to Jo. Don't let her go. Better take her indoors. This is serious.'

Jo wasn't going to be taken indoors. She squealed, and wriggled like an eel. Then she began to kick Dick viciously with her bare feet.

'Let me go! I'm not doing any harm. I only brought you that note!'

'Stop squealing and being silly,' said Dick. 'I don't want to hurt you, you know that. But you must come indoors.'

But Jo wouldn't stop wriggling and pulling and kicking. She looked scared out of her life. It was as much as Dick and Julian could do to get the little wriggler into the dining-room and shut the door. Anne followed, looking very frightened. Whatever was happening?

'Listen to this,' said Julian, when the door was shut. 'It's unbelievable!' He held out the typewritten note for the others to see as he read it out loud.

'We want the second notebook, the one with figures in, and we mean to have it. Find it and put it under the last stone on the crazy paving path at the bottom of the garden. Put it there tonight.

461

'We have got the girl and the dog. We will set them free when we have what we want from you. If you tell the police, neither the girl nor the dog will come back. The house will be watched to see that nobody leaves it to warn the police. The telephone wires are cut.

'When it is dark, put the lights on in the front room and all three of you sit there with the maid Joanna, so that we can keep a watch on you. Let the big boy leave the house at eleven o'clock, shining a torch and put the notebook where we said. He must then go back to the lighted room. You will hear a hoot like an owl when we have collected it. The girl and the dog will then be returned!'

This amazing and terrifying note made Anne burst into tears and cling to Julian's arm.

'Julian! Julian! George can't have come back from her walk with Timmy last night! She must have been caught then – and Timmy, too. Oh, why didn't we start hunting for her then?'

Julian looked very grim and white. He was thinking hard. 'Yes – someone was lying in wait, I've no doubt – and she and Timmy were kidnapped. Then the kidnappers – or one of them – came back to the house and shut the front door to make it seem as if George was back. And someone has probably been hanging round all day to find out whether we're worried about George, or just think she's gone off for the day!'

'Who gave you the note?' said Dick, sharply, to the scared Jo.

She trembled.

'A man,' she said.

'What sort of a man?' asked Julian.

'I don't know,' said Jo.

'Yes, you do,' said Dick. 'You *must* tell, Jo.'

Jo looked sullen. Dick shook her, and she tried to get away. But he held her far too tightly. 'Go on – tell us what the fellow was like,' he said.

'He was tall and had a long beard and a long nose and brown eyes,' rattled off Jo suddenly. 'And he was dressed in fisherman's clothes, and – he spoke foreign.'

The two boys looked sternly at her. 'I believe you're making all that up, Jo,' said Julian.

'I'm not,' said Jo sulkily. 'I'd never seen him before, so there.'

'Jo,' said Anne, taking Jo's brown little paw in hers, 'tell us truly anything you know. We're so worried about George.' Tears sprang out of her eyes as she spoke, and she gave a little wail.

'Serve that George-girl right if she's got taken away,' said Jo fiercely. 'She was rude to me – she's cruel and unkind. Serve her right, I say. I wouldn't tell you anything – not even if I knew something to tell.'

'You *do* know something,' said Dick. 'You're a bad little girl, Jo. I shan't have anything more to do with you. I felt sorry and unhappy about you, but now I don't.'

Jo looked sullen again, but her eyes were bright with tears. She turned away. 'Let me go,' she said. 'I tell you, that fellow gave me fifteen pence to bring this note to you, and that's all I know. And I'm *glad* George is in trouble. People like her deserve it, see!'

'Let her go,' said Julian wearily. 'She's like a savage little cat – all claws and spite. I thought there might be some good in her, but there isn't.'

'I thought so, too,' said Dick, letting go Jo's arm. 'I quite liked her. Well, go, Jo. We don't want you any more.'

Jo rushed to the door, wrenched it open, and fled down the hall and out of the house. There was silence after she had gone.

'Julian,' whispered Anne. 'What are we going to do?'

Julian said nothing. He got up and went into the hall. He picked up the telephone receiver and put his ear to it, listening for the faint crackling that would tell him it was connected. After a moment he put it back again.

'No connection,' he said. 'The wires have been cut, as the note said. And no doubt there's somebody on watch to see we don't slip out to give warning. This is all crazy. It can't be true.'

'But it is,' said Dick. 'Horribly true. Julian, do you know what notebook they want? I've no idea!'

'Nor have I,' said Julian. 'And it's impossible to go and hunt for it, because the safe has been mended and locked – and the police have the key.'

'Well, that's that, then,' said Dick. 'What are we going

to do? Shall I slip out and warn the police?'

Julian considered. 'No,' he said at last. 'I think these people mean business. It would be terrible if anything happened to George. Also, you might be caught and spirited away yourself. There are people watching the house, don't forget.'

'But, Julian – we can't just sit here and do nothing!' said Dick.

'I know. This will have to be thought about carefully,' said Julian. 'If only we knew where George had been taken to! We could rescue her then. But I can't see how we can find out.'

'If one of us went and hid down the bottom of the garden and waited to see whoever came to take up the notebook we could follow the fellow and maybe he'd lead us to where George is hidden,' suggested Dick.

'You forget that we've all got to sit in the lighted front room, so it would easily be spotted if one of us were missing,' said Julian. 'Even Joanna has to sit there. This is all very stupid and melodramatic.'

'Does anyone come to the house this evening? Any of the tradesmen, for instance?' asked Anne, again in a whisper. She felt as if people must be all round the house, listening and watching!

'No. Else we could give them a note,' said Julian. Then he gave the table a rap that made the others jump. 'Wait a bit! Yes, of course – the paper-boy comes! Ours is almost the last house he delivers at. But perhaps it would be risky to give him a note. Can't we think of something better?'

'Listen,' said Dick, his eyes shining. 'I've got it! I know the paper-boy. He's all right. We'll have the front door open and yank him in as soon as he appears. And I'll go out immediately, with his cap on, and his satchel of papers, whistling – jump on his bike and ride away. And none of the watchers will know I'm not the boy! I'll come back when it's dark, sneak round the garden at the bottom and hide to watch who comes for the hidden notebook – and I'll follow him!'

'Good idea, Dick!' said Julian, turning it quickly over in his mind. 'Yes – it's possible. It would be better to watch and see who comes rather than tell the police – because if these kidnappers mean business, George would certainly be in trouble once they knew we'd been able to get in touch with the police.'

'Won't the newspaper boy think it's odd?' asked Anne.

'Not very. He's not that bright,' said Dick. 'He believes anything he's told. We'll make up something to satisfy him and give him such a good time that he'll want to keep visiting us!'

'About this notebook,' said Julian. 'We'd better get some kind of book out of one of the drawers and wrap it up with a note inside to say we hope it's the one. The fellow who comes to collect it will have some kind of parcel to take off with him to give the kidnappers. It isn't likely he'd undo it and look at it – or even know if it was the right one or not.'

AN EXTRAORDINARY MESSAGE – AND A PLAN

'Go and hunt out a book, Anne,' said Dick. 'I'll be looking out for the newspaper boy. He's not due till half past seven, but I don't dare to risk missing him – and he may be early, you never know.'

Anne shot off to the study, thankful to have something to do. Her hands were trembling as she pulled out drawer after drawer to look for a big notebook that would do to wrap up in a parcel.

Julian went with Dick to the front door, to help him to deal with the unsuspecting newspaper boy. They stood there, patiently waiting, hearing the clock strike six o'clock, then half past, then seven.

'Here he comes!' said Dick, suddenly. 'Now – get ready to yank him in! Hallo, Sid!'

CHAPTER TEN

Sid's wonderful evening

SID, THE paper-boy, was most amazed to find himself yanked quickly through the front door by Julian. He was even more amazed to find his very lurid check cap snatched off his head, and his bag of papers torn from his shoulder.

'Here!' he said feebly. 'What are you doing?'

'It's all right, Sid,' said Julian, holding him firmly. 'Just a joke. We've got a little treat in store for you.'

Sid didn't like jokes of this sort. He struggled, but soon gave it up. Julian was big and strong and very determined. Sid turned and watched Dick stride out with his bright check cap sideways on his head, and his paper-bag over his shoulder. He gasped when he saw Dick leap on the bicycle that he, Sid, had left by the gate, and go sailing off up the lane on it.

'What's he doing?' he asked Julian, amazed. 'Funny sort of joke this.'

'I know. Hope you don't mind,' said Julian, leading him firmly into the sitting-room.

'Did somebody bet him he wouldn't deliver the papers?' said Sid. 'So he's taken the bet on?'

'You're clever, you are, Sid,' said Julian, and Sid beamed all over his round face.

'Well, I hope he'll deliver them all right,' he said. 'Anyway, there's only two more, up at the farm. Yours is the last house but one that I go to. When's he coming back?'

'Soon,' said Julian. 'Will you stay and have supper with us, Sid?'

Sid's eyes nearly fell out of his head. 'Supper with you folks?' he said. 'Coo! That'd be a rare treat!'

'All right. You sit and look at these books,' said Julian, giving him two or three story books belonging to Anne. 'I'll just go and tell our cook to make a specially nice supper for you.'

Sid was all at sea about this unexpected treat, but quite willing to accept a free meal and sit down. He sat beaming on the couch, turning over the pages of a fairy-story book. Coo! What would his mother say when she heard he'd had supper at Kirrin Cottage? 'She wouldn't half be surprised,' thought Sid.

And now Julian had to tackle Joanna, and get her to join in their little plot. He went into the kitchen and shut the door. He looked so grave that Joanna was startled.

'What's the matter?' she said.

Julian told her. He told her about the kidnapping of George, and the strange note. He gave it to her to read. She sat down, her knees beginning to shake.

'It's the kind of thing you read in the papers, Julian,' she said, in rather a shaky voice. 'But it's funny when it happens to *you*! I don't like it – that's flat, I don't.'

470

'Nor do we,' said Julian, and went on to tell Joanna all they had arranged to do. She smiled a watery smile when he told her how Dick had gone off as the paper-boy in order to watch who took the notebook that night, and described how surprised Sid was.

'That Sid!' she said. 'We'll never hear the last of it, down in the village – him being invited here to supper. He's a strange boy, but there's no harm in him.

'I'll get him a fine supper, don't you worry. And I'll come and sit with you tonight in the lighted room – we'll play a card game. One that Sid knows – he's never got much beyond Snap and Happy Families.'

'That's a very good idea,' said Julian, who had been wondering how in the world they could amuse Sid all the evening. 'We'll play Snap – and let him win!'

Sid was quite overcome at his wonderful evening. First there was what he called a 'smasher of a supper', with ham and eggs and chip potatoes followed by jam tarts and a big chocolate mould, of which Sid ate about three-quarters.

'I'm partial to chocolate mould,' he explained to Anne. 'Joanna knows that – she knows I'm partial to anything in the chocolate line. She's friendly with my mum, so she knows the things I'm partial to, that I like very much.'

Anne giggled and agreed. She was enjoying Sid, although she was very worried and anxious. But Sid was so comical. He didn't mean to be. He was just enjoying himself hugely, and he said so every other minute.

In fact, he was really a very nice guest to have. It wasn't everybody who could welcome everything with so much gusto and say how wonderful it was half a dozen times on end.

He went out to the kitchen after supper and offered to wash up for Joanna. 'I always do it for Mum,' he said. 'I won't break a thing.' So he did the washing up and Anne did the drying. Julian thought it was a good thing to give her as much to do as possible, to stop her worrying.

Sid looked a bit taken-aback when he was asked to play games later on. 'Well – I dunno,' he said. 'I'm not much good at games. I did try to learn draughts, but all that jumping over one another got me muddled. If I want to jump over things I'll play leap-frog and do the thing properly.'

'Well – we did think of playing Snap,' said Julian, and Sid brightened up at once.

'Snap! That's right up my street!' he said. And so it was. His habit of shouting snap and collecting all the cards at the same moment as his shout, led to his winning quite a lot of games. He was delighted.

'This is a smasher of an evening,' he kept saying. 'Don't know when I've enjoyed myself so much. Wonder how that brother of yours is getting on – hope he brings my bike back all right.'

'Oh, he will,' said Julian, dealing out the cards for the sixth game of Snap. They were all in the lighted sitting-room now, sitting round a table in the window – Julian,

Joanna, Anne and Sid. Anyone watching would see them clearly – and would certainly not guess that Sid, the fourth one, was the paper-boy and not Dick.

At eleven o'clock Julian left to put the parcel that Anne had carefully wrapped up under the stone at the bottom of the garden. She had found a big notebook she thought would do, one that didn't seem at all important, and had wrapped it in paper and tied it with string. Julian had slipped a note inside.

Here is the notebook. Please release our cousin at once. You will get into serious trouble if you hold her any longer.

He slipped down the garden and shone his torch on the crazy paving there. When he came to the last stone he found that it had been loosened. He lifted it up easily and put the parcel into a hollow that seemed to have been prepared ready for it. He took a cautious look round, wondering if Dick was hidden anywhere about, but could see no one.

He was back in the lighted sitting-room in under two minutes, yelling 'Snap' with the others. He played stupidly, partly because he wanted the delighted Sid to win and partly because he was wondering about Dick. Was he all right?

An outbreak of owls hooting loudly made them all jump. Julian glanced at Joanna and Anne, and they nodded. They guessed that it was the signal to tell them that the parcel had been found and collected. Now they could get rid of Sid, and wait for Dick.

Joanna disappeared and came back with cups of chocolate and some buns. Sid's eyes gleamed. Talk about an evening!

Another hour was spent in eating and drinking and hearing Sid relate details of all the most exciting games of Snap he had ever played. He then went on to talk of Happy Families and seemed inclined to stay a bit longer and have a game at that.

'Your mum will be getting worried about you,' said Julian, looking at the clock. 'It's very late.'

'Where's my bike?' said Sid, realising with sorrow that

his 'smasher of an evening' was now over. 'Hasn't that brother of yours come back yet? Well, you tell him to leave it at my house in time for my paper-round tomorrow morning. And my cap, too. That's my Special Cap, that is. I'm very partial to that cap – it's a bit of a smasher.'

'It certainly is,' agreed Julian, who was now feeling very tired. 'Now listen, Sid. It's very late, and there may be bad folks about. If anyone speaks to you, run for your life, and don't stop till you get home.'

'Coo,' said Sid, his eyes nearly falling out of his head. 'Yes, I'll run all right.'

He shook hands solemnly with each of them and departed. He whistled loudly to keep his spirits up. The village policeman came unexpectedly round a corner on rubber soles and made him jump.

'Now then, young Sid,' said the policeman, sternly. 'What are you doing out this time of night?'

Sid didn't wait to answer. He fled and when he got home there was his bicycle by the front gate, complete with checked cap and paper-bag. 'That was a bit of all right!' thought Sid.

He glanced in disappointment at the dark windows of his house. Mum was in bed and asleep. Now he would have to wait till morning to tell her of his most remarkable evening.

And now, what had happened to Dick? He had shot out of the house and sailed away on Sid's bicycle, with Sid's dazzling cap on his head. He thought he saw a movement in the hedge nearby and guessed someone was hidden there, watching. He deliberately slowed down, got off his bicycle and pretended to do something to the wheel. Let the watcher see his bag of papers and be deceived into thinking he was without any doubt the paper-boy.

He rode to the farm and delivered the two papers there, then down to the village where he left Sid's things outside his house. Then he went into the cinema for a long while – until it was dark and he could safely creep back to Kirrin Cottage.

He set off at last, going a very roundabout way indeed. He came to the back of Kirrin garden. Where should he hide? Was anyone already hidden there? If so, the game was up – and he'd be caught, too!

CHAPTER ELEVEN

Dick makes a capture

DICK STOOD and listened, holding his breath. He could hear no sound except for the rustling of the trees around, and the sudden squeak of a field-mouse. It was a dark night and cloudy. Was there anyone hidden nearby, or could he find a hiding-place in safety and wait?

He thought for a few minutes, and decided that there wouldn't be anyone watching the back of the house now that it was dark. Julian and the others would be in full view of any watcher at the front, seated as they were in the lighted sitting-room – there would be no need for anyone to watch the back.

He debated where to hide and then made a quick decision. 'I'll climb a tree,' he thought. 'What about that one just near the crazy paving path? If the clouds clear away I could perhaps catch a glimpse of what the man's like who comes to collect the parcel. Then I'll shin quietly down the tree and stalk him.'

He climbed up into an oak tree that spread its broad branches over the path. He wriggled down in a comfortable fork and set himself to wait patiently.

What time had that note said? Eleven o'clock. Yes – Julian was to go down at eleven o'clock and put the parcel under the stone. He listened for the church clock to strike. If the wind was in the right direction he would hear it clearly.

It struck just then. Half past ten. Half an hour to wait. The waiting was the worst part. Dick put his hand into his pocket and brought out a bar of half-melted chocolate. He began to nibble it very gently, to make it last a long time.

The church clock struck a quarter to eleven. Dick finished the chocolate, and wondered if Julian would soon be along. Just as the clock began to chime the hour at eleven, the kitchen door opened and Dick saw Julian outlined in the opening. He had the parcel under his arm.

He saw Julian go swiftly down the path and sensed him looking all about. He dared not give the slightest hint to him that he was just above his head!

He heard Julian scrabble about in the path, and then drop the big stone back into its place. He watched the light of Julian's torch bobbing back up the path to the kitchen door. Then the door shut with a bang.

And now Dick could hardly breathe! Who would come for the parcel? He listened, stiff with excitement. The wind blew and a leaf rustled against the back of his neck making him jump. It felt as if a finger had touched him.

Five minutes went by and nobody came. Then he heard the slightest sound. Was that somebody crawling through the hedge? Dick strained his eyes but could only make out a deeper shadow that seemed to be moving. Then he could most distinctly hear somebody breathing hard as they tugged at the heavy stone! The parcel was being collected as arranged!

The stone plopped back. A shadow crept over to the hedge again. Whoever had the parcel was now going off with it.

Dick dropped quietly down. He had rubber shoes on and made no noise. He slipped through a big gap in the hedge nearby and stood straining his eyes to find the man he wanted to follow. Ah – there was a shadow moving steadily down the field path to the stile. Dick followed, keeping close to the hedge.

He kept well behind the moving shadow till it reached the stile, got over it and went into the lane beyond. When it got there it stopped, and a perfect fusillade of loud owl-hoots came to Dick's startled ears.

Of course! That was the signal that the parcel had been collected. Dick admired the excellent imitation of a little owl's loud, excited hooting.

The shadow stopped hooting and went on again. It obviously did not suspect that it might be followed and, although it moved quietly, it did not attempt to keep under cover. Down the lane it went and into a field.

Dick was about to follow when he heard the sound of voices. They were very low, and he couldn't hear a word. He crouched in the shadow of the gate, which was swung right back, leaving an entry into the field.

A loud noise made him jump. Then a brilliant light dazzled him and he felt glad he could duck down behind the gate. There was a car in the field. A car that had just started up its engine and switched on its lights. It was going, moving slowly down to the gate!

Dick tried his hardest to see who was in the car. He could make out only one man, and he was driving. It didn't seem as if anyone else was in the car at all. Where was the other fellow, then – the one who must have collected the parcel and given it to the man in the car? Had he been left behind? If so, Dick had better be careful!

The car was soon out in the lane. It gained speed and then Dick heard it roaring off in the distance. He couldn't stalk a car, that was certain! He held his breath, listening for some movement of the other man who, he felt certain, was still there.

He heard a sniff and crouched lower still. Then a shadow passed quickly through the gate, turned back in the direction of Kirrin Cottage and was lost in the darkness of the lane.

In a trice Dick was after it again. At least he could track down *this* fellow! He must be going somewhere!

Down the lane to the stile. Over the stile and into the field. Across the field and back at the hedge that grew at the bottom of Kirrin Cottage.

Why was this fellow going back there? Dick was puzzled. He heard the shadow creeping through the hedge and he followed. He watched it go silently up the path and peer in at a darkened window.

'Going to get into the house again and ransack it, I

suppose!' thought Dick, in a rage. He considered the shadowy figure by the window. It didn't look big. It must be a small man – one that Dick could tackle and bring to the ground. He could yell loudly for Julian, and maybe he could hold the fellow down till Julian came.

'And then perhaps *we* could do a little kidnapping, and a little bargaining, too,' thought Dick grimly. 'If *they* hold George as a hostage, we'll hold one of them, too! Tit for tat!'

He waited till the shadow left the window, and then he pounced. His victim went down at once with a yell.

Dick was surprised how small he was – but how he fought! He bit and scratched and heaved and kicked, and the two of them rolled over and over and over, breaking down Michaelmas daisies in the beds, and scratching legs and arms and faces on rose bushes. Dick yelled for Julian all the time.

'Julian! JULIAN! Help! JULIAN!'

Julian heard. He tore out at once. 'Dick, Dick, where are you? What is it?'

He flashed his torch towards the shouting and saw Dick rolling on top of somebody. He ran to help at once, throwing his torch on the grass so that both hands were free.

It wasn't long before they had the struggling figure firmly in their grips and dragged it, wailing, to the back door. Dick recognised that wailing voice! Good gracious – no, it couldn't be – it couldn't be Jo!

But it was! When they dragged her inside she collapsed completely, sobbing and wailing, rubbing her scratched and bruised legs, calling both boys all the names she could think of. Anne and Joanna looked on in complete amazement. *Now* what had happened?

'Put her upstairs,' said Julian. 'Get her to bed. She's in an awful state now. So am I! I wouldn't have hit her like that if I'd known it was only Jo.'

'I never guessed,' said Dick, wiping his filthy face with his handkerchief. 'My word, what a wild-cat! See how she's bitten me!'

'I didn't know it was you, Dick; I didn't know,' wailed Jo. 'You pounced on me, and I fought back. I wouldn't have bitten you like that.'

'You're a savage, deceitful, double-dealing little wild-cat,' said Dick, looking at his bites and scratches. 'Pretending you know nothing about the man who gave you that note – and all the time you're in with that crooked lot of thieves and kidnappers, whoever they are.'

'I'm not in with them,' wept Jo.

'Don't tell lies,' shouted Dick, in a fury. 'I was up in a tree when you came and took that parcel from under the stone – yes, and I followed you right to that car – and followed you back again! You came back here to steal again, I suppose?'

Jo gulped. 'No, I didn't.'

'You did! You'll be handed over to the police tomorrow,' said Dick, still furious.

'I *didn't* come back to steal. I came back for something else,' insisted Jo, her eyes peering through her tangled hair like a frightened animal's.

'Ho! So you say! And what did you come back for? To find another dog to dope?' jeered Dick.

'No,' said Jo, miserably. 'I came back to tell you I'd take you to where George was, if you wouldn't tell on me. My dad would half kill me if he thought I'd split on him. I know I took the parcel – I had to. I didn't know what it was or anything. I took it to the place I was told to. Jake told me. And then I came back to tell you all I could. And you set on me like that.'

Four pairs of eyes bored into Jo, and she covered her face. Dick took her hands away and made her look at him.

'Look here,' he said, 'this matters a lot to us, whether you are speaking the truth or not. Do you know where George is?'

Jo nodded.

'And will you take us there?' said Julian, his voice stern and cold.

Jo nodded again. 'Yes I will. You've been mean to me, but I'll show you I'm not as bad as you make out. I'll take you to George.'

CHAPTER TWELVE

Jo begins to talk

THE HALL clock suddenly struck loudly. 'DONG!'

'One o'clock,' said Joanna. 'One o'clock in the morning! Julian, we can't do any more tonight. This child here, she's not fit to take you traipsing out anywhere else. She's done for – she can hardly stand.'

'Yes, you're right Joanna,' said Julian, at once giving up the idea of going out to find George that night. 'We'll have to wait till tomorrow. It's a pity the telephone wires are cut. I do really think we ought to let the police know something about all this.'

Jo looked up at once. 'Then I won't tell you where George is,' she said. 'Do you know what the police will do to me if they get hold of me? They'll put me into a Home for Bad Girls, and I'll never get out again – because I *am* a bad girl and I do bad things. I've never had a chance.'

'Everyone gets a chance sooner or later,' said Julian gently. 'You'll get yours, Jo – but see you take it when it comes. All right – we'll leave the police out of it if you promise you'll take us to where George is. That's a bargain.'

Jo understood bargains. She nodded. Joanna pulled her to her feet and half led, half carried her upstairs.

'There's a couch in my room,' she told Julian. 'She can bed down there for the night – but late or not she's going to have a bath first. She smells like something the dog brought in!'

In half an hour's time Jo was tucked up on the couch in Joanna's room, perfectly clean, though marked with scratches and bruises from top to toe, hair washed, dried, and brushed so that it stood up in wiry curls like George's. A basin of steaming bread and milk was on a tray in front of her.

Joanna went to the landing and called across to Julian's room. 'Julian! Jo's in bed. She wants to say something to you and Dick.'

Dick and Julian put on dressing-gowns and went into Joanna's neat room. They hardly recognised Jo. She was wearing one of Anne's old nightgowns and looked very clean and childish and somehow pathetic.

Jo looked at them and gave them a very small smile. 'What do you want to say to us?' asked Julian.

'I've got some things to tell you,' said Jo, stirring the bread round and round in the basin. 'I feel good now – good and clean and – and all that. But maybe tomorrow I'll feel like I always do – and then I wouldn't tell you everything. So I'd better tell you now.'

'Go ahead,' said Julian.

'Well, I let the men into your house here, the night they came,' said Jo. Julian and Dick stared in astonishment. Jo went on stirring her bread round and round.

'It's true,' she said. 'I got in at that tiny window that was left unfastened, and then I went to the back door and opened it and let the men in. They did make a mess of that room, didn't they? I watched them. They took a lot of papers.'

'You couldn't possibly squeeze through that window,' said Dick at once.

'Well, I did,' said Jo. 'I've – I've squeezed through quite a lot of little windows. I know how to wriggle, you see. I can't get through such tiny ones as I used to, because I keep on growing. But yours was easy.'

'Phew!' said Julian, and let out a long breath. He hardly knew what to say. 'Well, go on. I suppose when the men had finished you locked and bolted the kitchen door after them and then squeezed out of the pantry window again?'

'Yes,' said Jo, and put a piece of milky bread into her mouth.

'What about Timmy? Who doped him so that he slept all that night?' demanded Dick.

'I did,' said Jo. 'That was easy, too.'

Both boys were speechless. To think that Jo did that, too! The wicked little misery!

'I made friends with Timmy on the beach, don't you remember?' said Jo. 'George was cross about it. I like dogs. We always had dozens till Mum died, and they'd do anything I told them. Dad told me what I was to do – make friends with Timmy so that I could meet him that night and give him meat with something in it.'

'I see. And it was very, very easy, because we sent Timmy out alone – straight into your hands,' said Dick bitterly.

'Yes. He came to me at once, he was glad to see me. I took him quite a long walk, letting him sniff the meat I'd got. When I gave it to him, he swallowed it all at once with hardly a chew!'

'And slept all night long so that your precious friends could break into the house,' said Julian. 'All I can say is that you are a hardened little rogue. Aren't you ashamed of anything?'

'I don't know,' said Jo, who wasn't really quite certain what feeling ashamed meant. 'Shall I stop telling you things?'

'No. For goodness' sake go on,' said Dick, hastily. 'Had you anything to do with George's kidnapping?'

'I just had to hoot like an owl when she and Timmy were coming,' said Jo. 'They were ready for her with a sack to put over her head – and they were going to bang Timmy on the head – with a stick to knock him out – then put him into a sack too. That's what I heard them say. But I didn't see them. I had to creep back here and shut the front door, so that if nobody missed George till morning they'd just think she'd gone out early somewhere.'

'Which is what we did think,' groaned Dick. 'What mutts we are! The only clever thing we thought of was to stalk the person who collected the parcel.'

'It was only me, though,' said Jo. 'And anyway, I was

coming back to tell you I would take you to George. Not because I like her – I don't. I think she's rude and horrible. I'd like her to stay kidnapped for years!'

'What a nice, kind nature!' said Julian to Dick, helplessly. 'What can you do with a kid like this?' He turned to Jo again. 'Seeing that you wish George would stay kidnapped for years, what made you decide to come and tell us where to find her?' he asked puzzled.

'Well, I don't like George – but I do like *him*!' said Jo, pointing with her spoon at Dick. 'He was nice to me, so I wanted to be nice back. I don't often feel like that,' she added hurriedly, as if being kind was some sort of weakness not really to be admired. 'I wanted him to go on liking me,' she said.

Dick looked at her. 'I shall like you if you take us to George,' he said. 'However, if you deceive us, I shall think you're like one of those sour damson stones – only fit to be spat out as far away as possible.'

'I'll take you tomorrow,' said Jo.

'Where *is* George?' asked Julian, bluntly, thinking it would be as well to know now, in case Jo changed her mind by the morning, and became her wicked little self again.

Jo hesitated. She looked at Dick. 'It would be very nice of you to tell us,' said Dick, in a kind voice. Jo loved a bit of kindness and couldn't resist this.

'Well,' she whispered, 'you know I told you my dad had gone off and left me to Jake. Dad didn't tell me why – but

Jake did. He shut George and Timmy into our caravan, harnessed Blackie the horse, and drove away in the night with them both. And I guess I know where he's gone – where he always goes when he wants to hide.'

'Where?' asked Julian, feeling so astounded at these extraordinary revelations that he really began to wonder if he was dreaming.

'In the middle of Ravens Wood,' said Jo. 'You don't know where that is, but I do. I'll take you tomorrow. I can't tell you any more now.' She began to spoon up her bread and milk very fast indeed, watching the boys through her long eyelashes.

Dick considered her. He felt pretty sure she had told them the truth, though he was equally certain she would have told lies if she could have got more by doing so.

He thought her a bad, cold-blooded, savage little monkey, but he pitied her, and admired her unwillingly for her courage.

He caught sight of her bruises and grazes, and bit his lip as he remembered how he had pounced on her and pummelled her, giving her back kick for kick and blow for blow – he hadn't guessed for one moment it was Jo. 'I'm sorry I hurt you so,' he said. 'You know I didn't mean to. It was a mistake.'

Jo looked at him as a slave might look at a king. 'I don't mind,' she said. 'I'd do anything for you, straight I would. You're kind.'

Joanna knocked impatiently at the door. 'Aren't you

491

ready yet, you boys?' she said. 'I want to come to bed. Tell Jo to stop talking, and you come on out too, and go to bed.'

The boys opened the door. Joanna took one look at their solemn faces and guessed that what Jo had told them was important. She took the empty basin from the girl's hands and pushed her down on the couch.

'Now you go straight off to sleep – and mind, if I hear any hanky-panky from you in the night I'll get up and give you such a hiding you won't be able to sit down for a month of Sundays,' she said roughly, but not unkindly.

Jo grinned. She understood that kind of talk. She snuggled down into the rugs, marvelling at the warmth and softness. She was already half-asleep. Joanna got into bed and switched off her light.

'Two o'clock in the morning!' she muttered as she heard the hall clock strike. 'Such goings-on! I'll never wake up in time to tell the milkman I want more milk.'

Soon only Julian was awake. He worried about whether he was doing right or not. Poor George – was she safe? Would that scamp of a Jo really lead them to the caravan next day – or might she lead them right into the lion's mouth, and get them all captured? Julian simply didn't know.

CHAPTER THIRTEEN

Off to find George

JOANNA WAS the only one in the household who woke up reasonably early the next morning – but even she was too late to catch the milkman. She scurried downstairs at half past seven, an hour later than usual, tying up her apron as she went.

'Half past seven – what a time to wake up!' she muttered, as she began to make breakfast. She thought of all the happenings of the night before – the strange evening with young Sid, Dick's capture of Jo – and Jo's extraordinary tale. She had had a look at Jo before she went down, half expecting that lively young rogue to have disappeared in the night.

But Jo was curled up like a kitten, her brown cheek on her brown paw, her hair, unusually bright and tidy, falling over her tightly-shut eyes. She didn't even stir when Joanna scurried about the bedroom, washing and dressing.

The others were fast asleep, too. Julian woke first, but not till eight o'clock. He remembered immediately all that had happened, and jumped out of bed at once.

He went to Joanna's room. He could hear Joanna downstairs talking to herself as usual. He peeped round the open door of her bedroom. Thank goodness – Jo was still there.

He went and shook her gently. She wriggled away, turned over and buried her face in the pillow. Julian shook her more vigorously. He meant to get her up and make her take them to where George was as soon as possible!

Most miraculously everyone was down at half past eight, eating porridge and looking rather subdued. Jo had hers in the kitchen, and the others could hear Joanna scolding her for her manners.

'Have you got to stuff yourself like that, as if the dog's going to come and lick your plate before you've finished? And who told you to stick your fingers into the syrup and lick them? I've eyes in the back of my head, so just you be careful what you're doing!'

Jo liked Joanna. She knew where she was with her. If she kept on Joanna's right side and did what she was told, Joanna would feed her well and not interfere too much – but if she didn't, then she could expect something else she understood very well indeed – scoldings and even a sharp slap. Joanna was good-natured but impatient, and no child was ever afraid of her. Jo followed her about like a little dog when she had finished her breakfast.

Julian came out into the kitchen at nine o'clock. 'Where's Jo?' he said. 'Oh, there you are. Now, what about taking us to where your father's caravan is? You're sure you know the way?'

Jo laughed scornfully. 'Course I do! I know everywhere round here for miles.'

'Right,' said Julian, and he produced a map, which he spread out on the kitchen table. He put a finger on one spot. 'That's Kirrin,' he said. 'And here's a place called Ravens Wood. Is that the place you mean? How do you propose to get there – by this road, or that one?'

Jo looked at the map. It meant nothing to her at all. She gazed vaguely at the spot that Julian had pointed to.

'Well?' said Julian, impatiently. 'Is that the Ravens Wood you mean?'

'I don't know,' said Jo, helplessly. 'The one I mean is a real wood – I don't know anything about yours on this map.'

Joanna gave a little snort. 'Julian, maps are wasted on her. I don't expect she's ever seen one in her life! She can't even read!'

'*Can't* she?' said Julian, amazed. 'Then she can't write either.' He looked questioningly at Jo.

She shook her head. 'Mum tried to teach me to read,' she said, 'but Mum wasn't very good herself. What's the good of reading, anyway? Won't help you to trap rabbits or catch fish for your dinner, will it?'

'No. It's used for other things,' said Julian, amused. 'Well – maps are no good to *you*, I can see.' He rolled his map up, looking thoughtful. It was very difficult to know exactly how to deal with a person like Jo, who knew so little of some things and so much of others.

'She'll know the way all right,' said Joanna, scraping out a saucepan. 'They're like dogs, these folk – they can smell out any road they want.'

'*Do* you smell out your way like a dog?' asked Anne, curiously. She had come in to see what was going on, and was quite willing to believe that Jo really could smell her way here and there, as Timmy did.

'No, I don't,' said Jo. 'I just know the way I have to go. And I don't go by the roads, either! They take too long to get to a place. I take the shortest way, see?'

'How do you know it's the shortest way?' asked Anne.

Jo shrugged her thin shoulders. All this was very boring to her.

'Where's that other boy?' she said. 'Isn't he coming? I want to see him.'

'She's just crazy on Dick,' said Joanna, taking up another saucepan. 'Here he is – now you can go and lick his boots if you want to, young Jo!'

'Hallo, Jo!' said Dick, with one of his amiable grins. 'Ready to take us travelling?'

'Better go at night,' said Jo, staring at Dick.

'Oh, no!' said Dick. 'We're going *now*. We're not going to be put off like that. *Now*, Jo, now!'

'If my dad sees us coming he'll be mad,' said Jo obstinately.

'Very well,' said Dick, looking at Julian. 'We'll go by ourselves. We've found Ravens Wood on the map. We can easily get there.'

'Pooh,' said Jo, rudely. 'You can get there all right – but it's a big place, Ravens Wood is – and nobody but me and Dad knows where we hide the caravan there. And if Dad wants to keep George quite safe, he'll take her to our hidey-hole in the middle of the wood, see? You can't go without me.'

'Right. Then we'll get the police to take us,' said Julian, quite cheerfully. 'They will help us to comb the wood from end to end. We'll soon find George.'

'No!' cried Jo, in alarm. 'You said you wouldn't! You promised!'

'*You* made a promise too,' said Julian. 'It was a bargain. But I see you're not really to be trusted. I'll just get on my bike and ride down to the police station.'

But before he could go out of the room Jo flung herself on him and clung to his arm like a cat. 'No, no! I'll take you. I'll keep my promise! But it *would* be best to go at night!'

'I'm not putting things off any more,' said Julian, shaking Jo off his arm. 'If you mean what you say, you'll come with us now. Make up your mind.'

'I'll come,' said Jo.

'Hadn't we better give her another pair of shorts or something?' said Anne, suddenly seeing a tremendous hole in Jo's grubby shorts. 'She can't go out like that. And look at her awful jersey. It's full of holes.'

The boys looked at it. 'She'd smell a bit better if she had clean clothes,' said Joanna. 'There's that old pair of shorts I washed for George last week, and mended up. Jo could have those. And there's an old shirt of hers she could have, too.'

In five minutes' time Jo was proudly wearing a pair of perfectly clean, much-mended shorts of George's, and a shirt like the one Anne had on. Anne looked at her and laughed.

'Now she's more like George than ever! They might be sisters.'

'Brothers, you mean,' said Dick. 'George and Jo – what a pair!'

498

Jo scowled. She didn't like George, and she didn't want to look like her.

'She's even got George's scowl!' said Anne. Jo turned her back at once, and Joanna then got the benefit of the scowl.

'My word, what an ugly creature you are!' said Joanna. 'You be careful the wind doesn't change – you might get your face stuck like that!'

'Oh, come on,' said Julian, impatiently. 'Jo! Do you hear me? Come along now and take us to Ravens Wood.'

'Jake might see us,' said Jo, sulkily. She was determined to put off going as long as she could.

'Yes, he might,' said Julian, who hadn't thought of that. 'Well – you go on a long way ahead, and we'll follow. We won't let Jake know you're leading us anywhere.'

At last they set off. Joanna had packed them up a meal in case they wanted one. Julian slipped the package into a bag and slid it over his shoulder.

Jo slipped out the back way, went down to the bottom of the garden and made her way out to the lane through a little thicket. The others went out of the front gate and walked up the lane slowly, watching for Jo to appear.

'There she is,' said Julian. 'Come on. We must keep the little wretch in sight. I wouldn't be surprised if she gave us the slip even now!'

Jo danced on in front, a good way ahead. She took no notice of the others behind, and they followed steadily.

Then suddenly something happened. A dark figure strode out from the hedge, stood in front of Jo, and said something to her. She screamed and tried to dodge away. But the man caught hold of her and firmly pulled her into the hedge.

'It was Jake!' said Dick. 'I'm sure it was Jake. He was watching out for her. *Now* what do we do?'

CHAPTER FOURTEEN

Simmy's caravan

THEY ALL hurried up to the place where Jake had caught hold of Jo. There was absolutely nothing to be seen except a few broken twigs in the hedge. No Jake, no Jo. There was not a sound to be heard, either. Not a scream from Jo, not a shout from Jake. It was as if both had faded into the hedge and disappeared.

Dick squeezed through the hedge and into the field beyond. Nobody was there either, except a few cows who looked at him in surprise, their tails whisking.

'There's a little copse at the end of the field,' called back Dick. 'I bet they're there. I'll go and see.'

He ran across the field to the copse. But there was nobody there either. Beyond the copse was a row of huddled-up cottages. Dick looked along the untidy row, exasperated.

'I suppose Jake's taken her to one of those,' he thought, angrily. 'Probably lives there! Well, he won't let her go, that's certain. He most likely guesses that she's in with us now. Poor Jo!'

He went back to the others and they had a low-voiced conference in the lane. 'Let's tell the police now,' begged Anne.

'No. Let's go to Ravens Wood ourselves,' said Dick. 'We know where it is. We wouldn't be able to go the way Jo would have taken us – but at least we can go by the map.'

'Yes. I think we will,' said Julian. 'Come on, then. Quick march!'

They went on up the lane, took a field path and came out eventually on to a road. A bus passed them in the opposite direction to which they were going.

'When we come to a bus stop we'll find out if one goes anywhere near Ravens Wood,' said Julian. 'It would save a lot of time if we caught a bus. We'd be there long before Jake, if he thinks of going to warn Jo's father we're on the way! I bet Jo will tell him. You might as well trust a snake as that slippery little thing.'

'I hate Jo!' said Anne, almost in tears. 'I don't trust her a bit. Do you, Dick?'

'I don't know,' said Dick. 'I can't make up my mind. She hasn't really proved whether she's trustable or not yet. Anyway, she came back to tell us all she knew last night, didn't she?'

'I don't believe she *did* come back for that,' said Anne obstinately. 'I believe she was coming back to pry and snoop.'

'You may be right,' said Dick. 'Look, here's a bus stop – and a time-table!'

A bus did apparently go quite near Ravens Wood, and was due in five minutes' time. They sat down on the bus stop seat and waited. The bus was punctual and came rumbling down the road, full of women going to Ravens Market. They all seemed very plump women and had enormous baskets, so it was difficult to squeeze inside.

Everyone got out at Ravens Market. Julian asked his way to Ravens Wood. 'There it is,' said the conductor, pointing down the hill to where trees grew thickly in the valley. 'It's a big place. Don't get lost! And look out for the travellers. There's usually hordes of them there!'

'Thanks,' said Julian, and the three of them set off down the hill into the valley. They came to the wood.

'It's a proper wood,' said Anne. 'Nothing but trees and trees. I should think it gets very thick in the middle – like a forest.'

They came to a clearing where there was a little travellers' camp. Three rather dirty-looking caravans stood together, and a crowd of children were playing some sort of a game with a rope. Julian took a quick look at the caravans. All had their doors open.

'No George here,' he said in a low voice to the others. 'I wish I knew exactly where to go! I suppose if we follow this broad pathway it would be best. After all, Jo's caravan must have a fairly broad way to go on.'

'Can't we ask if anyone knows if Jo's caravan is anywhere about?' said Anne.

'We don't know her father's name,' said Julian.

'But we could say it's a caravan drawn by a horse called Blackie, and that a girl called Jo lives in it with her father,' said Anne.

'Yes. I'd forgotten the horse,' said Julian. He went up to an old woman who was stirring something in a black pot over a fire of sticks. Julian thought she looked very like a witch. She peered up at him through tangled grey hair.

'Can you tell me if there's a caravan in the wood drawn by a horse called Blackie?' he asked politely. 'A girl called Jo lives in it with her father. We want to see her.'

The old woman blinked. She took an iron spoon out of the pot and waved it to the right.

'Simmy's gone down-away there,' she said. 'I didn't sec Jo this time – but the caravan door was shut so maybe she was inside. What do you want with Jo?'

'Oh – only just to see her,' said Julian, quite unable to think up a good reason for going to visit on the spur of the moment. 'Is Simmy her father?'

The old woman nodded and began to stir her pot again. Julian went back to the others.

'This way,' he said, and they went down the rutted path. It was just wide enough for a caravan to go down. Anne looked up. Tree branches waved overhead.

'I should think they brush against the roof of a caravan all the time,' she said. 'What a funny life to live – in a little caravan day in and day out, hiding yourself away in woods and fields!'

They walked on down the path, which wound about through the trees, following the clear spaces. Sometimes the trees were so close together that it seemed impossible for a caravan to go between. But the wheel-ruts showed that caravans did go down the path.

After a time the wood became thicker, and the sunlight could hardly pierce through the branches. Still the path went on, but now it seemed as if only one set of wheel-ruts was marked on it. They were probably the wheels of Simmy's caravan.

Here and there a tree was shorn of one of its branches, and a bush uprooted and thrown to one side.

'Simmy meant to go deep into the wood last time he came,' said Julian, pointing to where a bush lay dying by the side of the path. 'He's cleared the way here and there. Actually we aren't on a proper path any longer – we're only following wheel-ruts.'

It was true. The path had faded out. They were now in a thick part of the wood, with only the ruts of the caravan wheels to guide them.

They fell silent. The wood was very quiet. There were no birds singing, and the branches of the trees were so thick that there was a kind of green twilight round them.

'I wish we had Timmy with us,' half-whispered Anne at last.

Julian nodded. He had been wishing that a long time. He was also wishing he hadn't brought Anne – but when they had started out, they had Jo with them to guide them, and warn them of any danger. Now they hadn't.

'I think we'd better go very cautiously,' he said, in a low voice. 'We may come on the caravan unexpectedly. We don't want Simmy to hear us and lie in wait.'

'I'll go a little way in front and warn you if I hear or

see anything,' said Dick. Julian nodded to him and he went on ahead, peering round the trees when he came to any curve in the wheel-rut path. Julian began to think of what they would do when they reached the caravan. He was pretty certain that both George and Timmy would be found locked up securely inside.

'If we can undo the door and let them out, Timmy will do the rest,' he thought. 'He's as good as three policemen! Yes – that's the best plan.'

Dick suddenly stopped and lifted up his hand in warning. He peered round the trunk of a big tree, and then turned and nodded excitedly.

'He's found the caravan!' said Anne, and her heart began its usual thump-thump-thump of excitement.

'Stay here,' said Julian to Anne, and went on quietly to join Dick. Anne crept under a bush. She didn't like this dark, silent wood, with the green light all round. She peered out, watching the boys.

Dick had suddenly seen the caravan. It was small, badly needed painting, and appeared quite deserted. No fire burned outside. No Simmy was sitting anywhere about. Not even Blackie the horse was to be seen.

The boys watched intently for a few minutes, not daring to move or speak. There was absolutely no sound or movement from the tiny clearing in which the caravan stood.

Windows and doors were shut. The shafts rested crookedly on the ground. The whole place seemed deserted.

'Dick,' whispered Julian at last, 'Simmy doesn't seem to be about. This is our chance! We'll creep over to the caravan and look into the window. We'll attract George's attention, and get her out as soon as we can. Timmy, too.'

'Funny he docsn't bark,' said Dick, also in a whisper. 'I suppose he can't have heard us. Well – shall we get over to the caravan now?'

They ran quietly to the little caravan, and Julian peered through the dirty window. It was too dark inside to see anything at all.

'George!' he whispered. 'George! Are you there?'

CHAPTER FIFTEEN

Anne doesn't like adventures

THERE WAS no answer from inside the caravan. Perhaps George was asleep – or drugged! And Timmy, too. Julian's heart sank. It would be dreadful if George had been ill-treated. He tried to peer inside the window again, but what with the darkness of the wood and the dirt on the pane, it really was impossible to see inside.

'Shall we bang on the door?' asked Dick.

'No. That would only bring Simmy if he's anywhere about – and if George is inside and awake, our voices would have attracted her attention,' said Julian.

They went quietly round the caravan to the door at the back. It had no key in the lock. Julian frowned.

Simmy must have got the key with him. That would mean breaking down the door and making a noise. He went up the few steps and pushed at the door. It seemed very solid indeed. How could he break it down, anyway? He had no tools, and it didn't look as if kicking and shoving would burst it in.

He knocked gently on the door – rap-rap-rap. Not a movement from inside. It seemed very strange. He tried the round handle, and it turned easily.

It not only turned easily – but the door opened! 'Dick!

508

ANNE DOESN'T LIKE ADVENTURES

It's not locked!' said Julian, forgetting to whisper in his surprise. He went inside the dark caravan, hardly hoping now to see George or Timmy.

Dick pushed in after him. There was a nasty sour smell and it was very untidy. Nobody was there. It was quite empty, as Julian had feared.

He groaned. 'All this way for nothing. They've taken George somewhere else. We're done now, Dick – we haven't a clue where to go next.'

Dick fished his torch out of his pocket. He flashed it over the untidy jumble of things in the caravan, looking for some sign that George had been there. But there was nothing at all that he could see to show him that either Timmy or George had been there.

'It's quite likely that Jo made the whole story up about her father taking George away,' he groaned. 'It doesn't look as if they've been here at all.'

His torch flashed on to the wooden wall of the caravan, and Dick saw something that caught his attention. Somebody had written something on the wall!

He looked more closely. 'Julian! Isn't that George's writing? Look! What's written there?'

Both boys bent towards the dirty wall. 'Red Tower, Red Tower, Red Tower,' was written again and again, in very small writing.

'Red Tower!' said Dick. 'What does that mean? *Is* it George's writing?'

'Yes, I think so,' said Julian. 'But why should she keep

writing that? Do you suppose that's where they have taken her to? She might have heard them saying something and scribbled it down quickly – just in *case* we found the caravan and examined it. Red Tower! It sounds most peculiar.'

510

'It must be a house with a red tower, I should think,' said Dick. 'Well – we'd better get back and tell the police now – and they'll have to hunt for a red tower somewhere.'

Bitterly disappointed the boys went back to Anne. She scrambled out from under her bush as they came.

'George is not there,' said Dick. 'She's gone. But she *has* been there – we saw some scribbled writing on the wall of the caravan inside.'

'How do you know it's hers?' said Anne.

'Well, she's written "Red Tower" ever so many times, and the R's and the T's are just like hers,' said Dick. 'We think she must have heard someone talking and say they were taking her to Red Tower, wherever that is. We're going straight back to the police now. I wish we hadn't trusted Jo. We've wasted such a lot of time.'

'Let's have something to eat,' said Julian. 'We won't sit down. We'll eat as we go. Come on.'

But somehow nobody wanted anything to eat. Anne said she felt sick. Julian was too worried to eat, and Dick was so anxious to go that he felt he couldn't even wait to unpack sandwiches! So they started back down the path, following the wheel-ruts as before.

It suddenly grew very dark indeed, and on the leaves of the trees heavy rain fell with a loud, pattering sound. Thunder suddenly rolled.

Anne caught hold of Julian's arm, startled. 'Julian! It's dangerous to be in a wood, isn't it, in a storm? Oh, Julian,

511

we'll be struck by lightning.'

'No, we shan't,' said Julian. 'A wood's no more dangerous than anywhere else. It's sheltering under a lone tree somewhere that's dangerous. Look – there's a little clearing over there; we'll go to that, if you like.'

But when they got to the little clearing the rain was falling down in such heavy torrents that Julian could see that they would immediately be soaked through. He hurried Anne to a clump of bushes, and they crouched underneath, waiting for the storm to pass.

Soon the rain stopped, and the thunder rolled away to the east. There had been no lightning that they could see. The wood grew just a little lighter, as if somewhere above the thick green branches the sun might be shining!

'I hate this wood,' said Dick, crawling out from the bushes. 'Come on, for goodness' sake. Let's get back to the wheel-rut path.'

He led the way through the trees. Julian called to him. 'Wait, Dick. Are you sure this is right?'

Dick stopped, anxious at once. 'Well,' he said uncertainly. 'I thought it was. But I don't know. Do you?'

'*I* thought it was through those trees there,' said Julian. 'Where that little clearing is.'

They went to it. 'It's not the same clearing, though,' said Anne at once. 'The other clearing had a dead tree at one side. There's no dead tree here.'

'Blow!' said Julian. 'Well – try *this* way, then.'

They went to the left, and soon found themselves in a

thicker part of the wood than ever. Julian's heart went cold. What an absolute idiot he was! He might have known that it was madness to leave the only path they knew without marking it in some way.

Now he hadn't the very faintest idea where the wheel-rut way was. It might be in any direction! He hadn't even the sun to guide him.

He looked gloomily at Dick. 'Bad show!' said Dick. 'Well – we'll have to make up our minds which way to go! We can't just stay here.'

'We might go deeper and deeper and deeper,' said Anne, with a sudden little gulp of fear. Julian put his arm round her shoulder.

'Well, if we go deeper and deeper, we shall come out on the other side!' he said. 'It's not an endless wood, you know.'

'Well, let's go straight on through the wood, then,' said Anne. 'We'll *have* to come out the other side some time.'

The boys didn't tell her that it was impossible to go straight through a wood. It was necessary to go round clumps of bushes, to double back sometimes when they came to an impenetrable part, and to go either to the left or right when clumps of trees barred their way. It was quite impossible to go *straight* through.

'For all I know we're probably going round and round in circles, like people do when they're lost in the desert,' he thought. He blamed himself bitterly for having left the wheel-ruts.

They made their way on and on for about two or three hours, and then Anne stumbled and fell. 'I can't go on any further,' she wept. 'I must have a rest.'

Dick glanced at his watch and whistled. Where ever had the time gone? It was almost three o'clock. He sat down by Anne and pulled her close to him. 'What we want is a jolly good meal,' he said. 'We've had nothing since breakfast.'

Anne said she still wasn't hungry, but when she smelt the meat sandwiches that Joanna had made she changed her mind. She was soon eating with the others, and feeling much better.

'There's nothing to drink, unfortunately,' said Dick. 'But Joanna's packed tomatoes and plums, too – so we'll have those instead of a drink. They're nice and juicy.'

They ate everything, though secretly Julian wondered if it was a good thing to wolf all their food at once. There was no telling how long they might be lost in Ravens Wood! Joanna might get worried sooner or later and tell the police they had gone there, and a search would be made. But it might be ages before they were found.

Anne fell asleep after her meal. The boys talked softly over her head. 'I don't much like this,' said Dick. 'We set out to find George – and all we've done is to lose ourselves. We don't seem to be managing this adventure as well as we usually do.'

'If we don't get out before dark we'll have to make up some kind of bed under a bush,' said Julian. 'We'll have another go when Anne wakes – and we'll do a bit of yelling, too. Then if we're still lost, we'll bed down for the night.' But when darkness came – and it came very early in that thick wood – they were still as much lost as ever. They were all hoarse with shouting too.

In silence they pulled bracken from an open space and piled it under a sheltering bush. 'Thank goodness it's warm tonight,' said Dick, trying to sound cheerful. 'Well – we'll all feel much more lively in the morning. Cuddle up to me, Anne, and keep warm. That's right. Julian's on the other side of you! This is quite an adventure.'

'I don't like adventures,' said Anne, in a small voice, and immediately fell asleep.

CHAPTER SIXTEEN

Visitor in the night

IT TOOK a long time for Julian and Dick to fall asleep. They were both worried – worried about George and worried about themselves, too. They were also very hungry, and their hunger kept them awake as much as their anxiety.

Dick fell asleep at last. Julian still lay awake, hoping that Anne was nice and warm between them. He didn't feel very warm himself.

He heard the whisper of the leaves in the trees, and then the scamper of tiny paws behind his head. He wondered what animal it was – a mouse?

Something ran lightly over his hair and he shivered. A spider, perhaps. Well he couldn't move, or he would disturb Anne. If it wanted to make a web over his hair it would have to. He shut his eyes and began to doze off. Soon he was dreaming.

He awoke very suddenly, with a jump. He heard the hoot of an owl. That must have been what wakened him. Now it would be ages before he slept again.

He shut his eyes. The owl hooted again and Julian frowned, hoping that Anne would not wake. She stirred and muttered in her sleep. Julian touched her lightly. She felt quite warm.

He settled down again and shut his eyes. Then he opened them. He had heard something! Not an owl or the pattering of some little animal's feet – but another sound, a bigger one. He listened. There was a rustling going on somewhere. Some much bigger animal was about.

Julian was suddenly panic-stricken. Then he reasoned sternly with himself. There were no dangerous wild animals in this country, not even a wolf. It was probably a badger out on a nightly prowl. He listened for any snuffling sound, but he heard none, only the rustling as the animal moved about through the bushes.

It came nearer. It came right over to him! He felt warm breath on his ear and made a quick movement of revulsion. He sat up swiftly and put out his hand. It fell on something warm and hairy. He withdrew his hand at once, feeling for his torch in panic. To touch something warm and hairy in the pitch darkness was too much even for Julian!

Something caught hold of his arm, and he gave a yell and fought it off. Then he got the surprise of his life. The animal spoke.

'Julian!' said a voice. 'It's me!'

Julian, his hands trembling, flashed his torch round. The light fell on a dirty dark face, with tangled hair over its eyes.

'Jo!' said Julian. 'JO! What on earth are you doing here? You scared me stiff. I thought you were some horrible hairy animal. I must have touched your head.'

517

'You did,' said Jo, squeezing in under the bush. Anne and Dick, who had both woken up at Julian's yell, gazed at her, speechless with surprise. Jo of all people here in the middle of the wood! How had she got there?

'You're surprised to see me, aren't you?' said Jo. 'I got caught by Jake. But he didn't know you were following behind. He dragged me off to the cottage he lives in and locked me up. He knew I'd spent the night at Kirrin Cottage, and he said he was going to take me to my dad, who would give me the worst hiding I'd ever had in my life. So he would, too.'

'So that's what happened to you!' said Dick.

518

'Then I broke the window and got out,' said Jo. 'That Jake! I'll never do a thing he tells me again – locking me up like that. I hate that worse than anything! Well, then I came to look for you.'

'How did you find us?' said Julian, in wonder.

'Well, first I went to the caravan,' said Jo. 'Old Ma Smith – the one who always sits stirring a pot – she told me you'd been asking for my dad's caravan. I guessed you'd go off to find it. So along I went after you – but there was the caravan all by itself, and nobody there. Not even George.'

'Where *is* George, do you know?' asked Anne.

'No. I don't,' said Jo. 'Dad's taken her somewhere else. I expect he put her on Blackie, because Blackie's gone, too.'

'What about Timmy?' asked Dick.

Jo looked away. 'I reckon they've done Timmy in,' she said. Nobody said anything. The thought that Timmy might have come to harm was too dreadful to speak about.

'How did you find us here?' asked Julian at last.

'That was easy,' said Jo. 'I can follow anybody's trail. I'd have come quicker, but it got dark. My, you did wander round, didn't you?'

'Yes. We did,' said Dick. 'Do you mean to say you followed all our wanderings in and out and round about?'

'Oh, yes,' said Jo. 'Properly tired me out, you did, with all your messing round and round. Why did you leave the wheel-ruts?'

Julian told her. 'You're daft,' said Jo. 'If you're going somewhere off the path, just mark the trees with a nick as you go along – one here and one there – and then you can always find your way back.'

'We didn't even know we were lost till we were,' said Anne. She took Jo's hand and squeezed it. She was so very, very glad to see her. Now they would be able to get out of this horrible wood.

Jo was surprised and touched, but she withdrew her hand at once. She didn't like being fondled, though she would not have minded Dick taking her hand. Dick was her hero, someone above all others. He had been kind to her, and she was glad she had found him.

'We found something written on the caravan wall,' said Julian. 'We think we know where George has been taken. It's a place called Red Tower. Do you know it?'

'There's no place called Red Tower,' said Jo at once. 'It's . . .'

'Don't be silly, Jo. You can't possibly know if there's no place called Red Tower,' said Dick, impatiently. 'There may be hundreds of places with that name. That's the place we've got to find, anyway. The police will know it.'

Jo gave a frightened movement. 'You promised you wouldn't tell the police.'

'Yes – we promised that – but only if you took us to George,' said Dick. 'And you didn't. And anyway if you *had* taken us to the caravan George wouldn't have been there. So we'll jolly well have to call in the police now and find out where Red Tower is.'

'*Was* it Red Tower George had written down?' asked Jo. 'Well, then – I *can* take you to George!'

'How can you, when you say there's no place called Red Tower?' began Julian, exasperated. 'I don't believe a word you say, Jo. You're a fraud – and I half-believe you're still working for our enemies too!'

'I'm not,' said Jo. 'I'm NOT! You're mean. I tell you Red Tower isn't a place. Red Tower is a man.'

There was a most surprised silence after this astonishing remark. A man! Nobody had thought of that.

Jo spoke again, pleased at the surprise she had caused. 'His name's Tower, and he's got red hair, flaming red – so he's called Red Tower. See?'

'Are you making this up, by any chance?' asked Dick, after a pause. 'You have made up things before, you know.'

'All right. You can think I made it up, then,' said Jo, sulkily. 'I'll go. Get yourselves out of this the best you can. You're mean.'

She wriggled away, but Julian caught hold of her arm. 'Oh, no, you don't! You'll just stay with us now, if I have to tie you to me all night long! You see, we find it difficult to trust you, Jo – and that's your fault, not ours. But we'll trust you just this once. Tell us about Red Tower, and take us to where he lives. If you do that, we'll trust you for evermore.'

521

'Will Dick trust me, too?' said Jo, trying to get away from Julian's hand.

'Yes,' said Dick shortly. He felt as if he would dearly like to smack this unpredictable, annoying, extraordinary, yet somehow likeable ragamuffin girl. 'But I don't feel as if I *like* you very much at present. If you want us to like you as well as to trust you, you'll have to help us a lot more than you have done.'

'All right,' said Jo, and she wriggled down again. 'I'm tired. I'll show you the way out in the morning, and then I'll take you to Red's. But you won't like Red. He's a beast.'

She would say nothing more, so once again they tried to sleep. They felt happier now that Jo was with them and would show them the right way out of the wood. Julian hardly thought she would leave them in the lurch now. He shut his eyes and was soon dreaming.

Jo woke first. She uncurled like an animal and stretched, forgetting where she was. She woke up the others, and they all sat up, feeling stiff, dirty and hungry.

'I'm thirsty as well as hungry,' complained Anne. 'Where can we get something to eat and drink?'

'Better get back home for a wash and a meal, and to let Joanna know where we are,' said Julian. 'Come on, Jo – show us the way.'

Jo led the way immediately. The others wondered how in the world she knew it. They were even more astonished when they found themselves on the wheel-rut path in about two minutes.

'Gracious! We were as near to it as that!' said Dick. 'And yet we seemed to walk for miles through this horrible wood.'

'You did,' said Jo. 'You went round in an enormous circle, and you were almost back where you started. Come on – I'll take you *my* way back to your house now – it's much better than any bus!'

CHAPTER SEVENTEEN

Off in George's boat

JOANNA WAS extremely thankful to see them. She had been so worried the night before that if the telephone wires in the house had been mended, she would most certainly have rung up the police. As it was, she couldn't telephone, and the night was so dark that she was really afraid of walking all the way down to the village.

'I haven't slept all night,' she declared. 'This mustn't happen again, Julian. It's worrying me to death. And now you haven't got George or Timmy. I tell you, if they don't turn up soon I'll take matters into my own hands. I haven't heard from your uncle and aunt either – let's hope they're not lost, too!'

She bustled about after this outburst, and was soon frying sausages and tomatoes for them. They couldn't wait till they were cooked, and helped themselves to great hunks of bread and butter.

'I can't even go and wash till I've had something,' said Anne. 'I'm glad you know so many short cuts back here, Jo – the way didn't seem nearly so long as when we came by bus.'

It had really been amazing to see the deft, confident manner in which Jo had taken them home, through fields

524

and little narrow paths, over stiles and across allotments. She was never once at a loss.

They had arrived not long after Joanna had got up, and she had almost cried with surprise and relief when she had seen them walking up the front path.

'And a lot of dirty little tatterdemalions you looked,' she said, as she turned their breakfast out on to a big dish. 'And still do, for that matter. I'll get the kitchen fire going for a bath for you. You might all be sister and brothers to that ragamuffin Jo.'

Jo didn't mind remarks of this sort at all. She chewed her bread and grinned. She wolfed the breakfast with no manners at all – but the others were nearly as bad, they were so hungry!

'It's a spade and trowel you want for your food this morning, not a knife and fork,' said Joanna, disapprovingly. 'You're just shovelling it in. No, I can't cook you any more, Julian. There's not a sausage left in the house nor a bit of bacon either. You fill up with toast and marmalade.'

The bath water ran vigorously after breakfast. All four had baths. Jo didn't want to, but Joanna ran after her with a carpet beater, vowing and declaring she would beat the dust and dirt out of her if she didn't bath. So Jo bathed, and quite enjoyed it.

They had a conference after breakfast. 'About this fellow, Red Tower,' said Julian. 'Who is he, Jo? What do you know about him?'

'Not much,' said Jo. 'He's rich, and he talks strange, and I think he's mad. He gets fellows like Dad and Jake to do his dirty work for him.'

'What dirty work?' asked Dick.

'Oh – stealing and such,' said Jo, vaguely. 'I don't really know. Dad doesn't tell me much; I just do what I'm told, and don't ask questions. I don't want more slaps than I get!'

'Where does he live?' said Anne. 'Far away?'

'He's taken a house on the cliff,' said Jo. 'I don't know the way by land. Only by boat. It's an odd place – like a small castle almost, with very thick stone walls. Just the place for Red, my dad says.'

'Have you been there?' asked Dick, eagerly.

Jo nodded. 'Oh, yes,' she said. 'Twice. My dad took a big iron box there once, and another time he took something in a sack. I went with him.'

'Why?' asked Julian. 'I shouldn't have thought he'd wanted you messing round!'

'I rowed the boat,' said Jo. 'I told you, Red's place is up on the cliff. We got to it by boat; I don't know the way by road. There's a sort of cave behind a cove we landed at, and we went in there. Red met us. He came from his house on the cliff, he said, but I don't know how.'

Dick looked at Jo closely. 'I suppose you'll say next that there's a secret way from the cave to the house!' he said. 'Go on!'

'Must be,' said Jo. She suddenly glared at Dick. 'Don't you believe me? All right, find the place yourself!'

'Well – it does sound like a tale in a book,' said Julian. 'You're sure it *is* all true, Jo? We don't want to go on a wild-goose chase again, you know.'

'There's no wild goose in my story,' said Jo, puzzled. She hadn't the faintest idea what a wild-goose chase was. 'I'm telling you about Red. I'm ready to go when you are. We'll have to have a boat, though.'

'We'll take George's,' said Dick, getting up. 'Look, Jo – I think we'd better leave Anne behind this time. I don't like taking her into something that may be dangerous.'

'I want to come,' said Anne at once.

'No, you stay with me,' said Joanna. 'I want company

527

today. I'm getting scared of being by myself with all these things happening. You stay with me.'

So Anne stayed behind, really rather glad, and watched the other three go off together. Jo slipped into the hedge to avoid being seen by Jake, in case he was anywhere about. Julian and Dick went down to the beach and glanced round to make sure the traveller was nowhere in sight.

They beckoned to Jo, and she came swiftly from hiding, and leapt into George's boat. She lay down in it so that she couldn't be seen. The boys hauled the boat down to the sea. Dick jumped in, and Julian pushed off when a big wave came. Then he jumped in too.

'How far up the coast is it?' he asked Jo, who was still at the bottom of the boat.

'I don't know,' said Jo, with her usual irritating vagueness. 'Two hours, three hours, maybe.'

Time didn't mean the same to Jo as it did to the others. For one thing Jo had no wrist-watch as they had, always there to be glanced at. She wouldn't have found one any use if she had, because she couldn't tell the time. Time was just day and night to her, nothing else.

Dick put up the little sail. The wind was in their favour, so he thought he might as well use it. They would get there all the more quickly.

'Did you bring the lunch that Joanna put up for us?' said Julian to Dick. 'I can't see it anywhere.'

'Jo! You must be lying on it!' said Dick.

528

'It won't hurt it,' said Jo. She sat up as soon as they were well out to sea, and offered to take the tiller.

She was very deft with it, and the boys soon saw that they could leave her to guide the boat. Julian unfolded the map he had brought with him.

'I wonder whereabouts this place is where Red lives,' he said. 'It's pretty desolate all the way up to the next place, Port Limmersley. If there *is* a castle-like building, it must be a very lonely place to live in. There's not even a little fishing village shown for miles.'

The boat went on and on, scudding at times before a fairly strong wind. Julian took the tiller from Jo. 'We've come a long way already,' he said. 'Where *is* this place? Are you sure you'll know it, Jo?'

'Of course,' said Jo, scornfully. 'I think it's round that far-off rocky cliff.'

She was right. As they rounded the high cliff, which jutted fiercely with great slanting rocks, she pointed in triumph.

'There you are! See that place up there? That's Red's place.'

The boys looked at it. It was a dour, grey stone building, and was, as Jo had said, a little like a small castle. It brooded over the sea, with one square tower overlooking the waves.

'There's a cove before you come to the place,' said Jo. 'Watch out for it – it's very well hidden.'

It certainly was. The boat went right past it before they

529

saw it. 'There it is!' cried Jo, urgently.

They took the sail down and then rowed back. The cove lay between two high layers of rock that jutted out from the cliff. They rowed right into it. It was very quiet and calm there, and their boat merely rose and fell as the water swelled and subsided under it.

'Can anyone see us from the house above?' asked Dick, as they rowed right to the back of the cove.

'I don't know,' said Jo. 'I shouldn't think so. Look – pull the boat up behind that big rock. We don't know who else might come here.'

They dragged the boat up. Dick draped it with great armfuls of seaweed, and soon it looked almost like a rock itself.

'Now, what next?' said Julian. 'Where's this cave you were talking about?'

'Up here,' said Jo, and began to climb up the rocky cliff like a monkey. Both the boys were very good climbers, but soon they found it impossible to get any further. Jo scrambled down to them. 'What's the matter?' she said. 'If my dad can climb up, surely you can!'

'Your dad was an acrobat,' said Julian, sliding down a few feet, much too suddenly. 'Oooh! I don't much like this. I wish we had a rope.'

'There's one in the boat. I'll get it,' said Jo, and slithered down the cliff to the cove below at a most alarming rate. She climbed up again with the rope. She went on a good bit higher, and tied the rope to something.

It hung down to where Dick and Julian stood clinging for dear life.

It was much easier to climb up with the help of a rope. Both boys were soon standing on a ledge, looking into a curious-shaped cave. It was oval-shaped, and very dark.

'In here,' said Jo, and led the way. Dick and Julian followed stumblingly. Where in the world were they going to now?

CHAPTER EIGHTEEN

Things begin to happen

JO LED them into a narrow rocky tunnel, and then out into a wider cave, whose walls dripped with damp. Julian was thankful for his torch. It was eerie and chilly and musty. He shivered. Something brushed his face and he leapt back.

'What was that?' he said.

'Bats,' said Jo, 'there're hundreds of them here. That's why the place smells so sour. Come on We go round this rocky bit here into a better cave.'

They squeezed round a rocky corner and came into a drier cave that did not smell so strongly of bats. 'I haven't been any farther than this,' said Jo. 'This is where me and Dad came and waited for Red. He suddenly appeared, but I don't know where from.'

'Well, he must have come from somewhere,' said Dick, switching on his torch, too. 'There's a passage probably. We'll soon find it.'

He and Julian began to hunt round the cave, looking for a passage or little tunnel, or even a hole that led into the cliff, upwards towards the house. Obviously Red must have come down some such passage to reach the cave. Jo stayed in a corner, waiting. She had no torch.

Suddenly the boys had a tremendous shock. A voice boomed into their cave, a loud and angry voice that made their hearts beat painfully.

'SO! YOU DARE TO COME HERE!'

Jo slipped behind a rock immediately, like an animal going to cover. The boys stood where they were, rooted to the spot. Where did that voice come from?

'Who are you?' boomed the voice.

'Who are *you*?' shouted Julian. 'Come out and show yourself! We've come to see a man called Red. Take us to him.'

There was a moment's silence, as if the owner of the voice was rather taken aback. Then it boomed out again.

'Why do you want to see Red? Who sent you?'

'Nobody. We came because we want our cousin back, and her dog, too,' boomed Julian, making a funnel of his hands and trying to outdo the other voice.

There was another astonished silence. Then two legs appeared out of a hole in the low ceiling, and someone leapt lightly down beside them. The boys started back in surprise. They hadn't expected that the voice came from the roof of the cave!

Julian flashed his torch on the man. He was a giant-like fellow with flaming red hair. His eyebrows were red, too, and he had a red beard that partly hid a cruel mouth. Julian took one look into the man's eyes and then no more.

'He's mad,' he thought. 'So this is Red Tower. What is he? A scientist like Uncle Quentin, jealous of uncle's work? Or a thief working on a big scale, trying to get important papers and sell them? He's mad, whatever he is.'

Red was looking closely at the two boys. 'So you think I have your cousin,' he said. 'Who told you such a stupid tale?'

Julian didn't answer. Red took a threatening step towards him. 'Who told you?'

'I'll tell you that when the police come,' said Julian, boldly.

Red stepped back.

'The police! What do they know? Why should they come here? Answer me, boy!'

'There's a lot to know about you, Mr Red Tower,' said Julian. 'Who sent men to steal my uncle's papers? Who sent a note to ask for another lot? Who kidnapped our cousin, so that she could be held till the papers were sent? Who brought her here from Simmy's old caravan? Who . . . ?'

'Aaaaaah!' said Red, and there was panic in his voice. 'How do you know all this? It isn't true! But the police – have they heard this fantastic tale, too?'

'What do you suppose?' said Julian, wishing with all his heart that the police *did* know, and that he was not merely bluffing. Red pulled at his beard. His green eyes gleamed as he thought quickly and urgently.

He suddenly called loudly, turning his head up to the hole in the ceiling. 'Markhoff! Come down!'

Two legs were swung down through the hole, and a short burly man leapt down beside the two startled boys.

'Go down the cliff. You will find a boat in the cove, somewhere – the boat we saw these boys coming in,' said Red sharply. 'Smash it to pieces. Then come back here and take the boys to the yard. Tie them up. We must leave quickly, and take the girl with us.'

The man stood listening, his face sullen. 'How can we go?' he said. 'You know the helicopter is not ready. You *know* that.'

'Make it ready, then,' snapped Red. 'We leave tonight. The police will be here – do you hear that? This boy knows everything – he has told me – and the police must know everything too. I tell you, we must go.'

'What about the dog?' said the man.

'Shoot it,' ordered Red. 'Shoot it before we go. It's a brute of a dog. We should have shot it before. Now go and smash the boat.'

The man disappeared round the rocky corner that led into the cave of bats. Julian clenched his fist. He hated to think of George's boat being smashed to bits. Red stood there waiting, his eyes glinting in the light of the torches.

'I'd take you with us too, if there was room!' he suddenly snarled at Julian. 'Yes, and drop you into the sea!

'You can tell your uncle he'll hear from me about his precious daughter – we'll make an exchange. If he wants her back he can send me the notes I want. And many thanks for coming to warn me. I'll be off before the police break in.'

He began to pace up and down the cave, muttering. Dick and Julian watched in silence. They felt afraid for George. Would Red really take her off in his helicopter? He looked mad enough for anything.

The sullen man came back at last. 'It's smashed,' he said.

'Right,' said Red. 'I'll go first. Then the boys. Then you. And boot them if they make any trouble.'

Red swung himself up into the hole in the roof. Julian and Dick followed, not seeing any point in resisting. The man behind was too sulky to stand any nonsense. He followed immediately.

There had been no sign of Jo. She had kept herself well hidden, scared stiff. Julian didn't know what to do about her. He couldn't possibly tell Red about her – and yet it seemed terrible to leave her behind all alone. Well – she was a sharp-brained little monkey. Maybe she would think up something for herself.

Red led the way through another cave into a passage with such a low roof that he had to walk bent almost double.

The man behind had now switched on a very powerful torch, and it was easier to see. The passage sloped upwards and was obviously leading to the building on the cliff. At one part it was so steep that a hand-rail had been put for the climber to help himself up.

Then came a flight of steps hewn out of the rock itself – rough, badly-shaped steps, so steep that it was quite an effort to climb from one to the next.

At the top of the steps was a stout door set on a broad ledge. Red pushed it open and daylight flooded in. Julian blinked. He was looking out on an enormous yard paved with great flat stones with weeds growing in all the crevices and cracks.

In the middle stood a helicopter. It looked very strange

and out-of-place in that old yard. The house, with its one tall square tower, was built round three sides of the yard. It was covered with creeper and thick-stemmed ivy.

A high wall ran along the fourth side, with an enormous gate in the middle. It was shut, and from where he stood Julian could see the huge bolts that were drawn across.

'It's almost like a small fort,' thought Julian, in astonishment. Then he felt himself seized and taken to a shed nearby. His arms were forced behind him and his wrists were tightly tied. Then the rope was run through an iron loop and tied again.

Julian glared at the burly fellow now doing the same to Dick. He twisted about to try to see how the rope was tied, but he couldn't even turn, he was so tightly tethered.

He looked up at the tower. A small, forlorn face was looking out of the window there. Julian's heart jumped and beat fast. That must be poor old George up there. He wondered if she had seen them. He hoped not, because she would know that he and Dick had been captured, and she would be very upset.

Where was Timmy? There seemed no sign of him. But wait a minute – what was that lying inside what looked like a summer-house on the opposite side of the yard? *Was* it Timmy? Surely he would have barked a welcome when he heard them coming into the yard, if it *was* Timmy!

'Is that my cousin's dog?' he asked the sullen man.

The man nodded. 'Yes. He's been doped half the time,

he barked so. Savage brute, isn't he? *Ought* to be shot, I reckon.'

Red had gone across the yard and had disappeared through a stone archway. The sullen man now followed him. Julian and Dick were left by themselves.

'We've muddled things again,' said Julian, with a groan. 'Now these fellows will be off and away, and take George with them – they've been nicely warned!'

Dick said nothing. He felt very miserable, and his bound wrists hurt him, too. Both boys stood there, wondering what would happen to them.

'Psssssst!'

What was that? Julian turned round sharply and looked in the direction of the door that led from underground into the yard. Jo stood there, half-hidden by the archway over the door. 'Pssssst! I'll come and untie you. Is the coast clear?'

CHAPTER NINETEEN

Jo is very surprising

'JO!' SAID the boys together, and their spirits lifted at once. 'Come on!'

There was no one about in the yard. Jo skipped lightly across from the doorway and slipped inside the shed.

'There's a knife in my back pocket,' said Julian. 'Get it out. It would be quicker to cut these ropes than to untie them. My word, Jo – I was never so pleased to see anyone in my life!'

Jo grinned as she hauled out Julian's sturdy pocket-knife. She opened it and ran her thumb lightly over the blade. It was beautifully sharp. She set to work to saw the blade across the thick rope. It cut easily through the fibres.

'I waited behind,' she said, rapidly. 'Then I followed when it was safe. But it was very dark and I didn't like it. Then I came to that door and peeped out. I was glad when I saw you.'

'Good thing the men didn't guess you were there,' said Dick. 'Good old Jo! I take back any nasty thing I've ever said about you!'

Jo beamed. She cut the last bit of rope that bound Julian, and he swung himself away from the iron loop and began to rub his stiff, aching wrists. Jo set to work on Dick's bonds. She soon had those cut through, too.

'Where's George?' she asked, after she had helped Dick to rub his wrists and arms.

'Up in that tower,' said Julian. 'If we dared to go out in that yard you could look up and see her. And there's poor old Tim, look – half-doped – lying in that summer-house place over there.'

'I shan't let him be shot,' said Jo. 'He's a nice dog. I shall go and drag him down into those caves underground.'

'Not now!' said Julian, horrified. 'If you're seen now, you'll spoil everything. We'll *all* be tied up then!'

But Jo had already darted over to the summer-house and was fondling poor old Timmy.

The slam of a door made the boys jump and sent Jo into the shadows at the back of the summer-house at once. It was Red, coming across the yard!

'Quick! He's coming over here!' said Dick, in a panic. 'Let's go back to the iron loops and put our hands behind us so that he thinks we're still bound.'

So, when Red came over to the door of the shed, it looked exactly as if the boys still had their hands tied behind them. He laughed.

'You can stay here till the police come!' he said. Then he shut the shed door and locked it. He strolled over to the helicopter and examined it thoroughly. Then back he went to the door he had come from, opened it, and slammed it shut. He was gone.

When everything was quiet Jo sped back from the summer-house to the shed. She unlocked the door of the shed. 'Come out,' she said. 'And we'll lock it again. Then nobody will know you aren't here. Hurry!'

There was nothing for it but to come out and hope there was nobody looking. Jo locked the shed door after them and hurried them back to the door that led underground. They slipped through it and half-fell down the steep steps.

'Thanks, Jo,' said Dick.

They sat down. Julian scratched his head, and for the life of him could not think of anything sensible to do. The police were *not* coming because they didn't know a thing about Red, or where George was or anything. And before long George would be flown off in that helicopter, and Timmy would be shot.

Julian thought of the high square tower and groaned. 'There's no way of getting George out of that tower,' he said aloud. 'It'll be locked and barred, or George would have got out at once. We can't even get to her. It's no good trying to make our way into the house – we'd be seen and caught at once.'

Jo looked at Dick. 'Do you badly want George to be rescued?' she said.

'That's a silly question,' said Dick. 'I want it more than anything else in the world.'

'Well – I'll go and get her, then,' said Jo, and she got up as if she really meant it.

'Don't make jokes now,' said Julian. 'This really is serious, Jo.'

'Well, so am I,' retorted Jo. 'I'll get her out, you see if I don't. Then you'll know I'm trustable, won't you? You think I'm mean and thieving and not worth a penny, and I expect you're right. But I can do some things you can't, and if you want this thing, I'll do it for you.'

'How?' said Julian, astonished and disbelieving.

Jo sat down again.

'You saw that tower, didn't you?' she began. 'Well, it's a big one, so I reckon there's more than one room in it – and if I can get into the room next to George's I could undo her door and set her free.'

'And how do you think you're going to get into the room next to hers?' said Dick, scornfully.

'Climb up the wall, of course,' said Jo. 'It's set thick with ivy. I've often climbed up walls like that.'

The boys looked at her. 'Were you the Face at the Window by any chance?' said Julian, remembering Anne's fright. 'I bet you were. You're like a monkey, climbing and darting about. But you can't climb up that great high wall, so don't think it. You'd fall and be killed. We couldn't let you.'

'Pooh!' said Jo, with great scorn. 'Fall off a wall like that! I've climbed up a wall without any ivy at all! There're always holes and cracks to hold on to. That one would be easy!'

Julian was quite dumbfounded to think that Jo really

meant all this. Dick remembered that Jo's father was an acrobat. Perhaps that kind of thing was in the family.

'You just ought to see me on a tight-rope,' said Jo earnestly. 'I can dance on it – and I never have a safety-net underneath – that's baby-play! Well, I'm going.'

Without another word she climbed the steep steps lightly as a goat and stood poised in the archway of the door. All was quiet. Like a squirrel she leapt and bounded over the courtyard and came to the foot of the ivy-covered tower. Julian and Dick were now at the doorway that led into the yard, watching her.

'She'll be killed,' said Julian.

'Talk about pluck!' said Dick. 'I never saw such a kid in my life. There she goes – just like a monkey.'

And, sure enough, up the ivy went Jo, climbing lightly and steadily. Her hands reached out and tested each ivy-stem before she threw her weight on it, and her feet tried each one, too, before she stood on it.

Once she slipped when an ivy-stem came away from the wall. Julian and Dick watched, their hearts in their mouths. But Jo merely clutched at another piece of stem and steadied herself once. Then up she went again.

Up and up. Past the first storey, past the second, and up to the third. Only one more now and she would be up to the topmost one. She seemed very small as she neared the top.

'I can't bear to look and I can't bear not to,' said Dick, pretending to shield his eyes and almost trembling with nervousness. 'If she fell now – what should we do?'

546

'Do shut up,' said Julian, between his teeth. 'She won't fall. She's like a cat. There – she's making for the window next to George's. It's open at the bottom.'

Jo now sat triumphantly on the broad window-sill of the room next to George's. She waved impudently to the boys far below. Then she pushed with all her might at the window to open it a little more. It wouldn't budge.

So Jo laid herself flat, and by dint of much wriggling and squeezing, she managed to slip through the narrow space between the bottom of the window-pane and the sill. She disappeared from sight.

Both boys heaved heartfelt sighs of relief. Dick found that his knees were shaking. He and Julian retired into the underground passage below the steep steps and sat there in silence.

'Worse than a circus,' said Dick at last. 'I'll never be able to watch acrobats again. What's she doing now, do you suppose?'

Jo was very busy. She had fallen off the inside window-sill with a bump, and bruised herself on the floor below. But she was used to bruises.

She picked herself up and shot behind a chair in case anyone had heard her. Nobody seemed to have heard anything, so she peeped cautiously out. The room was furnished with enormous pieces of furniture, old and heavy. Dust was on everything, and cobwebs hung down from the stone ceiling.

Jo tiptoed to the door. Her feet were bare and made no

sound at all. She looked out. There was a spiral stone stairway nearby going downwards, and on each side was a door – there must be four rooms in the tower then, one for each corner, two windows in each. She looked at the door next to the room she was in. That must be the door of George's room.

There was a very large key in the lock, and a great bolt had been drawn across. Jo leapt across and dragged at the bolt. It made a loud noise and she darted back into the room again. But still nobody came. Back she went to the door again, and this time turned the enormous key. It was well oiled and turned easily.

Jo pushed open the door and put her head cautiously round. George was there – a thin and unhappy George, sitting by the window. She stared at Jo as if she couldn't believe her eyes!

'Psssst!' said Jo, enjoying all this very much indeed. 'I've come to get you out!'

CHAPTER TWENTY

The adventure boils up

GEORGE LOOKED as if she had seen a ghost. 'Jo!' she whispered. 'It can't really be you.'

'It is. Feel,' said Jo, and pattered across the room to give George quite a hard pinch. Then she pulled at her arm.

'Come on,' she said. 'We must go before Red comes. Hurry! I don't want to be caught.'

George got up as if she was in a dream. She went across to the door. She and Jo slipped out, and stood at the top of the spiral staircase.

'Have to go down here, I suppose,' said Jo. She cocked her head and listened. Then she went down a few steps and turned the first spiral bend.

But before she had gone down more than a dozen steps she stopped in fright. Somebody was coming up!

In panic Jo ran up again and pushed George roughly into the room she had climbed into first of all.

'Someone's coming,' she panted. 'Now we're finished.'

'It's that red-haired man, I expect,' said George. 'He comes up three or four times a day and tries to make me tell him about my father's work. But I don't know a thing. What are we to do?'

The slow steps came up and up, sounding hollowly on

the stone stairs. They could hear a panting breath now, too.

An idea came to Jo. She put her mouth close to George's ear. 'Listen! We look awfully alike. I'll let myself be caught and locked up in that room – and you take the chance to slip down and go to Dick and Julian. Red will never know I'm not you – we've even got the same clothes on now, because Joanna gave me old ones of yours.'

'No,' said George, astounded. 'You'll be caught. I don't want you to do that.'

'You've *got* to,' whispered Jo, fiercely. 'Don't be daft. I can open the window and climb down the ivy, easy as winking, when Red's gone. It's your only chance. They're going to take you off in that helicopter tonight.'

The footsteps were now at the top. Jo pushed George well behind a curtain and whispered fiercely again: 'Anyway, I'm not really doing this for you. I'm doing it for Dick. You keep there and I'll do the rest.'

There was a loud exclamation when the man outside discovered the door of George's room open. He went in quickly and found nobody there. Out he came and yelled down the stairs.

'Markhoff! The door's open and the girl's gone! Who opened the door?'

Markhoff came up two steps at a time, looking bewildered. 'No one! Who could? Anyway, the girl can't be far off! I've been in the room below all the time since I locked her in last time. I'd have seen her if she's gone.'

'Who unlocked the door?' screamed Red, quite beside himself with anger. 'We've *got* to have that girl to bargain with.'

'Well, she must be in one of the other rooms,' said Markhoff, stolidly, quite unmoved by his master's fury. He went into one on the opposite side to the room where Jo and George crouched trembling. Then he came into their room, and at once saw the top of Jo's head showing behind the chair.

THE ADVENTURE BOILS UP

He pounced on her and dragged her out. 'Here she is!' he said, and didn't seem to realise that it was not George at all, but Jo. With their short hair, freckled faces and their similar clothes they really were alike. Jo yelled and struggled most realistically. Nobody would have guessed that she had planned to be caught and locked up!

George shook and shivered behind the curtain, longing to go to Jo's help, but knowing that it wouldn't be of the least use. Besides – there might be a chance now of finding Timmy. It had almost broken George's heart to be parted from him for so long.

Jo was dragged yelling and kicking into the room and locked in again. Red and Markhoff began to quarrel about which of them must have left the door unlocked

'You were there last,' said Red.

'Well, if I was, I tell you I didn't leave the door unlocked,' Markhoff raged back. 'I wouldn't be so fat-headed. That's the kind of thing *you* do.'

'That'll do,' snapped Red. 'Have you shot that dog yet? No, you haven't! Go down and do it before *he* escapes too!'

George's heart went stone-cold. Shoot Timmy! Oh *no*! Dear darling old Timmy. She couldn't let him be shot!

She didn't know what to do. She heard Red and Markhoff go down the stone stairway, their boots making a terrific noise at first, and then gradually becoming fainter.

She slipped down after them. They went into a nearby

room, still arguing. George risked being seen and shot past the open door. She came to another stairway, not a spiral one this time, and went down it so fast that she almost lost her footing. Down and down and down. She met nobody at all. What a very strange place this was!

She came into a dark, enormous hall that smelt musty and old. She ran to the great door at the front and tried to open it. It was very heavy, but at last it swung slowly back.

She stood there in the bright sunlight, peering out cautiously. She knew where Timmy was. She had been able to see him sometimes, flopping peculiarly in and out of the summer-house. She knew that because of his continual barking he had been doped. Red had told her that when she had asked him. He enjoyed making her miserable. Poor George!

She tore across the courtyard and came to the summer-house. Timmy was there, lying as if he were asleep. George flung herself on him, her arms round his thick neck.

'Timmy, oh, Timmy!' she cried, and couldn't see him for tears. Timmy, far away in some drugged dream, heard the voice he loved best in all the world. He stirred. He opened his eyes and saw George!

He was too heavy with his sleep to do more than lick her face. Then his eyes closed again. George was in despair. She was afraid Markhoff would come and shoot him in a very short time.

'Timmy!' she called in his ear. 'TIMMY! Do wake up. TIMMY!'

Tim opened his eyes again. What – his mistress still here! Then it couldn't be a dream. Perhaps his world would soon be right again. Timmy didn't understand at all what had been happening the last few days. He staggered to his feet somehow and stood swaying there, shaking his head. George put her hand on his collar. 'That's right, Tim,' she said. 'Now you come with me. Quick!'

But Timmy couldn't walk, though he had managed to stand. In despair George glanced over the courtyard, fearful that she would see Markhoff coming at any moment.

She saw somebody else. She saw Julian standing in an archway opposite, staring at her. She was too upset about Timmy even to feel much astonishment

'Ju!' she called. 'Come and help me with Timmy. They're going to shoot him!'

In a trice Julian and Dick shot across the courtyard to George. 'What happened, Jo?' said Julian. 'Did you find George?'

'Ju – it's me, George!' said George, and Julian suddenly saw that indeed it was George herself. He had been so certain that it was still Jo that he hadn't known it was George!

'Help me with Timmy,' said George, and she pulled at the heavy dog. 'Where shall we hide him?'

'Down underground,' said Dick. 'It's the only place. Come on!'

How they managed it they never quite knew, but they

did drag the heavy, stupid Timmy all the way across the yard and into the archway. They opened the door and shoved him inside. Poor Timmy fell over and immediately rolled down the steep steps, landing at the bottom with a frightful thud. George gave a little scream.

'He'll be hurt!'

But astonishingly enough Timmy didn't seem to be hurt at all. In fact the shaking seemed to have done him good. He got up and looked round him in rather a surprised way. Then he whined and looked up at George. He tried to climb the steep steps, but wasn't lively enough.

George was down beside him in a moment, patting him and stroking him. The two boys joined in. Timmy began to feel that things might be all right again, if only he could get rid of the dreadful, heavy feeling in his head. He couldn't understand why he kept wanting to lie down and go to sleep.

'Bring him right down to the caves,' said Dick. 'Those men are sure to hunt for him and for us too when they find Timmy gone, and us not in the shed.'

So down the narrow passages and into the little cave with the hole in the roof they all went, Timmy feeling as if he didn't quite know which of his legs to use next.

They all sat down in a heap together when they got there, and George got as close to Timmy as she could. She was glad when the boys switched off their torches. She badly wanted to cry, and as she never did cry it was most embarrassing if anyone saw her.

She told the boys in a low voice all that had happened with Jo. 'She *made* me stay hidden so that she could be caught,' she said. 'She's wonderful. She's the bravest girl I ever knew. And she did it all even though she doesn't like me.'

'She's an odd one,' said Dick. 'She's all right at heart, though – very much all right.'

They talked quickly, in low voices, exchanging their news. George told them how she had been caught and taken to the caravan with Timmy, who had been knocked out with a cudgel.

'We saw where you had written Red's name,' said Dick. 'That gave us the clue to come here!'

'Listen,' said Julian, suddenly. 'I think we ought to make a plan quickly. I keep thinking I hear things. We're sure to be looked for soon, you know. What can we *do*?'

CHAPTER TWENTY-ONE

A few surprises

AS SOON as Julian had said that he kept hearing noises, the others felt as if they could hear some, too. They sat and listened intently, George's heart beating so loudly that she was certain the boys would be able to hear it.

'I think perhaps it's the sound of the sea, echoing in through the caves and the tunnels,' said Julian at last. 'In the ordinary way, of course, we wouldn't need to bother to listen – Timmy would growl at once! But, poor old chap, he's so doped and sleepy that I don't believe he hears anything.'

'Will he get all right again?' asked George, anxiously, fondling Timmy's silky ears.

'Oh, yes,' said Julian, sounding much more certain than he really felt. Poor Timmy – he really did seem ill! There wasn't even a growl in him.

'You've had an awful time these last few days, haven't you, George?' asked Dick.

'Yes,' said George. 'I don't much want to talk about it. If I'd had Timmy with me it wouldn't have been so bad, but at first, when they brought me here, all I knew of Timmy was hearing him bark and snarl and bark and snarl down below in the yard. Then Red told me he had doped him.'

A FEW SURPRISES

'How did you get to Red's place?' asked Julian.

'Well, you know I was locked in that horrible-smelling caravan,' said George. 'Then suddenly a man called Simmy – he's Jo's father, I think – came and dragged us out. Timmy was all stupid with the blow they'd given him – and they put him in a sack and put us both on the caravan horse and took us through the wood and along a desolate path by the coast till we came here. That was in the middle of the night.'

'Poor old George!' said Julian. 'I wish Tim was himself again – I'd love to set him loose on Red and the other fellow!'

'I wonder what's happening to Jo,' said Dick, suddenly remembering that Jo was now imprisoned in the tower room where George had been kept so long.

'And do you suppose that Red and Markhoff have discovered that we've got out of that shed, and that Timmy has disappeared, too?' said Julian. 'They'll be in a fury when they do discover it!'

'Can't we get away?' said George, feeling suddenly scared. 'You came in a boat, didn't you? Well, can't we get away in that and go and fetch help for Jo?'

There was a silence. Neither of the boys liked to tell George that her beloved boat had been smashed to pieces by Markhoff. But she had to know, of course, and Julian told her in a few short words.

George said nothing at all. They all sat silently for a few minutes, hearing nothing but Timmy's heavy, almost snoring, breathing.

'Would it be possible, when it's dark, to creep up into the courtyard, and go round the walls to the big gate?' said Dick, breaking the silence. 'We can't escape anywhere down here, it's certain – not without a boat, anyhow.'

'Should we wait till Red and Markhoff have gone off in the helicopter?' said Julian. 'Then we'd be much safer.'

'Yes – but what about Jo?' asked Dick. 'They think she's George, don't they? – and they'll take her away with them, just as they planned to do with George. I don't see how we can try to escape ourselves without first trying to save Jo. She's been a brick about George.'

They talked round and round the idea of trying to save Jo, but nobody could think of any really sensible plan at all. Time went on, and they all felt hungry and rather cold. 'If only we could *do* something, it wouldn't be so bad!' groaned Dick. 'I wonder what's happening up at the house.'

Up at the grey stone house with its big square tower, plenty was happening!

To begin with, Markhoff had gone to shoot Timmy, as Red had ordered. But when he got to the summer-house there was no dog there!

Markhoff stared in the greatest amazement! The dog had been tied up, even though he was doped – and now, there was the loose rope, and no dog attached to it!

Markhoff gazed round the summer-house in astonishment. Who could have loosed Timmy? He darted across to the locked shed where he had tied Julian and

560

Dick with rope to the iron staples. The door was still locked, of course – and Markhoff turned the key and pushed it open.

'Here, you . . .' he began, shouting roughly. Then he stopped dead. Nobody was there! Again there was loose rope – this time cut here and there, so that it lay in short pieces – and again the prisoners had gone. No dog. No boys.

Markhoff couldn't believe his eyes. He looked all round the shed. 'But it was locked from the outside!' he muttered. 'What's all this? Who's freed the dog and the boys? What will Red say?'

Markhoff looked at the helicopter standing ready for flight in the middle of the yard, and half decided to desert Red and get away himself. Then, remembering Red's mad tempers, and his cruel revenges on anyone who dared to let him down, he changed his mind.

'We'd better get off now, before it's dark,' he thought. 'There's something strange going on here. There must be somebody else here that we know nothing about. I'd better find Red and tell him.'

He went in through the massive front door, and in the hall he came face to face with two men waiting there. At first he couldn't see who they were, and he stepped back hurriedly. Then he saw it was Simmy and Jake.

'What are you doing here?' shouted Markhoff. 'Weren't you told to keep watch on Kirrin Cottage and make sure the police weren't told anything?'

'Yes,' said Jake, sulkily. 'And we've come to say that

that cook woman called Joanna – went down to the police this morning. She had one of the kids with her – a girl. The boys don't seem to be about.'

'No. They're here – at least, they were,' said Markhoff. 'They've disappeared again. As for the police, we've heard they're on the way, and we've made our plans. You're a bit late with your news! Lot of good you are, with your spying! Clear off now – we're taking the girl off in the helicopter before the police come. How did anyone know where the girl was? Have you been spilling the beans?'

'Pah!' said Simmy, contemptuously. 'Think we want to be messed up with the police? You must be mad. We want some money. We've done all your dirty work, and you've only paid us half you promised. Give us the rest.'

'You can ask Red for it!' growled Markhoff. 'What's the good of asking me? Go and ask *him*!'

'Right. We will,' said Jake, his face as black as thunder. 'We've done all he told us – took the papers for him, took the girl – and that savage brute of a dog too – see where he bit me on my hand? And all we get is half our money! I reckon we've only just come in time, too. Planning to go off in that heli-thing and do us out of our pay. Pah!'

'Where's Red?' demanded Simmy.

'Upstairs,' said Markhoff. 'I've got some bad news for him, so he won't be pleased to see you and your ugly mugs. Better let me find him for you and say what I've got to say – then you can chip in with your polite little speeches.'

'Funny, aren't you?' said Jake, in a dangerous voice.

Neither he nor Simmy liked Markhoff. They followed him up the broad stairway, and then up again till they came to the room that lay below the spiral staircase.

Red was there, scanning through the papers that had been stolen from the study of George's father. He was in a black temper. He flung down the papers as Markhoff came in.

'These aren't the notes I wanted!' he began, loudly. 'Well, I'll hold the girl till I get . . . why, Markhoff, what's up? Anything wrong?'

'Plenty,' said Markhoff. 'The dog's gone – he wasn't there when I went to shoot him – and the two boys have gone too – yes, escaped out of a locked shed. Beats me!

'And here are two visitors for you   they want money! They've come to tell you what you already know – the police have been told about you.'

Red went purple in the face, and his strange eyes shone with rage. He stared first at Markhoff, then at Simmy and Jake. Markhoff looked uneasy, but Simmy and Jake looked back insolently.

'You – you – you *dare* to come here when I told you to keep away!' he shouted. 'You've BEEN paid. You can't blackmail me for any more money.'

What he would have said next nobody knew because from up the spiral stairs there came yells and screams and the noise of someone apparently trying to batter down a door.

'That's that girl, I suppose,' muttered Markhoff. 'What's

up with her? She's been quiet enough before.'

'We'd better get her out now and go,' said Red, his face still purple. 'Jake, go and get her. Bring her down here, and knock some sense into her if she goes on screaming.'

'Fetch her yourself,' said Jake, insolently.

Red looked at Markhoff, who immediately produced a revolver.

'My orders are always obeyed,' said Red in a suddenly cold voice. '*Always*, you understand?'

Not only Jake scuttled up the stairs then but also Simmy! They went to the locked and bolted room at the top and unlocked the door. They pulled back the bolt and door. Simmy stepped into the room to deal with the imprisoned girl.

But he stopped dead and gaped. He blinked, rubbed his eyes and gaped again. Jake gaped too.

'Hallo, Dad!' said Jo. 'You *do* seem surprised to see me!'

CHAPTER TWENTY-TWO

Jo is very smart

'JO,' SAID Simmy. 'Well, of all the . . . well . . . *JO!*' Jake recovered first. 'What's all this?' he said, roughly, to Simmy. 'What's Jo doing here? How did *she* get here? Where's the other kid, the one we caught?'

'How do *I* know?' said Simmy, still staring at Jo. 'Look here, Jo – what are you doing here? Go on, tell us. And where's the other kid?'

'Hunt round the room and see if you can find her!' said Jo, brightly, keeping on her toes in case her father or Jake was going to pounce on her. The two men looked hurriedly round the room. Jake went to a big cupboard.

'Yes – she might be in there,' said Jo, enjoying herself. 'You have a good look.'

The two bewildered men didn't know what to think. They had come to get George – and had only found Jo!

But how – why – what had happened? They didn't know what to do. Neither of them wanted to go back and tell Red. So they began to search the room feverishly, looking into likely and unlikely places, with Jo jeering at them all the time.

'Better take the drawers out of that chest and see if she's here. And don't forget to look under the rug. That's right,

Jake, poke your head up the chimney. Mind George doesn't kick soot into your eyes.'

'I'll get you in a minute!' growled Jake, furiously, opening a small cupboard door.

An angry voice came up the stairway. 'Jake! What are you doing up there? Bring that kid down.'

'She's not here!' yelled back Jake, suddenly losing his temper. 'What have you done with her? She's gone!'

Red came tearing up, two steps at a time, his eyes narrow with anger. The first thing he saw in the room was Jo – and, of course, he thought she was George.

'What do you mean – saying she's not here!' he raged. 'Are you mad?'

'Nope,' said Jake, his eyes narrow too. 'Not so mad as you are, anyway, Red. This kid isn't that fellow's daughter – the scientist chap we took the papers from – this is Simmy's kid – Jo.'

Red looked at Jake as if he had gone off his head. Then he looked at Jo. He could see no difference between Jo and the absent George at all – short hair, freckles, turned-up nose – he couldn't believe that she was Simmy's daughter.

In fact, he didn't believe it. He thought Jake and Simmy were suddenly deceiving him for some strange reason.

But Jo had a word to say, too. 'Yes, I'm Jo,' she said. 'I'm not Georgina. She's gone. I'm just Jo, and Simmy's my dad. You've come to save me, haven't you, Dad?'

Simmy hadn't come to do anything of the sort, of course. He stared helplessly at Jo, completely bewildered.

Red completely lost his temper. As soon as he heard Jo's voice he realised she was not George. Somehow or other he had been deceived – and seeing that this was Simmy's daughter, then it must be Simmy who had had a hand in the deception!

He went suddenly over to Simmy and struck him hard, his eyes blazing. 'Have you double-crossed me?' he shouted.

Simmy was sent flying to the floor. Jake came up immediately to help him. He tripped up Red, and leapt on him.

Jo looked at the three struggling, shouting men, and shrugged her shoulders. Let them fight! They had forgotten all about her, and that suited her very well. She ran to the door and was just going down the stairs, when an idea came into her sharp little mind. With an impish grin she turned back. She pulled the door to quietly – and then she turned the key in the lock, and shot the bolt.

The three men inside heard the key turn, and in a trice Jake was at the door, pulling at the handle.

'She's locked us in!' he raged. 'And shot the bolt, too.'

'Yell for Markhoff!' shouted Red, trembling with fury. And Markhoff, left down in the room at the bottom of the stairs, suddenly heard yells and shouts and tremendous hammerings at the door! He tore up at once, wondering what in the world had happened.

Jo was hiding in the next room. As soon as Markhoff went to the door and shot back the bolt she slipped out and was down the spiral stairway in a trice, unseen by Markhoff. She grinned to herself and hugged something to her thin little chest.

It was the big key belonging to the door upstairs. Nobody could unlock that door now – the key was missing. Jo had it!

'Unlock the door!' shouted Red. 'That kid's gone.'

'There's no key!' yelled back Markhoff. 'She must have taken it. I'll go after her.'

But it was one thing to go after Jo and quite another to find her. She seemed to have disappeared into thin air.

Markhoff raged through every room, but she was nowhere to be seen. He went out into the courtyard and looked round there.

Actually she had made her way to the kitchen and found the larder. She was very hungry and wanted something to eat. There was nobody in the kitchen at all, though a fine fire burned in the big range there.

She slipped into the larder, took the key from the outer side of the door and locked herself in. She saw that there was a small window, and she carefully unfastened it so that she could make her escape if anyone discovered that she was locked in the larder.

Then she tucked in. Three sausage rolls, a large piece of cheese, a hunk of bread, half a meat pie and two jam tarts went the same way. After that Jo felt a lot better. She remembered the others and thought how hungry they must be feeling, too.

She found a rush basket hanging on a nail and slipped some food into it – more sausage rolls, some rockbuns, some cheese and bread. Now, if only she could find the others, how they would welcome her!

Jo put the big key at the bottom of the rush basket. She was feeling very, very pleased with herself. Red and Simmy and Jake were all nicely locked up and out of the way. She didn't fear Markhoff as much as Red. She was sure she could get away from him.

She wasn't even sorry for her father, Simmy.

She had no love for him and no respect, because he was everything that a father shouldn't be.

She heard Markhoff come raging into the kitchen and she clambered quickly up on the larder shelf, ready to drop out of the window if he tried the door. But he didn't. He raged out again, and she heard him no more.

Jo unlocked the door very cautiously. There was now an old woman in the kitchen, standing by the table, folding some clothes she had brought in from the clothes line in the yard. She stared in the greatest surprise at Jo peeping out of the larder.

'What . . . ?' she began, indignantly; but Jo was out of the room before she had even got out the next word. The old dame waddled over to the larder and began to wail as she saw all the empty plates and dishes.

Jo went cautiously into the front hall. She could hear Markhoff upstairs, still tearing about. She smiled delightedly and slipped over to the door.

She undid it and pulled it open. Then, keeping to the wall, she sidled like a weasel to the door that led underground. She opened it and went through, shutting it softly behind her.

Now to find the others. She felt sure they must be down . in the caves. How pleased they would be with the food in her basket!

She half-fell down the steep steps, and made her way as quickly as she could down the slanting passage. She had no torch and had to feel her way in the dark. She wasn't in the least afraid. Only when she trod on a sharp stone with her bare foot did she make a sound.

The other three – Julian, Dick and George – were still sitting crouched together with Timmy in the centre. Julian had been once up to the door that led into the yard and had cautiously peered out to see what was to be seen – but had seen nothing at all except for an old woman hanging out some clothes on a line.

The three had decided to wait till night before they did anything. They thought maybe Timmy might have recovered a little then, and would be of some help in protecting them against Red or Markhoff. They half-dozed, sitting together for warmth, enjoying the heat of Timmy's big body.

Timmy growled! Yes, he actually growled – a thing he hadn't done at all so far. George put a warning hand on him. They all sat up, listening. A voice came to them.

'Julian! Dick! Where are you? I've lost my way!'

'It's Jo!' cried Dick, and switched on his torch at once. 'Here we are, Jo! How did you escape? What's happened?'

'Heaps,' said Jo, and came gladly over to them. 'My, it was dark up in those passages without a torch. Somehow I went the wrong way. That's why I yelled. But I hadn't gone far wrong. Have a sausage roll?'

'*What?*' cried three hungry voices, and even Timmy lifted his head and began to sniff at the rush basket that Jo carried.

Jo laughed and opened the basket. She handed out all the food and the three of them fell on it like wolves. 'Jo, you're the eighth wonder of the world,' said Dick. 'Is there anything left in the basket?'

'Yes,' said Jo, and took out the enormous key. 'This, look! I locked Red and Jake and Simmy into that tower room, and here's the key. What do you think of *that*?'

CHAPTER TWENTY-THREE

Markhoff goes hunting

GEORGE TOOK the big key and looked at it with awe. 'Jo! Is this really the key – and you've locked them all in? Honestly, I think you're a marvel.'

'She is,' said Dick, and to Jo's enormous delight he gave her a sudden quick hug. 'I never knew such a girl in my life. Never. She's got the pluck of twenty!'

'It was easy, really,' said Jo, her eyes shining joyfully in the light of the torch. 'You trust me now, Dick, don't you? You won't be mean to me any more, any of you, will you?'

'Of course not,' said Julian. 'You're our friend for ever!'

'Not George's,' said Jo at once.

'Oh yes you are,' said George. 'I take back every single mean thing I said about you. You're as good as a boy.'

This was the very highest compliment that George could ever pay any girl. Jo beamed and gave George a light punch.

'I did it all for Dick, really,' she said. 'But next time I'll do it for you!'

'Goodness, I hope there won't *be* a next time,' said George, with a shiver. 'I can't say I enjoyed one single minute of the last few days.'

Timmy suddenly put his head on Jo's knee. She stroked

575

him. 'Look at that!' she said. 'He remembers me. He's better, isn't he, George?'

George carefully removed Timmy's head from Jo's knee to her own. She felt decidedly friendly towards Jo now, but not to the extent of having Timmy put his head on Jo's knee. She patted him.

'Yes, he's better,' she said. 'He ate half the sausage roll I gave him, though he sniffed at it like anything first. I think he knows something has been put into his food and now he's suspicious of it. Good old Timmy.'

They all felt much more lively and cheerful now that they were no longer so dreadfully empty. Julian looked at his watch. 'It's getting on towards evening now,' he said. 'I wonder what all those fellows are doing?'

Three of them were still locked up! No matter how Markhoff had tried to batter in the door, it held. It was old and immensely strong, and the lock held without showing any sign of giving way even half an inch. Two other men had been called in from the garage to help, but except that the door looked decidedly worse for wear, it stood there just the same, sturdy and unbreakable.

Simmy and Jake watched Red as he walked up and down the tower room like a caged lion. They were glad they were two against one. He seemed like a madman to them as he raged and paced up and down.

Markhoff, outside with the other two men he had brought up to help, was getting very worried. No police had arrived as yet (and wouldn't either, because Joanna hadn't been able to tell them anything except that she knew Julian and Dick had gone to see a man called Red – but where he lived she had no idea!).

But Red and Markhoff didn't know this – they felt sure that a police ambush was somewhere nearby. If only they could get away in the helicopter before anything else happened!

'Markhoff! Take Carl and Tom and go down into those underground caves,' ordered Red at last. 'Those children are sure to be there – it's the only place for them to hide. They can't get out of here because the front gate is locked and bolted, and the wall's too high to climb. Get hold of the kids and search them for the key.'

So Markhoff and two burly fellows went downstairs and out of the door. They crossed the yard to the door that led to the caves.

They got down the steep steps and were soon stumbling along the narrow, slanting passage, their nailed boots making a great noise as they went. They hung on to the hand-rail when they came to the difficult stretch of tunnel, and finally came out into the cave that had the hole in the floor.

There was nobody there. The children had heard the noise of the coming men, and had hurriedly swung themselves down through the hole into the cave below.

They ran through into another cave, the sour-smelling one where bats lived and slept. Then round the rocky corner into the first cave, the curious oval-shaped one that led out to the ledge of rock overlooking the steep cliff.

'There's nowhere to hide,' groaned Julian. He looked back into the cave. At least it was better in there than out on this ledge, outlined by the daylight. He pulled the others back into the cave, and shone his torch up and down the walls to find some corner that they could squeeze behind.

Half-way up the wall was a shelf of rock. He hoisted George up there, and she dragged Timmy up too. Poor Timmy – he wasn't much use to them; he was still so bemused and so very sleepy. He had growled at the noise made by the coming men, but had dropped his head again almost immediately.

Dick got up beside George. Julian found a jutting-out rock and tried to hide behind it, while Jo lay down in a hole beside one wall and covered herself cleverly with sand. Julian couldn't help thinking how sharp Jo was. She always seemed to know the best thing to do.

But as it happened, Jo was the only one to be discovered! It was quite by accident – Markhoff trod on her. He and the other two men had let themselves down through the hole into the cave below, had then gone into the cave of bats, seen no sign of anyone there, and were now in the cave that led to the cliff.

'Those kids aren't here,' said one of the men. 'They've gone to hide somewhere else. What a horrible place this is – let's go back.'

Markhoff was flashing his torch up and down the walls to see if any of the children were crouching behind a jutting rock – and he trod heavily on Jo's hand. She gave an agonised yell, and Markhoff almost dropped his torch!

In a trice he had pulled the girl out of her bed of sand and was shaking her like a rat. 'This is the one we want!' he said to the others. 'She's got the key. Where is it, you little rat? Give it to me or I'll throw you down the cliff!'

Julian was horrified. He felt quite certain that Markhoff really would throw Jo down the cliff, and he was just about to jump down to help her, when he heard her speak.

'All right. Let me go, you brute. Here's the key! You go and let my dad out before the police come! I don't want him caught!'

Markhoff gave an exclamation of triumph, and snatched a shining key out of Jo's hand. He gave her a resounding box on the ear.

'You little toad! You can just stay down here with the others, and it'll be a very, very long stay! Do you know what we're going to do? We're going to roll a big rock over the hole in that other cave's roof – and you'll be prisoners!

'You can't escape upwards – and you won't be able to escape downwards. You'll be dashed on the rocks by the sea if you try to swim away. That'll teach you to interfere!'

The other two men guffawed. 'Good idea, Mark,' said one. 'They'll all be nicely boxed up here and nobody will know where they are! Come on – we've no time to lose. If Red isn't unlocked soon he'll go mad!'

They made their way into the heart of the cliff again, and the listening children heard their footsteps getting fainter. Finally they ceased altogether, as one by one the men levered themselves up through the hole in the roof of the last cave, and disappeared up the narrow, low-roofed tunnel that led to the courtyard.

Julian came out from his hiding-place, looking grim and rather scared. 'That's done it!' he said. 'If those fellows really do block up that hole – and I bet they have already – it looks as if we're here for keeps! As he said, we can't get up, and we can't escape down – the sea's too rough for us to attempt any swimming, and the cliff's unclimbable above the ledge!'

'I'll go and have a look and see if they *have* blocked up that hole,' said Dick. 'They may be bluffing.'

But it hadn't been bluff. When Julian and Dick shone their torches on to the hole in the roof, they saw that a great rock was now blocking it up.

They could not get through the hole again. It was impossible to move the rock from below. They went soberly back to the front cave and sat out on the ledge in the light of the sinking sun.

'It's a pity poor Jo was found,' said George. 'And an even greater pity she had to give up the key! Now Red and the others will go free.'

'They won't,' said Jo, surprisingly. 'I didn't give them the key of the tower room. I'd another key with me – the key of the kitchen larder! And I gave them that.'

'Well, I'm blessed!' said Julian, astounded. 'The things you do, Jo! But how on earth did you happen to have the key of the *larder*?'

Jo told them how she had taken it out and locked herself

in when she was having a meal there.

'I had to unlock the door to get out again, of course,' she said. 'And I thought I'd take that key, too, because, who knows? – I might have wanted to get into that larder again and lock myself in with the food!'

'No one will ever get the better of you, Jo,' said Dick with the utmost conviction. 'Never. You're as cute as a bagful of monkeys. So you've still got the right key with you?'

'Yes,' said Jo. 'And Red and my dad and Jake are still locked up in the tower room!'

But suddenly a most disagreeable thought struck Dick. 'Wait a bit!' he said. 'What's going to happen when they find they've got the *wrong* key? They'll be down here again, and my word, what'll happen to us all then!'

CHAPTER TWENTY-FOUR

A grand surprise

THE THOUGHT that the men might soon return even angrier than they had been before was most unpleasant.

'As soon as Markhoff tries the key in the door of the tower room he'll find it won't unlock it, and he'll know that Jo has tricked him!' said George.

'And then he'll be in such a fury that he'll tear down here again, and goodness knows what will happen to us!' groaned Julian. 'What shall we do? Hide again?'

'No,' said Dick. 'Let's get out of here and climb down the cliff to the sea. I'd feel safer there than up here in this cave. We might be able to find a better hiding-place down on the rocks in that little cove.'

'It's a pity my boat's smashed,' said George, with a sigh for her lovely boat. 'And, I say – how are we going to get old Timmy down?'

There was a conference about this. Timmy couldn't climb down, that was certain. Jo remembered the rope still hanging down the side of the cliff to the ledges below – the one she had tied there to help Julian and Dick climb up the steep sides of the cliff.

'I know,' she said, her quick mind working hard again. 'You go down first, Julian, then Dick. Then George can go

– each of you holding on to the rope as you climb down, in case you fall.

'Then I'll haul up the rope and tie old Timmy to it, round his waist – and I'll lower him down to you. He's so sleepy still, he won't struggle. He won't even know what's happening!'

'But what about you?' said Dick. 'You'll be last of all. Will you mind? You'll be all alone up on this ledge, with the men coming behind you at any minute.'

'No, I don't mind,' said Jo. 'But let's be quick.'

Julian went down first, glad of the rope to hold to as his feet and hands searched for crevices and cracks. Then came Dick, almost slipping in his anxiety to get down.

Then George climbed down, slowly and anxiously, not at all liking the steep cliff. Once she glanced down to the sea below, and felt sick. She shut her eyes for a moment and clung with one hand to the rope.

It was a dreadful business getting Timmy down. George stood below, anxiously waiting. Jo found it very difficult to tie Timmy safely. He was big and heavy, and didn't like being tied up at all, though he really seemed hardly to know what was going on. At last Jo had got the knots well and securely tied, and called out to the others.

'Here he comes. Watch out that the rope doesn't break. Oh, dear – I wish he wouldn't struggle – now he's bumped himself against the cliff!'

It was not at all a nice experience for poor Timmy. He

swung to and fro on the rope as he was slowly let down, and was amazed to find that he was suspended in mid air. Above him Jo panted and puffed.

'Oh, he's so awfully heavy! I hope I shan't have to let go. Look out for him!' she screamed.

The weight was too much for her just at the last, and the rope was let out with rather a rush. Fortunately Timmy was only about six feet up then, and Julian and George managed to catch him as he suddenly descended.

'I'm coming now,' called Jo, and without even holding the rope, or looking at it, she climbed down like a monkey, seeming to find handholds and footholds by magic. The others watched her admiringly. Soon she was standing beside them. George was untying Timmy

'Thanks awfully, Jo,' said George, looking up gratefully at Jo. 'You're a wonder. Tim must have been frightfully heavy.'

'He was,' said Jo, giving him a pat. 'I nearly dropped him. Well – what's the next move?'

'We'll hunt round this peculiar little cove a bit and see if there's any place we can hide,' said Julian. 'You go that way, George, and we'll go this.'

They parted, and began to hunt for a hiding-place. As far as Julian and Dick could see there was none at all, at least on the side they were exploring. The sea swept into the cove, swelling and subsiding – and just outside the great waves battered on to the rocks. There was certainly no chance of swimming out.

There was suddenly an excited shriek from George. 'JU! Come here. Look what I've found!'

They all rushed round to where George was standing, behind a big ledge of rock. She pointed to a great mass of something draped with seaweed.

'A boat! It's covered with seaweed – but it's a boat!'

'It's *your* boat!' yelled Dick, suddenly, and began to pull the fronds of seaweed madly off the hidden boat. 'Markhoff *didn't* smash it! It's here, perfectly all right. He couldn't find it – it was hidden so well with seaweed – so he just came back to Red and told him a lie.'

'He didn't smash it!' shouted Jo, and she, too, began to pull away the seaweed. 'It's quite all right – there's nothing wrong with it. He didn't smash it!'

The four children were so tremendously surprised and joyful that they thumped each other ridiculously on the back, and leapt about like mad things. They had their boat after all – George's good, sound boat. They could escape, hip hip hurrah!

A roar from above made them fall silent.

They gazed up, startled. Markhoff and the other two men were on the ledge far above, shouting and shaking their fists.

'You wait till we get you!' yelled Markhoff.

'Quick, quick!' said Julian, urgently, pulling at the boat. 'We've got just a chance. Pull her down to the water, pull hard!'

Markhoff was now coming down the cliff, and Jo

wished she had untied the rope before she herself had climbed down, for Markhoff was finding it very useful. She tugged at the boat with the others, wishing it wasn't so heavy.

The boat was almost down to the water when something happened. Timmy, who had been gazing at everything in a most bewildered manner, suddenly slid off the ledge he was on and fell straight into the sea. George gave a scream.

'Oh, Timmy! He's in the water, quick, quick – he's too doped to swim! He'll drown!'

Julian and Dick didn't dare to stop heaving at the boat, because they could see that Markhoff would soon be down beside them. George rushed to Timmy, who was splashing around in the waves, still looking surprised and bemused.

But the water had an amazing effect on him. It was cold and it seemed to bring him to his senses quite suddenly. He became much more lively and swam strongly to the rock off which he had slipped. He clambered out with George's help, barking loudly.

The boat slid into the water, and Julian grabbed at George. 'Come on. In you get. Buck up!'

Jo was in the boat and so was Dick. George, trying to clutch at Timmy, was hauled in, too. Julian took a despairing look at Markhoff, who was almost at the end of the rope, about to jump down. They just wouldn't get off in time!

Timmy suddenly slipped out of George's grasp and tore madly over to the cliff barking warningly. He seemed to

be perfectly all right. The sudden coldness of the sea had washed away all his dopeyness and sleepiness. Timmy was himself again!

Markhoff was about five feet above the ledge when he heard Timmy barking. He looked down in horror and saw the big dog trying to jump up at him. He tried to climb up quickly, out of Timmy's reach.

'Woof!' barked Timmy. 'Woof, woof, woof! Grrrrrrr!'

'Look out – he'll have your foot off!' yelled one of the men above on the ledge.

'He's mad – angry – he's savage. Look out, Mark!'

Markhoff *was* looking out! He was terrified. He clambered up another few feet, and then found that Timmy was making runs at the cliff to try and get up after him. He went up a bit further and clung to the rope with one hand, afraid of falling and being pounced on by the furious Timmy.

'Come on, Timmy!' suddenly cried George. 'Come on!'

The four of them had now got the boat on the waves, and if only they had Timmy they could set off and row round the rocks at the cave entrance before Markhoff could possibly reach them.

'Timmy! Timmy!'

Timmy heard, cast a last regretful look at Markhoff's legs, and bounded across to the boat. He leapt right in and stood there, still barking madly.

Markhoff dropped down the rope to the ledge – but he was too late. The boat shot out to the entrance of the cove and rounded it. In half a minute it had disappeared round the rocky corner and was out at sea.

Julian and Dick rowed steadily. George put her arms round Timmy and buried her face in his fur. Jo did the same.

'He's all right again, quite all right,' said George, happily.

'Yes, falling into the cold water did it,' agreed Jo, ruffling up his fur. 'Good old Timmy!'

Timmy was now snuffling about in the bottom of the boat joyfully. He had smelt a lovely smell. Jo wondered what he had found. Then she knew.

'It's the packet of sandwiches we brought with us in the boat and never ate!' she cried. 'Good old Timmy – he's wolfing the lot!'

'Let him!' said Julian, pulling hard at the oars. 'He deserves them all! My word, it's nice to hear his bark again and see his tail wagging.'

And wag it certainly did. It never stopped. The world had come right again for Timmy, he could see and hear properly again, he could bark and caper and jump – and he had his beloved George with him once more.

'Now for home,' said Julian. 'Anne *will* be pleased to see us. Gosh, what a time we've had!'

CHAPTER TWENTY-FIVE

Everything OK

IT WAS getting dark as George's boat came into Kirrin Bay. It had seemed a very long pull indeed, and everyone was tired out. The girls had helped in the rowing when the boys had almost collapsed from exhaustion, and Timmy had cheered everyone up by his sudden high spirits.

'Honestly, his tail hasn't stopped wagging since he got into the boat,' said George. 'He's so pleased to be himself again!'

A small figure was on the beach as they came in, half-lost in the darkness. It was Anne. She called out to them in a trembling voice.

'Is it really you? I've been watching for you all day long! Are you all right?'

'Yes! And we've got George and Timmy, too!' shouted back Dick, as the boat scraped on the shingle. 'We're fine!'

They jumped out, Timmy too, and hauled the boat up the beach. Anne gave a hand, almost crying with joy to have them all again.

'It's bad enough being in the middle of an adventure,' she said, 'but it's much, much worse when you're left out. I'll never be left out again!'

'Woof,' said Timmy, wagging his tail in full agreement. He never wanted to be left out of adventures either!

They all went home – rather slowly, because they were so tired. Joanna was on the look-out for them, as she had been all day. She screamed for joy when she saw George. 'George! You've got George at last! Oh, you bad children, you've been away all day and I didn't know where and I've been worried to death. George, are you all right?'

'Yes, thank you,' said George, who felt as if she was about to fall asleep at any moment. 'I just want something to eat before I fall absolutely sound asleep!'

'But where have you been all day? What have you been doing?' cried Joanna as she bustled off to get them a meal. 'I got so worked up I went to the police – and what a silly I felt – I couldn't tell them where you'd gone or anything. All I could say was you'd gone to find a man called Red, and had rowed away in George's boat!'

'The police have been up and down the coast in a motorboat ever since,' said Anne. 'Trying to spot you, but they couldn't.'

'No. Our boat was well hidden,' said Dick. 'And so were we! So well hidden that I began to think we'd stay hidden for the rest of our lives.'

The telephone rang. Julian jumped. 'Oh, good – you've had the telephone mended. I'll go and phone the police when you've answered this call, Joanna.'

But it was the police themselves on the telephone,

very pleased to hear Joanna saying excitedly that all the children were back safely. 'We'll be up in ten minutes,' they said.

In ten minutes' time the five children and Timmy were tucking into a good meal. 'Don't stop,' said the police sergeant, when he came into the room with the constable the children had seen before. 'Just talk while you're eating.'

So they talked. They told about every single thing. First George told a bit, then Jo, then Dick, then Julian. At first the sergeant was bewildered, but then the bits of information began to piece themselves together in his mind like a jigsaw puzzle.

'Will my father go to prison?' asked Jo.

'I'm afraid so,' said the sergeant.

'Bad luck, Jo,' said Dick.

'I don't mind,' said Jo. 'I'm better off when he's away – I don't have to do things he tells me then.'

'We'll see if we can't fix you up with a nice home,' said the sergeant, kindly. 'You've run wild, Jo – you want looking after.'

'I don't want to go to a Home for Bad Girls,' said Jo, looking scared.

'I shan't let you,' said Dick. 'You're one of the pluckiest kids I've ever known. We'll none of us let you go to a home. We'll find someone who'll be kind to you, someone like – like . . .'

'Like *me*,' said Joanna, who was listening, and she put her arm round Jo and gave her a squeeze. 'I've got a cousin who'd like a ragamuffin like you – a bad little girl with a very good heart. Don't you fret. We'll look after you.'

'I wouldn't mind living with somebody like you,' said Jo, in an offhand way. 'I wouldn't be mean any more then, and I daresay I wouldn't be bad. I'd like to see Dick and all of you sometimes, though.'

'You will if you're good,' said Dick, with a grin. 'But mind – if I ever hear you've got in at anyone's pantry window again, or anything like that, I'll never see you again!'

Jo grinned. She was very happy. She suddenly remembered something and put her hand into the little rush basket she still carried. She took out an enormous key.

'Here you are,' she said to the sergeant. 'Here's the key to the tower room. I bet Red and the others are still locked up there, ready for you to catch! My, won't they get a shock when *you* unlock the door and walk in!'

'Quite a lot of people are going to get shocks,' said the sergeant, putting away his very full notebook. 'Georgina, you're lucky to get away unharmed, you and your dog. By the way, we got in touch with a friend of your father's, when we tried to find out about those papers that were stolen. He says your father gave him all his important American papers before he went – so this fellow Red hasn't anything of value at all. He went to all his trouble for nothing.'

'Do you know anything about Red?' asked Julian. 'He seemed a bit mad to me.'

'If he's the fellow we think he is, he's not very sane,' said the sergeant. 'We'll be glad to have him under lock and key – and that man Markhoff too. He's not as clever as Red, but he's dangerous.'

'I hope he hasn't escaped in that helicopter,' said Dick. 'He meant to go tonight.'

'Well, we'll be there in under an hour or so,' said the sergeant. 'I'll just use your telephone, if I may, and set things going.'

Things were certainly set going that night! Cars roared

595

up to Red's house, and the gate was broken in when no one came to open it. The helicopter was still in the yard – but alas! it was on its side, smashed beyond repair. The children were told afterwards that Markhoff and the other two men had tried to set off in it, but there was something wrong – and it had risen some way and then fallen back to the yard.

The old woman was trying to look after the three hurt men, who had crawled from their seats and gone to bathe their cuts and bruises. Markhoff had hurt his head, and showed no fight at all.

'And what about Red?' the sergeant asked Markhoff. 'Is he still locked up?'

'Yes,' said Markhoff, savagely. 'And a good thing, too. You'll have to break that door down with a battering-ram to get him and the others out.'

'Oh no, we shan't,' said the sergeant, and produced the key. Markhoff stared at it.

'That kid!' he said. 'She gave me the key of the larder. Wait till I get her – she'll be sorry.'

'It'll be a long wait, Markhoff,' said the sergeant. 'A long, long wait. We'll have to take you off with us, I'm afraid.'

Red, Simmy and Jake were still locked up, and were mad with rage. But they saw that the game was up, and it wasn't long before all of them were safely tucked away in police cars.

'A very, very nice little haul,' said the sergeant to one

of his men. 'Very neat, too – three of them all locked up ready for us!'

'What about that kid, Jo?' said the man. 'She seems a bad lot, and as clever as they make them!'

'She's going to have a chance now,' said the sergeant. 'Everybody has a chance sometimes, and this is hers. She's just about half-and-half, I reckon – half bad and half good. But she'll be all right now she's got a chance!'

Jo was sleeping in Joanna's room again. The rest were in their own bedrooms, getting ready for bed. They suddenly didn't feel sleepy any more. Timmy especially was very lively, darting in and out of the rooms, and sending the landing mats sliding about all over the place.

'Timmy! If you jump on my bed again I'll slam the door on you!' threatened Anne. But she didn't, of course. It was so lovely to see old Timmy quite himself once more.

The telephone bell suddenly rang, and made everyone jump.

'*Now* what's up?' said Julian, and went down in the hall to answer it. A voice spoke in his ear.

'Is that Kirrin 011? This is Telegrams. There is a cable for you, with reply prepaid. I am now going to read it.'

'Go ahead,' said Julian.

'It is from Seville in Spain,' said the voice, 'and reads as follows:

"HERE IS OUR ADDRESS PLEASE CABLE BACK SAYING IF EVERYTHING ALL RIGHT – UNCLE QUENTIN".'

Julian repeated the message to the others, who had now crowded round him in the hall. 'What reply shall I give?' he asked. 'No good upsetting them now everything is over!'

'Not a bit of good,' said Dick. 'Say what you like!'

'Right!' said Julian, and turned to the telephone again. 'Hallo – here is the reply message, please. Ready?

"HAVING A MOST EXCITING TIME WITH LOTS OF FUN AND GAMES EVERYTHING OK – JULIAN".'

'Everything OK,' repeated Anne, as they went upstairs to bed once more. 'That's what I like to hear at the end of an adventure. Everything OK.'

Enid Blyton

is one of the most popular children's authors of all time. Her books have sold over 500 million copies and have been translated into other languages more often than any other children's author.

Enid Blyton adored writing for children. She wrote over 600 books and hundreds of short stories. *The Famous Five* books, now 75 years old, are her most popular. She is also the author of other favourites including *The Secret Seven*, *The Magic Faraway Tree*, *Malory Towers* and *Noddy*.

Born in London in 1897, Enid lived much of her life in Buckinghamshire and adored dogs, gardening and the countryside. She was very knowledgeable about trees, flowers, birds and animals.

Dorset – where som of the Famous adventure was a favo of he

Enid stories and lo millions of children (and grown-ups) all over the world. Visit enidblyton.co.uk to discover more.